About the Author

Jim is a proud father, grandfather, husband, brother and uncle. Having spent his executive career primarily in technology and education, his business interests continue as the chairman of an ed-tech company in Liverpool. Enduring passions are family, hiking the hills of Derbyshire's Peak District and beyond, fine food and wine, and he is a Derby County Football Club season ticket holder. He self-published a novel, *Paradigm Shift*, in 2013 and a novella, *Perception*, in 2018; also two anthologies of short stories: *Life's Journeys* in 2017 and *We Will Remember You* in 2018.

Dedication

Dedicated to my parents, Dick and Barbara Chambers, and also to my wife, Barbara's parents, Bill and Eileen Douglass, who always gave us their unstinting love and support throughout their lives.

Jim Chambers

THE HOPE AFFAIR

AUSTIN MACAULEY PUBLISHERS™

LONDON · CAMBRIDGE · NEW YORK · SHARJAH

A CIP catalogue record for this title is available from the British Library.

ISBN 9781398407015 (Paperback)
ISBN 9781398407022 (ePub e-book)

www.austinmacauley.com

First Published (2021)
Austin Macauley Publishers Ltd
25 Canada Square
Canary Wharf
London
E14 5LQ

Acknowledgements

My special thanks must be extended to my long-suffering wife, Barbara, for her encouragement and endurance in listening to my reading of early drafted chapters, and for her never-ending support of my business and writing endeavours throughout our married lives. I would also extend a special word of appreciation to my writing coach for her patience and forbearance and to the many business leaders, friends and colleagues who have unknowingly been a source of inspiration.

Contents

1. Westminster Scandal

September 2002

Christopher was mesmerised by the extensive live TV coverage of the unravelling political storm. He rubbed his febrile brow and ran a hand through his mop of thick black hair, troubled by the unfolding tragi-drama. Paul, his ex-finance director, watched with him, as the helicopter hovered in a bright-blue September sky filming the police door-stepping the suspect, search warrant in hand. The moment was captured and transmitted live as a minister of the Crown was cuffed and led away, guided to a waiting police car and bundled into the back. The scene was witnessed by a horde of press photographers, microphones thrust forwards in the quest for an interview that was not forthcoming. As the car sped away, all blues and twos, the police piled into the house. They later emerged with computers, printers, files and bulging holdalls.

Over the following hours, a similar scene was repeated in Berkshire; yet another minister spirited away in handcuffs. This time, the suspect was relieved of his tie, belt and shoelaces on the front drive of a large house.

'A bit gratuitous, isn't it?' said Paul.

'It's a show for the public. Someone clearly tipped off the BBC and the papers. It all feels pre-emptive, orchestrated. The police must be very certain of their ground, it shrieks of presumed guilt. The message is clear: no-one is above the law; the powerful elite can expect no favours. Exactly as it should be, I suppose, but I'm not sure about turning it into such a public spectacle.'

Holiday homes in the French Riviera and Majorca were similarly raided as part of a co-ordinated operation with continental counterparts, pictures rapidly reaching bulletins in this era of instantaneous news.

'This has to relate to Caroline Hope,' said Christopher.

'Why her?'

'The leaked note to her minister. All over the papers. Accusations of bullying, corruption, fraud—'

'You don't think we could be dragged into all this after all do you? What else could we have done?' demanded Paul.

'We're okay. No need to worry on a personal basis – at least I don't think so.'

'I get the link to her minister. But the talk is of paedophilia. What's that got to do with…?'

'Don't know. I tried to reach Xavier, but for once, he's completely off-radar.'

The next morning's newspapers inevitably led on the crisis that was now engulfing the government. Christopher had ventured out early to buy a broad selection:

'PAEDOS,' screamed a red top.

'SCANDAL at the HEART of CORRUPT GOVERNMENT,' proclaimed the Times with damning articles; exposés on fraudulent benefits gangs.

'DEN of INIQUITY,' blazed the Sun with tales of a bordello-styled bedroom, X-rated videos and explicit pornographic photographs emblazoned across the pages, censored to obscure genitalia and faces. Readers were assailed with unedifying, lewd speculation of the wanton activities that a fly on such a bedroom wall might have been treated to.

An inside page of the Daily Telegraph delved further into the details and one article in the broadsheet led with "FRAUD: steganography suspected", followed by a technical description of the ancient art re-invented and repurposed for a digital age. References to the terrorist outrages of 9/11 in the USA ventured that steganography had been the means of Al Qaeda communications. The co-ordinated terrorist attacks – two on the twin towers, one on the Pentagon, plus the failed attempt on the White House – had outraged the Western world.

It all made for grim reading for Christopher and Paul, who had once more joined him to offer support and friendship. Sipping freshly brewed coffee, Christopher's inner voice spoke loudly to him, *Thank God I resisted the temptation.* His company had brushed disconcertingly close to the scandal that was now gripping the nation…the words leapt off the page as the column inches grew. Amid the vivid descriptions of scandalous events were assertions about ministerial bullying, business greed and corruption: a seismic scandal of sex and corporate criminality. The business and political classes were submerged in controversy, under sustained attacks. Bitter recrimination, striking headlines and speculation of the imminent implosion of the government swiftly followed, the media baying like a pack of bloodhounds in pursuit of the prized stag. Christopher watched avidly, transfixed and appalled. But the outcome seemed inevitable…the downfall of the government on a matter that was the very antithesis of the prime minister's lofty preaching. Integrity, duty, scrupulous honesty were the watchwords for MPs as servants of the public – all such sentiments and good intentions now lying in tatters; claims invalidated by events.

Paul's mobile pinged: news of a prime ministerial statement within the hour.

Christopher hungrily devoured the news bulletin which reported of an emergency meeting of the cabinet. It was soon followed by pictures of the PM being swept away in his bulletproof car for an audience with Her Majesty Queen Elizabeth II. The tenure of the government seemed flimsy; commentators speculated as to the likely outcome. He could imagine his uncle, Xavier Townsend, the prime minister of the United Kingdom, and his hard-core group of loyalists in the cabinet as incredulous witnesses to the speed with which events had hurtled to this point. Power was slipping from their grasp; political aspirations and careers crashing around them.

'It is with a heavy heart that I speak to the Great British public this evening. The gravity of the situation is one that I bear personally as the prime minister of this great country—'

The PM stopped abruptly, reached for his glass of water and sipped slowly. Replacing his glass gently, he bowed his head as if in prayer as his fingertips came together. It seemed an age before he lifted his eyes back to the camera.

'We had assured the nation of our determination to change the caustic perception of politicians, we were determined to consign malign motivations to the past; to rid the political classes of obscene abuses of power; to remove rule by self-interest. We were resolute in our pursuit of the old-fashioned virtue of honourable public duty...'

'He's quitting,' said Christopher, as he took in his uncle's public announcement, hanging on the prime minister's every word, his dear uncle. Christopher's knuckles whitened, as he clung on to his coffee mug, the dregs now tepid.

Xavier Townsend continued in a scratchy voice to announce the downfall of his government. The prime minister described the challenges of self-serving egotism at the heart of the political classes and spoke earnestly about the policies undertaken to eradicate this cancer; the policies had failed, *he* had failed. Christopher shook his head gravely, the sting of tears in his eyes. He knew that Xavier Townsend would be hurting, the emotionally charged events would scar him deeply and he could hardly bear the thought. The prime minister paused again, cleared his throat and stared ahead in apparent contemplation, peering through the camera with unblinking eyes as if attempting to burn into the consciousness of the watching public; an attempt to connect, to communicate on an emotional level.

The silence spoke volumes to Christopher and weighed so heavily that his head throbbed. He felt a surge of anger and slammed his mug onto the table so hard that it shattered.

'Shit, Paul. I owe the man so much, and we've played a part in his downfall. Me, his *nephew*. After all he's done for me.'

'What are you talking about? Did you know what was really happening? *No*! Not beyond the immediate crisis we were focused on,' said Paul.

'But we knew right enough of the corruption playing out before our eyes. We knew this involved a minister, knew of the sophisticated techniques being deployed. We should have seen beyond the details to understand the toxic implications, the motivations, the evil...' And his father's words leapt back at him, you're a *useless, good for nothing piece of shit...*

'No. Stop torturing yourself. How will that help? We didn't know of the events that brought all this about, and anyway, you personally chose a path away...'

'We could have done more; we *should* have done more. I could have spoken to Xavier – reached out, taken advice, warned him somehow.'

'Warned him of what? And anyway, you did reach out to the most senior civil servant within our reach: Caroline Hope. But at no point could any of us have known of the events that would lead to this point. We still don't! Come on Christopher, this isn't like you. Stop being so illogical, so dramatic. It's too bloody self-indulgent. Snap out—'

Christopher raised a hand to silence him as his uncle continued the broadcast.

'This government has been sorely let down by the immoral and corrupt acts of close colleagues, which serve to discredit our government and tarnish our international reputation. The police will determine the charges to be levelled and the full power of the independent judicial system will be brought to bear on those responsible.'

Xavier Townsend sat back, bowing his head as if in shame, his once vibrant good looks now time-weary and sad. The burdensome responsibility of high office had taken its toll – the stress obvious, the bitter disappointment of failure taken personally.

'It's so cruel,' said Christopher.

'The opposition has declared its intentions to move for a vote of no-confidence in Her Majesty's government. As prime minister, I might be expected to resist such a call, to fight it...But I won't. They are right to bring the motion. We don't deserve to continue, having been brought into such disrepute. Consequently, I have ceded the vote and been granted leave to call a general election by Her Majesty. My party will submit itself to the British public in seeking re-election on a platform of radical political reform. Our mission will be to rid our nation of the very moral deprivation and malignancy that has brought about this crisis. I will be missionary in my zeal to return to the fundamentally important values of duty and public service, which will be at the heart of our manifesto. In the meantime, as the prime minister of Great Britain and Northern Ireland, I offer my personal, fulsome and unreserved apology for this turn of events. Good evening and God bless.'

'He didn't have a choice. I'd hoped he'd hang on and weather the storm, but it was impossible. He's done the right thing, the only thing he could do in the awful circumstances.'

'He'll bounce back,' said Paul.

'I'm not so sure. I wonder if his party will even let him lead an election campaign. It feels terminal, the end of an illustrious career. Brought down by corrupt villains on the make. It's disgusting.' Christopher's voice faltered. 'You know, Paul, this can't continue. The hallmarks of the last decade of...of drift and decline, punc...punctuated by the foul whiff of corruption,' Christopher stammered, fighting his emotions. 'Politicians of all persuasions have plumbed new depths; driven by vanity, a relentless thirst for power. The political giants of yesteryear have disappeared; respected leaders on the world stage replaced by minnows; high-minded principles and philosophy displaced by flaky populist pragmatism...'

'Mm. Feel better now? Sounds like a political speech. An idealist's at that. It's a complicated and dirty world out there – you know that. Is there still a place for such high ideals? What the hell can you do about it anyway?' Paul said.

'Someone somewhere has to stand up and be counted,' Christopher shot back at him. 'Look at the approval ratings of politicians – they're at an all-time low and the oldest parliamentary democracy in the world is now engulfed by public outrage and political inertia.'

'Your uncle tried to turn the tide and look what's happened,' insisted Paul.

'Yes,' Christopher acknowledged, shaking his head sadly. Just two years ago, Xavier Townsend had stood out as the one man with the courage and determination to face public condemnation of the political classes in embracing the need for urgent change; a quest to transform public perceptions. Election to the highest office in the land had given him the opportunity to address the core values and behaviours of government. He had set about his daunting task with a fervour which earned him both high praise and mocking opprobrium in equal measures, a hero in some quarters, a laughingstock in others.

But then, the inevitable happened...events which were to end his career, the damning newspaper headlines which, Christopher knew, would have been like punches to the solar plexus; blows Christopher also felt keenly. A parallel was drawn with the nineteen-sixties Profumo scandal, an affair that had led to the resignation of the Conservative minister of war in the Macmillan government in March 1963. That was followed by Harold Macmillan's subsequent resignation.

'I still reel from the overlap of our business venture. How events careened out of control,' said Christopher, gently shaking his head.

'But you can't wallow in self-pity, Christopher, and anyway, what about Caroline Hope?'

Christopher looked at Paul sharply, accepting the charge. Paul was not particularly renowned for his compassion but even he evidently found the head space to empathise with Caroline Hope rather than languish in morose self-pity.

'Respect! You're right, my friend. Need to get my act together,' he said, as he absent-mindedly set about the collection of his shattered coffee mug, studying the fragments in his hands. The remnants seemed somehow symbolic of his career. *Time to move on, Christopher George Townsend but first...*

2. Father Figure

Five Years Earlier: September 1997

Covent Garden was buzzing as drinkers spilled onto the pavements: office staff sharing a convivial drink with work mates, theatregoers and revellers enjoying the plentiful bars and restaurants. The evening shards of sunlight filtering through the fluffy cumulus clouds reflected off the contemporary glassed flats and Georgian buildings – a golden evening. The people-packed streets throbbed to the beat of pub music, mingling with the sounds of buskers; excitable chatter and laughter all adding to the vibrant cosmopolitan atmosphere. Christopher strode through the hubbub sporting his favourite black suit with gold-coloured tie, red braces and brown brogues. One hand in his pocket, he gave off the air of a young man at ease with the world.

Covent Garden held a special place in his heart, a place he had enjoyed as a young adolescent. His mum had often brought him to watch the performers: clowns and acrobats and jugglers. That was before his poor mum…now it was tainted with sadness which snagged at his cheerful mood. He quickly pushed the thoughts away. Forging on at a brisk pace, Christopher drew close to an older woman with white hair walking alongside a young woman in a short skirt. Squeezing by, *sorry – thank you*, a whining sound penetrated his consciousness. Moments later, a moped hove into his peripheral vision and before anyone could react, its rider grabbed at the older woman's handbag, yanking it from her grasp. With an anguished cry, she collided with the younger girl, and with Christopher, before falling to the pavement. The rider accelerated away, and Christopher sidestepped the fracas, striding on, before he had a chance to even think. It was only when he reached the corner and glanced behind him that he questioned his actions. He had just sidestepped around a person in need, deserting an old woman who might require medical assistance or at least reassurance – and he a senior manager in the caring profession. The words of his coach rang in his ears: *think, connect with people, empathise*. He guiltily retraced his steps, but by then, a small group had gathered to lend their support. He left them to it, reassured that he had at least tried to offer help, his conscience salved.

He was looking forward to seeing his Uncle Xavier but was intrigued as to exactly why his uncle was anxious to meet him. The supper rendezvous had been arranged around the minister's timetable: a vote in the House later that evening. Ducking through the doorway and sliding his slim frame through the alcohol-fuelled prattling throng, Christopher spotted him sitting at a corner table and waved his greeting.

'Hi, Uncle, sorry I'm a bit late. Covent Garden is soooo busy. I guess it always is, oh and some poor woman just got mugged, floored by some moron on a moped. Would you believe it? What a world. How are you?'

'Well hello, young man. Smashing to see you,' said Xavier Townsend, shunning his nephew's proffered hand to draw him into an affectionate hug. Townsend senior wore his trademark blue chalk-stripe suit with waistcoat and a Tory-blue tie over a crisp white shirt with gold cufflinks. Christopher noticed that his uncle had dispensed with hair dye, evidently more relaxed these days about his silver-grey locks. They gave him a distinguished air to suit his new-found prominence in the political world.

'How are you? In good form, I trust. Was she okay, not badly hurt I hope?'

'Oh, I'm sure she'll be fine. Great to see you, Unc...' said Christopher, with a beaming smile.

'How's the business world?'

'Up and down, I guess. It's not without its challenges and as for the bloody owner...well more of that later. Tell me what's happening in Westminster – much more interesting.'

'Westminster is Westminster – a cess pit of machinations and lies. Nothing changes there! But at least a few of us are managing to hold ourselves just above the melee, grinding the cogs of government. As the great man himself said, KBO: keep buggering on! Anyway, we should think about food!'

'How's Aunty Rose?'

'Desperate to know everything that's going on in your life – particularly your love life! You know how she adores a bit of gossip, especially from her favourite nephew.'

'Her *only* nephew! I need to pop around and see her. I will, I will. It's been too long.'

'You're going to have to give me some red meat, my boy. Who's your latest love interest or have you hooked back up with...well you know who—' said Xavier, stopping mid-stream when Christopher held up his hand up as if to say *stop, don't go there*.

'Give me a break,' said Christopher. 'Have to play the field a bit, don't I? Anyway, I was much too young to...'

His Uncle looked unconvinced. The disapproval that Christopher knew lay just below the surface caused him to bristle. He pulled a face, choking back the instinct to argue. *Why did he always have to bring this up? And why did it still strike a raw nerve?* He sighed, fiddled with his signet ring. It was true she had been special – the girlfriend epitaph had hardly cut it, but it was a while ago now. Others had come and gone but he had never known anyone like her. How typical of Xavier to bring this up, knocking him off balance in the process. He looked away, momentarily making eye contact with a pretty, young woman in the corner before dragging his focus back to his uncle.

'Let's not go there. Please.'

'Fair enough. Come on, let's get a drink. What's your poison? Beer? Glass of wine?'

17

Christopher had not seen his uncle for nearly a year, distracted, as he single-mindedly placed his business career centre stage. But he had maintained occasional telephone contact as Xavier rose through the ranks. Their closeness went back to when, as a young teenager, Christopher had struggled with the breakdown of his parents' marriage. He had stayed often with Xavier and Aunty Rose to escape the fall-out of his dad's frequent drunken binges. Eventually, he had disowned his father, and the resentment held to this day.

'My erstwhile brother's on the wagon, Chris, you'll be pleased to hear. At the moment anyway.'

'And how long's that likely to last? I really don't give a shit to be honest with you – after what he did to Mum, how all that ended.'

His dad had suffered a series of minor strokes over recent months. The doctors' most earnest advice concerned his need to change his lifestyle: eat healthily and forgo the take-aways, lose weight, give up the booze and exercise. Not a hope.

'Only natural that you feel that way, but he's still your dad.'

A particular day – *the* day seared in his memory – flashed back. He had come home from school to find his dad blind drunk, swearing and shouting. For once, his mum had answered him back, and his dad lost it completely. Hit her with the full force of his fist. Drew blood. Christopher had tried to intervene to protect her but was also hit. Told to *fuck off*.

'Apparently, I was a stupid, useless little bastard destined for the scrap heap, remember?'

His father had always told him that he was hopeless, ignorant, lacking in guts.

'Listen, I'm sorry,' said Xavier, shifting in his seat. 'You know how we feel about the whole thing. But there's something you need to know. He's had another stroke, Chris.'

Xavier spoke quietly, watching Christopher.

'I'm sorry to hear that, but he's only got himself to blame.'

'It's quite a serious one, I think. Come on, can't you consign the past to history? Who knows how much longer he's got?'

Christopher thought about his mother – she had been admitted into a psychiatric unit after suffering a mental breakdown, and her illness had migrated into dementia.

'Is it terminal?'

'They're still hoping for a recovery of sorts – but you can never tell, not even the medics.'

'I can't forgive him. How can I?'

'He's your dad, he needs you. It's not healthy to be consumed by hate, you know. Your Aunty Rose worries about you, we both do…'

'You can relax on that count. I choose not to think about him mainly. You're more of a dad to me than he ever was. I don't dwell on that period. But I can't forget what he did to Mum. Remember that bath? The colour of the water? I can't forgive him, I just can't. But I owe you and Aunty Rose everything.'

'And it's as a father figure that I ask you to reconsider. For you, if not for him. You may live to regret it otherwise. I'm not defending him. He gave you a torrid time as a kid and was never there for you – but he's still your dad.'

'He's beyond saving but I'll prove him wrong about me. I *will* succeed, Uncle. For myself and for you two. In a funny way – for him as well. I'll bloody well show him.'

'Your aunty Rose and I are so proud of you, so proud,' said Xavier with liquid eyes, reaching out to grasp Christopher's arm.

His uncle was a surprisingly sensitive man for a senior minister in the cutthroat world of politics. Some claimed it was his Achilles heel, but Christopher liked to think it showed his humanity – a rare trait in the modern political world.

The waiter placed before them plates of Lancashire Hot Pot with a mini Shepherd's Pie and a side dish of steaming green vegetables. They washed it down with a glass of Rioja. Xavier had declared that such a main course needed a robust wine and that a fine Burgundy or even a Claret would be lost.

'The Rioja will stand up to it well. Nice and chewy,' he said.

'Tastes silky to me. How's your moral crusade going, Uncle Xav?'

'I wouldn't quite call it that. And enough of the uncle bit, it makes me feel old…Xavier will do just nicely, Xav if you like.'

'Awesome. Xavier it is then. But as to your crusade – the tabloids call it exactly that, don't they? I hope you don't have too many indiscretions lurking in the dim and distant to come back and haunt you. Were you a tearaway in your prime? I imagine you sowed your wild oats and all that, eh?'

'Not on your life. I had a boring youth, fortunately. Met your Aunty Rose when we were both at University. A one-woman man, that's me. Dull, but there we have it.'

Christopher had closely followed Xavier Townsend's political career, as he rose to one of the great offices of state, that of Home Secretary. Xavier had embarked upon an attempt to persuade his parliamentary colleagues on a cross-party basis to rid themselves of the unsavoury reputation acquired over recent decades: to embrace old-fashioned virtues of public service and duty. The project was on the runway and he said he was confident it would take off and soar to new heights. Christopher wished him well in his endeavours but privately suspected the process would take decades at best; at worst, it would crash and burn taking the pilot down with it.

'About time you told me about your business career, Chris. How's it going at…remind me.'

'Skills World Limited. I joined as one of their Regional Managers. Good company if a bit old-fashioned, but generally well regarded. Mind you, progress is slow, much too slow. There's so much opportunity but trying to persuade the owner to change is a nightmare. The internal politics are acrimonious, a roller-coaster at the moment. And—'

'Hang on, I think I know them. Isn't it owned by Bill Taylor? A bit of an acquired taste, isn't he?'

19

'And I've yet to acquire it! He's so bloody controlling, pompous, arrogant and just damned well impossible. The dinosaur's attitude to technology is very last century. The modern world's left him behind, and he seems to be the only one who hasn't cottoned on to that. Can't tell you how bloody frustrating it is. Someone needs to get him to see sense, persuade him to hang his boots up.'

'And you're the one, are you? How's that working out?' asked Xavier, raising his eyebrows.

'Not great…'

'I can imagine but you must've known of his reputation when you took the job? It goes before him,' said Xavier.

'Knowing it and experiencing it…What would you have me do? Man-up, eh? Take the pain, bide my time? Is that the message? Give me strength. But there are good prospects for the business if only we can persuade Bill to let us get on with things. And I can see a path for future advancement personally, so I'll struggle on and see where we get to,' sighed Christopher.

He had a game plan but was exasperated at it being thwarted at every twist and turn.

'I could tell you a thing or two about Bill. A bit of a lady's man you know. But you have to give it to him; he's kept the business going a very long time and you don't do that without—'

'Yeah, yeah but times change.'

'There speaks an impatient, confident young man. Don't over-do it, Chris. Don't want you tripping yourself up. But it's a good thing to gain business experience before entering the world of Westminster,' said Xavier, 'too many career politicians these days with a background of Eton, Oxbridge and the inevitable PPE. No bloody experience of the outside world so this is all grist to the mill for you…'

'Who said I'm going down that particular route?' Christopher retorted, sitting back in his seat to take in what had been mooted, turning his dessertspoon over and over. And it somehow dragged up his university girlfriend's assertions *a restless soul, driven by a sense of higher purpose, a yearning for power…driving ambition, not always attractive though, Christopher George.* Such nonsense. But why did it still prick his conscience? Casting the thoughts to one side, he scanned the restaurant alighting on that same pretty girl in the corner, briefly returning a flirtatious smile. Yet again, Xavier had delivered a message that somehow resonated and disturbed in equal measures. He supposed this was the knack of an experienced politician. Or perhaps the filial perception of his surrogate father. Either way…

'Your destiny, my dear chap. Now you really must excuse me. Must get back for that vote. Look, it's been simply marvellous to see you. We must catch up again soon. Stay in touch…the bill please if you would be so kind,' he said to the passing waiter.

'Can I get that?' said Christopher, reaching for his wallet.

'Not on your life. Just do me one favour – please at least think about what I've had to say about your dad. Will you do that at least?'

'I can't promise to change my mind though…' with which Xavier scooped up the bill, shook Christopher's hand briskly, drawing him into a bear hug. Christopher watched him pay, nod to a passing acquaintance, shake a hand thrust in his direction and turn to wave goodbye before walking briskly into the hustle and bustle of Henrietta Street.

Christopher sat back and sipped his wine whilst reflecting upon their conversation. He did not want to think any more about his dad and it was too painful to think about his mum's demise. Forcing himself to pull away from his early teenage years, he thought about the more immediate business challenges at Skills World. He had his eye on a promotion to the managing director's position. Then he could lead the business, although he had the small matter of needing to persuade the old patrician, Bill Taylor, of his merits. As his mind floated over the various strands of the conversation that evening, he briefly allowed himself to reflect upon his old flame. Theirs had been more than a fling and he had let her escape, he reflected wryly. *Hey-ho Christopher George Townsend, you can't win them all.*

3. Caroline

Caroline faced her staff and scanned the utilitarian, open-plan office. Thirty or so heads stooping over papers, scribbling notes, scrutinising computer screens. Apart from the odd whispered aside, there was little interaction. She ignored the black looks thrown in her direction from Julie, who had needed to be reminded of her need to focus, concentrate on her work and stop giggling. The exchange had not endeared her to staff but then it was not a popularity contest. Just as well, she thought grimly. The atmosphere and scene never changed. Her section was reputed as being highly organised, efficient and effective. Caroline took a pride in that, but staff kept asking for transfers – why, was a mystery. They should be proud to be part of such a well-regarded team. Caroline's unrelenting attention to detail and steadfastness in delivering the tasks of the department had led to her promotion. But the promotional gloss and the boost to her sense of self-worth was fading as routine became ingrained in her daily life; a ration of mundanity and boredom laced with the onerous responsibility of maintaining a smoothly working machine.

Glancing at her watch, it was time for a break. With a sigh, she headed for the double doors, the escape route. Reaching for her grey coat, red, woollen scarf and hat, Caroline strode away, intent on braving the elements.

Behind her, there was a sudden commotion from the adjoining section, followed by a roar of laughter. 'Laters...' cried the offender, bursting through the doors and colliding with Caroline, a peel of laughter fading into the background.

'Sorry...Oh hi. It's Caroline, isn't it?' said Olivia, a diminutive, bubbly character who had been the evident source of the office hilarity.

'Causing mayhem again, Olivia?'

'Where you off to?'

'In search of a caffeine fix. Need to get out of this place,' Caroline groaned.

'Great idea. Mind if I join you?'

'Not sure I'd be good company. A rotten morning so if you don't...'

'Nonsense. Come on, let's go. Now just you wait till I tell you the office goss—' Olivia hooked her arm through Caroline's and marched them down the stairs out into Tothill Street. After a couple of twists and turns, they found their way to Victoria.

'What was all the hilarity?' asked Caroline.

'Just the girls taking the mickey out of Fran. Our bossy supervisor. Hey, look at that handbag. Isn't it just gorgeous?'

Olivia dragged her to the shop window. It struck Caroline that the two of them made a curious sight, a stark contrast. A small, pretty blonde extrovert chatting away non-stop alongside an ungainly, tall, withdrawn girl.

'Yikes, look at the price. I need to sweet-talk Julian. Pots of money he simply yearns to spend on me; doesn't know it yet mind! Come on – coffee.'

'And do I need that fix,' agreed Caroline, now adjusted to the notion of sharing her break with Olivia. At least she brought some brightness to lighten her day.

As they meandered on, Olivia continued the endless chat, pausing only to pop into a newsagent, soon emerging with a white plastic bag. Caroline followed her around the corner to a side-street where Olivia found a local tramp.

'Hi, Bel. How you doing? Here, get these inside you,' she said, reaching inside her bag and setting a sandwich and drink down on the bench beside Bel.

'Bless you, love,' was the croaked reply.

'Now remember to get a hot meal at that hostel we found. Get there in plenty of time though so you can enjoy a bath as well.'

'Stink, do I?' said the tramp, flashing a gummy smile.

'You mark my words, Bel. Promise?'

'Promise, boss. 'Ere – you ever been a headmistress, Miss Bossy Pants?'

'You've promised now! Lines for you otherwise…'

Caroline soaked up the chatter and the extraordinary scene with Bel, relishing the distraction and a change of pace; admiring the sheer humanity and warmth of Olivia towards someone most people were scurrying past.

Settling into a corner with their coffees, she was again struck by how pretty Olivia was with her Shirley Temple blonde curls cut short into the nape of her neck, almond-shaped hazel eyes and her slim, almost boyish figure. Olivia was popular, and it was not difficult to see why. The thoughts crossed her mind with a wave of wistful jealousy, and an instant stab of guilt. But the nose studs and eyebrow-ring? *Why would such a pretty girl want to pierce her own body?*

The two chatted about life generally before focusing on the department, Olivia's garrulousness rapidly filling any gaps.

'Your career's going great guns, isn't it? I mean it's only a couple of years or so since you were on the grad scheme. And now look at you,' said Olivia. Caroline's career did seem to be on a sharply ascending trajectory following her recent promotion, a reward for her diligence and dedication, efficiency and determination.

'It's okay, I suppose, but I don't know if this is me.'

'Why? You always seem so in control.'

'Some days, I love the sense of achievement. And the next—'

'What, Hon?'

'I'm not sure I fit in. Not sure how long I'll stay. What about you? Got your eye on that supervisory vacancy?'

'Too busy enjoying life.'

'Oh, that seems a waste.'

'Hey, lighten up. Take a chill-pill. Life's for living.'

Caroline lapsed into silence, her mind elsewhere.

'Do you have family down here?' probed Olivia.

'No. No one.'

'A bloke?'

'No.'

'So where is your family from?'

Caroline's mind skipped back to the rectory in Northumberland, and a day fixed in her memory. She had been just twelve when her world changed abruptly – the joy and light that was her mother suddenly extinguished; a candle prematurely snuffed out. Cancer. Suddenly, she was sharing her memory fragments with Olivia as if they had known each other for years.

'Must have been hard. More than hard,' said Olivia, with concern etched on her features.

'It was. But lots of people have to cope with much worse, so my dad said.'

'He must have been devastated?'

'I don't know really. He never spoke about her. Never showed any emotion. Just seemed to accept it as the mysterious purpose of God's will, a further test of his faith. Oh, I'm sorry. Just listen to me being all maudlin. Let's change the subject.'

'Refills and cakes – that's what we need,' announced Olivia, recovering some of her energy.

As Caroline watched Olivia making her way past the students that congregated noisily by the counter, she allowed herself to slip back in time, soon lost in her thoughts…

Returning with the coffee and pastries, Olivia cast her a look of empathy, taking in Caroline's melancholy. 'Sorry about your mum, babe. Poor you. It's terribly sad. I can't imagine what it must have been like.

'Thanks.'

'I mean, my mum's an absolute pain but I love her to bits. Always telling me off for going with the wrong blokes, partying too much, spending too much and all that. Mind you, she's usually right.' Olivia wrinkled her nose in mock annoyance, before breaking into a grin.

'You're quite the tonic, aren't you? And here I am banging on about death, being all doom and gloom. What about your life, Olivia? You obviously live it large.'

'Oh, you've got to—'

'Hang on, crikey look at the time – we need to get back,' interjected Caroline.

'If we must…' groaned Olivia. 'Tell you what, let's have a drink one night,' she suggested, as they pulled on their coats and headed back.

4. Night Out

Caroline had arranged to meet Olivia at the iconic Lamb & Flag pub, dating back to the early eighteenth century it had been a former haunt of Charles Dickens. Once hosting bare-knuckle fights, its nickname was 'Bucket of Blood'. Early evening drinkers were spilling out onto the cobbled street to enjoy the warm spring evening, and just as Caroline was summoning the courage to venture inside, she was assailed by Olivia's cheery greeting.

'Am I late? Sorry. You got a drink? No? Come on let's grab a G&T.'

Caroline smiled, enjoying the warmth of the greeting but also feeling a little disoriented by her friend's tactile, effusive manner.

Emerging a short while later from the packed interior, clutching their drinks, they muscled in to create space next to a small group of young men, perching themselves precariously on the edge of a wooden bench.

'Love your outfit,' said Caroline.

Olivia's style was bohemian – reminiscent of the nineteen-sixties, with facial piercings lending a modern-day twist. She wore knee-length leather boots and a tiny, black and white checked, Mary Quant-style mini-skirt. As Olivia balanced on the edge of her seat, shapely legs crossed, her mini skirt rode high. A simple top, strings of coloured beads slung around her neck and a small, red beret atop her blonde curls completed the extraordinary look. Caroline was not the only admirer. The youths at their table were taking a distinct interest, their conversation lapsing briefly, eyes wandering. Olivia seemed completely oblivious. Perhaps she was used to men reacting that way.

'Thanks, babe,' she said, pulling a slight face at Caroline's attire. 'You must come shopping with me, you know. Need to take you in hand. No offence.'

It was impossible to take offence with Olivia. But Caroline looked down at her flat shoes, grey woollen skirt and white blouse and protectively pulled her jacket tightly around her. She self-consciously ran her hand over her short mousy brown hair and touched her long, crooked nose. The gangly, gawky teenager who had felt so out of place at the youth club of her adolescence – who had viewed her contemporaries with lofty disdain as a fig leaf for her own inadequacy – was still alive and kicking. And it pained her to realise it.

'Mind you,' Olivia added quickly, I love that ring,' grabbing her hand to admire it more closely.

'My most treasured possession. It was my mam's – and hers before her.' Caroline splayed her long bony fingers to allow closer inspection of the sapphire and diamond ring, the stones sitting in a distinctive antique setting. She fought with thoughts of her mother's illness and passing, which had torn her to pieces.

But Olivia was such a conversational butterfly that they were swiftly off on to other topics: the best pubs, live music in Soho, the latest films and her boyfriend.

'Tell me about Julian then?' prompted Caroline. 'How long have you and he been an item?'

'He's gorgeous, but a bit clingy. Works in the City doing something or other intensely boring. Don't understand it really, but he's got loads of dosh. That helps. We've been going out about four months, I guess. That's long-term for me. He's at football with his insufferable mates. Chelsea is his main passion, I come a distant second to that,' she laughed. 'I insist on plenty of me-time in any case. Can't let him monopolise me.'

'And he approves of your, err, taste in fashion?'

'What *are* you suggesting, hon?'

'Not exactly corporate, is it? It's quite the rebel look, isn't it? Mind you, it gets you plenty of attention,' she observed, pointing to the reactions of those around them, 'and you look great. But what about the piercings?' Caroline raised an eyebrow which produced another fit of giggles from her friend.

'You don't approve! Well, he loves them – especially this one,' Olivia said, pushing her studded tongue out. 'And this.' She lifted her top slightly to reveal a navel piercing in the shape of a small heart dangling from a silver chain. 'And there's a *very* private one he likes even more,' she added, glancing downwards.

'*Olivia*…Anyway, tell me about your family. Are you close?'

'Changing the subject? Not much to tell, just a boringly normal family unit,' Olivia said. 'All the usual family stuff with arguments and dramas and tantrums…'

Caroline heard how Olivia's childhood and her own could hardly have been more different. Her new-found friend had grown up with siblings, a mam and dad and surrounded by wider family in a town in the midlands. To Caroline, this was anything but normal. Her parents had been middle-aged when she had come along, and the premature loss of her mam left her in a large house with just her elderly father.

'Enough about my boring family. Come on, I've told you about Julian – now what about your love life?' insisted Olivia, when she returned with another round of drinks.

'That'll be a short conversation.'

'No blokes in the recent past?'

'No,' she sighed. 'I told you a bit about my upbringing. And suddenly, I find myself in London. It's a world away from anything I've ever experienced,' Caroline reflected sadly, taking a sip of her Hendricks gin and tonic.

'What about uni?' asked Olivia.

Caroline soon found herself recalling university life, her friend listening intently. How at the tender age of sixteen, she had gone to Cambridge University, having obtained top grades at A level; landing in a new world she was ill-prepared for. She had not had a wide circle of friends, sport was not her thing, she was younger than the other students and so all she really did was study and play chess. Caroline recalled how she and her father had found a common interest in chess after her mam's death, their only mutual interest really. It was the solitary pastime that met with parental approval and which provided treasured father/daughter shared time. Caroline had excelled at the game and gone on to become the under-sixteen champion of the National School Chess Championship at the age of just fourteen and subsequently, the youngest ever winner of the Women's British Chess Championships.

'Wow. That's impressive.'

'It didn't help much socially though. I struggled a bit, if I'm honest, but threw myself into the one group I learnt to enjoy – the Poets' Society. That's where I met Cecil.'

Caroline described him as a dreamy, slightly dippy boy. He had regarded himself as something of a modern-day Byron and had aped the flamboyance of the notorious romantic poet. Inevitably, he was ridiculed by his fellow students, teased mercilessly, picked on. But the two of them had found common ground. Two social outcasts; kindred spirits turning to each other for succour in the face of hostility.

'He was a bit weird, now I come to think of it. Immature, but nice. Caring. Funny. Made me laugh.'

'Did you and he get it on?'

'Oh God, Olivia, you don't dance around the handbags, do you?'

Caroline let Olivia drag out of her the details of their short-lived relationship. After a few dates, they had entered an experimental phase.

'No discussion. Sex was much too embarrassing to discuss.'

What had followed had been educational but also clumsy and humiliating. At Olivia's encouragement and with the help of the alcohol, she gradually rid herself of her inhibitions to describe the uncertain exploratory groping, opportunity for research, a sexual apprenticeship.

'Following a particularly dull society meeting,' Caroline reminisced, 'we went to Cecil's room to, err, you know…' She lapsed into silence, as she recalled the events in that tiny student room…

'You can't leave me hanging like that. Come on, babe. The telling is therapeutic you know,' said Olivia.

'Oh, in for a penny, in for a pound I suppose,' Caroline responded, slurping her G&T before pressing on to describe the proceedings. 'If I'm honest, I was a bit keener than he was. Goaded him a bit but he'd got the, you know, thingies…'

'Johnnies, condoms.'

'Mm. I even remember the Byronesque exchange we had. *Pleasure's a sin,* he declared, with a mock frown and a raised finger of admonishment.'

'And you said?' prompted Olivia, flourishing an extended hand palm-side up in dramatic encouragement.

'I just completed the Byron line from Don Juan, *and sometimes sin's a pleasure*!'

Caroline described how their giggles had released some of the tension as they set about their agenda, with Lord Byron's image peering sardonically down at them. She described how a flustered Cecil whose nervousness had reached new heights struggled with his task, all fingers and thumbs only to climax prematurely as Caroline leant a helping hand. 'We both recoiled in horror – seemed to place a seal on the relationship.'

'Oh lovely,' Olivia exclaimed, pulling a face. 'Well, we've all got stories like that, babe. Hilarious. I don't suppose you ever stayed in touch?'

'No.'

Whilst Olivia went in search of the ladies toilet, Caroline mused on how she had been prepared to share even the most private experience with her friend, something she had never dreamed of doing. She had never had a close friendship, no one who was ever remotely interested in her. Other than the soppy Byronesque character that is, and he did not count. But the whole Cecil experience had awakened in her an awareness of her own sensuality. She had tried to repress her instincts and thoughts, considering them to be distasteful, dirty even. Certainly, her father would not approve; he would be horrified. But Olivia seemed to have a wholly different outlook on life which cast such matters in a new light and the libertarian, cosmopolitan world that she had landed in seemed to have a totally different moral compass.

Caroline pulled herself out of her reverie to notice that Olivia seemed to have acquired yet another admirer who had walked her back to their table, a handsome swarthy guy with a lean face. The two of them chatted animatedly and flirted outrageously before her male suitor moved away with a distinct bounce in his step.

'Friend of yours?' asked Caroline, intrigued.

'He is now. Marku. He's a Romanian, gorgeous, isn't he?'

'You mean he's just picked you up? You'd never met him before?'

'The picking up was mutual, but yeah.'

'I thought you were in a relationship, Olivia.'

'*Hello*. This is the twentieth century. He was cute. Does no harm to benchmark Julian occasionally.'

'Laters,' she shouted, responding to Marku's cheery wave. 'Back to you though. What brought you to London? How come you chose to work at the department of wank and poverty?'

She smiled and thought about the transition from rural Northumberland. Taking a sip from her drink, she then outlined to Olivia how she had been determined to escape the family home, commenting indignantly on the difficult exchange with her father about gaining a place on the graduate scheme. How dare he simply expect her to fall into the role of housekeeper as some sort of replacement for his wife? *Surely, she had a right to a career and to her own life?*

'Course you do, babe.'

Caroline was still bruised by his lack of support and his disinterest in her being selected on the scheme. He refused to congratulate her or enjoy her success and made clear his objection to Caroline moving away from her familial duties. He had been dismissive of London, muttering something about *a den of iniquity*. Caroline's resolve to move away had been strengthened by the exchange, hurt and dismayed though she was. She needed to find her own way in the world, perhaps career success would help her to feel better about herself, about life.

She lapsed into quiet introspection as Olivia was momentarily distracted by one of the guys on their table. She had quickly absorbed herself into the graduate scheme but found London desperately lonely. Gradually settling into the pace of life, she began to appreciate the diverse home of a myriad of ethnicities, cultures and religions which gave rise to a wide spectrum of activities and tastes. A place where almost anything went. Life in London was a completely new experience at so many levels. Caroline lived in Camden Town and would often wander around Covent Garden, through theatre-land and into Soho on her way home. People did not appear to judge each other's interests. So, she learnt that a brave step across the threshold to browse the shelves of a sex shop in Soho went completely unnoticed. She could further explore her sexuality without anyone judging her. Intrigued and emboldened, she set about accessing magazines, videos and various aids that interested her. No one cared so long as she paid for her goods…

'You struggling to adapt to the smoke?' Olivia probed, breaking into Caroline's introspection.

'Could say that. It's more than that though. I mean just look at me,' she exhaled in exasperation. 'Oh, I'm sorry this is all me, me, me. But it's so hard. It's all right for you, Olivia…'

'What, babe?'

'You're gorgeous, blokes fall over themselves, but hardly notice I'm here. I don't blame them, I mean look in the mirror and then look at me,' Caroline said. 'Fish out of water. Dowdy. Plain. Ordinary…I'm lonely for God's sake. The only good thing about my life is my career. And you, of course.'

'Well, I'm going to take you in hand. It really isn't that bad; life can be great. You just need to be shown how.'

Over the coming months, Olivia was true to her word and their friendship blossomed. They enjoyed some of the social life that London had to offer – cinemas, theatres, restaurants and pubs. Caroline had never laughed so much and felt a warmth and closeness that she had not known for too many years.

Olivia influenced Caroline's choice of music, fashion and makeup. She took notice of current trends and delighted in buying colourful, fashionable outfits in Covent Garden and Carnaby Street. Caroline learnt how to make the most of herself by shedding her drab clothes and low heels. Her social life developed from the confidence that her early friendship with Olivia slowly instilled. She enjoyed short relationships with a number of guys, but none were of a serious nature, few lasting more than a month or so. But life was becoming tolerable, enjoyable even.

5. Making an Impact

Not only was Caroline's social life looking up, but her professional world was becoming more interesting and fulfilling. Perhaps life was not so bad after all, she mused as she hurried back to her meeting after a short coffee break.

'So, in the red corner,' intoned Sebastian Frith, the minister attempting to sum up an impasse, 'we have the Job Centres claiming the current programmes are successfully returning the long term unemployed to the work force; that these must be delivered by the public sector. In the blue corner are the doubters who question the evidence. Caroline, you're the only person in the room yet to voice an opinion. What do you have to say?'

She had joined a high-level meeting, having been promoted to the role of deputy to the head of procurement at the tender age of just twenty-nine. It was chaired by the department's permanent secretary with the minister in attendance. The assembled protagonists were assessing the effectiveness of the programmes currently in progress and Caroline had listened intently to the arguments. She had been delighted at being asked to attend such a meeting, although the prospect had seemed daunting. Nonetheless, the personal recognition gave her a warm glow and it was also a welcome break from the grind of normal office routine. And the topic of the meeting was an area of interest to her; she had spent hours researching and thinking about the issues. Early programmes had been solely delivered by the Job Centres but there was a growing body of opinion in favour of changing this monopoly; that a new approach was needed. In recent times, contracts had been let to the private sector, but these represented a small fraction of the total. The Job Centre network still dominated delivery.

Attitudes were changing as first the US government took the view that welfare benefits for those out of work should be earned via work in public-service jobs. This American 'workfare' concept developed into a more empathetic approach in the UK with emphasis upon the support of unemployed adults; education and training programmes developed to support and equip unemployed 'clients' for the world of work. These were pioneering times and Caroline developed an insatiable appetite to analyse, learn and understand.

All of the meeting's participants, ragged from their arguments, turned to glare at her, perhaps unsure what to expect from this normally taciturn young official. The whole room waited on her contribution; she sensed hostility. Finding it difficult being the centre of attention, she was nevertheless confident of her subject, two counter-balancing notions. Here was an opportunity to begin to make her mark. Caroline fought inwardly to allow her confidence in the detail to percolate to the surface.

'Well, Minister,' she began, her palms moistening, 'I've been working on these questions for many months now. I've carefully studied all the available evidence.'

'And?' prompted the minister, raising a hand to silence Felicity Jenkinson, the senior representative of the Job Centre, who was sighing in exasperation, poised to re-enter the fray.

'Well, it's hard to avoid reaching uncomfortable conclusions if one looks at this dispassionately.' She paused and glanced around the table nervously, but despite her angst, she also felt a frisson of excitement at having such an audience hanging on her words.

'Yes? *Good*! And what are they? Spit it out,' he insisted, glancing at his watch. This particular minister might be a junior in the department, but he was expected to rise through the ranks to reach the cabinet. He had a developing reputation as someone who did not suffer fools gladly and tended towards a hectoring, impatient manner. But it seemed that he was also on the search for innovative solutions, so long as they could secure political capital to further his career of course. Caroline sensed rather than understood this but, in any event, she would deliver her conclusions whether they found favour or not; she knew no other way.

'Firstly, there's simply not the dataset to be completely confident about what works and what doesn't. Secondly, I'm not convinced that the Job Centre is best placed to deliver these programmes…' she began.

'Stuff and nonsense, you haven't got a clue what you're…' said Felicity.

'Oh, do be quiet, Felicity, will you?' the minister demanded. 'I'd like to hear what Caroline has to say. Please continue, come on, speak up, I haven't got all day.'

'On the whole, the Job Centre does a great job, but the performance metrics show glacial improvement. At this rate, there's no chance of policy objectives being achieved for years, if ever.'

'And you conclude what exactly?'

'We need to inject some creativity and imagination. In my opinion, we need to open up the programmes for wider participation by the private and third sectors…'

'Oh, this is intolerable. She's only a junior and is totally deluded—'

'Shut up, Felicity,' the minister said, provoking a sharp intake of breath amongst her team.

'As I was saying, Minister,' continued Caroline, losing some of her inhibitions to return Felicity's stare before re-focusing, 'the Job Centre can't, and shouldn't, do everything…'

She proceeded to advocate that it should focus on what it does best, that there should be a review and redefinition of the purpose of the Job Centre network and that they should open up the wider delivery of all welfare-to-work and vocational training programmes to open competition. She spoke of integrating vocational training, of having a payment by results approach and of engaging with the private and charity sectors to change delivery patterns.

'Oh, heaven preserve us…' proclaimed a member of the Job Centre team. Caroline glanced at him but continued. 'I fear we are inadvertently encouraging the creation of generational unemployment cultures and ghettos by our well-intentioned but failing policies…'

'Please spare us the lecture. Get off your moral soap-box will…' interjected an exasperated, seething Felicity, not able to contain herself any longer.

'Felicity! Do *shut* it. Please continue, Caroline,' barked the minister.

'I think we should also introduce a national dataset to record all interactions with every person who becomes registered as unemployed, however short that period is; however many times that person becomes unemployed; to build a profile of unemployment. A lifetime-record that tracks interactions with, for example, the Job Centres and employers; to record periods of work experience, vocational training qualifications and training programme participation. Only then will we create the intelligence and statistical data to know how and where to effectively deploy our scarce resources. Then we will know what works and what doesn't – not only across the entire cohort of unemployed people but sliced and diced to show empirical evidence of the effectiveness of our programmes by different age groups; to show geographical differences; to show results by different types of clients; and to—'

'Enough!' barked the minister, Sebastian Frith. 'A word please,' he spat out at Steven Garside. The two of them left the meeting, which dissolved into acrimony, sharp words being flung at Caroline from one direction whilst others defended her corner. For her part, Caroline sat back and allowed the arguments to wash over her. She could hardly believe she had managed to speak up and at such length. But she had worked hard at this policy agenda and had studied the evidence in both the USA and in the UK and applied her logical mind to the issues. All this gave her conviction and an appetite to contribute. She sensed that at last this was the big opportunity to make a difference, to do something really special and perhaps to further her own career in the process. *Then maybe you'll be impressed, Daddy? Be proud of me?* After all, at the heart of this are the Christian values of helping disadvantaged people. This was just a modern-day approach that would surely resonate with her father's faith. The thought was enough to make her realise that it was some time since she had tried to contact him. She would ring that evening, and perhaps arrange to spend a few days with him at home.

6. Building Bridges

As Caroline took her usual route home, she reflected on a rewarding day. It had been a long one with an early start to ensure her preparations were sufficient for the important meeting and a late one too; staying long after her staff had departed to catch up on paperwork. But who would have thought that she would have the minister and the perm sec hanging on her words? She could hardly wait to tell Olivia, but tonight she needed to ring her father. It was long overdue and today was a good day to do it. Caroline almost felt good about herself. He could not puncture that feeling today; she would not allow it. But first, she would step through Soho and buy a few magazines for later. And a bottle of wine to celebrate.

Letting herself in to her block of flats through the communal front door, she saw the old man of the downstairs flat just about to cross his threshold. He stooped to pick up a black and white cat purring around his ankles.

'Evening, Mr Green, how are you?'

He looked at her coldly, scowled, grunted and disappeared inside, slamming the door after him.

'How nice to see you too. Yes indeed, I'm very well, how good of you to ask and for once I've had a perfectly wonderful day,' she said aloud to his front door.

Having prepared a snack supper and poured herself a large glass of white wine, she sat down and thought about her father. He was probably lonely, which must be why he was always so gruff and impatient with her, so cold. But from what she could glean from his short letter, he was leading an ever more austere existence. His life seemed to be restricted to a diet of the bible and parish duties with occasional meetings with the bishop. His evenings were devoted to preparing sermons, listening to the radio and to reading classical fiction: Dickens, Dostoevsky, George Eliot. He did not seem to have a circle of friends and enjoyed no hobbies as far as she could tell.

After a while, she dialled the number, getting an answer on the third attempt.

'Yes,' spoke a voice laced with irritation.

'Daddy, how are you?'

'Caroline. I'm a bit busy right now.'

'But always a few minutes for your favourite daughter. Isn't that right, Daddy? Pleased to hear from me? I miss you so.'

'It's been a while and of course I'm pleased to hear from you, Caroline. And as you well know, you're my only daughter. Or was that supposed to be a joke? Maybe I'm not attuned to the humour of the sophisticates you meet in London these days.'

'I don't know about that. Just a…how are you?'

'I'm well enough, thank you.'

'That's good. Just wait until you hear what I've been doing today, Daddy. A meeting with a minister and the permanent secretary. What do you think about that? And they asked for my views on an exciting new policy. You'd approve as it's all about helping those without work and needing benefits and training and some money to tide them over. Very Christian, don't you think? And I've been promoted and—' But her attempts to inject some energy and Olivia-like bonhomie did not seem to be getting through.

'That sounds nice. Now I really am very busy. So, if you will forgive me—'

'Aren't you pleased for me?'

'Of course. Always. But you're still in London. I just don't understand…I mean, what would your mam have thought of your desertion…'

'I like to think she'd have been proud of me, Daddy. Why can't you be?'

'Don't be ridiculous.'

But just exactly what he thought she was being ridiculous about was a mystery and as for desertion, she could not trust herself with a response to the charge.

'How long is this phase going to last, Caroline?'

'Daddy! It isn't a phase, it's not some sort of adolescent preoccupation you know. This is my career we are talking about and—'

'I wish you well, Caroline. You know where home is when you come to your senses.'

7. Annual Dinner and Ball

Flush with the news of her promotion, Caroline prepared for the annual ball, this being attended by civil servants, various sponsors and lobbyists as a grand affair in the heart of London. Neither she nor Olivia had partners at that particular time so agreed to accompany each other.

Both had booked a day's holiday and set about spending it jointly in their preparations for a special evening. They met at an upmarket spa in Marble Arch for a morning of pampering over full body massages, detoxifying palm and foot therapies and waxing. After a light lunch served with a glass of pink champagne they spilled out of the restaurant, hailed a cab and next stop was a fashionable hairdressing salon in Knightsbridge. The day was unashamedly given over to unbridled luxury and dedication to the preparations for an evening of splendour.

Caroline's father would not have approved, but he had no concept of her life in London and expressed little curiosity about it either. She chose not to inform him, safe in the knowledge that he would neither understand nor see anything other than hedonistic excess. Some of these thoughts worried her normally, but today she would not submit to guilty feelings or misgivings. It was all about shameless, self-indulgent high-living.

The two linked arms as they glided into the Café Royale, one of London's most glamorous destinations in Regent's Street, in the very heart of the West End. They were welcomed formally and directed to the reception area where they entered a room of luxurious opulence with deep-piled carpets, Corinthian pillars and mirrored panels with heavily gilded frames. The Louis XVI style room also boasted a highly decorative ceiling depicting scenes of love and romance, from which hung large, pendulous crystal chandeliers.

As they entered the throng, glass of champagne in hand, they were greeted by Caroline's line manager, Simon Greening.

'Hello there, you two – how nice to see you. Let me introduce you to the permanent secretary. Steven, this is Caroline and Olivia who work in—'

'We've met, haven't we, Caroline? How nice to see you again? I thought you spoke up very bravely in front of the minister the other day,' said the permanent secretary.

Caroline mumbled a polite response and glowed inside.

The two of them sipped their drinks and Caroline inwardly gulped. It was one thing to speak out at a meeting on a topic she was confident in but quite another at such a lavish social occasion. And the permanent secretary's daunting reputation went before him.

'Hello, Steven, how are you?' greeted Olivia, proceeding to engage him in lively conversation. After a short while, he excused himself and drifted off to join another group.

'I didn't know you two had met,' gasped Caroline.

'Never seen him before in my life. Hey, loosen up, hon,' she said gleefully, lifting two more glasses of champagne from a passing waiter's tray. 'Here, this'll help. Let me introduce you to Freddie. Bit of a lad, if you know what I mean, but entertaining company.' She dragged Caroline off to a neighbouring cluster, breaking into their conversation with an effortless ease Caroline could only envy.

'Freddie, I thought you might be here. How's tricks? Caroline, this is that womaniser I was telling you about. Be wary of this man. No woman's safe in his company. Beware.'

'Olivia, what a joy. How are you?' said Freddie. 'Don't take any notice of her, Caroline, she talks utter garbage at times. Most of the time, come to think of it. Nice to meet you and do you know H? No? Let me introduce you. Now if you're looking for a rich, eligible bachelor...*and* he's an inveterate lady's man, I would have you know.'

'I'm not,' laughed Caroline, noticing H's distinctive attire complete with a white dinner jacket, burgundy-coloured bow tie and matching cummerbund. In a sea of black, he made quite a visual impact.

'Hello, pleased to meet you,' she said, shifting uncomfortably, self-conscious about her loftiness, almost wishing she had worn her flats.

'My pleasure entirely, Caroline,' H said with a beaming smile that revealed a cute dimple on his left cheek.

Introductions having been made, Caroline became stranded with H as Olivia and Freddie floated off. But he chattered pleasantly, and she did not have to do much other than listen, nodding and smiling in what she hoped were the right places. He seemed very amiable and quite the gentleman, almost old-fashioned in his attentiveness.

Just then, the master of ceremonies came to the rescue by announcing that dinner was served and, smiling to her companion, she drifted away as everyone began to shuffle towards their tables. The group of people she was destined to spend the next couple of hours with converged on table 'E' positioned in the middle of the grand room. Taking her seat, she sighed inwardly at the realisation that she was not to be sat next to Olivia, partners being seated separately being the social norm.

Caroline was soon engaged in pleasantries with a middle-aged man to her left who also worked in the department. As she turned to her right, she was surprised to see the person who had been introduced to her simply as H a few moments ago. He owned an information technology company which worked in the sector, he informed her conspiratorially. As he chatted freely, she was better able to take in his wavy, black hair, dark eyes and swarthy good looks; handsome, self-assured and dapper. Her attention briefly wavered at a peel of laughter emanating from her opposite number on the table: Olivia, who else? Her friend seemed completely at ease and was already the source of some attention, flanked by Freddie on one side and a severe looking elderly man on the other. She was in her element and flirted shamelessly with both. They obviously enjoyed the attention. Olivia was an attractive woman in her normal office attire and even in jeans and baggy jumper at a weekend – but this evening, she looked simply stunning, the champagne-induced glow adding to her allure.

Dragging her attention back to her dashing businessman, Caroline and he took in the excellent menu and chatted easily about the choice of food. Tonight, they could look forward to Lobster Bisque, Lemon Sorbet, Sole Veronique and Beef Wellington followed by a choice of desserts: Raspberry and Chocolate Torte or Fresh Pineapple and Mango with Coconut Ice Cream, finishing with Stilton, Celery and Grapes.

'Oh, look. The wines are to die for as well,' said H. 'I hope they meet with your approval,' he added. It was as if they were in a private restaurant and he was the paying host who would instantly change the selection to suit his guest's tastes.

'To be perfectly honest, I'm really not that well versed in wines,' she admitted, shyly smiling her admission.

'Then I shall make it my mission to encourage you in your research – a most pleasurable past-time I assure you,' he said, giving her a barely perceptible wink. She was suddenly not quite sure what to make of H. On the one hand, he seemed charming and a compelling raconteur so that she did not have to try too hard to fill any conversational pauses. But the wink was unsettling, and he was perhaps ten years older than her. He acted even older than that too but, yes, given his appearance and all things considered, she put his age at just the right side of forty. Too old? But he was engaging, considerate, chivalrous. She was not used to the attentions of such a good looking and suave male companion. And she noticed that the young woman to H's right received no more than the minimum of polite acknowledgement despite her model looks.

As the evening wore on, Caroline and H talked increasingly effortlessly, broken only by the after-dinner speeches. He quietly commented on how desperately dull they were, whispering various amusing asides to provoke stifled laughter. As coffee was being served, he leant closer to Caroline and whispered gently in her ear.

'Why don't we find coffee and a brandy elsewhere? It's impossible to talk here and no one will miss us.'

'That'd be nice but—'

'Splendid. Let's go then, I know just the place.'

Caroline allowed herself to be persuaded, smiled her agreement and stood. H gradually withdrew her chair to allow a smooth exit. Caroline glanced across the table and, gaining her attention, mouthed a "goodnight" to Olivia, who returned the message with a mischievous smile and arched eyebrows…

Fortunately, the weekend had allowed Caroline to deal with the inevitable hangover before another week commenced. At a coffee break on a dark, drab Monday morning, Olivia made a beeline for Caroline and drew her aside.

'Well?' she enquired, lifting those oft-used, metal pierced eyebrows to punctuate the question.

'Well what?' countered Caroline, with the merest hint of a smile creasing the corner of her mouth.

'Don't be coy with me. You know very well what. How did your evening finish up?'

'I had a wonderful time, Olivia. One of the best nights of my life.'

'Ah ha. So, the evening ended victoriously, did it? How was that old scam-artist? Bit of a creep, isn't he? Hope his performance didn't disappoint though.'

'Scam-artist? I don't even know what that is and…no, I don't even want to know. Creep? Not at all. What're you talking about? He was a perfect gentleman. Very Cary Grant.'

'Cary who? But, whatever, I don't believe it. Come on, level with me, babe. Give me the salacious details. I've a strong constitution. I can take all the gory details. What was he like? Marks out of ten?'

'*Olivia!* As I said, he was the perfect gentleman. He saw me home and—'

'I bet he did.'

'He saw me home, walked me to my door and then returned to the waiting cab before disappearing into the London night.'

'So, he didn't cross the threshold, let alone—'

'No, he did *not*,' interjected Caroline, quickly heading her off. 'He gave me a quick and very respectful peck on the cheek and waved goodbye – period.'

'Oh, poor you, what a disappointment,' said Olivia, grinning widely. 'Are you seeing him again? Where does he live? I understand he's impossibly rich.'

'Well, you obviously know rather more than me and yes he said he'd like to see me again…Hey, Olivia, I can hardly believe it. What a handsome hunk he is,' she suddenly gushed, lightening up now that she had dealt with the teasing interrogation of her friend. 'He's going to call me. God, I hope he does. Oops, we're getting dark looks. We need to get back. Come on.'

It was a full week before Caroline received the promised call, just as she was beginning to despair of it ever coming. She had half-persuaded herself that she had simply been duped by feigned interest and old-fashioned courtesy.

8. Living the High Life

Caroline was met by H and swept to a waiting black cab which proceeded to twist and turn through the busy London streets to their destination. As she stepped out, helped down by H, she stood back and took in the world he was introducing her to whilst he paid the fare. They were in the middle of St James's and about to enter a cocktail bar inspired by the famous mixologist, Salvatore Calabrese. Stepping over the threshold, door held ajar by a gentleman in a smart evening suit, its outlandish interior was soon revealed.

'I don't think you'll be disappointed, Caroline.'

'Wow. I've never been to such a place.'

'Come on then, here we go,' with which he gently hooked her arm through his. Wearing a perfectly tailored chalk-striped, blue suit with red tie and matching handkerchief which ballooned out of his top pocket, he led her through the front doors and up the sweeping marble staircase. She noticed the huge windows, sparkling crystal chandeliers, exotic paintings and plush, red carpets. It seemed to be modelled on a traditional, slightly risqué Parisian brasserie with undertones of the pulsating Soho scene. H spoke enthusiastically about what he described as a "happening scene" and promised her a sophisticated, upbeat cocktail bar also boasting a rare collection of the world's finest vintage cognacs and whiskies; a fun place to be where you can rub shoulders with celebrities. He declared it his favourite cocktail bar in London. As they entered the grand room, her senses were assaulted.

'Just savour all this, Caroline. I love it. I always like to pause on the threshold and behold the scene. What do you think?'

She took in the chattering hubbub, vivid colours, the whiff of expensive perfumes and intoxicating alcoholic fumes, the throb of music, shrieks of laughter and the theatrical mixing of drinks by expert bar staff. It was pure show business. She had to pinch herself. What was she doing in a place like this? And she a vicar's daughter from a rural Northumberland parish. H explained that the bar was famous for its contribution to mixology, the science of cocktail making. Caroline had never heard of such things but suspended her disbelief, as she savoured the lively surroundings and the joy of being in such debonair company. She could hardly believe her luck, as she sipped the concoction that he had ordered for her. What would Olivia say? *Live it large, babe.* What on earth would her father say? She dared not conjecture.

'Mm, this is delicious. What is it?'

'Bunny Bubbles, a mix of Benedictine, raspberry puree and Champagne. Have a taste of mine.' She smiled and sipped before exclaiming. 'That's good. Is that a champagne cocktail as well?' she asked pointing at his potion.

'Yes, with vodka, absinthe, and lemon juice, I believe. They say it has aphrodisiacal qualities,' he said, grinning mischievously, serving to display his dimple, and, with smiling eyes, added, 'all stuff and nonsense of course.'

Caroline looked around her, delighting in the atmosphere. She smiled as she imagined how Olivia might describe it – *positively buzzing, hon.* H pointed out various minor luminaries who wandered past, their needs catered for by attentive staff. It was clear even to Caroline's untutored eye that the alcohol-induced atmosphere was full of flirtatious liaisons, illicit dalliances, and blatant intemperance. H assured her that all manner of activities was being played out: business deals, high finance, politics, mistresses being plied with drink to ease the path to their eventual dénouement, gay couplings on similar journeys.

Caroline looked at H and pondered. What were his motivations? Perhaps she was also being led to her eventual sexual dénouement? The passing thought sent a shiver of excitement through her, spiced with anticipation. But she also felt strangely uneasy and out of place. Olivia spoke to her again – *lighten up, babe. Enjoy.* But the unease won out as she turned the conversation to safer ground.

'Tell me about your business, H. I understand it's an IT company?'

'Here and now? Surely not? I refuse to bore you with such things when in grand surroundings. If you will forgive me? It would turn perfectly glorious cocktails sour. Now come on, drink up. I have an exceptional restaurant lined up for you. Next stop is Le Gavroche, a two-starred Michelin restaurant in Mayfair. The head chef is the famous Michel Roux Jr. Followed in the footsteps of his even more famous father, Albert. The food's divine and we can continue to explore the fine wines of the world too. Now what do you say?'

'Another cocktail first is what I say.'

'Excellent idea…'

On this, as on the many previous dates over the months since first meeting him, H was the epitome of the English gentleman. He treated Caroline with old-fashioned courtesy. She felt pampered and liked the feeling. As they perused the menu, H declared that he was intent upon introducing her to some fine French wines, recalling their conversation at the December Ball on this matter. And so, it was that they progressed through the Puligny Montrachet white, burgundy, selected to accompany her king crab starter; a very fine Gevrey Chambertin Premier Cru to complement the roast suckling pig. As a grand finale, she sampled the joy of a dessert wine to savour alongside their rich apricot and Cointreau soufflé: a glass of Sauterne. Caroline firmly declined cheese and port in favour of a decaffeinated coffee but allowed herself to be persuaded to a small cognac. They chatted effortlessly throughout an evening which passed all too quickly.

Once again, he escorted her to the door of her flat and gently kissed her on both cheeks, as he bade her goodnight. She was left to totter inside, taking her alcohol-induced warm glow alone to her bedroom with a mild sense of disappointment clouding an otherwise excellent evening.

As the weeks wore on, her social life became turbocharged as H introduced Caroline to many of what he described as the finer things in life: Opera evenings at the internationally renowned Royal Opera House in Covent Garden and the London Coliseum in St Martin's Lane; ballet at Sadler's Wells; classical musical concerts at The Royal Festival Hall on the Southbank and at The Barbican and red carpeted film premieres in Leicester Square. They also enjoyed the theatre and the first play he took her to was Agatha Christie's Mousetrap, which had been playing continuously since the nineteen-fifties. Her social life became an exciting whirlwind with rarely a week passing without some special event or other. Her mind flashed back to her socially moribund university life and of her early days in London: all those lonely evenings with too much time to dwell on her empty life and her inability to make friends, all of which added to her acute lack of self-esteem. But in recent months, Olivia and H had shown her how to enjoy herself, introducing her to a world that had only previously existed in books and glossy magazines. The contrast was delicious. Intoxicating.

Their relationship developed over the following weeks as they became more romantically entwined. But the anticipated development of any physical manifestation of their feelings was slow in coming – all too slow for Caroline who was becoming mildly confused as to his intentions. How did he see their relationship? Did he seek a merely platonic social friendship? Perhaps he was not physically attracted to her? He could not be homosexual could he and simply enjoy her company as some sort of elaborate smokescreen? Surely not. *I don't know much about him either do I?* Why won't he talk about himself? She was becoming curious and soon resolved to test him.

Caroline summoned up the courage to take the initiative and when he rang to make arrangements for their next evening, she was insistent. She preferred a simple evening at home over a bottle of wine and a home-cooked meal.

'Well, that sounds perfectly splendid. But why don't I book a private room at the Café Royal or—'

'No. I'll cook for us and treat you to an evening for once. I won't take no for an answer,' she said. 'And you'd better be prepared to talk about yourself too. I want to get to know you, H.'

The arrangements were made, and she laid her plans. She was determined to find out once and for all where the boundaries of their relationship lay.

9. Leadership Election

February 2000

The nerves jangled and his stomach did somersaults as Christopher approached the famous black front door of 10 Downing Street. He had anticipated this moment for weeks and the sense of now treading in the footsteps of great political figures, of being touched by the hand of history, if only by proxy, was palpable, as he was ushered over the threshold. Larry, the celebrated mouser, took the opportunity to brush past his legs and into the warmth within, perhaps time for an afternoon snooze. An aide led Christopher into the study, otherwise known as the Thatcher Room – used by the great but controversial lady as her main office. He peered around, taking in the surroundings, but remained standing. It did not seem right to sit until invited to do so in this historic room.

After a few minutes, the door swung open and his uncle, the latest prime minister of the United Kingdom of Great Britain and Northern Ireland, bounced in.

'Sorry to keep you waiting, my boy. How are you? Wonderful to see you. Like a tour? Come on.'

The whirlwind that was his uncle led the way and soon Christopher found himself in probably the most famous room of all: The Cabinet Room. The large oval table had nearly thirty chairs around it and many more on the room's perimeter, presumably for aides or civil servants in attendance.

'It's great to see you, Xavier…Prime Minister—'

'Xavier,' he boomed, laughing his amusement. 'Now take a seat there,' he pointed to a chair in the centre.

'Are you sure? There's not some ancient law that will have me thrown into the Tower?' Christopher said, his angst dissipating with the warm welcome. He grinned. Always interested in history and passionate about politics, he had hoped for a sneak preview, but never imagined this.

'Go on, sit down. There…sharing the same position as the likes of Gladstone, Disraeli, Churchill, Attlee, Thatcher…'

'And now Xavier Townsend!'

'Yes. Hard to believe, isn't it? But come on, let's repair to somewhere a little more informal, shall we? Let's go upstairs to the flat. See if I can rustle up a pot of tea?'

Xavier led him to the private living quarters, sweeping up the Grand Staircase, photographs of all the previous prime ministers adorning the walls.

They eventually found themselves in more homely surroundings and were soon sipping their cups of Darjeeling and nibbling shortbread.

'Congratulations, Uncle Xavier. Sorry, I intended to say that straight away, but this place is a bit distracting. Awe inspiring even.'

His uncle frowned his disapproval of the reappearance of the familial term, but they were soon chatting amiably. Xavier had been elected leader of the Tory Party following the resignation of his predecessor due to ill health. Most of the opposing candidates had fallen by the wayside after an initial ballot and he had eventually secured the role by a huge majority.

'So where will the crusade feature in your priorities, Xavier? What with problems in the Middle East, a resurgence of expansionary Russia and the threat of world trade wars? To say nothing of the warring factions on Europe. Will our Party ever coalesce around a common policy on Europe?'

'I very much doubt it. The EU is destined to remain a thorn in our side for decades to come I suspect, but as for what you call the moral crusade – of course! Why would I throttle back now I can exert the authority of the role of PM? We must take notice of the public mood and they've had enough of the establishment lording it over them, of politicians feathering their own nests. Hopefully, I have a few years to get this agenda going.'

'When will the next election be?'

'It's scheduled for May 2003, but who knows? Anything can happen in politics. As Harold Macmillan reputedly once remarked, *events dear boy, events*. But enough of all this. How's business with you?'

'Good. In the main. In fact, I've managed something of a promotion myself, I'll have you know.'

'Excellent. Tell me …more tea?'

'No, thanks. Well, it doesn't compare with your own elevation—'

'Nonsense. Spit it out.'

'You are looking at the newly appointed Managing Director of Skills World Limited. It happened a few months ago now.'

'Congratulations, Chris, congratulations! Delighted for you. So how did you manage to convince that old aristocrat, Bill Taylor? I hope you managed to screw a good deal out of the old codger as well?'

'Mm. Bill gets no better, but he's been persuaded he should shape the business for sale and needs a young gun at the helm. Me! That family of his came good after all in persuading him of the need for change. I suspect that's because they smell a few million in the offing. But that's fine. The deal isn't bad and could be good if we manage to grow the business, which should be possible, although—'

'Don't tell me, the biggest obstacle to that is the old dinosaur himself.'

'That's about the size of it. But there's more – the company's attracting interest from an overseas provider with UK interests: Supreme. We think an offer may be imminent,' said Christopher. The two of them chatted about what that might mean for him, for SWL and of market developments. 'And I think it's about time government engaged to a much greater extent with the private sector on this whole employability and welfare to work agenda,' added Christopher.

'Interesting. Some of my advisers are advocating exactly that approach. Which reminds me, I have a meeting with the minister responsible for welfare.'

'Well, if he needs any private sector insights you know who you could direct him towards. The whole agenda of long-term unemployment, generational ghettos and the attendant issues are too big to hope the public sector can solve alone. Government needs some creative lateral thinking.'

'Points taken. Not that you have any commercial axe to grind here, eh?' Xavier laughed. 'You know I'm immensely proud of you, Chris. Your dad will be too.'

Christopher bowed his head briefly at mention of his dad, uncomfortably aware of his uncle's penetrating gaze.

'He's managing to hang on then?' said Christopher.

'He's confounded the medics but his quality of life's not great. It would mean the world to him if you popped in. Think about it…' Just then, there was a polite knock at the door and an official informed the PM it was time for his next meeting.

'Crikey, is that the time already? Sorry, Chris we're going to have to cut this short but let's meet again soon and please think about what I said. Come on, I'll show you out.'

As they stepped down the Grand Staircase, stopping occasionally to discuss one leader or another, they reached the bottom step just as the front door opened. Xavier sprang forward to warmly shake the hand of one of his ministers.

'Good to see you, Seb. Let me introduce you to a young man going places…my nephew, Christopher. Chris, please meet Sebastian Frith.'

'Hello, young man.'

'Pleased to meet you, Minister.'

The two shook hands in a cursory fashion, as Sebastian signalled that he needed an urgent word with the PM. The two politicians pulled away from Christopher and strode towards the Cabinet Room, Xavier throwing a cheery wave to his nephew before the door closed behind him.

10. A Night In

Caroline worked hard on her preparations, lavishing attention on her small flat and culinary preparations as well as upon herself. A visit to the hairdressers and to a spa for some cossetting to boost her self-confidence. She dressed in a short, black skirt and cream blouse, leaving the top three buttons undone to reveal a glimpse of cleavage. Not that she was particularly well-endowed, she thought downheartedly, self-consciously refastening one of the buttons. She had also treated herself to a pair of red Christian Laboutin high heels. Standing in front of the full-length mirror she thought she just about passed muster. *This is as good as it gets.*

H arrived proffering a huge bouquet of flowers and a bottle of champagne. He complimented her bijou flat and simply presented dinner table and remarked upon her "excellent choice" of music, as George Michael's 'Faith', played in the background.

He saved the lion's share of his appreciation, though, for his hostess. He doesn't miss a trick, Caroline thought. He was so smooth. Was it a little over the top? Perhaps, but where's the harm in that? She loved his generosity of spirit and his keen interest in her as a person. He showed interest in her professional life, unlike her father. It felt good to spend time with someone whose upbringing contrasted so greatly to hers: a successful and ultra-confident businessman, seemingly at ease with the world. She enjoyed being the centre of attention of such a charismatic, good looking, sophisticated man. There had not been too many of those in her life, she reflected wryly.

But occasionally, despite enjoying his attention, her previously suppressed doubts about H – provoked mainly by the comments of Olivia and others – percolated to the surface. *Watch out for that one, always on the make. What do you see in him?* And worse than that: *he's a misogynist; a creep.* She had seen no evidence of any of that. Quite the contrary. H was debonair, warm and friendly, full of romantic gestures. But was it quasi paternal? Platonic, even? Not a welcome thought. It strengthened her resolve and sense of purpose – she would not be deflected this evening.

Having enjoyed a simple meal and despatched a bottle of mediocre Medoc, they settled on the sofa. Caroline had long-since dispensed with her heels. As she poured two large brandies, she interrupted his chatter, looked searchingly into his eyes and announced that she needed some answers.

'Answers? To what? Fire away.'

'Who are you, H, and where do I fit into your life?' she asked, softly.

'Well goodness, what a question. Where do I start? Where do you think you should fit?'

'No! *You*! What do you think? What do you want? Who are you? Let's start with *you*. Every time I ask about what *you* do, about who *you* are you just change the topic, and we find ourselves talking about me or something or other – anything other than you!'

The verbal explosion even surprised Caroline. She had planned to say something but had not imagined she could do so with such passion, such vehemence. It came from deep within and the venting of pent-up feelings gave her an immediate sense of release. From his facial expression, it had obviously surprised H as well, but he quickly regained his equanimity.

'You're much more interesting, that's all, but I can see that you have a bee in your pretty little bonnet and—'

'Don't be so bloody patronising. Oh God, I don't mean to pick a fight with you…that's the last thing I want. I just don't know…'

'Sorry. I wouldn't hurt you for the world, couldn't bear the thought.' H paused and took a deep breath before proceeding carefully. 'Let me see if I can't give you a potted life history then. Where to start? Well, I was brought up in…'

He proceeded to give her an overview of his upbringing, family background, educational achievements and career, although some of the details still seemed vague to her. It was better than nothing though and she did not want to scare him away.

'That's a start,' she said. 'It makes a welcome change from talking about welfare-to-work agendas which are hardly inspiring, are they?'

'Au contraire, Caroline, I find you delightfully compelling and what you do is so *very* important. You shouldn't be so modest, you know. Look, having said that, I realise that I might seem a little evasive but some people, you know, err, are just uncomfortable talking about themselves.'

'I don't mean to pry. But why won't you open up? I thought we were close.'

'Oh, I do hope so. You're special to me. But I find this hard. There's one aspect of my personal life I've never shared with anyone…' he said, pausing to take another sip of his brandy.

'Yes?'

He looked intently at her. His eyes had dulled, and the dimple had disappeared. He seemed pensive; evidently experiencing inner turmoil, wrestling with what to say. The gap in conversation seemed unnaturally prolonged. She squeezed his hand in encouragement. Eventually, the silence was broken.

'Well – here goes. When I was a young teenager, I wasn't treated that well. I was, ahem, the target of physical abuse by my father. Oh, don't get me wrong. Many have fared far worse than me and it stopped short of anything other than, well, a bit of inappropriate petting, shall we say. I'm sure you get the picture. That left a mark, and my mother must have had an inkling as to what was happening. I recall some terrible rows in the ancestral homestead. In fact, my parents split up, whether as a result of this or something else I never did know. One doesn't speak of such things you know. Not quite the done thing.'

'Oh, poor you. I'm so sorry. I didn't want to open any old sores. What a terrible thing. I just can't think what to say. I—'

'Please, Caroline, I don't want to dwell on this, and nor should you read too much into it. In many ways, I had a very privileged upbringing. Our family is wealthy, and I had the advantage of an expensive education. And then, enjoyed the trappings of inherited wealth at an early age. So, there's no need for you to feel sorry for me. It's just that it has, shall we say, left an indelible mark. You don't easily overcome such things, but then we all have to live with whatever this world throws at us, don't we? Now, have I answered all your questions? I'd really rather talk about your life and, gosh is that the time, perhaps we'd better call it a day soon?'

'I do have one other question for you. I'm sorry but if I don't ask now, I may never again summon the courage.' Caroline looked keenly at him, as he turned sharply towards her. Taking a gulp of brandy for Dutch courage, stuttering slightly and colouring as she sought the right words, she spoke quietly.

'Where do I fit in? I know I'm not exactly pretty, not particularly attractive?'

'What utter tosh—'

'No, please let me get this out. It's just that you always seem so...so...so damned proper. Am I just a friend or something more? Where do I stand?'

H looked at her aghast and turned away, seemingly finding interest in an old print hanging on the far wall. Caroline flinched and was overcome with a sense of foreboding; she had overstepped the mark, scared him away. She looked down at her glass, swirling the contents distractedly. But he slowly turned back to her, gently lifted her chin and his eyes found hers.

'So much more than a friend. I didn't want to rush you. Let you get to know me. You seemed unhappy with life here and I wanted to show you a side to London you had not—'

'And you have, but I need more than friendship. Oh, God what will you think of me?' He shushed her and pulled her into a close embrace, wiping away a single tear.

'Love me, H. I need you to *want* me,' she whispered.

'I do want you so very much. May we...' He pulled her up and glanced towards the stairs.

'Here. Right here. Love me here.'

And, within minutes, clothes had been cast aside and they were physically expressing their desire, their need for each other. Caroline was soon pulling him into her, at first gently and then, with fingernails digging into his back and her long, lithe limbs encircling him, he thrust strongly...

Eventually, they subsided and lay prostrate on the floor, energies spent for the moment. Looking at each other they burst out laughing, all awkwardness dispelled.

Caroline eased herself up. She felt bold, brazen, brash even in her nakedness but strangely comfortable in her body for the first time ever. She headed towards the stairs and paused with one foot on the second rung. She looked around as he gazed up at her from the floor, propping his head up with his elbow embedded in the cushions that had served as their impromptu bed. Her insecurity had slipped away these last few hours, as if cast aside along with her clothes. She smiled and headed upstairs, soon followed by H where they resumed their lovemaking before eventually falling asleep entwined in each other's arms.

What a night it had been. His reaction to her questions and their energetic activities dispelled any misgivings. From a quasi-platonic relationship to a full-blown encounter in just one evening. H was a considerate lover but together they were also adventurous. It was the kind of intense gratification that Caroline had often imagined – often read about or observed in explicit videos – but never experienced.

Having breakfasted, she contentedly watched him adjust his tie and fluff up his pocket handkerchief so that it overflowed in the way he liked. With a careful combing of his wavy black hair and an adjustment of his jacket, he was impeccably dressed and ready for his business day. He kissed Caroline goodbye, revealing his cute dimple, as he beamed a smile at her and headed off. From the front doorstep, Caroline watched, as he strode along the streets of Camden Town. He paused briefly at the end of the road to extend a cheery wave, before briskly marching off, hailing a cab in the early morning rush hour traffic.

As the spring months melded into early summer, their relationship deepened, developing into a full-blown love affair. And the two of them gradually shared with each other the details of their lives. She was relieved to learn that he was not married, despite rumours to the contrary. H lived in Reading but spent a lot of time in a London flat owned by his family.

H told her about how he had built up his own company, HostIT, from scratch. It specialised in management information systems, hosting and consulting services together with an expanding technical consulting arm. This was not an area in which she had a great deal of interest or understanding; she also found some of the terms he used bamboozling. But having made such a fuss about wanting to learn more about his life she was happy that he shared this with her. She had always been a good listener.

Given that, Caroline had now secured a senior position in the procurement of welfare-to-work services she was only too pleased to have someone with whom to share her thoughts, concerns and preoccupations. Especially someone so much more experienced in life, who was so interested and expert in business matters. So, it was natural to talk about new programmes about to be introduced, contract management and procurement issues – usually towards the end of an expensive restaurant meal and sometimes during a lull in their strenuous lovemaking in the afternoons of a weekend. She was impressed that he had slowly become quite knowledgeable about the welfare-to-work and vocational training markets and engaged enthusiastically and perceptively. Caroline spoke about the need to attract entrepreneurial private companies to invest in the market and to procure services from the private and charitable third sectors in order to provide a counterbalance to the public sector's stranglehold. These were early days in the development of this market and Caroline operated at the forefront as her department grappled with the challenges, encouraged by ministers politically motivated to roll back the state sector.

In H, she found a useful sounding-board; someone who spoke eminently good commercial sense, whilst being sensitive to the challenges the new policies presented. He was gently encouraging of her approach and growing determination to identify newcomers and of supporting young, ambitious companies to invest in this space…

One summer's evening, she was pleased to receive a call from H as a welcome interlude to her domestic chores.

'I hope I'm not interrupting any great affairs of state in calling this evening?'

'Lovely to hear from you. I'll happily shelve my civic duties for a few moments – but not too long mind, these smalls won't wash themselves,' she laughed. Their maturing relationship made her feel better about herself and he lifted her spirits with his aristocratic accent, upper crust banter and gentle teasing.

'I was wondering if you could spare me half an hour tomorrow lunch time. What do you say?'

'I'm sure I can manage that. Why? Where?'

'Splendid. Very good of you. Meet me in Princes Square in Notting Hill one o'clock sharp and all will be revealed. Can you make that? You might find it quite an interesting visit.'

'What on earth do you mean? How? What are you up to? You can be quite enigmatic you know?'

'Oh, I do hope so! See you tomorrow, Caroline. Remember, one sharp. Must dash. Love and kisses and all that.'

'Wait a moment…' But it was too late. He'd gone. The bloody man was insufferable at times. Returning to her less than exacting duties, she grinned as her mind replayed the conversation.

11. Notting Hill

The sun streamed through the leafy trees that surrounded Princes Square as the mercury climbed; it was unseasonably hot. Two tramps were illicitly settled into a corner of the grassed area that lay within the inner sanctum, wrought iron railings and privet hedges marking the boundaries. They had somehow managed to circumvent the locked gates designed to limit access only to residents. Sprawling in the warm sunshine, they glugged from a shared bottle of cider, smoking and chuckling as Caroline walked by. The group of children playing in shade in the opposite corner brought a brief smile to her face, but her mind was elsewhere, and she did not spot the cyclist until it was almost too late, stepping out in front of him, forcing him to swerve dramatically.

Striding on, Caroline soon spotted her immaculately attired beau at the end of the street. He beamed as she approached, quite evidently pleased with himself. Having embraced her warmly, he reached into his pocket and with a great flourish produced a key which he dangled in front of her with an impish grin.

'What are you looking so smug about? You're being very mysterious.'

'Come on, no time to waste,' he answered, taking her hand and leading her up the steps of a nearby house.

A moment later, she was being spirited around a classy, expensively appointed flat with high ceilings and huge windows overlooking the square where the children still played. It was equipped with the very latest in music systems and highly fashionable furnishings. At the end of a corridor, he paused, flashing a smile before ceremoniously flinging open large double doors. She gasped at the exotic, boldly furnished bedroom. Stepping into the room, Caroline looked around in wonder. She had never been in a room like it. It was expensively decorated with a nod towards eroticism: walls decorated in a fabric wallpaper – bright red hibiscus prominent amongst green foliage, all set on a slate-grey background flecked with gold; an ivory cream wool carpet; luxurious, red velvet curtains.

'*H*! This is amazing, but it's a bit OTT, isn't it? A mirrored ceiling? *Really*?'

She threw herself down onto the bed, lying back to look at her reflection. Clasping her hand to her mouth, she laughed, half embarrassed, half thrilled.

'I hope you like it. It's an Emperor bed by the way. Plenty of room for recreation, if you catch my drift.'

'I catch your drift, all right,' she said, smiling broadly.

'Here's a key. Just for you. *Do* you like it? Our very own oasis in this hurly-burly world of ours.'

'The flat's stunning. But the bedroom…'

'Where's your sense of fun? It's about time we had a place to enjoy, just the two of us, when we're in that certain kind of mood, don't you think?'

'It's a wonderful idea, H, *thank you*, and as for the bedroom, well I can hardly wait to give it a test drive,' she said, blushing.

He smiled.

'But I'm keeping my own flat, H.'

'Absolutely. This isn't a home. It's simply a bolthole to use whenever the fancy takes us. Our personal respite from the trials and tribulations of business. Now what do you say – will you take the key?'

12. London Conference

April 2000

Not only was Caroline's private life on the up but her work was also was also becoming more rewarding which was helping to fuel some self-belief. Her role entailed her supporting new policy agendas and she was beginning to make headway. Her promotion gave her an elevated status from which she could help colleagues counter engrained prejudice; new policy gradually replacing perceived wisdom which favoured delivery by the State. But the resistance to this was strong within many corners of the department, as typified by the sharp exchange at that morning's review meeting.

'It's the function of the state and mustn't be opened up to greedy capitalists,' said Julie, an experienced manager.

'We have to open our minds to new possibilities, different solutions,' argued Caroline.

'Can't you see how offensive that is to most people?'

'Whose interests are you seeking to protect? Our clients or your staff?'

'That's insulting.'

'What's the answer though? The out-of-work unfortunate or the public sector worker delivering poor service?' said Caroline.

'The service is exemplary.'

'Against what yardstick? Certainly not the objectives of even your own department? How do you explain that?'

Caroline's brusque, direct questioning curried no favours and earnt her scant regard with many in the department. But it was viewed with respect in the higher echelons and as politicians and senior officials became ever more wedded to the new policy direction, they began to promote like-minded staff of that bent.

In her procurement role, she headed the team tendering the programmes designed by their colleagues in the neighbouring section, reporting to the head of procurement who was nearing retirement. He was happy to give her free rein. She did not know the providers well – but then at that stage, few did. But a steady stream of contracts was being let, mainly directed at job seekers who had been out of work for twelve months or longer: the long term unemployed.

'This is really exciting, H,' she enthused one evening. 'We seem to be making some headway.'

'I never doubted you would,' he chuckled, proceeding to pepper her with questions. 'Tell me more. Which providers are in the frame? What's it you're looking for? It's always a mystery to me as to why government chooses to contract with X but not Y. Do educate me.'

'Price is a big factor but it's not the only criteria…'

'Ah price. Cheapness rather than quality. Always the case with government, sometimes that's short sighted though,' said H.

'Maybe, but not here. Not in isolation anyway. Providers have to be prepared to invest and take on risk. Perhaps just as importantly, providers must demonstrate local knowledge. Locality is critically important. Sorry, am I boring you?'

'Never! So who will win out then?'

'Now that would be telling but in strict confidence you understand…'

'Yes of course. Mum's the word and all that, but if you're uncomfortable, let's change the subject. I was just interested that's all.'

'No, no it's okay. Let me see: Project2learn, Supreme, Skills World, Ulysses, Workalot – yes I know, a bizarre name…' Caroline continued in that vein and was thrilled he shared her interest. It was flattering that he was so attentive, so encouraging.

W2W Conference: Engage, Motivate, Inspire

Caroline was summoned to a meeting with Steven Garside, at which the minister was also present. He indicated how impressed he was with her fortitude in the face of vocal opposition to the new policy line and her own advocacy. Caroline could hardly believe her ears, as he went on to assert that she had a bright future – and all this with the minister present. He was as good as his word and she was soon promoted again, this time to the position of head of welfare-to-work, a role which spanned both procurement and implementation. She reported directly to the Director of Employment and Welfare, just two rungs below that of the Permanent Secretary, and this at the tender age of twenty-nine.

Caroline now had responsibility for pushing forward agendas to implement radical new policies. The approach became a hot political issue debated in parliament and on current affairs programmes. It thrust her into the vanguard of progressive reforms. She had never sought nor lusted after the limelight, having spent much of her life in the shadows. But she was ambitious and saw this as the price to pay for career development. Who knows, maybe even her father could one day be proud of her advancement. She pushed to the back of her mind his last discordant voice on the matter, *a phase you're going through…your place is at home…*She promised herself she would contact him again soon. She worried that his health was not good and although he denied the suggestion, he seemed weaker and even more withdrawn of late.

It was in her newly elevated capacity that she was thrust forward to speak at the conference on welfare reforms at which she would join the new secretary of state, none other than the Rt. Honourable Sebastian Frith MP, in the delivery of a keynote speech. The minister was widely tipped as a future party leader with the reputation of a man who got things done. He and Caroline seemed to be ascending their respective hierarchies in parallel.

She knew little about political matters, and cared even less, but now she needed to work increasingly with politicians, and it was Sebastian Frith she seemed destined to serve. Instinctively, Caroline disliked the man. He was impossibly pompous and overbearing, but they at least appeared to share similar views as to the urgency of the welfare-to-work agenda. For his part, Sebastian had latched onto the ideas that Caroline and others had offered. It seemed likely the minister perceived political advantage in the quest for power which she assumed trumped ideology and principle. Not for him the encumbrance of ideals or the constraints of core beliefs, not that she was about to share such thoughts with him.

The minister was welcomed to the podium by polite applause from the assembled audience of nearly one thousand. As they fidgeted in their seats and shuffled their papers, the Rt Hon Sebastian Frith stood before them at the podium. He calmly smoothed his shiny black hair, gently eased down his white shirt cuffs to show just below his jacket sleeves. Turning his gold cufflinks between index finger and thumb, he then shook an expensive looking watch into view with a brisk twist of his wrists. Silently scanning the conference attendees for a moment, he then spoke confidently in a manner that exuded authority and power.

'Ladies and gentlemen, this government remains committed to the radical development of policy in this important area. It is essential we reduce and eventually eradicate the dependency culture of the long-term unemployed, about which you all know and care so much about. The damage caused to the very fabric of our society by the fostering of generational unemployment, of deprivation and joblessness is a disgraceful inheritance bestowed upon the nation by the previous government. This is why, we are intent upon continuing to work with the job centres, colleges and local authorities on this agenda, but also why we will further extend our network to additionally embrace the third and private sectors.'

The minister continued in that vein, uttering grandly eloquent sentiments and issuing vague platitudes served in self-important, patronising tones. At last, he gave way to allow his senior civil servant to deal with the details, citing the need to rush back to the House for an important vote.

Caroline approached the podium hesitantly, taking a series of deep breaths to quell the butterflies. Her hair was tied in a ponytail and she had applied just a little make-up. She wore a simple white blouse tucked into a black pencil-skirt, a short, black jacket and flat shoes. Caroline's choice of outfit was intended to appear modest and business-like. She paused to allow the hubbub of her restless audience to recede. She knew full-well that her statement was likely to win both approval and indictment and steeled herself.

'If I may conclude this slot, conference. We are determined to build upon *your* success in this field…' She proceeded to generously recognise the excellent work of the various sections of the industry represented by her audience.

Continuing, she declared, 'Colleagues, we also seek to introduce an element of incentive to our providers by paying for results and offering bonuses for exceptional performance.' This provoked a murmuring in her audience.

Unlike Sebastian, Caroline was not a skilled or practiced public speaker; her anxiety, she feared, was obvious – her wavering voice and her flushed neck and cheeks. But as she warmed to her task and developed her carefully drafted speech to a set of well-researched slides, she felt herself becoming more fluent, gaining in confidence.

In the final few minutes of her short slot, she leant forward on the podium and having hesitated briefly, spoke urgently to release the anticipated news.

'Conference, the "Work Focus" programme is to be contracted to a range of private providers as well as public sector and charity organisations. The winners of this competition are now being displayed on the main screen. I congratulate them all and…'

Her words were drowned out by a thunderclap of noise peppered with lightning rod cheers from private sector victors. She looked up sharply, her wide eyes registering surprise, before scurrying back to her seat alongside the chair of the conference, the newsreader Archibald Fitzgerald.

Archibald was a mature and well-known broadcaster; avuncular and popular. He pulled a hand thoughtfully over his neat, closely cropped beard. The whiskers failed to disguise his fleshy jowls which wobbled, as he turned from the speakers to his audience. He wore a dark, shiny business suit, stretched tightly over his portly frame. He thanked Caroline for her contribution and announced they would conclude this conference with a Q&A session.

Joseph Potts was welcomed to the stage, the Head of Welfare of a local authority, a renowned left-wing member of the Labour party of the old school. Joseph was something of a firebrand and his extraordinary appearance seemed in keeping – unkempt, wiry grey hair which flared at all angles giving him a mad professorial appearance. He was a tall, angular man with a gaunt, pinched face and a booming, deep bass voice. He habitually wore jeans and tee shirts but today donned a tweed jacket with leather patches, a green frayed collared shirt and woollen tie. He joined Caroline in order to take questions, casting her a look of disdain.

'Conference, now is the opportunity to have your say and to pose questions to our two guests this afternoon if you would raise your hands…' said Archibald. 'Thank you. I will take three points, firstly from the lady at the back in red, then the gentleman in the centre in the black suit and then from you, sir, in the front row.'

'I'm appalled that we should let profit-mongering companies' muscle in and take advantage of the poorest in our society. It's disgusting that the minister won't stay and face the music; shame on him,' spoke the angry lady in red, who had announced herself as Alice Henning. She sat down to cheers and loud applause, some leaping to their feet to emphasise their agreement.

'Hear, hear,' echoed the black suit, adding, 'We need more resources – not gimmicky stunts.'

'And to you now, sir,' said Archibald, pointing to the front row.

'Hello. My name's Christopher Townsend, Managing Director of Skills World.'

'What's your question please, Christopher?'

'I certainly can't agree with the sentiments of either of the previous questioners. We have to move on, embrace change, raise our sights higher. The private sector will bring much needed creativity. I welcome this initiative as a first step in the right direction: a small step. The volumes involved are tiny and yet the investment required is large. I wonder what the panel has to say about this?' He had to raise his voice in order to be heard before sitting down to loud objections which easily drowned out applause from those sympathetic to the private sector's cause.

'Thank you for your remarks. But conference, I must also appeal for some decorum please,' said Archibald. 'Personal insults are not in order, so let's keep our cool and maintain our dignity, I urge you. I think we can roll those questions into a single answer from our panel. What do you have to say, Joseph?'

'I have a great deal of sympathy with the first two questioners,' he boomed, provoking cheering from his animated audience. 'The importance of this work can't be overstated. We need to address deep-seated and knotty problems which have their roots in long term societal decay and deprivation brought about by decades of failed government policy and lack of resources. Now is not the time to experiment by engaging the private sector. And the notion of companies making a profit out of the most underprivileged in our society is repugnant,' declared an ebullient Joseph, playing to the majority view. He evidently enjoyed his rapturous reception, as he glanced self-righteously at Caroline, who was now invited to comment.

'Colleagues, I must ask you for some sense of proportion here. Let's put this into context. These issues are too important to waste our time on populist rhetoric,' she declared, pausing to throw an accusatory glance at Joseph, who evidently struggled to retain his composure; positively bristling. Caroline continued, 'The challenges of generational unemployment and joblessness are severe and are getting worse despite the vast resources dedicated. These budgets have increased beyond inflation in each of the last ten years—'

'But it's not enough,' cried a dissenting voice.

'Quite right,' shouted Joseph, unable to contain himself any longer.

'Please conference, do continue, Miss Hope,' intercepted Archibald.

'Thank you. For how much longer can we afford to fund these programmes with such largesse? Where will the funds come from? It's incumbent upon us to cast our net wider—'

'No, no, no...' shouted the incandescent lady in red and the black suit in unison.

'*Yes*,' insisted Caroline, shaken by the reactions but refusing to be deterred, 'we *will* engage with the private sector. They seem to have different, more imaginative solutions to offer. Less than ten percent of the budget is spent with the private sector and even after this programme, it will be less than fifty percent. And the man in the front row is right. I can offer him some reassurances here at least.'

'Are you referring to the volumes; the size of contracts, Caroline?' clarified Archibald.

'Yes. Investment will only happen if private companies can be confident of being allowed to bid for contracts in the future before making long-term financial commitments to the market. The minister has authorised me to state very clearly that the contract awards announced today will be followed by a series of additional programmes – which *both* the public and the private sector may bid for. We will increase the size of these contracts as our confidence grows in the ability of the sector to deliver the required results. Colleagues, we are talking about the need for better quality support services, improved vocational training and better results in literacy and numeracy and, in particular, higher return-to-work figures. The government will place contracts with those providers that *deliver*. The clear message is that the results currently being delivered by today's public sector providers are *simply not good enough*.'

Caroline trotted out industry statistics to illustrate her points and referred to case studies of clients who had been failed by the complacent delivery of conventional services which had failed to cut through the underlying issues of joblessness. Her research was detailed, her case compelling, if unpopular. She eventually sat down to a cacophony of protestations and angry booing, but her persistent delivery had deflated the hyperbole of the smug Joseph Potts, who fumed in his seat. The session was allowed to overrun its twenty-minute slot, such was the high level of audience participation and the passions aroused.

As conference delegates dissolved noisily from the main auditorium to head to the refreshment hall and to breakout workshop sessions, Caroline made her way towards the exit, relieved that was all over. Time to head back to the office, shunning the free lunch available and instead opting to find relative solitude elsewhere; away from outraged, hand-wringing public sector servants and over-eager, thrusting private sector bosses. But as she neared the exit, her path was intercepted by a sharply dressed man who she vaguely recognised. She slowed and allowed him to shake her hand when it suddenly dawned on her that it was the guy who had asked a question in the main session earlier.

'Hello, Miss Hope. I wonder if I may introduce myself. Christopher Townsend, Managing Director of Skills World.'

'Sorry, I'm just rushing to another appointment.'

'I won't keep you a moment. I just wanted to say how brave I thought you were earlier. It's so important to break the status quo, mix things up a bit but that's easier for the likes of me to—'

'Thank you, but if you'll excuse me.'

'Of course, I hope to see you again soon.'

Caroline threw a snatched smile at him and was struck by his unblinking steel-grey eyes and easy-going manner. It occurred to her that he had also been brave in speaking up, although clearly motivated by commercial interests. Turning away, she took a couple of strides towards the door before suddenly turning full circle. 'I'm in the process of putting together a steering group for both public and private sector providers. It'll be a means of consulting with providers prior to framing programmes, brainstorming industry issues and the like. Would you be interested in joining such a forum?'

'Of course. I'd be delighted to do so,' Christopher said quickly.

'Good, you'll be hearing from me,' she said, before turning and marching through the doors into the busy Westminster streets.

13. Skills World Under Offer

June 2000

It was early as Christopher settled into his office chair, sipping the coffee he had grabbed on the way in as he surveyed his diary, mulling yesterday's events, turning his mind over today's schedule: meetings with Jane Smith, with Joanne Edwards and then with a number of his operational managers. On his way to meet Joanne, he passed the human resources director's office; one office that would remain unoccupied today, he knew.

'Morning Joanne, how are things?'

Joanne was their long-standing finance director, and always an early starter.

'Christopher. The accounts are looking very healthy. I've more work to do and will prepare you a short report. You'll have it by lunch time.'

'Let me see it before copying it anywhere else, won't you?'

Joanne threw him a wry look laced with meaning. 'Sorry to hear about your father, Christopher.'

'Thanks. That's nice of you. We aren't close but it's been a shock.'

'Will he be okay? He'll pull through, won't he?'

'No. At least that's not expected. Paralysed down one side, can't speak. I'm not sure he's aware of what's going on around him and, well, it's just a matter of time really. What can you do?'

'Be there with him?' Joanne suggested. 'You shouldn't be in work today. Why don't you go to him?'

'No. It won't change the old bastard's chances and I'm better at work. Look, I know how harsh that must sound but you don't know the half of it and…Thanks for your sympathy, Joanne. I really appreciate it, but can we just get on please?'

She looked at him carefully as if considering whether to push the point, reaching out briefly to place her hand on his as it rested on her desk, squeezing it briefly.

'Any further news on the Supreme offer?' Joanne asked.

'Oh, come on, you know even better than I do who monopolises that agenda. They'll be under instructions to speak to Bill – and only Bill. Bloody typical. He just won't let go.'

'He's still the owner, Christopher. You've got to be realistic.'

'At least he's not around today so we can get on with the preparations. Seeing Jane shortly, need to get our ducks lined up.'

Joanne raised her eyebrows, cocking her head slightly, whether to question his assumptions about Bill's whereabouts or at the news of a meeting with Jane he could not be sure.

'Oh well, better get on,' Christopher said, 'see you later.'

'Just before you go, have you thought any more about Samantha? You need to speak with Bill before acting. He's struggling to understand what she's supposed to have done wrong and she's been here so many years...'

'Too late for that. I met with her yesterday evening and executed the decision. The one endorsed by the board last week, you will remember. I wasn't going to give him another chance to change his mind. A decision is a decision.'

'I see. You know that isn't how Bill thinks or works, don't you? If I were you, I'd prepare for a reaction,' Joanne said. Her tone was matter of fact, cautionary, and her eyes flashed warning signals before she pulled her reading glasses down from their temporary position atop her head to resume the task in hand, conversation over. Her loyalty to Bill was legendary, despite him treating her with utter contempt whenever it suited his mood. Christopher could never understand why she put up with it.

In anticipation of the meeting with Jane, their corporate legal adviser, he went through some papers before sitting back to recall their last encounter. SWL had received several expressions of interest in buying the company. Following a recent difficult meeting with one of their potential suitors, Christopher and Jane had allowed business to morph into social: dinner at a particularly good Chinese restaurant where they shared a decent bottle of sauvignon blanc with the dim sum and then opted for brandy rather than lychees or Chinese tea. They had both flirted with each other remorselessly, the conversation punctuated with sharp wit and laughter, as he revelled in her company; they seemed to occupy the same wavelength and the evening passed all too quickly. He recalled how tactile Jane had become, as they slumped in the back seat as the taxi sped towards her place.

'Lovely evening, Jane. A coffee would cap it off very well, don't you think?'

'Thanks for dinner but coffee keeps me awake...' she had said with sparkling eyes.

'De-caffeinated? Or I'm sure we could think of something else.'

'I'm perfectly sure you could but a girl's got her reputation to think of and yours goes before you, Christopher Townsend.'

'Can't think what you mean, libellous. Know a decent lawyer?'

'Slanderous actually. Get it right. And how on earth could I be expected to resist those sexy doe eyes of yours. Another time. Goodnight, Christopher.' With which she uncrossed her shapely legs and stepped out of the taxi, leaning back in to kiss him goodnight, tantalisingly flicking her tongue between his lips before pulling away with a mischievous grin. On reaching the top of the steps, she blew a kiss and waved before disappearing inside.

A sharp rapping on his door snapped him out of his reverie – the arrival of his first appointment: Jane Smith from Entwistle Partners. She greeted Christopher breezily, shaking his hand with a glint in her eye. The handshake underlined the professional purpose of the meeting but her sparkling eyes suggested recollections of their recent social liaison. She was immaculately attired in a dark-grey matching skirt and short jacket, the skirt modestly riding to just above the knee on sitting opposite him. Christopher took his suit jacket off, hung it on the back of the chair and joined her in a bucket seat around a glass coffee table.

'Good to see you, really good. I suppose we should focus on business?' More a question.

'I gathered that was the general idea, yes,' she said.

'Let's get to it then.'

Jane brushed her blonde curls back from her face, as she sat forwards, reaching for the draft sale and purchase agreement and articles of association which had been put forward by Supreme Services following their offer to buy SWL. They proceeded to walk through the documents dealing with the various technicalities: class A shares, shareholder's rights, share capital, voting rights, drag along rights; subject matter dry but the importance high. Various amendments which they would seek as part of the negotiation process and follow-on actions were agreed.

Glancing at her watch, Jane indicated she was running short of time and gathered up her things, easing her jacket on. As they shook hands, Christopher held on to hers, turned it over and brushed the index finger of his left hand lightly down her long slender fingers. Their eyes connected and she allowed a half-smile before slipping free.

'Can we see each other again, Jane?'

'Of course. We've just set the next meeting date, haven't we?'

'You know what I mean. It was a really good evening, a great evening actually.'

'Not at all bad. Had worse,' she whispered, flashing him a coquettish smile.

'Well then?'

'Maybe.'

'I know this wonderful restaurant…'

'Let's take a rain check, Christopher.'

'I'll call you.'

'You don't give up easily, do you?' As she reached his office door, one hand on the handle, she turned back and said brightly, 'Make this deal happen and I will gladly help you celebrate. I've a weakness for a good Bollinger – makes a girl quite squiffy, weak at the knees even.'

In the midst of his round of operational meetings, Christopher was summoned to meet with the Chairman. His personal assistant was flushed and fidgeted uncomfortably as she relayed the message. *The Chairman was most insistent.* Christopher's immediate presence was demanded.

Approaching the hallowed surroundings of Bill's beloved boardroom, he knocked briefly, respectfully, before venturing inside. It was like stepping back into a parallel universe of faded glory: threadbare carpets, tired anaglypta wallpaper, a gallery of pictures – of Bill meeting royalty, of Bill at conferences, of Bill smiling benevolently, as he presented certificates of achievements to young people down the ages. Large, dark and forbidding oil paintings of Bill's family ancestors glared down from the walls, their eyes seemingly assessing the inadequacies of the poor souls lured into the deified presence of the Chairman.

'I heard about your father, young man. My sympathies,' he muttered, whilst shuffling his papers. Christopher was struggling to come to terms with news of his father's latest massive stroke and the likelihood of his imminent demise, unsure how he should feel or behave given their chequered past. *He's still your dad...*

'Sit down,' Bill said.

An instruction rather than an invitation.

'Thank you. It's come as quite a shock.'

'Quite. But business goes on. I hear you've sacked Samantha.'

The words were spat at him with barely concealed contempt, and the change of tack was unexpected. The depth of his sympathy for his father's predicament was underwhelming; Christopher struggled to swallow his irritation but should not have expected otherwise. There was no sign of sympathy, no hint of humanity, all seemingly beyond Bill's reach.

'No one has *sacked* Samantha. We're restructuring our human resources department and re-defining roles. Samantha doesn't have the requisite skills or experience and she's agreed to take voluntary redundancy.'

'Something about appointing a Talent Director, I hear. What the hell's that?'

'You know very well what the role is, Bill. You've seen the job spec.'

'Modern stuff and nonsense. Samantha has been a faithful, hugely successful member of staff. You will kindly reverse the restructuring and restore her to her rightful position.'

They had been through all this at the board meeting a week ago. They had eventually agreed all elements of the strategy and Bill's brooding acquiescence had been secured, Christopher reminded him, referring to the minutes.

'You aren't listening, young man. I *own* Skills World...'

'And *you* promoted *me* to the position of managing director, to *run* it. Since when our fortunes have been transformed, the turnaround dramatic.'

'Rubbish. Will you carry out my wish and reinstate Samantha or not?' Bill demanded, slamming his diary shut. He leant forward, placed his large bony hands flat on the table and leveraged himself upright to glower down at his MD threateningly.

'Err, *not,* I think.' Christopher was enraged and struggled to retain his composure, failing to control a wavering in his voice as a bile of anger surfaced.

'Then you are relieved of your command as of now. Please see Joanne, who will deal with the formalities.'

That evening, he was assailed by waves of anger and dismay, of loathing and disgust. His managing director's appointment had seemed to presage a glittering business career and the sale of SWL to Supreme would open the door to boundless opportunities. And to potential riches. But now, his career and dreams seemingly lay in tatters. Christopher could not leave it at this. He would not. But what could he do? He allowed the cogs in his brain to turn over, sipping a malt whisky, he twirled his signet ring around and around, staring into space. The cogs turned slowly, lazily – they were deeply ingrained, corroded, difficult to shift. As they reluctantly settled, he examined every option, but they all seemed flawed, bound to fail. *Click.* Another turn allowed a new perspective, and a thought came to him. He leapt to his feet, grabbed his whisky glass and took a gulp, the contents warming his throat. He was alert now, his tiredness and despair despatched by an adrenalin surge, serving as lubrication to his now rapidly whirring mind. Might it work? He examined the idea from every angle, as he paced up and down, considering the potential reaction it might provoke. Yes, it really might just do the trick. Dare he make the call? What the hell had he got to lose?

After a troubled night's sleep and endless nerve-wracking as to whether the call would make the slightest bit of difference, he agonised over alternative options. He could always throw his lot in with one of the competitors, but that would be giving in. A change of career? Career? Ha – he no longer seemed to have one.

Brooding over his reduced circumstances and uttering profanities, he set about a morning of domestic chores – an opportunity to catch up on washing, shopping, maybe even some dusting and cleaning. Hardly uplifting. From a busy executive's life to one of mundane domesticity. He looked momentarily at the whisky bottle but resisted the temptation. He would not be reduced to a daytime drinker, tempting though it was. He grabbed his wallet, his mobile and slung his coat on, slamming the front door behind him. The supermarket called, he supposed. Later that morning, letting himself back into his flat, laden with shopping bags he dumped them in the hall as his mobile trilled: Joanne. Could he meet with Bill this afternoon? *No, he bloody well could not.* It might be worth his while suggested Joanne who proceeded to imply change afoot. She was not to be drawn further.

Christopher knocked and entered the boardroom to find Joanne with Bill and Alexander Russia, the Strategy Director of Supreme. Interesting. Perhaps the call had not been in vain after all.

'Sit down,' said Bill.

Christopher shook hands with Alexander and nodded to Joanne before doing so. Alexander seemed as inscrutable as ever. There was no exchange of pleasantries, just grim expressions. Bill wore an expression of thunder. Joanne sought out Christopher's eyes and seemed to convey caution, pleading for restraint. The atmosphere was toxic, leaden with tension.

'Our friend at Supreme wished to meet with the three of us,' explained Joanne.

'Indeed,' confirmed Alexander, turning to Bill. 'I'll get straight to it. Am I to understand that you've dismissed Christopher?' he asked.

Bill seemed surprised by the directness of the question delivered on his home turf.

'You understand correctly. How do you know?' asked Bill.

'May I ask why?'

'With respect, why is that a matter for Supreme – and how do you know of this?'

'It matters enormously to Supreme. In seeking to acquire your company, we are buying into Christopher and his team.'

'Well if you must know, he sacked his HR director, Samantha which—'

'Good call,' said Alexander to a startled Bill. Joanne raised an eyebrow. Christopher stayed stony-faced, surprised at the brutality of the intervention, delivered with clinical efficiency, shorn of emphasis or emotion.

'I will ignore the discourtesy you're displaying for the moment, but kindly refrain from commenting on my internal matters. This is wholly between me and my executives and a decision has been made. It's irrevocable. I do own this company, may I remind you.'

'Is that your last word?'

'Let's put this all behind us, as we concentrate on managing the acquisition to completion. Now if you will excuse us, Christopher, I have business to conduct with Alexander that is no longer of interest to you.'

'Well in that case,' interjected Alexander, silently signalling to Christopher that he should stay put, 'I have no option other than to withdraw our offer. We will write formally to confirm.'

'What? We've been working on this for…Why? For God's sake, man, be bloody reasonable,' spluttered Bill.

'In bidding for your company, we were backing management. Christopher's leadership is pivotal. Georgina Harris, our CEO, you will recall—'

'I know who she is.'

'…has instructed me to make our position crystal clear.'

He had certainly done as instructed.

14. The Supreme Group PLC

July 2000

Christopher and the team assembled in the board room of Supreme, a multinational support services and information technology group. Headquartered in London, their two-billion-pound operation focused primarily on mainland Europe, with a substantial footprint in Australasia. Tea and coffee, water and juices were all on hand; the offer of chilled Chablis was politely declined. As the minutes ticked away the initial chatter subsided. Bill Taylor soon broke the quiet to declare that once their hosts arrived then business would be quickly concluded, and the vintage champagne would soon flow.

'They know a great business when they see one, they won't prevaricate.'

His assertions did not release the growing tension in the room and not even Bill's bombast could pull off the attempt at optimism. Christopher shuffled in his seat and surreptitiously wiped moist hands on his trousers. He fidgeted with his ring, every now and then getting up to prowl around the room, straightening a picture here, a book there and picking up a business magazine to flick through before carelessly discarding it.

'For goodness sake, sit down. Hold your nerve, young man,' said Bill.

Here to finalise the details on the sale of the business to Supreme Group for forty million pounds, the stakes seemed high: freedom from the oppressive owner together with the prospect of making some serious money. Despite his proffered positivity, Bill's mood seemed sour and it would not help to provoke an outburst from the chairman at this stage, so Christopher brooded privately. *Why are our hosts so late? What's afoot?* A tense silence engulfed the team. He reflected on the two calls from Alexander Russia during which he had been assured of the regard with which he and his team were held by the acquirers. Supreme's plans post-acquisition were to support SWL in a bold and exciting strategy to be led by Christopher. The young MD allowed the shadow of a smile to pass over his features, earning scowled disapproval from Bill, as Christopher spoke silently to himself, *survive this last period, get this over the line and then the world's my oyster.*

Dragging his mind back to the present, he quietly took in his surroundings: plush, deep-pile burgundy carpets, wood-panelled walls, polished mahogany boardroom table, black leather chairs, crystal chandeliers, iPads and sleek modern B&O telephones: an eclectic combination of traditional and contemporary. He did not much care for this corporate style but the contrast to the offices at Skills World Limited was striking. As one team member after another sighed, coughed and fidgeted, the clock noisily ticked away the minutes.

'Where *are* they?' Joanne suddenly asked. Christopher looked at her quizzically, it being unusual for her to display feelings. Joanne had joined the business ten years ago during a difficult trading period and more recently had supported Christopher in the turnaround strategy: the youthful, exuberant MD and a seasoned, stalwart finance director.

'You have to wonder what's going on,' Christopher ventured, looking directly at Joanne.

'Just remember your place as a minority shareholder, Christopher. Leave the deal to us,' interrupted Bill. His MD's view mattered only in respect of operational details, he was further reminded. 'Just conform to the script and do your duty.' Bill was strong on duty.

Also attending the meeting were the legal advisers from Entwistle Partners. The effervescent Jane Smith and the nervous intellectual Ernest Caruthers were an incongruous team. Ernest was tall and skinny. He had pinched features and wore tortoise-shell spectacles which slipped down his long-pointed nose to give him an avian-like bearing, accentuated by his nervous, high-pitched twittering voice. Ernest appeared to wake up and chirruped, 'I'm sure they'll be here soon. It'll be fine, mark my words.'

'Well, if they don't show up in the next five minutes, I'm heading back. They will have missed the biggest opportunity of their lives,' said Bill.

What are they up to? The process has gone too well hasn't it? Too good to be true? The tardiness of their hosts seemed like a portent of the unexpected. But such thoughts were abruptly interrupted, as the door swung open and the Supreme executives swept in.

'I apologise for keeping you waiting,' uttered Georgina Harris, the vivacious redheaded businesswoman who led Supreme. She was accompanied by Strategy Director Alexander Russia.

The expected courtiers, Georgina's professional advisers, were not in attendance and after the curtest of salutations, Georgina announced that the meeting was to be chaired by Alexander; she expected it to be a short session.

Christopher and Joanne exchanged impotent glances. Jane had a brief whispered aside with Ernest but neither spoke up. Bill grunted, sat forward and clasped his hands in front of him as if in prayer.

'Good afternoon all,' began Alexander in his quietly spoken manner, pausing to treat each member of the team to a lingering but unsmiling glance. His tone and demeanour suggested revelation and change. The irritatingly loud buzzing of a bluebottle, as it careened around the room seemed amplified and the temperature appeared to have risen.

'I'll get straight to it and relay to you our board's decisions,' began the strategy director.

'And?' said Bill.

Christopher felt a sense of foreboding and looked at Jane, whose eyebrows arched.

'We have concluded that Skills World Limited would enhance the business interests of Supreme, given the strategic positioning of both companies and the obvious synergies.'

This was met with an audible sigh of relief from both Joanne and Bill. Christopher remained dutifully silent. This was hardly fresh news. *Was a coup de grace about to be delivered?*

'As you know,' continued the unflappable Alexander, 'we have previously offered a valuation of forty million pounds for the entire share capital of Skills World Limited. This is conditional upon Christopher continuing to lead the company; all subject to our process of due diligence, which nears completion. Having reviewed the position with our board we are now able to firm up our offer. We are pleased to clarify the final details.'

He paused as the SWL team fidgeted. He permitted the semblance of a half-smile to play around his lips, the smile never reaching his eyes.

'Upon the exchange of final contracts, we will transfer to the current shareholders of Skills World Limited a sum of *thirty* million pounds. This will potentially increase to *fifty* million over a two year earn-out period.'

This was the first time there had been any mention of such a mechanism. It had not been anticipated, although in the corporate world of mergers and acquisitions it was not unusual. Alexander paused, as a ruddy-faced Bill rose angrily from his chair in protestation.

'For Christ's sake, man, you can't change the deal now. We've been at this for six months.'

Bill's objections prompted a sage nod from Alexander, as if conceding the wisdom Bill conveyed. A benign, sympathetic smile of understanding was cast in Bill's direction – but the only reason offered for the change was that of perceived risk. All entreaties to return to the previous headline sum were politely but firmly rebutted. Ernest asked for a few moments to allow the team to take the news in; to consider a response…

In an adjoining room, Bill ranted about the lack of integrity in the modern-day corporate world *especially given the entry of bloody women into a male domain.* Christopher looked daggers at Bill before turning to Jane and Joanne, but they seemed to receive the comment without surprise or complaint. They were well-versed in his prejudices and obviously chose to remain focused on the issues before them, showing admirable restraint. It was eventually agreed that Ernest and Jane should lead the next session for Skills World in an attempt to explore angles; to try to find leverage with a view to negotiating improved terms.

On reconvening, despite their best efforts, Alexander simply held his ground. He politely stonewalled all objections, reiterating the board's final decision. He declined to be drawn into a wider discussion. There appeared no room for manoeuvre. Christopher focused his attention on Georgina who watched the exchange passively, allowing Alexander to parry the arguments. She was no doubt gauging the reactions and body language of the participants. Throughout this exchange, Bill had been uncharacteristically, moodily silent. The constant rubbing of his temples was an apparently futile attempt to dispel a tension-headache. Finally, Georgina leant forward and fixed her emerald-green eyes on the team, turning sharply to focus on Christopher with laser beam intensity.

'I'd like to hear your views, Christopher.'

The room fell silent. All eyes turned on the MD. Christopher glanced briefly at Bill, who was visibly shaking with rage, then to Joanna, whose expression was unfathomable, before locking eyes with Georgina. Gathering his thoughts, he breathed in deeply. Georgina was about to become his boss. The contrast with the current one could hardly be starker. How to respond? The success of any earn-out period would largely be determined by a contract with Ulysses which was of enormous significance, as she full-well knew. How likely was it that SWL would successfully conclude a deal with Ulysses? It was not a slam dunk, but Christopher was confident. If Skills World were to reject Supreme's offer, then it would condemn the team to more years under Bill and might even jeopardise the partnership with Ulysses. The thought that Christopher's response might determine whether a deal could be struck today struck him like a thunderbolt. Bill would ultimately decide as the majority shareholder, of course. His MD's acquiescence was not needed, nor anyone else's. But Bill now knew the value that Supreme attached to the executive team under Christopher's leadership and Bill would know that he could not manage the company alone. All that had been built up over the last few years could quickly disappear with any fall-out. And with it thirty million pounds. A shiver of anticipation tingled down Christopher's spine. The future suddenly seemed to rest in his hands.

What was the decision to be? Georgina or Bill? He and the team had an inherent belief in their future prospects. Skills World was on the cusp of great things that could only be countenanced under new, liberating ownership. The only pause for thought was whether this would be possible under Georgina's regime? She had a reputation as talented and successful but hard-nosed; a powerful, self-assured businesswoman with an intimidating character. Life would not be easy under her leadership, but her ambition, drive and successful track record was also part of the attraction. To decline this opportunity would be to condemn the business to mediocrity. The choice was obvious. After a long pause, Christopher leant forward and looked directly into her sparkling orbs, his nerve endings jangling.

'Then you're about to spend ten million pounds more than originally offered. It's an excellent deal. We *will* max out on the earn-out arrangement, of that I'm *very* confident.'

Bill seethed.

Jane and Ernest breathed more easily.

Joanne allowed a small, almost imperceptible raising of one eyebrow.

Georgina let the semblance of a smile lighten her features and slowly nodded her approval. This was presumably what she had hoped to hear.

Phew!

15. Skills World – Post Mortem

Savoy Hotel

The deal was quickly agreed following the meeting with Georgina Harris and Alexander Russia, despite the initial huffing and puffing of Bill. As they worked with Supreme's legal team, Entwistle Partners soon became engaged in re-writing history to better match Bill's perspective for the all-important press release.

Trying to secure Bill's focus on legal clauses in the terms and conditions of the sale and purchase agreement proved nigh on impossible. Not even the important matter of warranties he was required to sign could draw his attention away from the public relations presentational layer. It was left to Christopher and to Bill's faithful servant, Joanne, to look after his best interests. Rather than being appreciative, he dismissed the work as being merely operational detail. *Mm, I wonder what you'd think if the company breached the conditions and warranties were invoked? That would be very costly indeed.* It fell to Ernest Caruthers to explain to Bill the legal implications of what he was about to sign, an unenviable task. Meanwhile, Jane worked closely with Christopher and Joanne on the commercial and contracting terms. The three of them made progress, negotiating some worthwhile concessions from the acquirer's team and eventually the deal was done, the legal paperwork signed, and firm handshakes ensued.

The Skills World team had planned a special meal, all bar Bill readily agreeing that a celebration was more than warranted. It was a fabulous deal and would deliver higher returns to Skills World shareholders than the original had promised. Ninety-seven percent of the value would accrue to Bill, and Christopher would enjoy some modest returns. *Not exactly a fortune…but not bad for a useless bastard, eh Dad?*

'It's a good deal,' Christopher suggested carefully.

'At a multiple of six times profit, even the base deal is good and that's before any earn-out is factored in,' said Ernest.

'We agreed to sell for forty million and you lot all caved in to rob me. *Ten million pounds.* How can you all look me in the eye? Daylight bloody robbery. As for women in business. *Ha!*'

On securing the maximum pay-out, as Christopher was confident of delivering, then the multiple would increase to ten. An extremely healthy return indeed, in the upper quartile of deal multiples at that time, Jane reminded the team.

'We should remember our profits were only around one million a few years ago. There's been quite a turnaround,' suggested Joanne, taking everyone by surprise, and earning a glare for her intervention. But there was no convincing Bill. Profits had increased to around five million on a turnover of sixty million pounds. Bill would not accept this version of reality; profits had merely been depressed previously because of difficult market trading, he insisted.

'There's some truth in that...' began Christopher.

'Don't be impertinent. I don't need any lectures from the likes of *you.*'

'Whether you like it or not the plain truth is that previous profits were never in the history of the company greater than one-point-five million on turnover no higher than forty million,' responded Christopher. His sharp response earnt him an autocratic glare and a dismissive wave of the hand.

'I suggest we look at it in another way, Bill. The minimum guaranteed thirty million return is five times greater than what you could have reasonably anticipated just two years ago,' suggested Jane.

For this turnaround in company performance, the owner had sacrificed only three percent of the equity, Christopher being allocated just one percent, the rest spread amongst the team. Bill bitterly resented ever having been persuaded to dilute his equity, however, and made this known. He refused to acknowledge the efforts of his young team and denied that driving turnover and profits higher had increased the value of the business. Dinner was, therefore, destined to be a relatively muted and comparatively sober affair and the team had wished each other good night by ten-thirty.

The bell chimed to room 565. Christopher entered with a winning smile, eager anticipation, the hint of Hugo Boss aftershave, a bottle of Bollinger and two champagne flutes. The private assignation was to be the highlight of his day, one Christopher had keenly anticipated for much of the evening.

Jane had been the instigator of this rendezvous, tantalising him with some provocative under-table exploratory footwork focused on the trouser department. Her toes provocatively delved and probed, whilst simultaneously engaging her colleagues in conversation, with just the occasional enigmatic smile cast in Christopher's direction. *Naughty girl!* It proved to be a stimulating and distracting accompaniment to his wild sea bass with orange and fennel. Never had a fillet of sea bass required such powers of concentration.

As she passed him en route to the bathroom, she had leant over his shoulder to daintily remove a strand of fennel from his tie, holding it aloft as some sort of trophy, to the amusement of the team. She slipped a note into his pocket, tapping it lightly to draw his attention.

In a lull in the conversation, he had discreetly extricated the scrap of paper and devoured its contents. His eyes opened wide, hardly believing. Jane's eyes sparkled expectantly as he raised his head and looked in her direction. She had his full attention now.

The note simply read:

'Room 565. 11.30. Be there! J.'

The adventurous romp that had followed in the plush surroundings of Jane's bedroom in the Savoy had effectively been funded at Bill's expense, an enjoyable additional thought given his mean-spirited attitude that evening and throughout the entire process. It had prompted a second bottle of champagne during a brief lull in proceedings. Christopher would remember this deal for the rest of his life, of that he was certain.

16. Post-Acquisition

Earn-Out Arrangements

At last, Christopher was released from Bill's clutches – well, almost. There was still the important matter of the earn-out period to be navigated. Once the erstwhile owner had come to terms with the realities of the changed deal, surely Bill would come to understand the massive financial upside? *I damn well know what's in it for me…*

Christopher's mobile trilled – Jane.

'Hi, Jane. Great to hear from you. Wonderful night. Wasn't it?'

'Another time Chris – this is strictly business and I'm a bit tight for time, if you'll forgive me?'

'What's on your mind?'

'Earn-out arrangements.'

She proceeded to map out an incentive scheme the family had persuaded Bill to offer; to ensure continuing influence over the business following the transaction. Christopher was to be incentivised to urgently pursue an optimal outcome.

'Well, that's a welcome surprise, although I s'pose it means I'll still have to deal with the old—'

'Yes. I suggest we meet with him at his house.'

'Okay, if we must.'

'And I would implore you to be on your best behaviour, please count to ten every time he says something incendiary. The chemistry between you two is—'

'Point taken. Not that it'll be easy.'

'I know but he's taken a bit of cajoling to agree this deal. It's a good one for you. But then I can only offer advice.'

'I appreciate it. Really. And perhaps we could find a little restaurant afterwards? Just you and me. It *was* a special night wasn't it? Perhaps we could find further reason to—'

'Not sure that's such a good idea, Chris…' she said, pausing before continuing, 'And by the way, why is it you blokes always need reassuring after your conquests…'

'Oh, I wouldn't say…' But she had gone. *Why was she so tetchy?*

Christopher soon found himself once again in Bill's ancestral home in Epsom Downs in rural Surrey. The obligatory lunch was served by his housekeeper in the dining room, with lashings of inconsequential, boorish small talk. This was the standard formula applied by Bill to meetings he deemed important enough to be held in his home. Having completed the ritual, they repaired to the library where a formal desk served as the boardroom table.

Bill started formal proceedings by delivering a long introduction, an updated pocket-history of the company. At least that afforded Christopher an overview as to how history had been redrawn, together with his glossy rationale of the recent transaction. Bill featured large in the overview and Christopher was but a footnote, one that would no doubt be erased as events unfolded. Poor old Joanne was not even mentioned. Her corporate rescue act of ten years ago was overlooked, as was her part in delivering a massive return on investment for the family. Christopher had over the years learned that it would be a waste of time to attempt any challenge of such an account. But he was uncomfortable about Joanne's treatment.

'I had expected Joanne to join you, Bill. How is she? On holiday perhaps? I hope she's well?'

'Not much for her to do now you know and, ah-hem, she's done enormously well out of this family for a long time so deserves her retirement. She's been well-treated, very well-treated, as you can no doubt imagine. Anyway, let's get on with it, shall we?' It was highly likely that he had cast aside his loyal finance director and a family friend of many years standing with barely a thank you, let alone any financial reward.

'Given the earn-out structure,' began Jane, taking her cue, 'we would like to agree with you an additional arrangement which would see you personally share in the benefit of any upside. It seems to Bill that it's only right and proper you have this opportunity.'

'Bloody generous too. All comes out of the family's pockets,' Bill said.

'Indeed, the family's largesse is greatly appreciated. Isn't that right, Christopher?'

'All shareholders did rather well from the turnaround strategy,' said Christopher, just about keeping his irritation in check.

'My dear chap, we have all benefited from the strength of the market and, of course, from the longevity and success of this revered family firm, would you not say?'

'Gentlemen, I suggest we move this discussion on,' Jane interceded swiftly. She then proceeded to outline a deal whereby Christopher would enjoy an additional bonus based on the upside quantum at the end of the earn-out period, to be calculated by a pre-determined formula.

'Gentlemen, let's consider the optimum position, shall we, and tease out what this means for all parties. Let's assume that the maximum earn-out position is secured. The current deal's already paid out three-hundred thousand pounds for your one percent, Christopher—'

'Bloody good for such a young man—'

'Please, Bill. As I was saying…' Jane proceeded to spell out the deal mechanisms and the financial rewards that would accrue to all parties. Christopher would secure almost an additional one million pounds, three quarters of this funded by the bonus scheme that was proposed in Bill's name.

'Ha! A princely sum which makes you a millionaire – for doing what? And out of my pocket too…Three-quarters of a million…' said Bill.

Christopher looked aghast and turned to Jane who gave a barely perceptible shake of her head, her blonde curls moving gently as if caught by the whisper of a breeze.

'That's very generous of you,' Christopher mumbled. His words did not convey much conviction. 'All to our mutual benefit I'm sure. But for God's sake man, you get even richer. Spell it out, will you please, Jane? Before I say something which we may all regret?'

'All in all, you will have secured forty-seven million, seven hundred and fifty thousand pounds net of the incentive payment to Christopher,' she said to Bill.

'By my reckoning that's over ninety-five percent of the total deal.'

'Correct,' agreed Jane swiftly, before adding, 'So of the additional twenty million pounds at the maximum earn-out you will enjoy an uplift of nearly nineteen million pounds, Bill.'

'Mm. And do I need to remind you that I've spent my entire life building this company? A lifetime, young man. And you've been here five minutes…You're bloody lucky, unlikely to ever come across another family like ours again.'

'And on that at least we are in full agreement. I've one final question.'

'Yes?'

'You promised to make small gifts to a number of loyal and long-serving members of staff upon completion of the deal. You will recall that, at your request, you and I discussed names and amounts on numerous occasions and I have a copy of the final list you agreed. When will this be paid?'

'Christopher, you really must adjust to the new reality. You are now operating in a company with a different set of owners. I could not possibly interfere with your new masters in this way. It would also compromise you personally, I suggest. Now if that is it—'

'*No*. I have *not* finished, and you haven't answered the question. Not satisfactorily at least. We spent hours talking about this. You know we did. The cost would be about one-hundred thousand pounds in total – less than half of one percent of the sale proceeds to date. Surely, you aren't going to renege?' Christopher was incensed. The old tyrant had dined out on numerous occasions, basking in the glory of his intended benevolence; to Gill, Iain, Jeremy and a small number of other hard working, intensely loyal and relatively poorly paid staff. People who Bill had, on so many occasions, spoken of in the warmest possible terms. Even the small sums involved would make a significant difference to their lives and to their impending retirements.

'I will hear no more of this. The stress of your new responsibilities is clearly getting to you, playing tricks with your memory. We spoke about the possibility of recognising the contribution of these wonderful people but it's no longer my obligation. It's *yours*.' With which Bill shuffled his papers and stood, signalling the end of the meeting.

Christopher was ashen with rage and determined to have the last word on the matter.

'Then I will personally stand your corner. *Shame on you*. Goodbye…'

17. Birthday Girl

As Caroline went through her normal daily routine, the doorbell rang. She padded through the hallway in fluffy slippers with a piece of toast in her hand. On opening the door, she was faced with a huge bouquet of flowers, behind which a deliveryman offered her a cheery *happy birthday*. He pointed to the open card within the cellophane wrap emblazoned with the message, before disappearing down the steps, whistling tunelessly.

Meandering back to her kitchen, grabbing the post on her way, she hummed to the song that played on the radio in the background. She thrust the flowers in a bucket of water – they would have to wait until later to be arranged in vases – and extricated the message. He had remembered, of course he had. He could always be relied upon. Glancing at the post, she discarded the circulars and the bills and reached for two cards. One was from Olivia with an irreverent, cheery message and reminder of their lunch date. Just then, her mobile rang.

'Hello?'

'Happy Birthday, Caroline. How are you, birthday girl?'

'Thanks for the flowers, H. They're beautiful. You know how to spoil a girl.'

'All set for this evening? A splendid surprise lined up.'

'What? Where?'

'Aha, you will just have to wait and see, won't you? Oh, and one other thing. I have a surprise day out lined up for the weekend. Tell you all about it tonight. Must dash. Busy day at the corporate helm you know. Love and kisses.'

'H, wait…' But he was gone, mysterious as ever. The bloody man, she grinned. But time was marching on, anyway, and she needed to get ready for work. But first, she turned her attention to the second card. Whom could it be from? H and Olivia were the only significant people in her life. There really was not anyone else who would send her a birthday card through the post. Taking a knife, she slit the envelope open and eased the card out. The front cover proclaimed the milestone birthday; nothing unusual or surprising about that. But the celebratory message contained a word that made her pull up short: *daughter*. He *never* sent cards. She plopped down in a chair and gingerly opened it up. Sure enough, it was from her father.

Happy Birthday Caroline, darling.
I miss you desperately.
When are you coming home – if only to visit?
Love,
Daddy, x.

She read the card over and over again and soon her whole body was shaking, wracked by deep, relentless sobs as her emotions took hold. A tear dropped onto her father's writing. *Oh no!* She reached for the tissues and tried to make good his now smudged writing, but it only made matters worse. His message soon became illegible. Her tears flowed freely. *Oh, Daddy!* He had never expressed any emotion, not even at her mam's funeral. On so many occasions, she had come close to abandoning all hope she would ever be able to reach across the chasm of misunderstanding that had opened between them. He was so irascible, so intolerant, so disinterested in her achievements, dismissive of her choice of career and life. And yet, and yet. *He's my father. And I need to try harder, much harder.*

'Hi hon, happy birthday,' Olivia said, embracing Caroline tightly. 'You okay? Where have you been this morning?' They were meeting in a small restaurant in Covent Garden, Olivia's treat for her birthday. Caroline had tried to disguise the red eyes but knew that Olivia had not been fooled, as she held her at arm's length to study her closely.

'What's wrong?'

'I'm fine. Couldn't face work today.'

'Come on, tell Aunty Liv.'

'A card from my father.'

'Well, of course. That's great, isn't it?' And Caroline was soon pouring out her innermost thoughts and emotions, her guilty feelings. She revealed her concerns about his health, although she had no tangible evidence anything was wrong, and he denied any problem. But he seemed weaker and more fragile somehow. They had spoken occasionally in recent months, but the conversation never flowed, and he always seemed so miserable and unforgiving – of anyone, but particularly of her. She was beginning to despair.

'Have you rung him, babe?'

'I daren't. I can't trust myself to do so yet. Oh, look at me, thirty today and I'm an emotional wreck. Thank God for you and H.'

Eventually, Olivia's sympathy gave way to lighter, cheerier topics and Caroline eventually came around, as the conversation moved on. Olivia confided in Caroline that she was seeing Marku quite regularly.

'You remember, the good-looking hunk.'

'So, Julian's history, is he?' asked Caroline.

'No, not at all and don't you pull that face. A girl has to enjoy herself. Anyway, Marku is an exciting, mysterious character. Brings a bit of spice to my life. You should hear what he's doing. All undercover you know. Dangerous as hell...'

Caroline was soon distracted from her woes and intrigued by Olivia's news. It seemed that Marku was an investigative reporter and had infiltrated a gang illegally importing Eastern Europeans into the country. He suspected some sort of benefits fraud as well.

'Isn't that dangerous?'

'Incredibly. Told you it was exciting. My very own James Bond.'

'Doesn't much look like 007 from what I can recall, but I can see he's got you all shaken if not stirred,' laughed Caroline.

'Oh, get you! But you're right, he can shake and stir me any time he likes. Often does.'

'Olivia!'

'It helps that he's of Romanian descent himself, speaks the lingo.'

'So how come you get to see him? I mean where—'

'There's some slum in Hackney that seems to have been turned into a sort of hostel. Marku works in the kitchen there and is wheedling his way into the gang. Bogdan something or other seems to be the leader but Marku thinks this is just one cell in a large network. And he's feeding information back to the department through his favourite Bohemian girl.'

'Really? I wondered why you'd moved to the fraud section. I always thought that was dull.'

'It is in the main, not very taxing really but that suits me fine. Besides, it's suddenly turned me from being some sort of rebel in their eyes into a modern-day heroine – well nearly.'

'Mm. Struggle to see you as some Joan of Arc figure.'

'Me too. Come on, drink up, some of us have got work to do today.'

18. High-Powered Review

Caroline had dressed carefully – her sharpest suit – for the review meeting with the minister and Permanent Secretary Garside. She nipped to the ladies for some last-minute adjustments to her make-up, a smoothing of her black skirt and a final check in the mirror. She took a deep breath in a futile attempt to control the butterflies and having checked her watch for the umpteenth time decided it was time to enter the fray.

Caroline joined two colleagues from her section and Felicity Jenkinson and a colleague of hers from the Job Centre team. Given past skirmishes, Caroline and Felicity greeted each other guardedly, the atmosphere frosty. They quietly charged their cups with standard issue instant coffee and helped themselves to a biscuit, a rare treat signalling the imminent attendance of luminaries. They were soon joined by Permanent Secretary Steven Garside and Minister Sebastian Frith.

'Good morning everybody. I'd like to extend a warm welcome to the minister who joins us today. He has a tight schedule so let's press on, shall we? Minister, I think you wanted to say something at the outset, if you would be so kind.'

'Thank you. First of all, let me express my appreciation of your endeavours in this challenging area. Good progress is being made. I'd be grateful if you'd pass on such sentiments to your hard-working teams.'

A few nervous glances were exchanged as the minister paused, allowing his words to drift down on his audience like the first snowflakes of winter before settling softly on terra firma. The permanent secretary smiled his acknowledgement; the other attendees did their best to conceal their surprise. The minister was not given to engaging in pleasantries let alone expressing appreciation or bestowing compliments. Sebastian Frith gulped his coffee, attacked his biscuit and then continued.

'As you know, we've been debating the various policy options and I acknowledge that a number of you have expressed concerns about our direction of travel. You and yours especially, Felicity. But the government's course is now determined. We've contracted with the private and charitable third sectors increasingly over the last year or so and now we'll pick up the pace—'

'Might I just enquire, minister…Sorry, through the chair, permanent secretary—'

'No, you may not, Felicity,' the minister answered. 'You must accept the policy direction and commit to a redefined role for the Job Centre network. And I want to see larger contracts awarded to private companies prepared to invest in the market. We need to contract with fewer companies to get the concentration of expertise and economies of scale required to drive higher performance levels.

I expect you to draw up the specifications and tender documents accordingly. I know I can rely upon your expertise and professionalism to undertake this and I look forward to reviewing the draft documentation very soon,' he added.

Caroline sat back in her chair and remained silent. The minister made her nervous, apprehensive. She observed the exchange of anxious glances and whispered asides between Felicity and her colleague, who were clearly still exercised by the implied changes to their organisation.

'I'm sure we all greatly appreciate the minister confirming the policy direction of travel and his kind words. The steer from government is now very clear, which is tremendously helpful, minister. I propose that you all now devote your time to reviewing the market performance statistics and to determining the actions required to build upon the success to date,' said Steven Garside, smoothly stepping into the awkward lull in proceedings that followed the minister's broadside, whilst simultaneously distancing himself from the operational task.

'I will bow out at this point – but I'd appreciate a few minutes of your time, Caroline,' said the minister, not waiting for an answer as he bade everyone a brusque goodbye and bounded to the door. Caroline received a brief nod from her boss. They found a small meeting room and sat opposite each other. Caroline sat quietly awaiting the minister's words. She interlocked her hands and willed them to stay still in her lap.

'Just a word to the good, Miss Hope. You did very well at the spring conference and should have a bright career ahead of you – but you need to be a bit more flexible. Need to take your cue from your superiors, if you know what I mean.'

'I'm not sure I do, minister. But I strongly welcome your policy pronouncements and—'

'Good, but frankly whether you agree or not isn't the point,' he said leaning forward and glaring at her. 'Your reluctance to award the contracts to the right players in the last round was noted. I don't expect you to challenge my decisions in future.'

'Right players?'

'Those I choose, having taken into account your recommendations,' he said, clearly exasperated.

'But, minister, all we are doing is managing the process. I absolutely understand that policy is government's sole preserve; the department will of course do your bidding. But it's our job to execute the processes which fall under European procurement rules. I'm not sure there's scope for even ministerial preferences to be applied, is there?' Caroline sat back, surprised that she had summoned up the courage to say this, even if her voice had been wobbly.

'Miss Hope, I'll give you the benefit of the doubt on this occasion and put your rudeness down to youthful naivety. But listen to me carefully. My decisions are *final*. These procurement processes provide the framework within which judgement must be exercised.' He appeared to be struggling to maintain his equilibrium, his face flushing.

'Yes, minister. Sorry,' Caroline mumbled.

Sebastian rose to his feet, wagged his finger at her then said, 'Don't let me have to cover this ground again, Miss Hope. I don't take kindly to being defied. I trust we understand one another now.' Sebastian Frith glowered belligerently at her one last time then turned on his heels and left the room, slamming the door behind him. Caroline stared after him aghast, shaking with shock. He'd spoken sharply to her previously but never quite like this.

Later that evening, Caroline poured herself a large glass of wine and reached for her mobile.

'Hi, babe, how are you? What you up to?' answered Olivia in that inimitably bright and breezy way of hers.

'Okay, I guess. How's your day been, Olivia?'

'Ooh you sound down. What's wrong? Tell Aunty Liv. Come on now. I can always tell. Hang on, let me grab a bottle…that's better. Oops – well most of it landed in the glass. Now tell…' insisted her friend.

'Oh, just a run-in with my minister. Stunned me really, scared me a bit to be completely honest. At first, he was almost sweetness and light in front of the perm sec. Well almost, as nice as he gets anyway. Then he demands to speak to me alone and he was…he was…'

Gradually, Caroline relayed the exchange, taking several gulps of the chilled Chardonnay along the way. Olivia was a surprisingly good listener for one so extrovert and always seemed to find an irreverent comment to prick the tension. She did not fail this time either.

'He's a bully and probably hadn't been able to get it up this morning. All mouth and no trousers. Sod him and well done you for giving him a piece of your mind. Don't let him get to you. Speaking of the trouser department, tell me about H, babe. Marks out of ten for performance? Originality? He's not disappointing I hope?'

19. Henley

She had set the alarm early but need not have bothered. Such was her excitement at the prospect of a day at Henley Regatta – her birthday treat – that she'd even breakfasted before the alarm sounded. H promised her a day to remember, telling her bits and pieces about Henley; enough to whet her appetite for this very English social event – Caroline's first such experience. She was well-prepared and full of eager anticipation when H arrived at her door.

'How beautiful you look,' he said with a flourish. Caroline had been warned of the strict dress code, so was attired in a suitably modest, below the knee navy-blue dress and had also bought a hat for the occasion, which H admired in his customary expansive manner. He was resplendent in his blazer and flannels with a smart old school tie to complete his outfit.

H reached up and kissed her lightly before stepping to one side to announce, waving his arms excitedly, 'Your chariot awaits…' Caroline gasped in surprise. A stately car displaying the distinctive Spirit of Ecstasy purred in the centre of her road. It was too large to park in any of the available spaces in her suburban street.

'Oh, my goodness. What on earth—'

'A 1957 Rolls-Royce Silver Shadow drop head coupe, I would have you know. I've even arranged the promised blue sky and sunshine. We shall arrive at the premier event of the English social calendar in style, my dear.'

'I didn't even know you could drive and look at the size of the thing; it's enormous.'

The car looked incongruous in its shiny, spotless powder-blue livery and grey leather interior alongside the Minis and Sierras and white vans that lined the street.

'Indeed. Quite a challenge around here but my man, James, is frightfully good you know,' said H. On cue, a small man wearing a peaked cap opened the passenger door and, raking the seat as far forward as it would go, the couple were able to slide into the back.

'Now before we enjoy the wind in our hair, I thought you might appreciate this,' said H, handing Caroline a blue silk headscarf.

'Oh, very Audrey Hepburn. You think of everything, don't you? You certainly know how to spoil a lady I must say. This is quite something.'

'Nothing's too good for you and I promised a special day out. We also have tickets to the Stewards' Enclosure on the Berkshire bank for the day. Very hard to come by, you know. Invitation only.'

'How've you managed that?'

'Contacts. It's all about contacts. Now shall we get the show on the road. What do you say? Yes, off we go then…Henley, my man, if you please,' announced H, who seemed completely oblivious to the stares of a passing dog-walker and the local paper boy taking in the scene, surprise etched on their features.

'Yes, sir,' responded James, with a doff of the cap, easing the car forwards regally.

Their arrival gave them sufficient time to enjoy a glass of bubbly at the Champagne & Oyster Bar before locating their reserved place in the luncheon tent for a sumptuous three course meal. The wine flowed and they were soon chatting animatedly with fellow diners on the long tables. In one lull in the conversation, H excused himself. Caroline was soon engaged in a tête-à-tête with a lady next to her who seemed intrigued to hear about Caroline's work in the DWP and the world of the *poor workless darlings*. Victoria went on to make various disparaging and wholly inappropriate comments about their plight which served to display her ignorance. But no one was going to spoil Caroline's day and she allowed the comments to wash over her without complaint or correction. Out of the corner of her eye, she spotted H in conversation with two men at the entrance. There was something familiar about one of them, but she was soon distracted by an elderly man sitting opposite her. He sported a large Jimmy Edwards-style handlebar moustache curled upwards at the ends and insisted on sharing his knowledge about Henley whilst topping up her glass.

H soon returned and after a coffee they made their way towards the Members' Grandstand.

'I thought this was just for members?' asked Caroline.

'Quite so, my dear.'

'Are you then?' she asked.

'Am I what, dearest?' he answered.

'A member.' He could be so obtuse sometimes.

'Not strictly speaking. No,' H said, taking her hand, as they threaded their way through the assembled throng. 'Come on let's get ready for the race,' he added. He nodded to one or two people along the way and was briefly waylaid by a tall gent in a vivid blazer he apparently did business with.

'Sorry, Caroline. Business does so intrude, but nearly there.'

'Who was that and by the way who were you chatting to earlier during lunch?'

'No one in particular, just a business contact. Frightfully boring sort, you know.'

'He looked a little bit like my minister. Do you know him?'

'No. The tall chap in the blazer? That was just Freddie, an IT Director in a small company.'

'Not him, the one from earlier in the tent.'

'A minister? I don't know about that. I've no political contacts I can think of. He's a dealer in the City, I believe. Awfully rich and a frightful windbag or I'd have introduced you. Here we are. Just in time for the Grand Challenge Cup. Have a sip of that my dear; rusty nail.' He handed a hip flask to Caroline.

'What on earth's that?'

'Whisky and Drambuie. A marvellously rich, warming concoction.'

'I don't think so. Anyway, I'm quite warm enough.'

'Don't know what you're missing…'

The race seemed almost incidental to the social gathering, but Caroline enjoyed the spectacle and witnessed The Australian Institute for Sport beat Leander Club & Queen's Tower Boat Club by one and a half lengths. All too quickly, it was time to head back to their car park, find James and begin the slow but luxurious ride back to London. As they inched forwards in the voluminous traffic, the sun beating down on them on this glorious English summer's day, H turned towards Caroline, grabbed her hand and said, 'I hope you've enjoyed yourself. I've had a simply wonderful time and you are so very special to me you know.'

'Oh, H, I can't tell you what a difference you've made to my life and today has been wonderful. I don't want it to end really,' Caroline answered, before adding in a lighter tone. 'But I think you may have had too much to drink. A rusty nail too far?'

'Stuff and nonsense. Look, it's much too early to end the day. Why don't we find somewhere for supper and then aim for Notting Hill?' He said this with a glint in his eye, lifting her hand gently to brush his lips in that old-fashioned way he had, his eyes never leaving hers.

'I can't think of anything I'd like more,' she enthused. 'But I've eaten enough, why don't we settle for a snack and a glass of wine?'

'Good idea. I know just the place.'

'You always do,' she laughed, snuggling up to him.

They were deposited on the outskirts of London where they piled into a private taxi and watched James drive away happily. He'd been the grateful recipient of a wad of notes thrust in his direction. They soon found themselves in a quiet corner of a gastropub on the edge of Notting Hill. H ordered a bottle of Chablis, two glasses and a few snacks: calamari with lemon mayonnaise, arancini balls, humous, taramasalata and flat bread.

'Thanks for a perfect day, H.'

'My pleasure. It's always been a high spot in the English sporting and social calendar; right up there with Wimbledon, Cowes, Ascot…' he said, taking a sip of his Chablis before turning to her.

'You said there was something you wanted to ask me?'

'Did I?'

'In the car on the slow drive back. Something about political masters?' said H. He looked at her quizzically, arching his eyebrows.

'Yes, but I don't want to spoil the day and by the way, that Roller was just the icing on the cake,' Caroline said, her smile slowly giving way to a more sombre expression.

'I'm all ears. Here we go, a splash more, my dear. No? Very well, but it's frightfully good. You were saying? Do press on…'

'Okay. I may be being a bit paranoid here, but I'm worried about my minister. How he treats me. You're a man of the world. You seem to know how things work.'

'Spit it out, my dear,' he encouraged kindly, squeezing her hand reassuringly.

'It's just that he seems inclined to interfere in contract awards. It's the job of politicians to determine policy; ours to execute it within the legal framework.'

'I thought you and he were in agreement about what you're trying to achieve? Private sector contracts to achieve better results in returning the poor unwashed and out-of-work souls to honourable employment?'

'I wouldn't put it quite like that. It sounds more than a bit patronising and unsympathetic to their plight…but essentially…yes.'

'Forgive my clumsiness. I'm clearly not cut out for your line of work,' he said smiling, his dimple reappearing.

'No, you aren't. You'd have a riot on your hands in no time,' Caroline said quickly, flashing a half-smile at him. 'And yes, the minister and I are in complete agreement as to the direction of travel. But that's not the point. Even if I disagreed with him, I'd be duty-bound to execute the policy. The issue is that he seems to know which companies he wishes to award contracts to. He seems a bit cavalier about the rules of the tendering processes. He shouldn't be directly involved in any of that other than to hold us to account for implementation. He's becoming very directive and rude. Almost bullying. It upsets me. How should I deal with this? What do you think?'

'I don't know if you aren't imagining an issue. It sounds as if you're both on the same page; you both want the same outcomes and are pushing hard to that end. I know you're passionate and resolute in your approach. Aren't you just feeling the heat from the minister's similar enthusiasm and resolve? Clashing a bit? I'm afraid, my dear, that in the male form, this often comes out as being a bit pushy; testosterone-fuelled you might say. Not attractive, but we chaps rarely understand how it's perceived, but there you are. No harm intended. Isn't it just a case of him being a tad overzealous and you feeling under pressure? Anyway, if he instructs you to do X or Y, then you're protected in merely following instructions, aren't you?'

'Possibly, although I answer up the line in the department. Mind you, having said that, my boss is a million miles from any of this.'

'So, in effect, you have dual masters. Always challenging. I have two pieces of advice for you, if I may be so bold?'

'Yes, please,' she said, reaching forward to take an arancini ball, nibbling absent-mindedly.

'Firstly, there's a golden rule in business: to proactively manage your bosses. Most wait for their superiors to set the pace, the more enlightened manage upwards.' Caroline looked doubtful but listened attentively. Continuing, H added, 'And I strongly suggest you relax a little. In the real world, shortcuts are taken, risks are run and there's no harm in that. It's the way of the world. After all, you're both trying to get to the same end point it seems…now come on, drink up and let's head back to our little oasis, shall we?'

20. A Small World

November 2000

Christopher and Paul Dart, his recently recruited finance director, entered the grand office where they were met with a warm welcome by Horatio Pilkins, the CEO. He was also greeted by Gregory Jones and Eleanor Strong, the commercial director and finance director of Ulysses. Their plush, stylish office was located in a technology business park in Reading. It was part of the M4 corridor, often referred to as the UK's Silicon Valley which ran either side of the motorway and linked towns like Windsor, Maidenhead, Reading, Newbury and Bracknell; home to technology goliaths such as Microsoft, Oracle, Cisco, Vodafone and the like.

The heating was working overtime on this bitterly cold winter's day to the point where Horatio's office was uncomfortably hot. The décor was an eclectic mix of styles, from Art Deco, through to the sixties and seventies and into the new century: all black and cream leather, chrome and glass. Lurid Andy Warhol prints hung on the walls and sculptures of golfers in full swing were dotted around the room, although none of their executives seemed remotely sporty. The room boasted a long sideboard, scattered with decanters of whisky, gin and brandy – all very much in keeping with some of their larger, wealthy corporate neighbours.

'Well, it's simply marvellous to see you again, my friend. How are things with your new owners? Supreme are a splendid company, I should say. Shall we see if we can't get this show on the road? See if we can't put a bit of flesh on the bones?' began Horatio, rubbing his hands together briskly.

'Blimey, it's hot in here, don't you think so, Christopher? Horatio, do you mind?' said Gregory Jones, as he strode over to adjust the thermostat.

'Good call, Gregory. We couldn't be happier to be part of the Supreme empire, which should make us an even more attractive partner to Ulysses,' said Christopher. 'We're also keen to get things moving contractually, but some of the details about our proposed partnership were a little vague last time, with due respect.'

For some time, SWL had been in negotiations with Ulysses about a strategic partnering arrangement. Not only was this important for future business growth but it had significance in driving towards a maximum position in SWL's earn-out structure too. This pending deal was therefore a high priority and a major focus in the post-acquisition period. This would entail SWL becoming a primary strategic partner of Ulysses where it was proposed they would take on full operational responsibility for the front-line delivery of some of Ulysses' contracts.

'Well splendid. Tickety-boo. Gregory, why don't you outline our latest thoughts?'

'Yes, of course. We think we should now firm up our plans to move beyond the strategic partnering language to a full commercial deal, if that meets with your approval?' began Gregory, before giving way to Eleanor.

'But your price for the contracts in the South West of England are much too high. Unless you can be more reasonable, then I doubt there's much for us to talk about.'

'What the dear lady is quite rightly saying is that we're keen to secure a good deal where both parties are able to enjoy the proceeds in a fair and equitable manner. Ulysses recognises that economies of scale are likely to be a factor here,' said Horatio, in clarification. 'Gregory, please summarise what's in our minds.' Horatio ignored the pained expression this interjection had prompted from his finance director, who sat back and scowled.

'As you may know, the government is poised to massively expand the contracting out of programmes of training and employment. We believe this presents a significant opportunity for both companies. It would make sense to combine operations to secure efficiencies and economies of scale,' said Gregory.

'True, although we can't be clear how far or how fast the government will push this agenda, can we?' said Christopher, not wanting to imperil the deal but wanting to ensure perspective in their deliberations.

'Oh, don't you worry on that score, my friend. We *do* know,' asserted Horatio, smiling knowingly whilst his forefinger tapped the side of his nose.

'So, to continue,' said Gregory. 'We've previously discussed Skills World delivering a number of our contracts in the one region and of our two companies co-operating across all of our other regions, as you will recall.'

'But what this means in actual delivery and financial terms is unclear to us. There's no detailed specification, no contract volumes. Pricing is difficult without more details, so we are bound to err on the high side,' pointed out Paul, with a nod to Eleanor's earlier point.

'Quite so. Gregory?' invited Horatio.

'Ulysses offer to Skills World the unique opportunity to deliver *all* of our training and employment contracts in London, the South East of England and Wales as well as the region that has hitherto been under discussion – but you'll have to sharpen your pencil.'

'Oh! Really? I see. Well, that would clearly change matters considerably,' agreed Christopher, failing to conceal his surprise. This was an exciting, potentially game-changing twist in commercial negotiations.

'And there's one further piece of news you might like to hear,' said Horatio, quietly. He allowed a beaming smile to illuminate the room.

'Strictly hush-hush you understand. No names, no pack-drill…The outcome of the recent competitive tendering round will see Skills World awarded the contracts for the North West and the East Midlands; Ulysses the four regions of London plus the West Midlands. Now what do you think about that?'

'How on earth can you know? The results aren't due for another two weeks.' Christopher's response and tone betrayed his incredulity.

'Trust me. Mum's the word. Now why don't you and I have a private chat while these chaps do the business? Come on, let's take a wander.'

He led a bewildered Christopher out of the office and headed to the boardroom. As Christopher settled into the leather armchair at the far end of the room, Horatio turned to the side-table before pausing. He studied his watch with an exaggerated movement.

'Well, Christopher, the sun's over the yardarm so it's high time we quenched our thirst. Scotch, yes? On the rocks? Right oh. Splendid…There we are.'

He thrust the glass at Christopher, two ice cubes chinking against the cut glass. He was still thinking about the news that they wanted a bigger and deeper based relationship than had been envisaged. This was a potential game-changer; his head was buzzing with possibilities.

'I have a further proposition which should clinch the deal, I should think. Brace yourself; this will make a fundamental difference.'

'I'm all ears, you have the floor. Oh, and cheers.'

'Quite so. Down the hatch. Now, where was I?'

'Clinching the deal.'

'Oh, yes…As you know, we've developed with our partners – at considerable cost, I would have you know, we've invested millions – the most advanced computer system in the market. We'd like to make this available to Skills World to operate, not only across all of our contracts but your own too. Makes sense, surely? A single system and all that. Yes?'

'That's a big change, Horatio. Why? You must know that we have our own. It's tried and tested; embedded in our processes. It would be a huge change process to replace it. But thanks for giving us the option. We'll consider the implications and let you know.'

'Perhaps I need to be a little clearer. The point is, well, we see this as a requirement, a contractual condition if you will.'

'What? We've never discussed…It feels like a big change with all sorts of cultural and operational ramifications and complex technical considerations.' His mind flashed back to yesterday's meeting with Georgina Harris where they had reviewed progress of the proposed partnering with Ulysses: *Make it happen.*

'But neither have we offered you all of our contracts before either, you must admit.'

'True enough,' said Christopher.

'I tell you what, why don't I invite our IT lady up to discuss this with you?'

He made the telephone call and whilst they awaited her arrival, it gave them a few minutes to reflect on this turn of events.

'This needs a lot of consideration and I can't promise…' began Christopher.

'Quite, quite. Don't worry so, my dear fellow. Now let me tell you about this wretched IT woman. I'm afraid she's quite insufferable but, well, the thing is she's bloody good at what she does. Or so I'm told. So, one just has to humour her. One of these feminists you know. No sense of humour, no respect for authority. Wants to take over the world and she wears her morals on her sleeves.

Young, too. I shouldn't be surprised if she doesn't vote for some liberal, limp-wristed party, eat vegetarian junk, is teetotal and a lesbian to boot! Get the picture? Another swift dram to prepare you. No? Well, okay, don't say I didn't warn you.'

A sharp rap on the door had signalled her arrival.

'Come in, my dear. Now, Liz...'

She stepped towards the two of them, then abruptly stopped in her tracks.

'You!' she said.

'Elizabeth?'

Horatio looked quickly from one to the other, as if watching a tennis match before saying, 'Well, I can see that you know each other. What a surprise. I was just singing your virtues, Liz praising you to the hilt, wasn't I, Christopher?'

His uncle's words leapt back at him, *you're a bloody young fool to let her get away.*

'Your comments were certainly illuminating, Horatio,' he muttered, trying to regain some composure from yet another surprising turn of events.

'Tell you what, why don't we call it a day,' said Horatio. 'Yes, that's what we'll do. I'll leave you two to catch up on old times and why don't we meet later in the week? Yes?'

With which, he abruptly stood up, vigorously shook Christopher's hand and bounded out of the room.

Christopher and Liz – *Elizabeth* – sank back into their chairs and just stared at each other, quite dumbfounded.

Reunion

Christopher was shocked to see the former love of his life and by the look of things, Elizabeth felt similarly. His stomach was turning somersaults, his hands clammy.

'Elizabeth! I'd no idea you were...how *are* you? Long-time no see.'

'Quite.'

'What brings you...sorry, I don't know what to say.'

'Not like you to be short of words, Chris.'

'No, I guess not. I was thinking of you just the other day actually,' he said, rubbing a hand through his thick black hair, shifting in his seat.

'So, you greet me with a lie. Really?'

'I actually was. I was with Xavier, my uncle, if you recall. He still remembers you. Gives me a hard time about...you know...'

'The adult of the Townsend family. I always liked him. Voted for him actually.'

Elizabeth spoke brusquely, but her face suggested wry amusement. She had always been difficult to read – but she somehow reached parts of him that others never could, and the way her sharp tongue would turn to good humour in the blink of an eye was disconcerting. Even after all this time, her sudden appearance was enough to rupture his natural self-confidence.

'Good to see you, Elizabeth. Really good,' he eventually managed.

'And you. But I can't think why I should be pleased to see you. You disappear off the radar, you're totally unreliable, unhealthily ambitious and self-serving.'

'A ringing endorsement. Love you too,' Christopher responded, daring a smile.

'And they're your good points. Just wait 'til I get to the other stuff.' And then, her sternness filtered away, slowly replaced by the hint of a smile that drifted to her eyes. She leant forward and studied him intently, the smile now blossoming. His heart missed a beat at the appearance of the Elizabeth that he had loved and lost. Bit by bit, the tension levels subsided, and they began to chat more freely, steering clear of the tentacles of old times that threatened to ensnare him. After a while, Christopher hesitantly floated the idea of finding somewhere for an early evening drink.

Finding a relatively quiet corner, they settled into brown leather squashy chairs around a rustic wine-barrel that served as a table. A candle-wax encrusted Asti Spumante bottle sat in the middle, the naked flame of a spluttering white candle adding to the lava flow. Christopher struggled back from the bar through the early evening crowd of business suits carrying a large glass of Chablis for Elizabeth and a glass of St Emilion claret for himself.

'Hope this place is okay. All very nineteen-seventies,' he said, handing her the wine and retrieving some olives and nibbles from the bar.

'Thanks, I need this. What a surprise seeing you, Chris. I couldn't believe it. Mind you, life at Ulysses is full of surprises, I can tell you.'

'So – what have you been doing with yourself since uni? I'm sorry we lost touch.'

'I did write, you know, but I guess you were too busy making your way in the business world to worry about me.' She looked at him accusingly.

'I know, I know. I'm terrible at keeping in touch and – well, I kept meaning to pick the phone up or write but by the time I got around to it...I just got caught up. Sorry,' he said wryly, adopting a doe-eyed little boy look of contrition.

'Actually, I'm not sure you ever did get around to it,' Elizabeth said, quietly, her pretty features darkening into a scowl.

'No, I guess not, damned fool that I was.'

The two talked about their time at university and of their relationship in the two crossover years. They had been well-suited, shared similar passions and a zest for life. They'd fallen in love, but Christopher was careful not to say as much.

'So why did we—'

'Not make a go of it?' he interjected, pulling a face.

'You just couldn't—'

'Let me get more drinks before we get into that, shall I?'

'Okay, but then if you want to talk about this, you'd better let me finish a bloody sentence!'

Elizabeth's fiery nature was never far from the surface, Christopher recalled, as he struggled through the evening throng. On his return, Elizabeth quietly reflected on why their relationship might have foundered. It had always seemed to her, she pointedly insisted, that he had some sense of higher purpose, a yearning for power and influence, a driving ambition. His keen sense of social injustices in need of correction were his saving grace, according to Elizabeth. His active interest in politics had suggested that a political career beckoned; a man driven by a heightened sense of destiny.

'You must've been talking to Xavier. He trotted out much the same nonsense recently. You haven't, have you? Spoken with him.'

'I doubt you've changed much, Chris. Business may be your current outlet for your ambitions but...'

The sentiment was left to hang in the air. Persisting, she referred to an ill-defined something or other he was in search of, an aching void that would need to be addressed one day.

'That's why you allowed our romance to drift after I'd left my university lifestyle behind,' she said. A cutting edge had returned to her voice and the smile had dissolved. He shifted uncomfortably. *I really don't need to listen to this stuff yet, again, do I?* But his uncle's words echoed in his head, *bloody young fool to let her get away.* He was right, damn him. So, Christopher eventually conceded that her leaving university to plough her own furrow was just too convenient to label as a causal event. The two lapsed into thoughtful silence, as they reflected on what might have been. Elizabeth looked sadly at Christopher and with a barely perceptible shake of her head changed tack.

'How are the political interests these days then? Still active on that front?' she asked.

'Well...I still take an interest in local politics as a member of the Tory party and of course track the national issues of the day. The trouble is I just don't have the time to devote to it that I would like. Business, you know, gets in the bloody way, but it pays the bills.'

'Why don't you stand for election to become an MP?'

'I'm not sure they'd have me. An oik like me – I don't come from the right bloodstock and I didn't go to the posh schools either. I seem to have misplaced that silver spoon,' he said, laughing with her. 'And the biggest problem is that you need to find a few people to vote for you.'

'You don't fool me, and I see the charm switch still works, Christopher George Townsend.'

'Haven't got a clue what you're talking about and can't we just drop the George bit...hate that name. Always reminds me of the black sheep of the family...'

'Not a chance, Georgie Boy!' she hurled back at him with a broad grin.

'What about you, Elizabeth? Tell me what you've been up to. How come you've ended up at Ulysses?'

'Changing the subject again?'

'Mm, perhaps. Deflecting onto more interesting topics, I'd say. *You*! I want to know what you've been doing since you gave me the big E,' he said flashing a provocative grin.

'Ha! Well, I'll come back to the so-called big E, Georgie Boy, but okay – a potted version. On leaving uni, I got a graduate scheme placement with IBM, which was great experience. I really enjoyed that. Made some good friends, learnt a lot, grew up a bit too. Come to think of it, you should try doing that.'

'Ouch.'

'I was based in London but travelled throughout the UK and also spent some time in California, which I loved. Then I got a position of Information Services Manager reporting to an IT Director in an education services business. Stayed for three years before joining Ulysses. Not too sure how long I'll stay there though.'

'And…are you…with anyone?' he asked, clumsily, he realised as soon as the words were out of his mouth.

'Where the hell did *that* come from? You know you really do take the biscuit. I'm not sure there's much point to all this, Chris so if you'll—'

'No, please don't go. I'm sorry, Elizabeth, but seeing you again has knocked me for six. I didn't mean to pry, I've no right to.'

'No, you haven't. I mean whatever makes you think—'

'Hey – I'm sorry…I shouldn't…' but he broke off, as her flash of anger morphed into laughter.

'It's good to see I can still get a rise out of you. The answer is no, not really, not at the moment. You?'

'Nope. I've not really had a stable relationship since you and I broke up or drifted apart should I say.'

'Played the field?'

'Well, I wouldn't quite say that but…let's not talk of others, Elizabeth. Why don't we drink up and find a restaurant for dinner? Unless of course you have plans,' he added quickly.

'Let me make a quick call, but that would be nice. Let's do that. You can buy – as a down payment on the bill for failing me all those years ago,' she laughed. 'Then you can tell me what you've been up to.'

Leaving the dark barrel-vaulted wine bar, they braved the elements with the first snow of the winter beginning to fall as they navigated the streets of Reading to find the restaurant Elizabeth had suggested, her local knowledge serving them well. They found a table for two in a popular French bistro and the evening passed quickly as they reminisced about old times, catching up on news of each other's lives. After a few glasses of wine, the conversation turned back to their stalled relationship. It was Christopher who raised the matter.

'You know, I thought we had something special, Elizabeth. It's such a shame we let it slip away.'

Elizabeth slung herself back in her chair, her cheeks flushing, her arms raised in animated exasperation. 'I don't believe you. What planet are you on? Get real! What we had didn't just slip away or drift or whatever other euphemism you care to dream up. You simply broke up with me in the cruellest way.'

'Oh, that's not true, is it? I don't recall any bust-up or anything.'

'And that, Chris, is exactly the point. It was the most passive of break-ups imaginable. Left me dangling on the end of a string. You didn't respond to my letters, my calls or even to messages sent through our friends. We did have something special. You broke my bloody heart, you moron.'

'Oh, shit. I'd never really looked at it like that. Life just seemed to roll on and I missed you a lot but was caught up in—'

'*Yes* – bloody politics, beer and girls!'

'Please let's not argue over something we can't change. Let's just agree that I was that moron. Come on, Elizabeth, let's not spoil a lovely evening. Can we see each other again?'

'Let's see. Anyway, we should briefly touch on business.'

'Yes – but not now. It would spoil a good evening. Why don't we meet in the morning over breakfast? I'd like to hear about Ulysses, and we need to turn our mind to the IT topics I suppose. I'm a bit surprised by what Horatio is demanding, although excited about the opportunities it opens up.'

'You should be horrified. Be careful there, I suggest. Okay, breakfast would be good. Tomorrow then.'

21. Mixing Business with Pleasure

Christopher pushed through the door to the already busy tearooms for his breakfast meeting with Elizabeth, his mind in turmoil. The re-entry of her into his life was uppermost in his mind when attention to the Ulysses deal deserved his undiluted focus.

Elizabeth soon joined him, quickly dispensing with gloves, scarf, woolly hat and winter coat. He rose hesitantly not quite knowing how to greet her: a kiss might be presumptuous? A more formal handshake slightly ridiculous? She soon settled that conundrum, cheerily entering his presence and reaching up to kiss him lightly.

'Morning, Chris. You're early I see. Nice and eager, good for a girl's fragile ego.'

'Mm, you fragile? An interesting thought. Always keen to start the working day, you know,' he smiled, sitting back down. 'Lovely evening,' he added, fidgeting in his seat.

'A surprising day for both of us.'

She seemed to be at ease, and gradually that permeated his mind-set, as the two were soon recalling carefree student days. They broke off briefly to place their orders with a grumpy middle-aged waitress who they decided was not to be messed with. A muesli with fresh fruit for Elizabeth; poached eggs and crispy bacon for him; orange juice and tea for them both.

Their conversation majored on their personal lives, despite original intentions to concentrate on business, like the rest of the power-dressed, sharp suited, busy executive clientele surrounding them. Finally, Christopher slipped into business mode. Summoning up the resolve to grapple with his misgivings about the conditions, Horatio was seeking to apply to their deal.

'What do you think, Elizabeth? You're on the inside; must afford you a grandstand view? You seemed anxious about Ulysses last night. Your comments were a bit cryptic, as I recall.'

'You first, Chris. What's *your* problem with it?'

'It's this IT piece.'

'SWL being required to implement Dragonfly, the Ulysses system?' Elizabeth asked.

'Yup. Actually, I really like the idea of a single system, despite Paul being vehemently opposed to it. It makes a great deal of commercial sense.'

'So, what's your problem then?'

'I don't like it when the conditions of a deal suddenly change. That makes me wonder what's going on. But I have to say that I like the concept and the commerciality. Mind you, we'd need time to do this as we aren't just talking about a piece of equipment, you know. Our system is embedded into the business; it's part of the fabric of Skills World, part of our culture…'

'Yes. I do understand the cultural impact of such matters. *Hello*! Who's the IT director here?'

'Sorry. Teaching granny to suck eggs, was I?' he grinned.

'Well, that's not the most flattering of analogies and I know I'm a bit older than in our uni days…' she said flashing a scowl, but with laughing eyes.

'We will probably comply. Crazy not to. But I wonder about the results Ulysses has been achieving. They're staggeringly good, almost *too* good. In my experience, things that are too good…'

'So, you think the results are dodgy?' Elizabeth asked.

'No reason to. But I've begun to wonder why they want to outsource their operations to us at all when their performance stats are so much better than ours. It doesn't quite add up despite their insistence that it's all about strategic direction and a bigger game-plan – which sounds like ego stroking bollocks to me. I like to understand the motivations of everyone in any deal and I just don't quite get it on this one. And tell me how Horatio can know of the results of a procurement process before it's actually been announced and I—'

'What're you talking about?' she interjected, sitting forward, reaching out to grip his arm mid-flow.

Christopher proceeded to tell her of the conversation that had taken place in yesterday's meeting, prior to her being summoned to the boardroom. She quizzed him sharply, her brow furrowing, eyes narrowing. Elizabeth then shared with him her own anxieties about the political clout Horatio seemed to enjoy. He seemed to move in highly influential circles and Ulysses was certainly successful in securing government contracts beyond that which most market experts forecast. She also expressed her own doubts about the Dragonfly system and the complicated architecture with its reliance upon interactions with other systems in the hosted environment.

'So, again Elizabeth, what do *you* think's going on?'

'I don't know, but I *do* know that the performance statistics produced are better than I can independently verify. That of course drives revenues, given the reward-by-performance nature of our contracts, as you will know.'

'But the government's own system processes the returns, doesn't it? Surely, you're not suggesting—'

'No. Of course not…I don't think so…No…'

'You don't sound so sure to me.'

'I've no evidence whatsoever of anything improper but, like you, my guts tell me something's not quite right. I've said as much to Horatio and to that slime-ball, Gregory Jones. I've also demanded access to the other system providers and…hey look at the time. We must dash – I must anyway. Let's keep this conversation to ourselves, Chris.'

'Yes, of course. But before you disappear, can we see each other on Saturday-week? Let's spend the day together, come on what do you say? What would you like to do? Where shall we go? Why don't we spend a weekend in the hills? Pretty little country pub, glass of wine, log fires – you get the picture.'

Elizabeth flashed a half-smile, which soon gave way to an expression he struggled to decode.

'Look, it's been great to catch up and perhaps one day we can recapture something of what we once had. But let's just see how it goes. I'll help with this IT thing and if you'd like a night out sometime soon, that would be nice. Now I, at least, have a busy day ahead. Must dash,' she said firmly, recovering her poise. 'Bye, Chris.'

He rose slowly, disappointed, but trying to hide it. As Elizabeth pushed her chair back, she shrugged her jacket on, stood and reached over to give him the briefest peck on his cheek. She took a couple of strides away before momentarily pausing to flash a smile of apology to him. She then turned and struggled her way through an incoming group of noisy businessmen. His spirits sank as he lowered himself back into his chair disconsolately. He suddenly snapped himself out of his trance, thrust money into the hands of the waitress and ran after Elizabeth. Catching her up, just as she got to the end of the road, he caught her elbow and she spun around towards him.

'It doesn't have to be a whole weekend. I get it. Too early for that. Let's go for a walk, or to the theatre or to catch a film,' he said, between gasped breaths.

'Call me, Chris.'

The week's scheduled meetings followed hard on the heels of the revelations earlier that week. The broadening of the contract to embrace all of Ulysses areas was a huge opportunity. The conditions placed in respect of the IT contract perplexed Christopher but the more he thought about it the more the idea appealed: the economies of scale and efficiency gains would be transformative on their bottom line. And the importance of that in pleasing his new boss, whilst making his earn-out numbers, was an attractive notion. But his team were troubled at the prospect of replacing their own IT systems with Dragonfly and the scale of the challenge in rolling this out across all contracts. His mind reverberated with the contradictions: disruption versus opportunity; cost of change versus profitability; practicality of a single system versus the implementation challenge. But why is it so important to Ulysses that Horatio must make it a contractual condition? This nagged away at him, snagging on the threads of his cognitive processes.

Meantime, the pressures to secure this deal were growing more acute. Pressure from his new boss, the redoubtable Georgina; from the old dinosaur who wanted his maximum earn-out; from Horatio, his explanation as to the rationale for embracing Dragonfly making eminently good sense. Paul also admitted to the urgent investment required in their own system, which might now be avoided. And then, there was the burden he placed himself under in his quest to succeed for personal reasons. But other, more negative pressures weighed against the deal: Elizabeth's qualms about Ulysses and their intentions, his own nagging doubts about Horatio's motivations, and Paul's opposition to any major change initiative that might distract focus and resources from a challenging

95

agenda. His finance director's opposition to the proposal to take on Dragonfly was clear. But logic, commercial imperatives and the building pressures all recommended the merits of proceeding, as Horatio was demanding.

22. Skills World Management Meeting

Birmingham

The week started early, as they needed to prepare for further meetings with Ulysses whilst pushing on with the usual day-to-day hurly-burly of the management of SWL: the day job.

'Good morning, Paul. All well? How was your weekend?' Christopher greeted his finance director, Paul Dart, whilst pouring two cups of coffee.

'Thanks. I need that. A heavy night last night and, yes, a very good weekend thanks. Despite City losing yet again. They drive me to distraction – the same old story. We were one up until the seventieth minute and still managed to lose to three late goals.'

'You should support a real football team,' said Christopher. 'A bunch of no-hopers your lot, if you ask me.'

'Unlike Derby County, you mean?'

'Remind me, which team was relegated last season? Second tier football for you now whilst the Rams are playing with the big boys.'

'We'll be back. Just a blip. You lot are still living on the old Cloughie glory days…'

'Hey, I was just a babe when Brian Clough's Rams were first champions. Would have loved to have seen them but…' The two continued their football banter, Paul harping back to the golden era of Manchester City with the likes of Bell, Summerbee and Lee; Christopher to that of the Rams of the McFarland, Todd, Hector era under Brian Clough, the eccentric manager of that period in the nineteen-seventies…

'Come on, let's get down to business. What do you make of the Ulysses opportunity?' asked Christopher.

'Perplexing.'

'It's huge and tantalisingly within reach. There for the taking if we can price keenly and agree terms, surely,' pressed Christopher.

'I agree.'

'Then why the furrowed brow? You look as if someone's handed us a poisoned chalice.'

'I hope not but I'm worried about the conditions being attached to the contract, particularly in respect of the IT system. So much upheaval, so many risks and technical challenges to navigate and then there's the cultural challenge too. It just doesn't feel quite right. And why?'

'I must admit I've been asking myself the same questions, but the logic and the commercial advantages are overwhelming, aren't they? Let's focus on these first,' Christopher said brightly. 'How far have you got with the business plan and the numbers?'

They spent the rest of the morning reviewing the business model with colleagues from the various functions. At the end of the session, Paul summed up the position...

'Given our forecasts, we can be confident of a turnover of around one-hundred million pounds with a profitability of about nine to ten. Cash flow looks challenging, but I'm sure we'll be able to secure the support of our parent company in the early years and I'd expect us to build this into our price negotiations with Ulysses,' said Paul.

'Contingency?'

'These figures are net of operational and financial contingencies. The deal looks good, Christopher. It looks *very good* indeed. This will transform the company, take us to the next level.'

'Yes. So, what's wrong? You still look as if you've been sucking a lemon', said Christopher.

'You know what. Dragonfly!'

'Look – Elizabeth has also spoken of her misgivings and I share some of your anxieties: the insistence that we utilise their IT system is bugging me.'

'Elizabeth?'

'Ulysses' IT Director – remember, I told you.'

'Well, surely if *she's* concerned, for God's sake?' said Paul.

'I know. They're also insisting we use Dragonfly across our own contracts. Why? I want to talk further to them and see what movement we can get. I'd be much more comfortable if we had the option to exclude this requirement from the negotiations.'

'Just call their bluff,' said Paul.

'I'm not sure it's a bluff. They seem deadly serious. Remind me what the development of our own system will cost irrespective of Dragonfly?'

'A cash outflow of over one million.'

'And if we succumb to the Ulysses demands, surely we avoid this cost?' said Christopher.

'Yes, but the cost of implementing Dragonfly across our business is bound to cost something of that order. Wouldn't you rather have control of *our* systems and their interactions with government IT than cede to Ulysses?' asked Paul.

'Let's not rush into a decision. I'll talk to Elizabeth – but so far, she has only vague worries and concerns she can't corroborate. There's simply no evidence that there's anything untoward.'

'Untoward? Who suggested there was anything...? Please don't tell me...' said Paul, as he paced around the office, always a sure sign of rising anxiety levels.

'Enough. I understand that on balance you'd refuse their demands on this point. Elizabeth seems to be signalling her concerns too. Let's see if we can make progress on negotiating some wriggle room but until I see any evidence…I won't sacrifice this opportunity on the back of vague concerns', said Christopher.

Ulysses
Reading

Christopher had a pre-meeting with his team to prepare for the round of commercial, financial and contractual discussions. Paul's team would lead on financial and contractual matters, meeting with Gregory Jones and Eleanor Strong. Christopher's Romanian human resources director would meet with her counterpart to discuss personnel issues. A transfer of staff from Ulysses would be required and this posed some tricky pensions and contract of employment challenges. Meanwhile, he would meet with Horatio on strategy. Christopher had also requested a special meeting to discuss their options in respect of IT systems.

Towards the end of the day, Horatio hosted a session to hear of reported progress.

'Well, you've evidently had a good day's work, ladies and gentlemen. Splendid progress, it seems to me. Now, if I understand correctly – and do please let me know if I've lost the plot along the way, won't you, old chap?' he said, pausing to address Christopher directly, before continuing. 'You now need a few days to re-work the numbers into your business plan. We need to get the lawyers working on the final contract terms too and, let me see, how long will that take? A month?'

'That should be sufficient time for us on the business plan, but that runs us into Christmas and New Year, so I suggest the end of January as a backstop. We've got quite a lot of modelling and planning to do—' said Paul, but before he could continue, Horatio cut in.

'Okay. We can live with that, I suppose. Now before we break for the day, may I tempt you all to a glass of something or other? A wee dram perhaps?' he asked, half rising in his chair. Christopher stopped him in his tracks with a discordant note though. 'No, I don't think so, Horatio, although that's very generous of you. There's one area of disagreement we have yet to resolve.'

'Oh, dear me. Don't tell me we still don't see eye to eye on this IT matter, Christopher, my dear fellow?'

'I'm afraid so. We seem to have reached an impasse for now.'

'Well, what a shame. I really had hoped we might make this happen. It really is most dreadfully unfortunate if this has become an insurmountable obstacle.'

'You need to take this condition off the table, Horatio. There are significant obstacles to us agreeing this, I'm afraid.'

Christopher was conscious of Paul's eyes boring into him. The standoff between the two leaders seemed to send the temperature in the room plummeting. Their discussions during the course of the day had been held in a business-like, professional manner interspersed with occasional light humour as the team members got to know each other, relaxing into the negotiations. But any such bonhomie was now suspended as a blanket of tension enveloped them all.

Horatio fell silent. He looked downwards, shaking his head before jumping to his feet with new-found energy to declare to Gregory Jones.

'Well, there's nothing for it but to wheel in our reserve team. Will you see to that please, Gregory?'

Turning to Christopher, he calmly, deliberately, and evenly, concluded the day's meeting.

'Chris, I may call you Chris, may I?'

No! Only Elizabeth calls me that. But the thought remained silent; he reluctantly nodded.

'Good. Thought so. Anyway, the thing is, old chap, we simply require a single IT system in this contract. Let me know by Christmas at the latest if you can agree. If not, then we'll contract elsewhere. You'll respect the confidentiality clauses we signed, I'm sure.'

Christopher sat back in shock at Horatio's ultimatum; Paul seemed similarly affected. The stakes had just been raised considerably and in that moment, Christopher saw in his mind's eye an ex-owner angry at the disappearance of his earn-out fortune, and the prospect of failing to deliver on his promises to Georgina. The CEO of Supreme worried him more than an angry dinosaur.

'I do so hope you can find it within yourself to change your mind on this point. You and your splendid team are the people we'd most like to do business with but, I guess, you will have to make your own minds up. Now if you would be so good as to excuse me, I have a rather pressing engagement at the golf club with an up-and-coming minister. Mustn't keep our political masters waiting, must we? What-ho! Speak soon. 'Night all.' That said, he breezed out, his colleagues in tow.

The Skills World team watched the exodus in bewilderment, suddenly tired and deflated.

23. Girlie Night Out

'Hi, Olivia, it's been weeks, what have you been up to?' said Caroline, as they hugged.

'Hiya babe, and goodness me you look well. Love the outfit and that ring of course. How're things back in the department and what about that devil, H? Are you still seeing him?' said Olivia, as they strolled, arm in arm, through the busy streets of Covent Garden, past the iconic Royal Opera House. It had been a few months since they had last seen each other, and Caroline had looked forward to an evening on the town with the opportunity to catch up.

'Tell me where you've been, but let's get a drink first. Come on let's go in here,' she said, seizing her friend's hand and pulling her into a pub that was situated just down from the opera house towards The Strand. Olivia grabbed a table that a group of young early revellers were just vacating, and Caroline pushed her way through the crowd to the bar, returning a few minutes later armed with two large G&T's and a wide grin.

'You've changed, babe,' noted Olivia. 'Bottoms up by the way,' she exclaimed, raising her glass and chinking with Caroline's.

'Not me. I'm still the same old dowdy northerner of old,' was the swift retort, but delivered with a knowing twinkle in the eye.

'Nonsense. You look great and what is it about you? Something different's going on. You've an air of confidence I've not seen before and since when did you take the lead socially by the way. It's great to see,' she added, flashing a beaming smile.

'It has more to do with the Dutch courage I downed before I left the flat, I suspect. Anyway, tell me what you've been up to. Come on, I want to hear it all.'

Olivia updated her on a temporary move to a satellite office in the East End of London. Olivia told her that the reason was all to do with Marku, her undercover Romanian investigative reporter. She had moved so she could be closer to his Hackney assignment, better able to see him and document his information and leads. The Department was attempting to track the illicit transactions involving falsely claimed benefits.

'And we're talking millions, hon, there's a huge racket going on.'

'And they trust you to—'

'Can't think what you're implying,' she said, talking over Caroline. 'A responsible, upstanding citizen like me. The bonus is that it takes me closer to Markus the hunk. The poor lad is under so much pressure I do what I can to relieve his stress.'

'I can imagine.'

'Well, he's decided to tell the story through one unfortunate young guy called Flaviu. It's heart-breaking really. The guy's got a young wife and a baby called—'

'Should you be telling me all this?' asked Caroline.

'Probably not. Anyway, Flaviu told Marku all this stuff late at night when Bogdan and his thugs weren't around. I mean, can you imagine the poverty and desperation that would drive him to leave a wife and beautiful baby daughter in search of paid employment in the UK? Apparently, he scrimped and saved and stole back home in Bucharest to pay for transportation and promised employment, shelter and the services of an interpreter. Hardly speaks a word of English. He expected to be sending money home to his family within a couple of weeks; even low paid, menial work in the UK is paid at levels which can only be dreamt of in Bucharest. Am I boring you?'

'No! But where's this all going. What's happening now? But only tell me if you're allowed to. Don't want you getting into trouble.'

'There's not much more yet. He's surrendered his passport to Bogdan and is just sitting around waiting for work to turn up. This is just one of dozens of Romanians and Bulgarians coming and going through this one hostel. And Marku is convinced this is just one in a large network. Isn't it exciting?'

'Not for poor Flaviu, I don't imagine,' said Caroline.

'No, course not. Poor lad. But that's about it for now. Stand by for the next instalment. There you go, that's why I've been a bit remote these last few months.'

'Hard to take in. Makes my life seem a bit dull. So, are you back in London for the foreseeable?'

'Yeah. Dotting between here and Hackney for a while.'

'And apart from James Bond, are you still seeing that Julian chap? Wasn't he a stockbroker or something?'

'Good memory but no, alas that relationship fell apart when I moved over to the East End. Oh, we both insisted all would be well and he was full of good intentions but' – she paused to take a swallow of her G&T before continuing, waving her arm dismissively – 'you know what blokes are like. The very first sight of another pair of tits and off they go.'

'Olivia!'

'Well, it's true, isn't it? No self-control and I can hardly complain. Shall we find a restaurant, I'm famished.'

Having placed their orders at Luigi's and their waiter having opened a bottle of Barolo, Olivia declared, 'So I've told; now it's your turn – and where *did* you get such a taste for fine wine by the way. This is delicious, so smooth. You're not still seeing that scally, H, are you? I don't believe you answered me earlier. You don't get away with being coy; strictly banned. I want to hear all the spicy details. Don't spare me, my constitution's strong.'

Caroline was delighted to have the spotlight turned on her, as she relished bringing her friend up to speed with her love life and her promotions at work. She filled her in on some of the details but stopped short of describing quite the erotic nature of her burgeoning relationship, although she did admit to the existence of their shared flat, which Olivia thereafter referred to as a love nest.

If only she knew the full details. She was a good friend, but Caroline did not know how to even begin to allude to the nature of their urgent activities, let alone articulate the details. Some things were just too private to share. Even with Olivia; too private to share with anyone.

'I hear that H moved on from his company a couple of years ago, didn't he?' said Olivia, during one brief lull in the conversation.

'No. No, he's the owner of HostIT. Wherever did you hear such a thing?'

'From a normally reliable source. Are you sure? I was told he'd sold out and made a bomb. Now the MD of a growing company operating in your welfare-to-work market. Your department has awarded them contracts of late too. You ought to be careful you know.'

'Whatever do you mean?'

'Oh, you know what the press are like. Always quick to cast aspersions on government officials and all that. Inside knowledge, pillow-talk, tip-offs from lovers. That sort of thing,' she giggled, the Barolo coming hard on the heels of their G&T's now beginning to take its toll.

Caroline was taken aback. She fell silent, as her alcohol-befuddled brain began to race involuntarily and wildly in uncontrolled directions. She suddenly felt horribly uncomfortable, as she recollected some of their business conversations. Next moment, various images of herself and H enacting some of the more challenging of the Kama Sutra positions under their mirrored ceiling flitted across her mind. It suddenly and forcefully struck her as being shockingly unsavoury behaviour. Unsavoury? Where did that thought come from? She'd never thought of it like that before; exciting – *yes*; daring and erotic – *yes*, oh *yes*, but unsavoury – never. Surely, she had not been…No – such doubts could not be allowed to permeate her consciousness. It was just too horrendous to contemplate. *I know my H, love my H; we share everything. Don't we?*

Caroline was suddenly aware of her friend waving her hands in front of her eyes to demand her attention, gently prodding her under the table with her sharply pointed black stiletto heels.

'Hello, hello, anyone home? Have you gone to sleep?'

'Ow. Oh – sorry, Olivia. I was miles away,' she said, breaking out of her trance. She cast such ridiculous notions to the darkest recesses of her mind, from where she hoped they would never dare venture back.

'Goodness that wine's good, isn't it – must be stronger than I thought. But what about another drink. You need to set your source straight. Who is it by the way? Anybody I know?' said Caroline.

'I don't think so and he's obviously mistaken. If anyone would know then it's you. I'll mark his card. Hey – what about dessert? I fancy a tiramisu.'

24. Government Business

Caroline was attending to a stack of paperwork: expenses to authorise, tender documents to review, auditors' verdicts to note, reports to prepare. There was a mountain of work to get through, but her focus was interrupted by the commotion of staff scurrying hither and thither. She irritably called for quiet when in her peripheral vision she caught sight of Sebastian Frith striding down the corridor, heading in their direction; evidently, the cue for junior officials to take their leave. Staff preferred not to be in his presence, although it was doubtful that he could care less about that. His demeanour was one of self-importance, and not for the first time she wondered how he managed to get people to actually vote for him. He never seemed remotely interested in currying favour, in listening to alternative views or in considering different approaches. Popularity did not seem to feature high on his list of priorities. Except at election time of course.

'Good morning, minister,' greeted Caroline.

'Let's get on with it, shall we? I haven't much time and it looks straightforward. Take me through your recommendations, Caroline.'

A central plank of the government of the day's electoral mandate was to reduce unemployment and to support the creation of re-entry skills and welfare-to-work programmes. Significant investment was being expended towards this end. Ministers were always going to be involved in the decision-making processes and the likes of Sebastian Frith were determined to ensure their views prevailed.

'I'm happy with most of your recommendations and content to sign-off on the contracts for Scotland, the North East, North West, Yorkshire and Humber, the South West and East Midlands.'

'Minister, the tendering process rules are clear. These aren't merely recommendations but the definitive, calculated results. Only by exception can we vary the outcomes.'

'But I'm unhappy with the recommendations in respect of the four regions of London and the West Midlands,' he said, ignoring her strictures. 'We need to see radical change in the market, and I want to see bigger companies awarded the contracts given the scale of investment they'll need to commit to.'

'We can't change the procurement rules now, minister. The conclusions of the process are clear – all subject to ministerial discretion of course,' she added, observing his body language. She did not wish to provoke another volcanic outburst.

'*Quite.* I see you have Ulysses in second place in the rankings in most of these areas. They meet the strategic objective and investment criteria, so we should award the contracts to them.'

'But, minister, they are a distant second in most of these regions and, as you know, Skills World have also won the North West and East Midlands.'

'What's that got to do with it?'

'We understand that Ulysses and Skills World are in advanced stages of negotiating a strategic partnership, some form of alliance or even merger perhaps. To award the four London regions plus West Midlands to Ulysses, together with Skills World's contract wins, would give them a dominant market position.'

'Even better.'

'We can't do it. I have to advise you, minister. The rules don't allow it. We also have concerns about Ulysses' performance statistics in similar contracts. They seem questionable. We're just about to send an audit team in to investigate.'

'I'd have thought you'd be the last person to want to draw attention to *that*!'

'What on earth do you mean, minister?' said Caroline, sitting back in her chair.

'You know exactly…Look, I simply don't have time for this, Caroline. Re-assess the results of the process and you will find that Ulysses is the winning provider. As to sending in auditors, well that's stuff and nonsense. It'll be a waste of time and money, but that's a matter for your department. You can't let that affect the decision of a contract procurement process anyway.'

'I'm very reluctant, minister. I don't know how we can do this.'

'Caroline, if you value both your career and your professional reputation, just do it. Do you understand me?'

The tone was icy, and the threat was clear. Caroline was shaking involuntarily, panic-struck. She recalled the words of her friend. What was it she had said? Something about the perils of government officials leaking commercially sensitive information; something about insider knowledge and pillow-talk. She had also said that H had such commercial interests, that he was the Managing Director of a company in this market space. But that was not true. H had been clear about his business interests. Surely, he would not deceive her? And anyway, how would the minister know about any such inadvertent indiscretions? It did not seem at all likely. Perhaps she was jumping to conclusions, establishing links that did not exist. And yet, what else could he have meant? Perhaps she would have to do as instructed. His message had been delivered and received. She feared that the message was also now understood. As these thoughts hurtled through her mind, the door slammed as the minister departed. *Oh God, I can't believe this.*

Caroline needed some air and was in urgent need of a caffeine fix. Pulling her coat from the stand, she headed for the door, waving her security badge at officials manning the security at the front door to emerge into Tothill Street. Negotiating her way around New Scotland Yard, she found her preferred café on Victoria Street to enjoy an Americano with an extra shot, her thoughts crowding in on her in disordered confusion. The coffee helped but she needed time to think and urgently needed to clear her head. As she often did at stressful times, she navigated her way through the busy streets to St James's Park, walking briskly around the duck pond trying to order her thoughts and emotions.

She had to find out whether H was lying to her. But how if all he did was deny any such involvement in the market? He had been crystal clear that he owned and managed HostIT. But then again Olivia had cast doubts on that assertion. What if Olivia was right? Might she have been guilty of inadvertently sharing confidential information? Would she have to resign from office? If so, that would signal the end of her career. At the very least, her reputation would be tarnished. Should she instead turn the tables? But how? Perhaps she should report the minister's bullying and instructions to distort the procurement process? She winced. She was so utterly out of her depth and felt so vulnerable. Sighing, and with a sense of foreboding, she made her way back to the office, resigned to implementing the bullying will of her minister. To do her master's bidding. How she loathed the man.

25. Moral Compass

Christopher whistled tunelessly, as he examined himself in the hall mirror and pulled a comb through his thick mop of black hair, noticing one or two errant silver strands, before grabbing his keys. Slamming the door behind him, he strode briskly down the path and climbed into his waiting taxi. He had looked forward to this evening with Elizabeth – goodness knows, it had taken him long enough to persuade her to have dinner with him. He had seen her over the last few weeks but only in brief snatches: a lunch time sandwich here, an after-work drink there, and the occasional work meeting as SWL continued to grapple with Ulysses on their deal. He was almost camped out in Reading these days and had rented a flat, ostensibly to be on hand for the Ulysses negotiation but his real motivation was other than business. Was she playing hard to get? It certainly felt like it, but he supposed he deserved that.

'Hi, Elizabeth, lovely to see you. You look great by the way,' he said, reaching over to kiss her on the cheek.

'And you're late.'

'I know, bloody traffic. Let's get a drink and peruse the menu, shall we?'

Settling into a corner of the bar area, they caught up with each other's news, steering clear of work topics, over which they seemed to clash. The atmosphere in Lombardi's, an upmarket Italian, was serene, as background operatic music played to a half-empty restaurant in this lull before the Christmas rush. The waiters were attentive, and they were soon nibbling on sweet Sicilian green olives, mini cheesy mortadella fritters, assorted crostini whilst sipping Prosecco. Having been shown to a corner table, complete with linen tablecloth and candles, to enjoy the delights of their classy Italian food: Roman-style gnocchi with black truffle for Christopher and pasta and borlotti beans for Elizabeth; saltimbocca and beef fillet with Frascati Wine, and for dessert, they shared a Cherry and ricotta cheese tart. A bottle of Barbera accompanied the meal. As they drank coffees, Christopher asked Elizabeth about her plans for the forthcoming festive season.

'I'm heading to my folks for a quiet family Christmas. They've had a tough year with Mum's cancer. The treatment and recovery affected her more than the illness. Mum loves Christmas, so I'm sure the old traditions will still be rolled out, though it'll be a fairly quiet affair. My sister's away so it'll just be me. And you?' she said.

'Nothing planned. Was hoping you and I might spend some time together.'

'If you can bear it, come and join us. My folks would love to see you again. Don't worry, I never told them how you left me in the lurch,' Elizabeth added, smiling as Christopher shifted in his seat.

'I'd love to. It would be great, but you'll have to give me some clues on presents.'

They chatted about her mum and dad and how Marjory was coping with the aftermath of her breast cancer. *She's coping but they've become a bit reclusive. Only natural. Dad's as taciturn as ever, keeps his anguish and pain to himself.* They discussed the logistics and Christopher was delighted with the invitation and told her so.

'So, where have you got to with Horatio?' asked Elizabeth, changing the subject.

'Ah. A bit difficult really. But are you sure you want to talk shop?'

'Dragonfly?'

'Yeah. He's insistent. Let's not spoil—'

'Then tell him what to do with his contract,' Elizabeth said, speaking over him, eyes ablaze.

'I've tried to, and he's given us an ultimatum. We've been through this before, Elizabeth. I don't want to fall out with you, but I simply can't let this Ulysses deal pass me by just because you and Paul don't like it. You've never given me anything concrete to go by. I know, I know – before you remind me yet again: Horatio is not to be trusted, Gregory's a slime ball and you can't correlate the numbers. But there are millions at stake here. You must see that.'

'But between you and me, I'm pretty sure there is something fraudulent going on. There, I've said it: the F word! You can't ignore that.'

'And your evidence?'

'Working on it.'

'Thought so – none, even after all these months.'

'So, you're prepared to take the risk despite the advice of your FD and the IT Director of the company you're contemplating getting into bed with. And for what? Financial gain. How do you square that, Chris? And if I'm right, there'll be no gain. In fact, you could be dragged into criminality.'

'Now you're being dramatic.'

'But is it worth running the risk? Is the gain that big?'

'Yes, it is. It could be transformative. It will change lives – *our* lives if you let it, Elizabeth. Think about it. We could go anywhere, do anything. Opt out of the real world if you like. We could—'

'There is no *we*, Chris. And if you think I'm going to live off dodgy money…You have a decision to make – on the one hand financial gain, ambition and ego versus an ethical call to do what's right.'

'And that's called loading the dice to get the answer you want. Look, I'm not ignoring your concerns, nor Paul's advice. I'm seeking to negotiate an opt-out from this requirement, or at least a way of pushing the timescales for implementation out a year or so.'

'I thought you were better than this.'

'Oh, for God's sake. Aren't you being a bit bloody sanctimonious? Prove to me there's something dodgy going on and I will take it to the authorities myself. I knew we shouldn't have talked shop. I'm sorry. Let's just agree to differ and play this out. I'll try to negotiate a delay that buys you time to marshal your evidence. Agreed?'

'I suppose.'

'And are we still on for Christmas? Then we could party at New Year. How about that?'

'Let's see.'

Christopher sighed and tried to change the topic, but the evening had been marred by the exchange and Elizabeth was unusually solemn as a Ulysses shaped black cloud hovered. Normally, stormy exchanges with Elizabeth soon blew over but this one had left her quietly brooding and the evening squally.

Christopher slept uneasily following the evening with Elizabeth. She was so difficult at times, but she still awoke in him a medley of conflicting thoughts, passions and emotions. He knew he had to win over her trust in order to rekindle a relationship, one he found addictive, intoxicating. *Oh, for God's sake, man, stop beating around the bush – I love her, I need her to love me.* He ached for her to melt, but as soon as she showed signs of doing so, something in her snapped. And the trigger was usually Ulysses and Dragonfly; or recollections of the hurt he had previously inflicted upon her – upon them both. He knew what she wanted him to do on the Dragonfly matter but how could he? Everything he had worked for over the last few years, the significance of the Ulysses deal to his earn-out and to his new boss. And his father's words still haunted him: *useless little bastard destined for the scrap heap.* His promotion to managing director, he had forlornly hoped, would prove his worth and allow him to cast aside his father's harsh assessments. Then the SWL deal and the rewards attached to that. But none of this allowed him to escape his recurring flashbacks. However, surely a deal with Ulysses, a successful earn-out and a bank balance measured in the millions would consign the nightmare to the dustbin of history? Once and for all. He would have proven his worth to himself and to those around him; earnt the love and respect of his uncle and perhaps even of Elizabeth. He was not wholly convinced. But he *hoped.* And how could he walk away from such rich rewards on whims and feelings – even if they were from the only woman in the world, he could imagine a future with. But, right now, he needed to pull himself together and prepare for a summit meeting.

Christopher was pensive, as he shook hands with Horatio and Gregory, although Horatio was his usual smooth welcoming self – chatting about the market, competitors and future contracting possibilities. Eventually, Christopher was asked to deliver his verdict on the Dragonfly issue. Horatio sat back and smiled benevolently, as Gregory took the lead for Ulysses. Christopher was determined to find a way of deferring the system requirement, arguing that such a major change process needed to be planned meticulously and implemented incrementally if they were to avoid disruption and operational failure. Gregory pushed back firmly. The arguments raged back and forth until Horatio joined the fray:

'Christopher, my dear chap. We want to do this deal with you; we've given you more time than we wanted to as a measure of our support and good faith. It's decision time. What's your problem? The real problem? Not all these lame excuses you would have us swallow.'

'I've been telling you: it's risk, cost, disruption—'

'And we don't buy it. Your challenges, yours to resolve if you want to sign the agreement with Ulysses. It really is that straightforward,' said Horatio.

'Okay…But I need your cast-iron assurances that you won't take this outside this room.'

'Of course.'

'We're concerned about all the things we've been talking about – they aren't lame excuses. But I'm troubled because I don't understand either your motivation or your vehemence. Why? And why are your performance stats so much better than anyone else's in the market? And why would you wish to contract with SWL to deliver your contracts when even our stats are so much less impressive than yours. How are you doing this? Is it all, err, is it all—'

'Spit it out, man,' said Gregory.

'Is it all kosher? Even your IT Director has expressed reservations.'

'Has she indeed?' said Horatio, leaning forwards.

'Confidentially, yes.'

'And her evidence?'

'Mm.'

'You have no evidence because there's none to have. She's the IT Director for goodness sake. If there were anything wrong, wouldn't you expect her, of all people, to have the evidence at her fingertips?' said Gregory.

'Splendid point, Gregory,' said Horatio. 'Spot on. Look my dear chap, I know you and this Liz woman go back, but she really is a bit paranoid you know. Oh, she's good and I'm sure she's the most delightful of companions but…Okay here's what we'll do. If you have any evidence of any wrongdoing or errors or anything tangible at all, then we'll reconsider. Of course, we would always want to be completely above board. We *are* completely above board. Look, Christmas is nearly upon us and, in showing our support and belief in you as a partner, we've already extended the decision-making point to the end of January. Plenty of time to satisfy yourself that all is well, that you can cope with the operational planning. Can't say fairer than that, can I?'

26. Festive Interlude

Having wrapped things up at the office to allow an early get-away for the Christmas holidays, Christopher was now throwing a few clothes into a case and doing some last-minute present wrapping for Elizabeth and her folks. The last few weeks had been busy but had not changed things to any great extent on the Ulysses deal front: Paul remained opposed to the Dragonfly condition, Elizabeth similarly, despite the continuing absence of any evidence of wrongdoing let alone of fraudulent practice. At least their personal relationship had survived the row in Lombardi's and Elizabeth had even apologised for her stubbornness – not that she had changed her mind or advice in the slightest.

The journey down to her parents' house in the South Hams area of South Devon was slow in the get-away holiday traffic but it allowed the two of them to catch up; they readily agreed that the topic of Dragonfly was to be taboo for the three-day break. Elizabeth was in a festive mood and insisted upon the playing of traditional Christmas music – mainly hideous popular classics from Slade's 'Merry Xmas Everybody' to Bing Crosby's 'White Christmas'.

They arrived late evening and Elizabeth's mum and dad gave them a warm welcome, Marjory evidently in good spirits, although a little frail, and Ben fussing around his daughter. Elizabeth soon took charge of the kitchen, and supper was later served in their formal dining room with Christmas cards and discreet decorations adorning the fireplace and sideboard. Marjory managed half a glass of wine, and Ben made up for her abstinence. The evening soon passed as the family caught up with each other's news and Christopher was made to feel welcome. Soon, the two of them were left alone in the living room, as her parents declared themselves exhausted and headed upstairs. The lights were doused, and they snuggled up on the sofa listening to soft classical music with the twinkling Christmas tree lights and crackling log fire providing a warm glow to accompany that of the evening's claret and brandy.

'Happy?' asked Christopher.

'Happy but worried. Mum's putting a brave face on it but she's not well and Dad's obviously deeply concerned. I cornered him earlier and he allowed slip that the cancer's returned. Another bout of chemo is scheduled in January, but she's so weak.'

'I'm so sorry. Let's do what we can to make this a special Christmas for them. I'm happy to don the whites and take charge of the turkey.'

'You? No way, she's got enough on her plate without food poisoning adding to her woes. I'll be the head cook, you can be the bottle washer and general factotum,' Elizabeth said, laughing.

'Fair enough. Oh look, it's snowing now.'

'Is it? I just love the snow,' she said skipping over to the window. But the rain was relentless now. The usual British Christmas weather: mild and wet.

'Liar.'

'Where's your imagination? Come back, snuggle up and pretend.'

'Time for bed I think.'

Christopher dragged himself up and reached for her; she did not demur, and they kissed passionately in front of the tree before Elizabeth gently pulled away. Christopher followed her up and reached for her at the top of the stairs.

'Elizabeth, let's be together. Tonight. It's been so long, and I do—'

'No, Chris. It's too soon. Sorry. Please don't let it spoil anything though.'

'No,' he said, careful not to let his disappointment show. 'I won't, sleep well.'

She kissed him on the cheek, smiled and walked towards the bedroom, turning as she opened the door. He gave her the best smile he could muster, before glancing at his watch and mouthing – *Happy Christmas.*

The big day itself followed a familiar pattern: present opening in front of the tree, coffee and mince pies, G&T's, turkey and all the trimmings, the Queen and silly games. Christopher and Elizabeth even managed to navigate an awkward exchange with her parents over the Christmas meal.

'How long have you two been back together? You were always a great couple, made for each other. Goodness knows why you broke up,' was Marjory's opener.

'Mum!'

'Well, you can't fool me…'

'Marjory,' said Ben, his tone one of a warning grumble.

'Oh, it's Christmas and we can all pretend but we don't know how many more I might have…and no, I won't be shushed, Ben. You'll just have to humour me. A mother knows best and you, young man,' she said, pointing at Christopher, 'should get your act together and marry the girl.'

'Marjory!'

'Mum!'

'I've said it now. Said what most people think too. What have you got to say for yourself, Christopher?'

Before he could reply, Elizabeth interjected and tried to change the subject, but there was no diverting her mum.

'You aren't the first person to say that to me, Marjory. My uncle has given me so much grief and I must say I care about your daughter very much. I—'

'You care about me? *Care?*' interrupted Elizabeth. Christopher looked at Elizabeth with a wry smile playing around his mouth and then turned his attention to Marjory and addressed her directly.

'I'm doing everything I can. You do know, I assume, just how intensely annoying and obstinate your daughter can be?'

'Just like her mother,' said Ben, chuckling. Marjory nodded her agreement.

'I love your beautiful daughter, but I blotted my copy book a few years ago; incurred her wrath. I'm doing penance for that, but one day—'

'Georgie boy – one more word from you and it'll be your last!'

112

'Long memories, these women, you have my sympathy, son,' said Ben. He sat back sipping his wine and seemed to be enjoying himself.

'And as for you, Father Dearest.'

The matter was allowed to drop, and it appeared that it had quite exhausted Marjory who opted for a nap in the chair whilst the three of them cleared the dishes and washed up.

Prior to heading back to Reading, Christopher and Elizabeth managed a walk on the beach during a period of respite from the westerly that had brought persistent rain. They walked happily hand in hand along the shoreline and laughed about the exchange with her parents. And still, the taboo topic was avoided. At the far end of the beach, they embraced and agreed that the few days had been magical, despite all the worries about her mum's illness.

'Why don't we arrange that weekend, Elizabeth? A few days in the hills. All muddy walking boots, log fires, pub meals – you know the formula. It used to work. What do you say?'

'I'd love that, Chris.'

27. The Pull of the Hills

January 2001

Christopher's plans for a weekend's escape with Elizabeth from the trappings of corporate life began on the Friday, as they headed for the hills. They agreed that they deserved the rejuvenating tonic of an escape from hectic business agendas and, to Christopher, the weekend away with Elizabeth felt hard-won. Whatever the pressures from Ulysses and the demands of Georgina at Supreme, he could put those to one side for a weekend. And the clean air of Derbyshire's Peak District beckoned, an area they had hiked on many previous occasions. He had taken up her offer to organise the walking route and itinerary, having opted for the valleys and peaks in their favourite part of the world.

He met her at New Street station in Birmingham and after a brief embrace relieved her of the rucksack.

'I thought we deserved something special, so I've left the Vauxhall Cavalier in the garage.' Turning the corner, he led her towards an iconic Aston Martin Virage resplendent in racing green and now glinting in the sunshine. It had also drawn a crowd of admiring youths who slowly circled the car. When Christopher and Elizabeth approached, they drifted away, one muttering, 'Nice wheels, man.'

'Oh, just the ticket for a weekend of country pursuits, Christopher Townsend. Look at the size of the boot. Where are you going to put the rucksack? Whatever possessed you? Did you not think a Land Rover might have been more sensible?' she asked. He could see that she was, nonetheless, impressed and it would certainly add a dimension to their weekend. He smiled as she declared, 'But nice gesture, Georgie Boy!'

They eased out of Birmingham in the late afternoon rush-hour traffic before hitting the A38. At last, he could open the car up to enjoy the deep, throaty roar of the Aston Martin V8 soundtrack, as they accelerated towards Derby. He veered off onto the A61 towards Chesterfield and from there on to the Peak District National Park. Elizabeth directed him through the pretty village of Baslow and on to Calver crossroads where the Aston announced its arrival with a deep growl, as he turned right and gunned the car up the hill towards Froggatt. From here, it was but a few minutes to their booked accommodation, the atmospheric Grouse Inn sitting high on the moors at Longshaw, near Froggatt Edge: one of the gritstone escarpments that were a magnet for walkers and climbers alike.

By the time they reached their destination, it was early evening; time to enjoy a drink in the rustic country pub that was to be their overnight stay for the weekend. They dumped their bags in their rooms before heading to the bar. Elizabeth had booked two singles, dashing any hopes of a more intimate arrangement.

Christopher ordered a pint of the excellent local draught beer for himself and a glass of chardonnay for Elizabeth. They settled into a corner of the bar close to the open log fire, a welcoming sight on this cold, January evening. It was spent over a few drinks and a hearty pub meal in the busy bar and passed quickly as they reflected on their Christmas break, Elizabeth's mum's latest treatment regime and then they allowed themselves to reminisce about the various Peak District outings of their student days.

'Fancy a night cap, Elizabeth?' he asked, as the clientele began to thin out, the car park slowly emptying.

'No, I don't think so. We need to be able to enjoy tomorrow and I'm absolutely whacked. You have one, but I'll leave you to it.'

'So, what are the plans for tomorrow then?'

'Ah ha, that would be telling. Let's meet for an English breakfast in the morning at, let's say, eight o'clock. Now I'm going to leave you in peace and rest my weary head. See you in the morning, Georgie Boy. Eight sharpish, mind.' Standing on tiptoe, she reached up and pecked him on the cheek.

Christopher sighed internally, as she walked out of the bar and headed for her room; he was pleased to be away from the stresses and strains of SWL, Ulysses, Dragonfly and delighted to be spending time with Elizabeth but he had rather hoped they might be able to enjoy the weekend as a couple. As she disappeared, he picked his way to the bar to order a whisky. Sipping his large Glenmorangie with a splash of water and a chunk of ice, he contentedly stretched out in front of the fire and reflected. There was no question that Elizabeth had deeply stirred his innermost feelings. Why had he allowed their relationship to drift? He had known that it was special; he had never felt for anyone else what he instinctively and naturally felt for her. Very few people in this world had ever reached or touched him so profoundly. And history was repeating itself in their reunion. It was proving so hard to resume from where they had left off but at least the two of them seemed to be finding their way, bit by bit.

Having breakfasted at the pre-ordained time, they enjoyed a coffee as Elizabeth chattered excitedly, mapping their day out. She collected a flask of coffee and a pre-ordered packed lunch, placing it in Christopher's rucksack. They donned their walking boots and headed off.

They were treated to a frosty but clear blue-sky day, as they tramped the three edges of Curbar, Baslow and White Edge – choosing to divert to Baslow to wander around the picturesque village. Retracing their steps, they headed back up the steep path until they reached Wellington's Monument where they stopped to enjoy the views over towards the Chatsworth estate. Sitting on the steps of the memorial, they reached for the flask of coffee and snacks.

'Get that down you, lover boy,' said Elizabeth, handing him a Tupperware container. 'You're in for…' but before she could finish her sentence, he had pulled her playfully towards him and planted a huge smacker. Breaking away, he held onto her as she exclaimed, 'Goodness, what provoked that?' laughing, as she caught her breath.

'Well, if that's what you insist on calling me, it's time I lived up to the epitaph, don't you think?'

'*Fool*! Now where was I before being so rudely interrupted? Oh, I know. Let me introduce you to a partnership made in heaven.'

'You and me, you mean?'

'Steady now,' she countered with laughing eyes and a wry expression. 'Look inside – what do you think?'

'Pork pie?' he said raising his eyebrows.

'Yes. You've heard of roast beef and Yorkshire pudding, stilton and celery, gin and tonic, smoked salmon and lemon—'

'Yes, okay I get the picture – but coffee and pork pie? Have you lost your mind, woman?'

'Try it – it works. Honest, it's a combo made for the Gods. What do you think?' He did as instructed. *Surprisingly good.*

'Well?'

'Disgusting! I thought you were supposed to be the sophisticated, cultured one in our relationship. Anyway, what's that delicious smell? Look, Elizabeth. Your coffee and pork pie is being well and truly trumped over there.'

Behind them, a young couple had set up a make-shift picnic. A small pan sat on a primus stove where the unmistakeable smell and sound of sizzling bacon assaulted their senses. The young couple had also opened a bottle of white wine, which they were sloshing into plastic cups.

'Now that's what I call a marriage made in heaven – freshly cooked bacon butties eaten on the hills and washed down by a chilled glass of Sauvignon Blanc. Puts our so-called treat in its place, don't you think!'

The playful repartee continued in that vein as they meandered on over the heather-clad moors towards White Edge, carefully navigating their path around a herd of shorthorn Highland cattle sprouting menacingly long, curved horns. But the docile beasts ignored their presence, as they grazed. Plodding on, all thoughts of business deals and IT systems seemed a million miles away.

Having enjoyed a picnic lunch perched on the rocky outcrop of the edge, overlooking the Derwent Valley lying resplendent below, they spotted the fountain of Chatsworth Park in the far distance and as their eyes scanned westwards, they caught sight of the stone quarries and rooftops of the village of Stoney Middleton. Then the glorious Hope Valley with the picturesque villages of Hathersage and Hope nestled between the folds of green hills in the distance, a perfect setting.

It was late afternoon when they wearily ambled back into the Grouse for a restorative drink in the dying embers of daylight, looking up towards the edge they had descended half an hour ago. Having retrieved his mobile phone from his room, Christopher noticed that he had several missed calls. Well, the day had *almost* been free of the distracting and disruptive immediacy of modern-day life, he sighed. He wandered off to a corner of the car park to listen to his messages, his heart sinking as he did so. His frustration must have been written all over his face, as Elizabeth immediately demanded to know what was wrong.

'I've been asked to attend a meeting in London tomorrow morning – an early meeting at that.'

'On a Sunday? Well, they can go and whistle, can't they? It's your weekend, and besides which you have to entertain me,' she said brightly. But she failed to lighten his mood. It transpired that Georgina Harris had requested an urgent meeting – one that could not wait until Monday. This was the first time she had called him at a weekend. It was impossible to ignore the call. There was nothing for it but to curtail their rural pursuits and head back to the city…

As they drove south, they both expressed disappointment at having their weekend curtailed; the atmosphere was somewhat subdued.

'What do you think the meeting's been called for?'

'I can only imagine that somehow she's heard about the difficult session with Horatio the other day, although I'm not sure how. An argumentative meeting. He just piled on the pressure about the Dragonfly deadline. I argued the point but he's not for being moved and was a bit more strident in doing so. The deadline is real, do or die.'

'Perhaps Paul called Georgina?' she ventured.

'No, I really don't think he'd do that. Besides which I also had a message to say that he'd also been asked to attend the meeting. He's as nonplussed as I am.'

'Do you believe him?'

'Absolutely. It can only be that she's heard from elsewhere or, failing that, it's about another matter altogether, but it's all a bit perplexing. And bloody annoying.'

'So the negotiations on Dragonfly are at an impasse?'

'Yup!'

'What does Paul have to say about it? Have you worked out your options?'

'Paul thinks we should stand our ground and risk the termination of negotiations for the wider contract with Ulysses. He sees risk and disruption despite the logic and commercial attraction of running a single system.'

'And your view hasn't changed? Still putting ambition and financial gain ahead of—'

'*Please*! Not again. Show me some evidence… I share some of Paul's angst about operational difficulties and you know I still worry about motivations, but the upside is so much greater than the potential downside that…but you know all this.'

'What'll you do?'

'My options are stark – accept the condition and do the deal or reject it and see the contract awarded elsewhere; I don't seem to have any option.'

'Mm. Can't you seek a piloting arrangement?'

'We've explored that and they're adamant – all or nothing. The best I can get them to agree to is a phased implementation programme, but the phasing they've accepted is to implement across all contracts within six months of the deal being signed, with stiff financial penalties for any delays.'

'Wow! That's incredibly tight, Chris.'

'I know, I know. But my team tell me that whilst it's an aggressive plan it's just about doable.'

They drove on in silence, as Christopher ruminated before Elizabeth eventually surfaced to say quietly, 'I really worry about this system you know, Chris. I still have nothing concrete to support my underlying claims, but it seems to be at the epicentre of your pressure cauldron, so I ought to share with you my theory. Please hear me out – I'm not trying to reprise our previous fight.'

'Okay. I'm all ears.'

'I may be wrong but here goes. As I've mentioned before, I can't verify the numbers being returned to the government. Therefore, I can't be sure the financial payments to Ulysses are valid. The conversion of data performance into pound notes.'

'Indeed – bloody complicated system as well. Incidentally, Skills World has been working in this market and with the same client base for longer than Ulysses and we've a pretty slick operation, but we can't even get close.'

'Quite! I've had no credible answers to my questions, and I'm being stonewalled by Horatio and his sidekick. The statistics of clients returning to the work force and the sustainability of jobs are ten to fifteen percentage points above the nearest competitor in the market.'

'And it's Skills World in second place to Ulysses.'

'The extraordinary high level of performance is also similar in the reporting of achievement levels in vocational training programmes. I know that Ulysses has a good reputation but how credible is it that they're so far ahead of *all* the competition? I don't believe it. But despite spending hundreds of hours in trying to work out what the correct returns should be manually, I'm working with partial information and having to make so many assumptions you could drive a coach and horses through my figures. My instinct tells me there's something seriously awry though; that the system is massaging and falsifying the actual data. Given the stonewalling and hostility my questions are provoking, I can't help but think the directors not only know about this but may be the architects.'

'If you're right, then what you're saying is that Ulysses is in receipt of funds for which it isn't entitled – in other words, that dreaded *F* word.'

'Yes – *fraud* – fraudulent practice for financial gain. I did try to warn you about such a possibility when we were at that posh Italian restaurant. I might have used intemperate language which came over as overly dramatic to you, but I've done more work on this and I really think you should be concerned,' she said.

'Goodness me, if you're right…do you have any idea what order of magnitude the embezzled sums might add up to?'

'It could very well be millions.'

'And now they want to extend it to Skills World, implicate me and my team and distance themselves from it operationally. Well, that hardly helps my decision-making, does it?' he exclaimed.

'I would have thought it makes it easier. Could you not simply walk away?'

'Come on, Elizabeth. How many more times? Can't you understand the magnitude of what you're asking me to do? This contract is simply the one chance of achieving our earn-out. I've got the ex-owner breathing down my neck, my current boss and my finance director too. Our entire business plan depends on this deal. All I can muster by way of argument is Paul's inherent caution, my gut instinct and your speculations. I can't tell you the pressure I'm under. Shit.'

'Oh, my poor love. I know I've been difficult—'

'Yup.'

'…but it was only with your best interests at heart. Look, just a thought, but if you sign the deal, then we could work on a plan to verify once and for all whether there really is any credence in our fears and suspicions.'

'Go on – what's in your mind.'

'If you don't sign the deal, I'll move on. I've a number of irons in the fire and I'd welcome the distancing of my career from Ulysses. However, if you sign up, then is it not likely I would be transferred to your company?'

'Very,' he confirmed.

'Then we could work surreptitiously on this. I have a fall-back plan.'

As they sped south, Christopher insisted on taking Elizabeth back to her Reading flat. The rest of the evening was spent over a take-away Chinese meal in Elizabeth's flat, as the two of them concocted contingency plans. It was nearing midnight when Christopher said his goodnights, apologising once more for their disrupted weekend and promising to make it up to her soon.

'You'd better, lover boy,' she answered with a twinkle in her eye before adding, 'And it will cost you too – no rustic Derbyshire pub next time. More like the Savoy.' Inwardly, Christopher's mind flashed back to his last evening spent at the Savoy Hotel and his mind was briefly filled with vivid recollections of the urgent activities of that evening. *Perhaps the Dorchester then, or, for that matter, almost anywhere else.*

28. Sunday Revelations

Paul met Christopher at his hotel, The White House, near Regents Park. Over coffee, orange juice and a cooked English breakfast they compared notes and discussed at length the deal with Ulysses. Christopher further explained some of Elizabeth's doubts about the IT system, but not the full extent of her suspicions, which he knew would simply send Paul into panic mode.

'That puts a different complexion on it,' Paul said.

'Oh thanks, pal. So, my misgivings count for little but when shared by someone else—'

'Not just anyone – their IT Director. That Ulysses' IT Director could have such suspicions about their own system is significant,' Paul countered. 'So, you have misgivings, Elizabeth has doubts about the veracity of their returns, and you know of my objections. Remind me why we're even thinking about this?'

'You know full well. We've discussed this many times and you know my thoughts on the matter: we press on unless we have concrete evidence that would demand we walk away from the deal. You have nothing; Elizabeth has nothing. Let's be analytical about this.'

Paul nodded his acquiescence and they agreed that all they had were unsubstantiated qualms and vague theories. It did not change the current dilemma but made matters more challenging. They now had further reason to be cautious, but no evidence whatsoever upon which to place an argument in the face of conditions attached to the deal deadline Ulysses had issued. They could hardly name Elizabeth as being the source of such allegations, as that would simply expose her to their wrath – and in any case, she had spoken in the strictest confidence. Christopher shifted uncomfortably in his seat as he recollected the comments that he had made to Horatio, but he could not take those back now.

Turning their minds back to the imminent meeting with Supreme's CEO, neither of them could imagine what had caused Georgina to call such a meeting on a Sunday. They guessed that it must have something to do with the Ulysses deal.

'Unless they are about to issue a profit warning to the City or are about to be acquired or something along those lines,' offered Paul.

'To hell with it. Let's just get over there and find out from the horse's mouth,' said Christopher, taking a last slurp of coffee.

On entering the conference room, they were greeted by the CEO and Alexander Russia. The pleasantries were brief and business-like, but cordial, as they poured coffees from the flasks provided and helped themselves to mineral water.

'I thank you both for making yourselves available. I'm sorry about disrupting your weekends, but I hope you'll be pleased with what we have to say. I have very little time this morning, as I need to prepare for a round of wretched meetings in the City – presentations to pimply analysts barely out of short trousers. Anyway, that's my problem. Let me tell you why we need to meet. I'll be brief and then leave you all to discuss the details. Alexander, perhaps you would pass the papers?' Christopher raised his eyebrows on seeing the front page – 'Skills World Equity Share.'

'We're delighted with the progress you've shown in these early days. We always envisaged Skills World becoming the key vehicle for our assault on the welfare-to-work and vocational training marketplaces in the UK and we'd like to firm up our plans in this regard. I propose the transfer of our small number of UK contracts in this space to you. Skills World will become a subsidiary company of the group, with management owning a substantial minority shareholding. Alexander…'

Taking his cue, the Strategy Director elaborated.

'We offer the opportunity for Skills World management to purchase a twenty percent share in the equity of Skills World, with forty percent of that share being offered to you, Christopher, as CEO, and twenty-five percent to you, Paul.'

That meant that Christopher would own eight percent and Paul five percent of the total shareholding of their company. 'The remaining equity will be available for other management shareholders you may wish to nominate,' added Alexander.

'That sounds interesting,' responded Christopher, trying to conceal his surprise.

'You will need to write cheques to purchase your equity stake. The agreement sets out a valuation mechanism and a share buyback agreement so that Supreme will acquire your shareholding at the end of the three-year period, or earlier by mutual agreement,' Alexander summarised.

'If you achieve your current business plan of taking the company to a fifteen-million-pound level of profitability, then you will achieve a handsome return on your investment…' added Georgina, her emerald green eyes fixing on his.

'Goodness. How interesting. We'd no idea this was why you wanted to meet. I rather assumed it would concern the Ulysses deal,' responded Christopher, scanning her face for any reaction. None was forthcoming.

'The Ulysses deal is a matter for you. We're assuming this will happen anyway. You've been most encouraging on this point. I'm sure you'll get it done. We have every confidence. I certainly wouldn't disturb your weekend for such an operational matter.'

'I see. Can you run through the numbers with us?'

'Alexander will cover the details.'

He proceeded to do so, concluding that on achieving the business plan projections the value of the minority stake would be worth around ten million pounds. 'That's having offset the threshold profitability that we bought Skills World for.'

'Five million,' said Paul, unnecessarily.

Alexander nodded his affirmation before adding flatly, 'I'll let you crunch the numbers through to calculate what they mean to each of you personally.'

'What multiple of the profit net of the threshold are you offering?' asked Paul.

'Five times.'

'Only five?'

'Yes. You'll find the potential valuation compelling enough.'

Christopher computed the numbers in his head and presumed that Paul would be doing the same. For Christopher, the cost of his eight percent was fixed at two-hundred and forty-five thousand pounds: a substantial outlay. If they subsequently secured their business plan target, then his shares would be worth around four million pounds; Paul's about two point five million. These were life-changing sums. Paul and Christopher exchanged bewildered glances but before they had time to say anything, Georgina stood up, declaring, 'Now gentlemen, you'll have to excuse me. I have some homework that awaits, so I'll leave you in the hands of Alexander. Oh, just one last thing. I need to hear by eleven-thirty tomorrow morning that you're in agreement and committed to completing the contracts to procure your minority stake within one calendar month.'

'But we need to review the contractual terms, Georgina. I'm sure that, at the very least, you will have contracts and articles of association for us to wade through.'

'We've taken the liberty of alerting Entwistle Partners with whom you worked previously. I understand that both Ernest Caruthers and Jane Smith will be here by lunch time to begin that process. Now, I really must dash. Goodbye gentlemen.'

They replenished their cups for a much-needed caffeine fix before re-joining Alexander. The offer was good. Very good indeed. He and Paul discussed the details and technicalities with Alexander over the next hour: class of shares, voting rights, articles of association, threshold profits, valuation formulae and the like, prior to then reviewing with Ernest and Jane.

Towards the end of the afternoon, they had made good progress and it was time to head for home. Christopher and Jane soon found themselves alone, their colleagues having departed to catch trains. This was the first time they had seen each other since the meeting with Bill Taylor to thrash out the earn-out incentive arrangements.

'How's life treating you, Christopher? It seems a while since our celebrations at The Savoy, doesn't it?' Jane said, flashing a mischievous smile. Ever forthright, the observation simultaneously shocked and delighted him as images of their evening sped through his mind. Jane was as alluring as ever and given her coquettish nature, quite the temptress.

'That was quite some evening, wasn't it?' he said slowly, assaulted by vivid memories of their energetic and passionate coupling.

'It certainly was,' she acknowledged, running a fingertip lightly across his hand, before slowly adding, 'We should welcome the prospect of another deal opportunity – who knows, we may yet have cause for further celebration.'

The comment provoked lustful stirrings and he briefly lapsed into silence, savouring the electrical charge between them.

'Mm. Now there's a thought. Life's full of opportunity, risk, challenge and complexity at the moment...' Christopher paused and cast his eyes downwards, wrestling with conflicting thoughts speeding through his mind before reconnecting. 'But I always savour the chase of a deal; gets the adrenalin flowing first and then—'

'The champagne,' said Jane, finishing his sentence for him.

'Who knows? Something to aim for though, isn't it?'

'Go for it, Christopher,' she answered brightly, with raised eyebrows. With that, she grabbed his arm, breathed a gentle kiss on his cheek and whispered in his ear, 'Must dash. See you soon.'

He was left alone with his thoughts.

As he headed back to his hotel, he realised with a jolt that he now had not just a single deadline but two to face tomorrow.

29. Decision Time

Having found the quiet of his hotel room, mind buzzing, he reached for his mobile and made the first call...

'Hi, Elizabeth. I need to talk to you.'

'How nice of you to ask. I'm very well indeed thanks. Apart from having my weekend disrupted that is. And being spoken to like a lackey. I might remind you that I don't work for you – not yet at least, and even if I did...'

'Sorry. I'm in a bit of a lather. The heat's just been turned up yet further. Can we talk about that contingency plan of yours we sketched out last night?' he said, in business-like mode.

'I thought we'd done so already.'

It dawned upon him that he had completely misjudged the conversation. He had fixated on the decisions before him and the lack of time. The pressure to give way to the condition that stood in the way of a successful deal with Ulysses; to sign up to the equity deal with Supreme; the need to maximise the earn-out for Skills World ex-shareholders and current management shareholders was intense. His options seemed stark. The decision seemed obvious to everyone other than him, but his resolve was holding firm, although he had wavered. But the Supreme equity offer had just served to strengthen his resolve and even Paul seemed more ambivalent in his advice. Yet, he could not ignore his gut feeling and Elizabeth's speculation served only to add fuel to the fire.

'Can we start again? This is all coming out wrong.'

'Good idea,' Elizabeth said.

'Look first of all, I'm so sorry about ruining our weekend. I can't recall when I've enjoyed myself more and, well, it's as if a corner of me has been rediscovered. I'd not realised how much I'd missed you and how much you mean to me.'

'Steady now, lover boy. Don't say anything you may regret. Can't have you making commitments, can we?'

'Let's meet soon and talk about us. I need to see you, but I have to sort this business thing out first.'

'Okay – to business then,' she sighed.

They spent the next hour on the phone during which time they put some flesh on the skeletal bones of their contingency plan.

'I wonder if you'd be prepared to document this for us Elizabeth...Only if you're happy to do so of course,' he added.

'It seems that I'm to be that lackey after all, eh Chris?'

'I'd really appreciate...'

'I'm joshing really, but just you mark my words, Christopher Townsend, I'll help you do this but only in the right spirit. And because it suits me too. As soon as you treat me like a lowly subordinate, then you can go to hell. I'm doing it for both of us – I want to get to the bottom of all this just as much as you. I despise those Ulysses guys and just know they're on the take. How, I'm not yet sure, but let's find out. But as soon as—'

'Stop. I get the message,' he assured her.

His next port of call was his finance director. Christopher persuaded Paul they needed to thrash this out face to face and had booked another room in his hotel. By the time Paul got there, he had also taken a room in the business suite, ordered flasks of coffee, sandwiches and snacks and had mapped out a decision tree on the flip chart. They were set for an all-night vigil.

'Let's get to it,' said Christopher.

'I suggest we summarise the decision points before us – area by area. Firstly, there's the Supreme equity proposal and then the earn-out question,' suggested Paul.

'I don't think they're on the critical path. The key question concerns Ulysses.'

'Okay. So, what happens if we don't sign up to the Ulysses deal?' said Paul.

'Our chances of fulfilling the earn-out are slim and we disappoint Bill. I don't much care about that frankly, but we'll also fall short on our budgets and business plan agreed with Supreme.'

'And you won't secure your own earn-out bonus,' Paul pointed out, clearly playing devil's advocate now. Or was he warming to the risk of rolling out Dragonfly after all? Amazing how a big incentive and personal financial gain can focus the mind.

'That's true but it isn't reason enough to do a bad deal with Ulysses per se.' Christopher looked at his FD carefully, scrutinising the apparent internal agony he seemed to be experiencing. Until the Supreme offer he had been implacably opposed to Ulysses' ultimatum because of perceived risk.

'But what will Georgina have to say about that? And how will that affect the equity deal she's just offered?' countered Paul. Christopher smiled first, Paul's comments seemingly confirming his changing of perspective on risk. But as the point settled, he winced, acknowledging that his credibility would be seriously undermined.

'And she'll almost certainly pull the plug on the equity deal too. She may even simply replace thee and me, Christopher. Let's face it, she has track record.'

'Indeed. What's the downside of signing up to the Ulysses deal? Let's assess the pros and cons.'

The two continued in this vein until they had finally thrashed it through to a conclusion that they could both agree was in the best interests of all parties – and where the associated risks could be mitigated. Eventually, the two of them retired to their rooms at five o'clock in the morning to grab a couple hours sleep…

The clock struck eleven as Christopher and Paul were shown into the inner sanctum where an impatient Georgina paced the room. Alexander Russia sat quietly in the corner.

'About time. You've cut it fine,' was her terse welcome.

'Good morning, Georgina,' said Christopher looking at her quizzically.

'I have ten minutes, gentlemen, so let's cut to the chase, shall we? Then I can go and wow those pimply youths in striped suits. What's your answer?'

'Why the sudden rush and the impossible deadline?' asked Christopher. He spoke sharply, bristling at the aggressive tone and demeanour of Supreme's CEO.

'This is all upside to you and your team,' pointed out Alexander.

'With large cheques to sign. We can't do that overnight. It's a lot of money to us.'

'We aren't asking you to sign anything today, merely to give us your decision. Do you wish to proceed or not? I would also remind you the business plan this is based upon is yours,' said Alexander.

'And I had you down as a decisive executive. Make your mind up,' said Georgina.

'Yes,' responded Christopher.

'And thank-you,' added Paul quickly.

'But I don't like being pushed around,' added Christopher, his body language displaying his discomfort and anger.

'Good. Deal with this will you and meet me in ten minutes, Alexander. I must dash.' her flashing, emerald-green eyes her parting shot. The message seemed to be clear – get on with it. She did not seem to even register Christopher's objections. With that, she reached for her jacket, grabbed her handbag and pushed through them, managing the briefest of half-smiles on her exit.

They covered the ground required with Alexander, who took a more placatory line. It helped to calm Christopher down and Alexander proceeded to assure them that the details would be provided to their legal representatives later in the day to allow the deal to complete at the end of the week.

'Your funds need to be provided and lodged in escrow for subsequent forwarding on completion,' confirmed Alexander. 'We also need confirmation of the other management shareholders and their share. And their funds too,' he added.

'That's fine,' confirmed Paul, passing him a list.

'It really is a great offer to you, Christopher. Now if you will excuse me, gentlemen.'

He ushered them through the door as he glided off to join his demanding CEO.

Paul stared after him before turning to Christopher. 'Well, what do you make of that?'

'Don't like it. Makes me think we're being manipulated. Just pawns being moved around. A bigger game at play than we realise perhaps? It doesn't smell right, Paul. Let's insist on that parachute clause even if we do have to fight tooth and claw for it.'

'It'll no doubt cost us though. I can't see them increasing the multiple to a more acceptable seven times and agreeing to this.'

'Let's push hard on the multiple and give way in return for the parachute payment.'

'Are you sure that's the right way around?'

'Yes.'

'Okay, we need to set Jane on that, but Georgina won't like it.'

'Tough. And what the hell was wrong with Madam this morning. Let's go back over our game plan – there are still a few days before the die is cast.'

'Oh, for God's sake, Christopher. How many times do we have to rake over the same old coals? She's probably just had a bad night. Some bad news. Got out of bed the wrong side. Who knows? We've got our plan – let's just execute it,' he implored.

'That as maybe, but I'm not signing this without the parachute clause, however attractive the gains might be. Mark my words, Paul.'

'Got it. Come on, let's go and meet with Ulysses, shall we?'

'I suppose so,' muttered Christopher. His mood was downcast though, despite the imminent deal that represented the key to transforming the fortunes of the company – and personally. He was tired from their night shift, troubled by the scene with Georgina and they now faced the question of the Ulysses deal.

'Keep to the plan,' urged Paul again, as they hailed a cab to take them to the station and from there onto their next decision point in Reading...

Ulysses

Monday: 14:30

'Well how nice to see you, my dear chaps,' said Horatio, as they entered his Ulysses enclave.

'Horatio. Gregory,' greeted Christopher, accompanied by brisk handshakes, all smiles.

'Now what's it to be, my dear friends? Coffee? Perhaps with a little chaser? After all, the sun is well and truly over the yard arm. What do you say?' Horatio poured the malt whiskies anyway.

The monologue continued as Horatio declared, 'Your very good health, gentlemen,' raising his glass and taking a healthy slug.

'Ah. That's better. Now what's it to be, Christopher? Are we to drink to our partnership or is this to be a parting drink of friends and, alas, soon-to-be commercial adversaries? I do so hope you've managed to conclude positively. What do you say?'

Christopher sipped the warming whisky and sat back, looking intently at Gregory and Horatio. His body language suggested a negative outcome...But then, a smile gradually replaced the frown, as he offered his response.

'What I think is that this is rather a good Speyside. Am I right, Horatio, or have I just revealed my ignorance?'

'You clever old thing. Spot on. Tamdhu. More than decent, isn't it? And I've an even better eighteen-year-old malt lurking if we are to celebrate?'

Christopher paused and looked at Paul thoughtfully before turning back to Horatio.

'It would be a shame for that to gather dust, wouldn't it?'

Christopher smiled his assent to the deal. The bottle was swiftly retrieved, and generous glasses poured; the deal was struck.

30. Signed, Sealed and Delivered

Despite Christopher's qualms, the equity participation scheme establishing his team as shareholders of Skills World was duly completed within the agreed timeframe. Cheques were signed and monies paid; the largest outlay any of the team members had ever made. They reminded themselves the potential rewards were life-changing; committed now and little point looking backwards or harbouring doubts.

On completion, Christopher and Paul joined Georgina and Alexander for a celebratory toast. Champagne glasses were filled, congratulatory messages exchanged, glasses chinked, and the contents savoured. Christopher took in Georgina's marked change in attitude from their previous meeting. She was sweetness and light. Christopher thought she was especially striking today as her eyes sparkled from beneath her auburn mane. And unusually tactile, occasionally resting her hand on Christopher's arm to emphasise a point.

Later, Christopher admitted to being hugely relieved at the signing of the deal and compared notes with Paul about the changes in Georgina's approach.

'Chalk and cheese,' said Christopher.

'She got what she wanted,' suggested Paul.

'I guess so – but why did it matter quite so much? On the face of it, this deal might be mega for us but it's a tiddler to her.'

'Who knows,' responded Paul, 'ours not to reason why.'

'Ah, but it is. We need to be on our guard, my friend. First, she pulls off the Skills World deal – fair play. Great news as we rid ourselves of the Tyrannosaurus. But then, she offers us the equity agreement – voluntarily, mind you, and under no compunction other than vague promises made during the acquisition. And she's also handed over the Supreme welfare-to-work contracts as well.'

'Mm. And she applied subtle pressure on finalising the Ulysses deal too.'

'Not so bloody subtle if you ask me!'

'But, Christopher, the contracts from all three companies make us the biggest player in the market with huge potential for growth. We are staring at an open goal with the opportunity to make ourselves rich in the process. It's almost too good to be true.'

'Yes, it is, isn't it? And you've changed your bloody tune.'

The strategic partnership with Ulysses was also signed, sealed and delivered and the team set about absorbing the various contracts of both Ulysses and Supreme into their operation. The biggest challenge was to manage the migration to a single IT system, Dragonfly.

As expected, Elizabeth was transferred across to Skills World and became a senior member of the management team. Christopher knew that her expertise was going to be critical in the complex task ahead. Elizabeth told them that her technical team had expected the de-commissioning of the old Skills World system to be mapped out as a key part of the challenge. But that was not their plan. The system was not only continued for all Skills World contracts, including the new ones awarded by the Department of Work and Pensions, but also for Supreme and Ulysses. A prolonged period of dual running of systems was initiated across all contracts as the weeks elapsed and the programme was rolled out…

'All going to plan, Elizabeth?' asked Christopher.

'Not at the speed we need. We don't have sufficient resources.'

'What do you need?' asked Christopher.

'Over and above the additional staff we've already taken on, I need a full parallel team if we're to do this properly and swiftly.'

'That will dent our profitability. I'm not sure it's affordable. Let's just take it a little slower,' said Paul. As finance director, he was the custodian of the company's finances and cash flow and was ever mindful of delivering the budget agreed with the parent company. Christopher's response was to release the wider management team from the meeting leaving just the three of them to confer. He then leant forward and spoke earnestly.

'We have to get to the bottom of this and quickly. We're in contravention of our contractual terms with Ulysses and I worry that we're somehow being cynically used – possibly by both Supreme and Ulysses. There's something amiss. It doesn't smell right. Do you still harbour doubts about the validity of the returns, Elizabeth?' Christopher knew that she did but wanted her to emphasise the point for Paul's benefit.

'More than doubts. It's good to see you come on board at last, Chris. We've a contingency plan and we need to devote the resources…'

'Let's not rehearse old arguments. Do it, Paul. Provide the resources Elizabeth needs. You and I will have to manage the inevitable scrutiny of Georgina and her henchmen, but Ulysses won't yet have visibility of this. Hopefully. Horatio is so bloody smug and up himself, he won't even notice. He assumes we're in his pocket already and hasn't a clue what we're doing.'

'But let's not underestimate Gregory,' warned Paul.

'Or Eleanor Strong,' added Elizabeth. 'She has a nose for these things and an eye for detail.'

31. Assignations in Notting Hill

Caroline played her part in the awarding of a continuous stream of new programmes, mainly to the private and third sectors in the wake of policy announcements by government. Work pressures intensified, increasingly taking place in a febrile atmosphere; the controversial nature of the policy creating internal divisions and even hostility in some quarters.

So, it was that Caroline made the most of her opportunities to escape the pressure cauldron for some rest and recuperation. She headed once or twice a week for their shared oasis – a refuge which provided respite from their departmental and business lives in the splendid surroundings of Notting Hill, a part of London that was known for its Bohemian, cosmopolitan, creative soul.

Caroline regarded these visits as her escape from reality and looked forward to them eagerly. She insisted on referring to them as assignations rather than dates, much to H's amusement and delight. It seemed to her more in keeping with their erotic lovemaking in that bordello-creation of a bedroom.

Caroline's many forays to the sex shops of Soho had a new sense of purpose: the explicit magazines and DVDs she daringly selected had become a staple part of their time together. And any sense of shame or guilt had long since disappeared. *We're both adults*, she told herself. *Willing, adventurous, consenting adults.*

H had recently suggested that they take their own pictures – record their increasingly uninhibited antics. For their own pleasure. It was something that Caroline was initially reluctant to embrace. But gradually, her unease dissipated – elbowed out of the way by her thirst for new horizons. She had also been persuaded by the promise that H would develop the pictures himself and the two of them swore to each other that the outputs of their photographic work would remain strictly private. They certainly were *very* private. The camera and its richly intimate harvest were kept in a wall safe, in the flat that only the two of them had access to.

One afternoon, as they were relaxing over a glass of Sauvignon Blanc, propped up on the silk-covered, luxuriously plump feather pillows, Caroline asked H to tell her more about HostIT.

'What?' he said. 'Why on earth do you want to talk about that? It makes more sense to decide where we should go for supper. How about Raymond's?'

'No, seriously, I'm interested. How's business? You don't say much about it.'

'Mainly because it is so *boringly* tedious. But if you insist...' and he proceeded to tell her a little about his colleagues, his customers' demands and some of the wider business opportunities.

'Are you sure you're interested in this stuff, Caroline?' After a while, H changed course and said in his inimitably clipped manner, 'So – enough about my firm; what about yours? What are you up to these days? And no holds barred now. A verbal equivalent of our previous you-show-me-yours and I'll-show-you-mine game, my dear.'

She dug him playfully in the ribs.

'Oh, steady on, now,' he cried, as wine slopped onto their dishevelled playground. 'Look what you've done; the sheets will be even stickier now.'

'Don't be disgusting, it doesn't suit you.'

She proceeded to tell him proudly about her rise through the ranks, reminding him that she had told him all of this before and that he really ought to listen. Caroline shared her frustrations about office politics and spoke wistfully about how she wished there could be more focus on the issues and less on the greasy pole which everyone seemed so intent on climbing.

'How are the new programmes coming along?'

'For the long term unemployed, you mean? Early days, but I'm convinced we're heading in the right direction. I just wish we could move quicker. We need to engage much more with the private and third sectors.'

'Third sector?'

'Charities. Do pay attention.'

'Oh, of course. Yes, I would have thought that must be right. Do I understand you've contracted again with private companies?' he asked, raising his eyebrows.

'Oh yes. We've allocated contracts worth millions. We need to do more though to reach more and more unemployed clients.'

'Clients?'

'The unemployed. We're respectful of people who have found themselves in this predicament. It's the term we prefer to use. We've already awarded many contracts to providers and there's a debate within the department about the scale of these programmes; the extent to which we should encourage and invite yet more bids from the private sector. I expect a flow of such contracts over the next couple of years. It's a big opportunity for private providers. Anyway, we've discussed all this before...'

'Yes indeed. Now come on – supper. Let's get dressed shall we. Unless of course...'

The conversation meandered on for a while until H insisted their activities had given him an appetite; for food, he added, with a wicked grin. Caroline readily agreed and after a shower, she pulled on denim jeans and a woolly sweater. H opted for a more refined look with finely pressed grey flannels, a white shirt, a navy-blue blazer with gold buttons, the look completed by a natty paisley silk cravat tied at the neck. Closing the door on their shared abode, they headed off for an informal meal at a local bistro, where they continued to chat about life in general and business in particular.

'I hear you've sold your business and moved on. Is that right?' she asked on his return from a visit to the gents, having recalled and brooded on the conversation with Olivia of a few evenings ago. No matter how she tried to put the conversation to the back of her mind, it insisted on resurfacing.

'Who on earth have you been speaking to, my dear?' parried H, momentarily allowing a frown to crease his forehead.

'That hardly matters, does it? Tell me…'

'I'm afraid your source hasn't got this right. Now what about coffee and a brandy? What do you say?'

'Coffee, yes; brandy, no. But don't change the subject.'

'I wasn't aware I had. Your information is simply wrong. I can't see what else there is to say on the matter.'

'So, you still own HostIT?'

'Guilty as charged.'

'And you don't own another company of which you're MD?'

'Come on now, what is this? Some sort of trial? Where on earth has all this come from? Who's been filling your head with such fanciful ideas? I rather thought there was complete trust between us? After all, we could hardly be more intimate partners, could we? Are you sure you won't have that brandy?'

'Oh, I'm sorry, H. I don't know what's got into me and yes a brandy might be what I need after all.'

'That's the ticket. I say, excuse me young man,' his comment directed at the passing waiter…

As she headed for her own flat in the cab that H had hailed for her, she reflected further on their relationship. Other discussions in the recent past sprang to mind. Had Olivia heard correctly? Had her source simply got it completely wrong? At least she had broached the matter with H, and he could hardly have been more emphatic, could he? Surely, that put an end to the matter, and she could rest more easily? Their relationship was indeed special, and it was good to be able to benefit from his worldly-wise business experience; to share her thoughts and work challenges with him. It was entirely reciprocal, and it felt good. So why could she not dispel her unease? And what had the minister meant?

32. Hypothesis

Christopher had taken to meeting every Friday morning with Paul and Elizabeth over a coffee, to review the week's events, assess progress against the contingency plan and decide upon actions. They gathered in Christopher's office, a Spartan, utilitarian space devoid of status symbols. It contrasted with the trappings of power so beloved of Supreme's CEO, Georgina Harris, or indeed that of Horatio at Ulysses with his malt whiskies, plush sofas and the ambience of a high-end Mayfair flat. So it was that the three of them assembled around the light teak conference-table with simple padded wooden chairs, supping instant coffee from mugs adorned with the company logo.

Week after week, Elizabeth had reported good progress in aligning systems in executing the contingency plan. But nothing conclusive had been unearthed as yet, despite running the two systems in tandem.

'So, they're reporting similar outcomes,' asked Paul. 'Nothing sinister to report? No discrepancies? No dodgy algorithms?' He sounded disappointed, dejected.

'No, but we've been digging into the code base and have a theory,' said Elizabeth.

'Which is?' enquired the finance director. 'We need something tangible to justify our extravagant investment.'

'I'm beginning to wonder if there isn't a tie-up between Dragonfly and the government's systems which only manifests itself on submitting actual returns,' said Elizabeth, 'but this is only a hypothesis.'

'How do we prove it?' asked Christopher.

'By hitting the button to transmit.'

'But we can only do that from one system, otherwise we'll be guilty of claiming double bubble,' scowled Paul, throwing his hands in the air in exasperation.

'Never play poker, my friend,' said Christopher. 'But you're obviously correct. What do we do next, Elizabeth?'

It transpired that she had not only developed her theory but had elicited some expert assistance. One of her previous colleagues in Ulysses had fallen out with the company and set up on his own. He had become a consultant IT expert in forensic analysis and data mining. Elizabeth had taken the opportunity to employ his services. He had been responsible for large chunks of the code of the system they had inherited: Dragonfly.

'And at what daily rate, dare I ask? Come on, hit me with it.'

'Expertise like this is rare,' she pointed out.

'You're worrying me. Please tell me it isn't over one thousand.'

Elizabeth winced. 'He's really good, Paul.'

'Oh my God.'

'He's also been the architect of a particularly important part of the Dragonfly system.'

'The statistical returns?' ventured Christopher.

'Yes. He wrote much of the code.'

'You still haven't answered the question though.' Paul was nothing if not persistent, a real dog-with-a-bone approach to life, almost a pre-requisite in a finance director thought Christopher.

'Give it a rest, Paul. You can hang, draw and quarter our IT Director if she doesn't deliver the goods. Let's move on.'

'Look,' said Elizabeth, leaning forwards, 'you need to know there are risks here, guys.'

'What?' said Paul, wearing his tormented expression.

'Just listen for once in your life,' snapped Elizabeth. 'This is important, hear me out. Mo is working for us is in contravention of his restrictive covenants with Ulysses. And they've issued legal letters which threaten all manner of retribution if he contravenes them. He can't work for us directly so—'

'But I thought you said—'

'Give her a break, Paul,' said Christopher.

'So, he works for "Hell Hath No Fury", which…Please Paul, I'll explain. It's a company I've formed, owned partly by me and partly by a friend of mine. Of course, I expect Skills World to reimburse me.'

'That won't cover our tracks for long.'

'But for long enough if my hypothesis is right. And do you, or do you not, want to know what my theory is?' She threw Paul a hostile glare.

'Interesting company name,' observed Christopher.

'Yes – it seemed apt somehow.' The sharpness of her response was unmistakeable and found its target with unerring accuracy.

'Ouch.' Christopher grimaced, feeling the barb whilst not quite fully understanding.

'And I would have you know that I've also reached out to another friend of mine who is arranging a meeting with Caroline Hope for you and I, Chris.'

'That's dangerous, isn't it?' said Christopher, just beating Paul to the draw. They all knew who Caroline was and of her seniority and influence in the Department of Work and Pensions.

'I have it on good authority she'll see us, and we can probably engineer this as an 'off-the-record' meeting, but our leader will need to marshal what little charm he may be able to muster from days gone by.' Elizabeth smiled coquettishly and fluttered her eyelashes, managing to amuse both of her colleagues and release some of the tension.

'I can hardly keep up with your mood changes…Tell us more,' sighed Christopher. She had leapt well ahead of her brief. But at the same time, someone needed to grapple with this and get beyond the current impasse. He admired her tenacity and decisiveness, but his brow furrowed at the thought of a premature meeting with officials when they did not yet have a proper handle on the issues.

'I'm sorry, Elizabeth, that would be madness. What on earth would we have to say? I'm not prepared to venture into the lion's den without something conclusive, some sort of protection. And I don't believe you actually set out the details of your hypothesis. Find me some proof, then we can decide the next steps.'

'Will this help then?' Elizabeth asked lightly. Her eyes sparkled, as she played her ace, the semblance of a smile dancing around her lips. Christopher examined the report which showed the likely impact on returns if her hypothesis was correct. The figures were eye-watering.

'But it's still a long way short of proof.'

'Mm. You're right but the meeting's at the request of the department in light of the exceptionally high results being shown in our statistics; in Ulysses' statistics, to be precise. They stand out like a sore thumb. If we don't agree to a meeting, they may demand one anyway. Wouldn't we rather be proactive and position ourselves as the good guys?'

'I'll think about it. I know you're confident in your assertions but there's nothing convincing yet. Our position will become exposed if we can't provide the details and then any control of this agenda will be fleeting.'

'And you're right about the risk,' said Paul, 'on the one hand Ulysses find out we're in contravention of our contractual terms or sue us for employing this Mo character; on the other we fall foul of the DWP.'

The summary was sobering, but not even Elizabeth could summon up any objections. All they could do was play out their plans and trust in Elizabeth and her experts.

33. Romance Blossoms

April 2001

Despite the busy business agenda, Christopher and Elizabeth continued to see each other as their relationship blossomed. Having spent an evening at the theatre, they found a small restaurant in Covent Garden. A light supper of grilled sea bass and green salad served with a zesty glass of Semillon was just what was called for as they chatted about the play. Whilst sipping their coffees, Christopher changed the subject. 'Fancy a short break. And being your birthday on Saturday, let's celebrate in style. What do you say?

'Sounds exciting. Why not?'

'It's all booked so bring your passport. We fly off for the weekend on Friday afternoon.'

'What? Where?'

'You'll have to wait and see.'

'Come on, Georgie Boy, spill the beans.' Elizabeth pulled on his sleeve like an excited, young girl.

'Can't spoil the surprise. Pack a bag for the two nights and we'll leave work early. Your benevolent new boss has granted permission. A three o'clock flight,' he said, grinning from ear to ear. Elizabeth tried to wheedle out of him their destination and plans, but to no avail. They eventually decided to draw the evening to a close as an early start beckoned for both.

'Oh, just one thing, you romantic fool,' she said over her shoulder, as she headed for home.

'Yes?'

'My birthday's a week on Saturday,' she laughed, as she skipped away.

They entered the terminal building at Heathrow and still he had kept their destination secret, despite the grilling received on their journey to the airport. Surveying the boards, she dug him in the ribs and the interrogation was renewed.

'So where to then? Rome? Copenhagen? Munich? Madrid? I've always wanted to go to Madrid but…oh come on. Where?'

'Or the other departures at around that time like Oslo, Stuttgart, Paris, Florence?'

'Now you're just teasing me! But not even you would be so bloody corny as to choose Paris in the Spring, Christopher George Townsend. No – my guess is Madrid. You have to know that's the city I've always wanted to…'

He felt himself deflating, his smile evaporating.

'What's the *matter?*' she asked.

'I don't seem to be able to get anything quite right, do I?'

'You mean you *are* being corny? We have to endure the Champs-Élysées, all those wretched museums, French bistros—'

'You *guessed*! You know.'

'Well, you've informers in your office is all I can say. And Paris in the spring is bloody marvellous.'

He smiled, then beamed, as Elizabeth wrapped herself around him.

'Just one thing,' Christopher said quietly, pulling a little away from her. He held her shoulders and looked beseechingly at her.

'And what might that be?'

'I've booked one room, but I've checked, and the hotel has—'

'I'm sure we can cope, lover boy. It's been too long.'

They embraced again, kissing passionately, losing themselves in one another as the crowds swirled around them. '*Someone's* clearly pleased…' Elizabeth murmured, as he hardened against her.

As Christopher and Elizabeth strolled through the Île Saint-Louis and Île de la Cité, the sun shone brightly on a crystal clear but cold spring morning. It was a romantic meander along the quaint streets full of old-world boutiques and bookshops, taking in every nook and cranny. Next on their itinerary was the Cathedral of Notre-Dame where the splendour of the stained-glass windows was at their best as the spring sunshine streamed through…

Afterwards, they took the opportunity to relax on a bench beneath the cherry blossom in the gardens of Square Jean XXIII alongside the Seine to plan their next stops. The Palace of Versailles was definitely on their agenda and Elizabeth insisted on seeing the impressionist paintings at the Musée d'Orsay.

'Okay, let's head there next, shall we?' agreed Christopher. He leant forwards on the bench, searched and found Elizabeth's eyes. Taking her hand, he crouched down on one knee and reached into his pocket to retrieve a small gold-embossed black box.

'Elizabeth, I'm no good at expressing my feelings. I lost you once and I don't ever want to lose you again. I love you. I want to spend the rest of my life with you—'

'Chris—'

'No – please let me say this…'

But she slipped her hand free and encouraged him to get up. Enclosing the jewellery box with her hand, she gently prised it from him and slipped it back into his pocket. He looked at her, waiting, his heart beating hard in his chest.

'Not now, Chris. Not yet.'

'Elizabeth? Please don't say you're refusing me?'

'No,' she quickly asserted, 'you haven't asked me, have you? Look, Georgie Boy, I can't remember a time I've enjoyed more in my life. Let's enjoy the moment and just see where it takes us.'

'But—'

'*Chris*, I can't imagine spending my life with anyone else. I love you too and always have, despite everything. It's just that it's too soon and there's too much unfinished business.'

'I thought we'd agreed not to speak about Ulysses?'

'There just seems so much at stake. I have to prove those crooks Horatio and Gregory are on the take. If we can't prove it but the department does… We could be charged with fraud, you realise?'

'I'm under no illusions and I share your concerns. Of course, I do – I'm first in the firing line, aren't I? But, Elizabeth, whatever happens, I want to spend my life with you.'

'It's not just the business thing, troubling though that is. It's you, Chris. I need to learn to trust you again and I need time, whatever my yearnings and whatever my heart's telling me. You've changed, we both have, I guess. But once upon a time, you put your principles first and foremost and now…'

'I've grown up, come to understand the real world isn't binary as imagined in our student days. I've promised you that if we find anything untoward – *when* we do – I'll be the first to report it to the authorities. I'm still that principled guy you once knew; I still love you and this time, I won't let you go, I won't take no for an answer, love.'

'I don't want you to either. It's not a no, it's a not yet,' Elizabeth said encircling his hands tightly with hers, a silent tear sliding down her cheek.

'I won't fail you, Elizabeth. We need to be together. I've never felt so certain of anything in my life,' he said self-consciously, as they became aware of the attention their scene was giving rise to. He lapsed into an awkward silence before recovering to say in exasperation, 'Oh I'm sorry, I'm bloody useless at this sort of stuff…'

Elizabeth smiled, and reached up to kiss him on the cheek before saying, 'Then ask me when this whole thing is over – whatever the outcome. Please, let's not spoil things. Let's just enjoy the weekend. Now where are you taking me this evening? Somewhere nice and romantic I hope?'

'A rather nice seafood restaurant, I thought. All French chic and candles. Can't lose my corny reputation, can I?' he grinned, trying to recover his equilibrium.

34. Quest for Work

Caroline had promised herself an evening of abstinence, a time to think coolly, calmly, unemotionally about H's response to her challenge. Did he still own HostIT? Or did he, in fact, run a company winning contracts in her market? Had she compromised her position? Had H taken advantage of her for commercial gain? He had been adamant and convincing in his denial, but then Olivia's contact had been equally sure of his facts apparently. Was she convinced by H? She would like to be. She needed to be. Did she need proof? Yes. The phone rang shrilly, to disturb her thought processes.

'Oh, hello, Liv…yes of course…come on over…okay, see you soon.' Olivia in need of advice. And from Caroline. On what she could not imagine but it would make a change and she was determined to keep a lid on her own worries for once.

By the time Olivia reached Caroline's, the tea had been consumed and cleared away; Earl Grey was not her friend's drink. Reaching for the wine glasses and a bottle of chilled chardonnay, she was resigned to a boozy evening. So much for abstinence.

'Hi, babe,' said Olivia. Caroline looked at her askance. The words were right, but the energy was absent, and the expression veered more towards glum – a first.

'Something's wrong. Would you like a glass of wine?'

'Would I ever,' Olivia said, grabbing the proffered glass, taking a big gulp and slumping on Caroline's sofa. It transpired that she had become worried about Marku. The last time Olivia had met with him he sported a black eye, a split lip, abrasions and an arm was in a sling.

'He looked scared. Never seen him like that before. Just thrust his report into my hands, told me I knew what to do with it and skedaddled, scrammed. He just said something about having been caught by Bogdan's henchmen but insisted he'd managed to convince them he was kosher. Here, read it for yourself, mind if I top this up? I told you about that first bit, but you can see how Marku described it…the story told through Flaviu'. There are many like him, all with harrowing experiences, all being ripped off.'

Over a period of weeks, I struck up a rapport with a young man from Romania, Flaviu. This is what I learnt. The journey from the outskirts of Bucharest had taken longer and been more arduous than Flaviu had anticipated. Travelling with a dozen other bedraggled hopefuls in the back of a blue transit van, they had crossed the continent to eventually reach their destination: a terraced house in Hackney. Employment in the gloomy, depressed city of

Bucharest was hard to come by so he had spent all his meagre savings on the promise of work in England. Transportation, employment, shelter and the services of an interpreter were his purchases. His motivation? To find a way of supporting his young wife, Taara and their baby daughter, Dannie. Flaviu spoke dreamily of his beautiful baby with big, dark eyes and a ready smile. He expected to be sending money home to his family within a couple of weeks; he had learnt that even low paid, menial work in the UK paid at levels only dreamt of in Bucharest. Leaving his family was an emotional wrench, traumatic – but he did not know how else to support them.

'It's hard to imagine. Can I get you something else, Olivia? I've never seen you like this. Something to eat, chocolate, a biscuit?'
'Read on. Read it aloud.'

The Victorian house he now found himself in was a substantial building in a deprived area of Hackney, gentrification yet to reach these parts. It was crowded, most of the rooms having been converted to bedrooms to accommodate the two dozen or so inhabitants. Illegal immigrants trafficked across Europe were crammed into rooms which housed between four and six each. None of them had any money. None of them spoke English beyond a few words. They were promised meals until they had established themselves. A basic kitchen prepared the fare, the meagre food dished-out in the Spartan canteen by scruffy helpers. It was essentially a hostel providing the basic needs of their beholden guests: shelter, warmth, food and water. Whilst being free to come and go as they wished, to all intent and purpose they were imprisoned.

'Marku knows of at least eight other hostels from his research. Remember he's writing this as an exposé for his newspaper and also for the DWP,' said Olivia.

Flaviu's Romanian passport had been a backup for the journey, had they been detained, but the traffickers knew where the weak points in the borders were and once within the European Union it was not going to be a problem until they reached the UK. It isn't clear how they managed to evade border control here, only that they did. The suspicion is of corrupt officials taking handsome bribes. Throughout the journey, his passport was retained by his "hosts" for safekeeping. In return, they issued another identity to him. His first day in London was to prove to be a busy one, along with most of those he'd travelled with. The interpreter and chauffeur, Bogdan, took him to a Job Centre where his new driving licence enabled him to obtain the all-important national insurance number. An on-line bank account was set up, Bogdan controlling this process. The next port of call was to Nottingham to the offices of HM Revenue and Customs where, armed with the relevant records and the obligatory bank account, Bogdan helped him to complete claims for child tax credit and child benefits. Three children. At the end of the day, Flaviu and his fellow compatriots returned to their hostel, somewhat bemused by the day's events, not really understanding what was going on. But at this point, he told me, it felt like progress. As he sipped a watery meat and vegetable soup and chewed on stale chunks of bread and cheese, the chatter with his compatriots was largely positive. They had been promised transportation to England, shelter from the elements and food until such time as they could find work. They had also been helped to register claims for benefits. Their hosts were delivering on their promises. Flaviu and the others were confident employment would swiftly follow. He would soon be able to send money back to Taara and Dannie. Such thoughts were taken to his bed, where he pulled rough blankets over his shoulders and soon drifted off despite the thin mattress, lack of sheets and cacophony of farts, coughs and belches from his fellow roommates. I bore witness to him soon accompanying them with his own soundtrack.

'How can he be so sure of all this?' asked Caroline.
'Part of his job was to feed the so-called guests and then bed down with them.'
'You said he was attacked?'
'Read on,' said Olivia.

Time passed all too slowly for Flaviu, who remained workless. Bogdan gave him a little money each week, his benefit support he was told; it was barely enough to enable him to even buy a few snacks to top-up his meagre diet. He had been led to believe that benefits payments in the UK were generous; his experience suggested otherwise.

It was clear that his spirits were sinking. Flaviu had next to no money, no employment, nothing to do. The weather was as miserable as his mood. It rained day after day. The battleship-grey cloud hung low, reaching down to envelope him, emitting light rain and drizzle. The weather was unusually dismal for this time of year, as drab and unproductive as his life: grey, wet, chilly. Added to this, he was seriously homesick, desperately missing Taara and Dannie. He dwelt on the plight of his family. Over and over, he returned to this theme, tortured by the likely consequences of his failure on his young family. Left with very little money to tide them over, they would be in dire straits by now. Unless he did something quickly, unless he managed to send money, he would lose them. But how was he to do that?

Taara's choices would be stark. He told me that neither Flaviu nor his young, beautiful wife had family within striking distance and Taara's had disowned her on marrying him: the price of love. He knew of others in a similar plight who had resorted to crime and now languished in a cell somewhere, their children joining the gangs of feral kids roaming the streets. Other desperate women had opted for selling the only thing they had of value: themselves. Flaviu was becoming frantic with worry.

'Poor Flaviu and whatever will become of Taara and Dannie? No wonder he was at his wits end,' said Caroline, reaching over to Olivia who was struggling to maintain control of her emotions.
'Don't know, Marku doesn't know. It's just so evil, so...'

A number of the guests had disappeared over recent weeks, to be replaced by other Romanians, Poles, Bulgarians. Some simply floated away, presumably onto the streets of London. Others were shipped off-site by Bogdan and his henchmen – to where was a mystery. I continue to try and uncover this dimension. But back to Flaviu and his compatriots. Relationships with their hosts had deteriorated, hope and expectation replaced by despondency and resignation. Flaviu had come to regard them as his jailors rather than his saviours and spoke with venom about them whenever he could talk to me.

After a troubled night tossing and turning, I was woken by a member of the gang roughly rousing Flaviu at around five-thirty and was told to get ready.

'For what?' he demanded to know in his native language.

'You'll find out. Let's get going,' said Bogdan sourly. 'You too,' he added, pointing at me. 'You can travel in the back with him. You seem to be all chummy.'

I just shrugged and got to my feet and before I could say anything Flaviu had confronted Bogdan.

'No! I don't think so...' Flaviu's jaw setting to grimly defy his captors. He half-turned away from Bogdan, but a restraining hand pulled him up sharply, dragging him back face to face. He never saw the fist, but was floored by its sickening, crunching impact. His knees buckled and he collapsed in a heap. The next moment, two of them had bundled him out, tying his hands behind his back, brusquely dumping him into the back of the blue transit van. I was about to speak when they set about me, accusing me of treachery. I suffered cuts and bruises to my head and a broken arm. I was lucky to escape with my life.

'Oh, God, Olivia. Here, take these,' Caroline said, handing her tissues and pouring more wine.

Flaviu was bruised and battered from the assault although he had fared better than me – but at least I was not shackled. The journey painfully exacerbated his ailments as he was bounced around with hands tied fast. I did not dare undo them; to do so would only serve to destroy the last shred of hope I had of convincing them whose side I was on. The journey was wretched, nausea getting the better of him as he threw up, rolling over and over in his own filth. Eventually, the van drew to a halt and the back doors were flung open, momentarily providing welcome relief as the sweet fresh air diluted the fetid atmosphere: vomit, sweat and urine. He was unceremoniously hauled out and unshackled. Flaviu was relieved of his false driving licence, given twenty pounds, a ferry ticket and the return of his passport. He stared at Bogdan, clearly in shock at the turn of events.

'No work. Passenger terminal two miles down that road. Go home, Flaviu,' Bogdan said.

Looking at the cross-channel ferry ticket, he exhaled loudly, fighting back tears.

'And how do you suggest I get from Calais to Bucharest?' he asked, spreading his arms wide in despair, his voice wavering. Flaviu's pleading was

answered with a disinterested shrug as Bogdan and his companion turned away and climbed back into the van. He stared after them as they disappeared up the hill.

'What happened to Marku? Where's Flaviu now?'

'Marku told me that he managed to persuade them he was one of them, that they were mistaken. I'm not sure if he really succeeded and I know he's scared. But they allowed him back in the van, took him with them and warned him against getting too close to the guests. He's been told they will have a test for him to demonstrate his loyalty.'

'And? I hardly dare ask. Is he okay? What's he got to do?'

'I've no idea. I've not heard from him for a week. What should I do, Caroline?'

'Well, obviously talk to your superiors, the police. Get him out of there.'

'He's begged me not to do that. I think he fears for his life. These are evil bastards perpetrating dreadful crimes. They don't take prisoners. Marku told me he's sure this is a small part of a big syndicate. It's a nation-wide social security fraud, a complex operation with millions at stake. He believes there are UK politicians behind this too but won't say why he thinks that. I'm so scared for him.'

35. Audit Reverberations

June 2001

Christopher and Elizabeth were in conference when a call came through for Elizabeth; an Adam Harness was in reception from the DWP audit team. She relayed the news to Christopher who recoiled.

'I guess it's an unscheduled spot check audit. They've been threatened in the market, but I've never come across one before,' said Elizabeth. Christopher frowned and traced his fingers up and down his trademark red braces.

'Unannounced? Why? Bloody Ulysses? I really don't like the sound of this.'

'I'll get down there and report back,' she said, and left him to his speculation.

Half an hour later, Elizabeth returned to report that the scope of the audit was to sample their files on a random basis, which was perfectly normal. To object or insist upon a delay would only invite suspicion, so she had instructed her staff to give the audit team access to both paper and electronic files. A small office was provided for Adam and his colleague, Cheryl.

Christopher reflected upon the timing and the implications, wondering about the motivations of the DWP. Whilst doing so, they were interrupted by an unexpected call from Horatio. It was brief, and Christopher slammed the receiver down.

'A problem?'

'It seems that news travels fast.'

'You mean the audit?' asked Elizabeth.

'Yes.'

'But they've not been in the building more than an hour. How could he know?'

'I wonder. Do you have a mole in your department, Elizabeth? How come he has inside-knowledge yet again?'

'My team were hand-picked,' she bristled. 'It could just as easily be the receptionist, or whoever.'

'Okay. You're right, I guess,' said Christopher.

'We should be more concerned about what they're likely to uncover. I've already established they want files related to both Ulysses and Skills World.'

'What about the Supreme contracts we inherited? Are they in scope?' asked Christopher.

'I don't think it's dawned on them we manage those as well, so for the moment no – but let's assume they'll be scrutinised too. If my hypothesis is right, they may find nothing untoward whatsoever.'

'Tell me more. I could do with some optimism, some positivity.'

'I can't prove this, remember. Not yet anyway, although Mo is busily strutting his stuff behind the scenes. Basically, I suspect the system and paper files will all align. There are bound to be a few minor glitches and errors but that's perfectly normal and to be expected,' she explained.

'So, in a way, the audit might be good news and confirm your theory that the scale of payments can only be explained by the interaction of Dragonfly with the government's system? What the hell's it called?'

'STRAP – an acronym of statistical returns and payments. Imaginative huh?'

'Quite,' said Christopher.

'So, with a fair wind, we may come out of this okay. Thank goodness we've decided to meet with Caroline Hope,' Elizabeth said.

'Mm…'

'Don't tell me you've changed your mind?'

'No…but first let's get some feedback from the audit team at the end of the day. Meanwhile, I have to go and meet Horatio. God knows what I'm to say to him. But you'll have to come with me.'

'Happy to provide the expert backup, Georgie Boy. But let me just check how the audit guys are getting on first.'

Just then, Christopher's mobile chirruped with the specially designated Sherwood Forest ringtone alert announcing the caller.

'Her Majesty calls, I hear, so I'll leave you to the delightful Georgina.'

Ulysses Offices in Reading: 12:30

'Good to see you, Christopher. And you too, dear lady, err, Liz,' Horatio said, as they swept into his grand office.

'*Elizabeth*, if you please.'

'Quite, quite, my dear.'

Christopher placed a calming hand on Elizabeth's forearm, his eyes flashing a plea for restraint, knowing that Horatio's patronising tones were like a red rag to the proverbial bull. She silently acquiesced, settling for a daggers-drawn glare hurtled in Horatio's direction. The entire room seemed to flinch, bar Horatio, who seemed oblivious.

'It's good to see you too, Horatio. Hello, Gregory, Eleanor,' greeted Christopher quickly.

Pleasantries were exchanged but the atmosphere was brittle, hardly helped by Eleanor's scowling presence and hostile body language, and Gregory's grumpiness. Horatio's personal assistant busily arranged jammy dodger and bourbon biscuits, pouring coffees and mineral water, as the awkward small talk meandered aimlessly.

'Ahem, to business, shall we? What do you say, chaps? Yes, let's,' Horatio decided, answering his own rhetorical question. 'The thing is, err, my dear chap, we would greatly appreciate an update and, well, why don't you take it from there, Gregory?'

But he was beaten to the draw by a feisty Eleanor. 'What the hell's going on? That's what we'd like to know.' She punctuated her verbal assault with a spot of table thumping.

'It's called managing a business, Eleanor. I thought we were supposed to be partners here. Why the aggression?' demanded Elizabeth.

'Now, now ladies. Gregory, if you please…' interjected Horatio, as if a high court judge calling the protagonists to order.

'What news of progress, Christopher,' asked the Commercial Director, evidently struggling to find a more conciliatory path; his body language and facial expressions suggested he was firmly in Eleanor's camp. Christopher ignored the sharp exchanges to report in a flat tone, setting out the bare facts with little in the way of detail. Early teething challenges in implementing new systems and procedures in this larger operation were being experienced, but that was to be expected.

'So, all's going according to well-laid plans?' enquired Gregory.

'On track, I would say,' confirmed Christopher, who helped himself to a jammy dodger and munched on it noisily.

'So why are you running two systems in parallel?' demanded Eleanor.

'All part and parcel of implementation,' said Christopher.

'But how do you know about that?' demanded Elizabeth, leaning forward.

'For God's sake, let's cut the bullshit. We know you're running both systems across not only your own Skills World contracts but also ours and Supreme's. And why haven't you reported the government's audit?'

'Eleanor, a confrontational style is not going to assist us. Let's keep this civilised please,' demanded Christopher. Horatio had sat back in his chair and until this point had seemed disinterested, bored with proceedings, but now cocked his head to one side, scrutinised Christopher's face and smiled before re-entering the fray.

'I wholly agree. You're quite right. We must be civil. We are all friends and partners. Let's conduct ourselves accordingly.' Horatio turned towards Eleanor and smiled sympathetically before continuing, 'Over to you, Gregory.'

Eleanor fell into a prolonged sulk, glaring at Elizabeth, as she slunk down in her chair.

'Can we get to the bottom of all this please. We feel you haven't exactly levelled with us. I don't want to quote contractual terms, but both parties did enter into an agreement and we simply wish to see that honoured in good faith,' said Gregory. He changed his focus from Christopher back to Horatio as if to check the acceptability of the line. But Horatio had fallen back into his own private reverie and was once more apparently disengaged. Christopher sat quietly, his fingers twirling his signet ring. He looked thoughtfully from Gregory to Horatio and back, glancing briefly at Elizabeth.

'We obviously need to dual-run and test the application of the new system to verify the results being achieved,' said Elizabeth, filling the tense silence.

'This isn't a new system. It's tried, tested and approved by the Department of Work and Pensions,' Gregory responded.

'As is the system we've been using,' countered Elizabeth.

'But our agreement is that you replace your system with Dragonfly whether you like that or not…'

'Understood,' interrupted Christopher. 'We have a contract and will fulfil it in good faith and to the letter.'

'Never doubted it, my dear chap. Well, that's all right then, isn't it? All tickety-boo. Shall we conclude there?' said Horatio, suddenly awake and alert.

'There is the little matter of the audit,' Gregory reminded the meeting. 'How's that proceeding?'

This time, Elizabeth picked up the baton with alacrity.

'When there's something to say, then we will tell you. They haven't yet reported their findings. When they do so, we will consider what they have to say, clarify accordingly and determine our next steps. At that point, we may have something to report. Unless of course you have advance knowledge as to a pre-ordained outcome, Horatio?' Elizabeth glowered at Horatio questioningly, ignoring everyone else.

'I can't think what you mean, dear…err, Liz.'

'Elizabeth.'

'Yes of course, how frightfully forgetful of me. I've no idea what the audit will reveal or why they even considered one necessary. How could I?' His ingratiating smile quickly reasserted itself, although his eyes appeared to convey an altogether different message: one of personal distaste with the "dear lady" perhaps.

'I suggest that concludes matters unless there's anything else. Horatio? Gregory?' said Christopher, ignoring a brooding Eleanor Strong.

Piling back into a taxi, they headed to the station. Christopher breathed a sigh of relief.

'Well, we just about got through that. What is it about Horatio that brings out the very worst in you? You were bloody rude.'

'Oh, other than his ingratiating, patronising, oily nature you mean? Not forgetting the misogynistic, sexist attitude and old-school bollocks,' she countered, not wilting in the face of the challenge.

'I know he's trying, but we do have a contract and a delicate situation to manage.'

'I told you when you set out on this journey, Christopher Townsend, he and Gregory are crooks.'

'We don't know that.'

'But we soon will. Mark my words. Where are we going now? Back to Birmingham?'

'London.' Christopher indicated that their next stop was a meeting with Georgina Harris, which promised to be every bit as challenging. He sat back and mused on the uncomfortable exchange until Elizabeth broke the silence.

'This meeting was troubling. How did they know the auditors had visited? And how did they know we were dual-running systems? What do we do now, Chris?'

'We remain focused on our plan. Re-double our efforts to reach a conclusion. Find the proof. I'm even more persuaded of our doubts given their approach;

your assertions of illicit activity must be correct. I'm persuaded of that – but we need the proof.'

'That's not what you said in there.'

'No,' he smiled. 'The hostility of Eleanor was almost certainly stage-managed, although she fits the role rather well.'

'Wretched woman,' agreed Elizabeth.

'But their very approach to this meeting has convinced me they're hiding something and feeling the pressure. We're getting close, Elizabeth. Keep up the good work.'

'Will do, boss,' she laughed, digging him in the ribs before reaching across to deliver a smacker on his cheek.

'I can't bloody well keep up with you. One minute—'

'Oh, quit the complaining. Are you still on for tonight or do I need another suitor?'

'What? Oh, yes of course. Very much looking forward to it.'

'You've damned well forgotten. Men…'

Supreme Group's HQ in London: 16:40

As they waited for admittance to Georgina Harris's inner office, Christopher wondered as to what sort of welcome was in store. Which Georgina was he to see today? The flirtatiously charming, hypnotic businesswoman oozing power and sexual magnetism? The highly driven CEO totally fixated with the business issue of the day? Or the high-powered, demanding, threatening Georgina that Paul and he had encountered recently? It somewhat belatedly occurred to Christopher that the mix of Georgina and Elizabeth might be dangerously toxic. Too late to worry about that beyond seeking assurances that she would exercise restraint. But he was not too convinced she would be able to help herself if Georgina became aggressively assertive.

The opening exchanges were perfectly amicable. Christopher proceeded to give an overview of the progress of the business following the recent share participation agreement and the strategic partnership with Ulysses.

'So, let's talk about Ulysses, Christopher. But I'd appreciate a one-to-one session with you, as originally planned.'

'Okay, no problem…'

Georgina looked disdainfully at Elizabeth before turning towards her number two. 'Alexander, I wonder if you'd be good enough to take Elizabeth on a tour? Entertain her for half an hour, will you?'

Christopher winced.

'I can save him the bother. I've better things to do and certainly don't need entertaining.' She rose from her chair, grabbed her papers and marched towards the door. As she opened it, she paused to deliver a final parting shot. 'Enjoy your high-powered, executive conference.' The door was shut firmly as if to accentuate the point, leaving Georgina looking bemused. Christopher opened his arms wide and shrugged his shoulders as if to say *who knows what's eating her?*

It was early evening before Christopher returned to his office in Solihull looking somewhat bedraggled and weary from the day's stresses and strains. He just wanted to catch up on any final business before calling it a day. *I really do need to head back, shower and change before my date-night with Elizabeth.* Apparently, they had agreed to go out to dinner, but he really wished they had not. A shower would doubtless refresh him, and Elizabeth was always invigorating and energising company. *But much more than that.* Just then, the door opened and there she was.

'Penny for them,' Elizabeth offered.

'They aren't worth it,' he responded with a smirk.

'I bring my high and mighty lord and master some news.'

'Oh, God, what now. It's been quite a day you know.'

'Well, if you don't want to know about audits and software skulduggery…' Elizabeth shrugged her shoulders and turned on her heels.

'Elizabeth! Please…you really are especially insufferable today, aren't you?'

'I aim to please,' she answered, effecting a little-girl sickly sweet smile.

'I'd love to hear your news,' he sighed.

'Well, the headline is that we are in the clear from our audit. Squeaky clean. So far anyway.'

'So, your theory's spot on.'

'Steady now. This doesn't prove anything, but it does lend weight to our hypothesis. But there's more. Mo thinks he's found something. Oh, and you'll be pleased to know that you were right, oh great one. We do have a mole.'

'Who?'

'Duncan Mills. He came across from the original Ulysses team.'

'Do you have proof?'

'Of course.'

'Let me have it and I'll sack him tomorrow.'

'No, you won't.'

'Elizabeth…'

'I've beaten you to the draw,' she announced smugly, a broad smile lighting up the room. 'An enjoyable task for once too,' she added.

'Well, that's good. Well done…'

'Steady – such praise may go to my head you know…'

'Tell me about what this Mo guy has got,' he continued. She was clearly in a good mood, pleased with herself. Elizabeth abruptly got to her feet, reached for Christopher's coat and threw it to him. 'Later. Come on, Georgie Boy.'

'What?'

'Home. Who knows – it could be your lucky night!'

Her eyes twinkled; she grabbed his hand and led him outside. Having found a black cab, the driver was instructed to head for Christopher's flat. 'Grab a change of clothes and then we'll head back to mine,' she said.

Elizabeth had moved to Birmingham following her transfer from Ulysses and was a fifteen-minute taxi ride from Christopher's place.

'I thought we were going to that little French restaurant you like?'

'Change of plan. You can shower and change whilst I cook. No arguments. You look done in. We can catch up on the developments over a steak and a bottle of claret. Okay?'

'Sounds great.'

'Oh, and don't forget your PJ's,' she said. Suddenly, the tension that had gripped him for much of the day dissolved...

The day's events meant they could not avoid talking shop as he caught up on the audit news, which seemed to verify their input returns with the paper files. Apparently, Adam Harkness had called in reinforcements. They had visited several clients at their places of employment to establish they were actually working as declared: that they did indeed exist. In two cases, the individuals had left their employers, but these were the exceptions to the general findings and were easily explained. In one case, an individual, an Arnold Harrison and an ex-inmate of Her Majesty's Prison Blantyre House in Goudhurst, Kent, had been dismissed for theft. In the other case, Jen Hurst had repeatedly reported for work late, and often with a chronic hangover, due to her alcohol dependency issues. Her employer had lost patience and summarily terminated her employment.

Elizabeth also discussed the work of Mo in a little more detail, as they sipped their St Julien claret and picked at the cheese.

'What's he found?' enquired Chris.

'Evidence of hidden code in Dragonfly in each of the Ulysses, Supreme and Skills World installations.'

'Hidden?'

'It's a practice called steganography,' explained Elizabeth.

'I thought that was a form of shorthand used in courts of law?'

'That's stenography – I'm talking about steganography.'

'Well, that's as clear as mud. You're going to have to dumb this down for me.'

'Basically, it's the ancient art of hiding messages. In a picture for example, the modern incarnation being digital.'

'So, the piece of code is hidden in an image?' said Chris, beginning to grasp what she was saying.

'I think I just said that didn't I? And we've found it in our company logos. If you remember, we refreshed these recently and embedded them in the systems, all perfectly normal.'

'Let me get this straight. You're saying the code is hidden in the logo in our systems? Those used for statistical returns?'

'Yes, and those are the returns which are validated by the government's STRAP system and processed into payments to providers based on horribly complex funding formulae.'

'So, we now know that our actual returns are accurate. There isn't anything dodgy going on as far as the audit team is concerned; inputs are correct so if payments are inflated—'

'Which can only be the result of something illicit happening elsewhere,' said Elizabeth, interrupting his flow.

'Then how's this hidden code working? What's it doing?' pressed Christopher.

'Precisely,' confirmed Elizabeth.

'What do you mean *precisely*?'

Elizabeth chuckled and annoyingly ruffled his hair much as a doting aunt might her lovable nephew's. 'Your questions are precisely those we are now addressing but we are beginning to understand that the hidden code is somehow massaging data once it encounters STRAP.'

'But we don't have the proof?'

'Not yet. Patience. We're making progress. This is incredibly sophisticated, complex work. To give you some sort of idea, steganography is often used covertly for espionage purposes; sometimes by terrorist groups to conceal communications about planned outrages. One theory has it that the practice has been used in planning the various Al Qaeda terrorist attacks of recent years. The counter measures, otherwise known as anomaly-based detection, are still in their relative infancy.'

'Wow. Who's done this? And for this to work, wouldn't the government's system also have to have been penetrated or hacked or whatever the right term is?'

'That's almost certainly true,' she confirmed. 'Clever boy!'

Christopher was taken aback. If they could prove this, then the likelihood was that very advanced techniques had been deployed by highly skilled experts. Had the government's system been hacked? Had the feature been embedded in the software when it had been developed? Who had done it? Who was behind it? What sort of gain was involved? Was this not likely to be fraud on a large scale? It could extend to other systems in the market, could it not? The questions reverberated in his mind and their conversation pinged back and forth.

'There seem to be even more questions posed by this discovery,' Christopher sighed, wondering just where all this was headed.

'I know, but we can now be fairly certain of a number of things. Firstly, our internal processes, paper and electronic files are valid; secondly, we know that somehow the returns we make are being manipulated to pay inflated sums; thirdly, that there is rogue code embedded in all three of the Dragonfly systems. This is progress.'

'Do we actually *know* that the returns are being inflated by rogue code? Do we have *proof*? Are you sure about this?'

'Not definitively. We can be very confident from our work, from the audit's failure to find anything wrong this end and from Mo's investigation. But that falls short of proof, I agree.'

'Can we be certain that malign code is embedded somewhere in the government's IT system too?' asked Christopher.

'We think so. And we now need to meet with Caroline Hope, don't we Chris?' pressed Elizabeth.

'Mm. We need to be careful but let's prepare our ground and then seek that informal, off-the-record meeting. You win.'

'Just one more thing. Mo is wobbling a bit. It seems that someone has noticed what he's doing and possibly what he's uncovered,' explained Elizabeth, carefully.

'How?'

'No idea but he's been receiving threats. Three now in the past day or so…Watching you…Beware of the shadows…Look out for your health, Mo…That kind of thing.'

'Has he alerted the police?'

'He's hardly likely to do that is he, given what he's been doing? It isn't exactly kosher.'

'See what you mean. Oh well, let's worry about that tomorrow.'

'You're all heart,' she said, digging him in the ribs.

'Oh, I'm done in. Can't think straight. Now please, let's put work to one side. Here – have another glass of wine and what about that film you were threatening me with?' he suggested.

Elizabeth accepted the wine, sipped it and then stood up.

'Come on, Georgie Boy, I've got a better idea,' she said, taking him by the hand and leading him upstairs.

36. Home

Caroline decided to take annual leave and head home to her native North East. It had been a long time since she had been home and she felt guilty, especially as she knew that her father's health was ailing. He had been unwell just recently, but she did not know the details – he had been evasive when Caroline had called a couple of weekends ago. He was still "just about managing" to work, attending his dwindling flock, now no more than a handful, apparently. She had intended to get home earlier in the year, but with one thing and another…

Stepping over the threshold, she made a beeline for his study. Knocking briefly, she ventured inside intending to be upbeat, cheery even, but as he turned around, she stopped in her tracks, open-mouthed.

'Caroline.'

'Daddy. How are you, what are you doing? Oh, you don't look well and—'

'Stop mumbling, girl. What's wrong with you?'

He had always been wiry and lean in stature, steely and a little forbidding in attitude. Now he was positively gaunt and had developed a pronounced stoop. His demeanour seemed no less severe, though. She went to him and embraced him, noting he was all skin and bones, angular, hard-edged. He eased her away, muttering something about needing to return to his work.

'Please tell me what's wrong. I can tell you aren't well.'

'Very perceptive of you.'

'You seem so…so…'

'Yes?'

'Frail.'

'Getting old, you'll find out—' But he was interrupted by a hacking, rasping cough.

'Let me make you a cup of tea,' she said, leaving him in his study.

Large tracts of the rambling vicarage had long-since been mothballed, her father restricting himself to just the space needed. Many rooms had been sealed off for years, although Caroline's old bedroom had been resurrected. His housekeeper had done her best to dust and clean, make the bed up, air the room. Edith's efforts were appreciated but she was even older than her father, had failing eyesight and spent only a couple of half days per week in attempting to look after the sprawling Victorian house.

It was from Edith she learnt that the reverend had become ever-more withdrawn from society, ever-more devout in his worship of the Lord, ever-harsher in delivering his verdict on the modern world from the pulpit. He had long-since dispensed with the television and as far as she could glean, spent his evenings simply reading the bible or classic literature or listening to the ancient radio. Despite repeated attempts to persuade him to follow clinical advice, Edith's pleas had fallen on deaf ears, she explained. Not that Caroline imagined Edith a powerful or convincing advocate.

'What's exactly wrong with him, Edith? He won't talk to me. He looks so poorly.'

'Cancer. Lung cancer. Poor sod. Nasty. Doesn't talk much to anyone, lass. Not that he's ever been a talker, has he now?'

'What treatment's he's on?'

'A few pills and potions.'

'Radiotherapy? Chemo?'

'Refuses.'

'Oh, God. I didn't even know it was lung cancer although I had my suspicions. He just wouldn't say anything, shut me down.'

'Yes?' said Edith, raising her eyebrows.

'I've been a terrible daughter, I feel so—'

'Expect you do, but he doesn't talk to anyone. Not me. Not the Bish. Don't blame yourself.'

Caroline sat with him in the evenings and tried to re-establish some sort of relationship, tried to get through to him. 'Daddy, please listen to me. We all love you and—'

'Really?' he said, his voice hoarse. 'You have a funny way of showing it, Caroline.'

'I'm sorry, I'm so sorry. I've neglected you.'

'Mm.'

'I've tried to call, but you're hard to reach. And I suppose I've been busy with…busy with life.'

'In that place.'

'London, yes. But it's where my career is, Daddy. It's important to me. You must get that. Oh, be pleased for me. Can't you be proud? I like to think that Mam would have been.'

Her father gave her a withering look and reached for his bible, but Caroline stayed his hand. 'But more importantly, how are we going to get you better? Dr Robertson wants you to have this radiotherapy treatment. And Nurse Gladys. And Edith.'

'The Lord's will—' The sentence was unfinished, as his body was convulsed by a coughing fit.

Caroline was no more successful than Edith, Dr Robertson, Bishop Langley or Nurse Gladys. She was horrified and sickened that she had been so oblivious to his sufferings whilst leading a busy life so far away. She was ridden with guilt; distraught but utterly powerless.

In desperation, Caroline rang the one person in the world she could always turn to: Olivia.

'Hi, babe. How is he?' said Olivia. Her exuberance and cheery manner were a stark contrast to Caroline's mood, to the depressing surroundings. That was all that was needed to provoke an outpouring from Caroline, a stream of consciousness. 'Olivia, it's just awful. He's so ill. Lung cancer. He's got this horrible cough; spits blood and his voice is so weak, but he refuses to have the radiotherapy and chemo treatments he needs. He has no chance of remission without the treatment. He seems so unhappy yet won't help himself let alone accept help from others. He was always a serious person, not exactly the life and soul if you know what I mean, but he just seems to have lapsed into this morose catatonic state. Almost wears his illness like a hair shirt. Won't listen to anyone, least of all me. I've utterly failed him as a daughter—'

'Hey, gal, give yourself a break. Don't be so hard on—'

'I mean it. Seriously, Liv. I've been so focused on my career, on my life, on coping with a world I don't really belong in. And what am I doing? Living a life my father is whole-heartedly appalled by. If he knew the half of it, he'd more than likely disown me, renounce me.'

'You need some tough loving, hon. Snap out of it. Feeling sorry for yourself, taking all the blame – how's that going to help anyone?'

'I so desperately want to help him, even at this late stage. But what can I do? He's stubborn, dismissive of any offer of support and rudely rejects sympathy. He's completely withdrawn from the world at large and simply disinterested in anything that even his own daughter has to say; *especially* anything I have to say.' She simply had to face the reality that he was determined to face his fate stoically in servitude of the Lord and would truck no argument to the contrary or seek help.

'I'm sorry, Liv, all me, me, me. You've your problems too, haven't you?'

'I'm cool, babe. Just worried about you.'

'Any news about Marku?' said Caroline.

'Nothing. Let's not go there. Listen, babe, when are you coming home? Let's have a night out – drink away our sorrows. Nothing a few drinks, a laugh or two and getting laid won't sort out.' Olivia's attempt to prick the mood with her irreverent humour usually worked – but not this time. Caroline's mood was set.

'See you soon, Olivia.'

Caroline had a few more days at home and so busied herself with domestic chores and spring-cleaning to remove the grime that had escaped Edith's failing attentions. It was a largely solitary period even when in the company of her father; an opportunity to reflect deeply upon her own life. She was in little doubt that her father's was ebbing away and that brought a sharp focus to her thoughts. She tried to recall happy times in the family home and nearly all of those that immediately sprang to mind were with her mother, before she became ill, her life so cruelly shortened. Prior to then, there had certainly been laughter and fun at home, even if her father had been peripheral to it all. But the period after her mother's death had been devoid of happiness and love. Her studies had not been allowed to suffer, perhaps they had even benefitted – her father encouraging her at every stage, and helping her, too, to become an expert player of chess.

She had not appreciated the atypical nature of her family background at the time. It was only with the benefit of hindsight and exposure to other norms that a dawning realisation emerged.

She had largely adjusted to this reality over the last few years and had developed a more normal life, due in large part to her friendship with Olivia and, of course, with H. These years had been so successful and so busy that she had thought the gawky, socially immature, if intellectually gifted Caroline of her adolescent and early adult years had been consigned to the past. She thought she had moved on undamaged.

She had even learnt how to cope with her less than glamorous appearance. *Let's face it at best I'm plain looking.* She sighed in exasperation. How desperately unfair it was, although she had learnt how to disguise her almost masculine features with cosmetics, fashionable hairstyling and well-chosen clothes, thanks to Olivia. Now she was suddenly less sure that she had consigned these matters to the past, that she was now normal. How can one escape the reality of the formative childhood years? And anyway, what is normal? How many so-called normal people desert their parents in their hour of need? How many have so few friends? Have such interests in unseemly pleasures of the flesh? How normal is it to frequent sex shops, enjoy pornography and to indulge their interests with a man ten years her senior? Come to think of it, how many young women did she meet on her seedy shopping forays into Soho? And what of her relationship with H? How they energetically conducted their proclivities in their glass ceilinged bedroom, all of which now suddenly seemed so sleazy and sordid; so dirty. Did he love her? He had never declared so. Did she love him? She thought so – but what does love mean? Had she ever been loved? *Yes! My mam.* Did she know how to love? All these thoughts crowded in on her; she felt lonely and helpless, lost in a heaving, stormy sea without navigational aids to call upon…

After a troubled night's sleep, her head was spinning with desperate thoughts about her father's health, about her own lifestyle and what the future might have in store. But there was nothing she could do, so her distressed thoughts increasingly turned to the other man in her life. And not just to the nature of their relationship, but to the overlap with her professional life. Caroline was unsettled by the revelations about H, despite his subsequent denials. The extraordinary exchange with Sebastian Frith had also shocked and disturbed her, his behaviour bullying, threatening even. H's assertions that her minister was simply a man of the world acting a little brusquely to get what he wanted, as men are inclined to do, no longer reassured. The contents of countless conversations with H were now recalled with unambiguous clarity; the mists were clearing, and the emerging picture was deeply troubling. She had shared with him confidential and commercially sensitive information: about contracts, competitors, competitive tendering bids. Millions of pounds worth of contracts had been awarded, most of this under her ambit, much of which she had discussed with him. What if Olivia's source was correct? What if she had unwittingly provided him with confidential information? The thought horrified her. But it suddenly seemed plausible. She had been immature, socially and professionally inept, naïve; completely and utterly deceived – taken for an absolute fool. It seemed she had inadvertently and naively strayed from the straight and narrow. It had been noticed. Just how much trouble was she in? She needed some air.

Taking to the country lanes, she took herself off for a walk on this cool, damp summer's morning. She briefly enjoyed the weak rays of sunshine penetrating a swollen sky with bruised, brooding clouds gathering over the purple heather-clad Northern hills, the harbinger of the threatened summer thunderstorm. Northumberland felt wild but familiar; the vast expanses and big skies so different to the claustrophobia of the urban streets she inhabited these days. On another day, she might have been cheered by her native county with all its familiar smells, the Geordie accents, the angry North Sea and the salty tanginess of the air. As a child, she had always loved the country strolls with her mother; the shoreline ambles along the dunes; the outings to Lindisfarne. On another day, she would have found it nostalgic. But her mood today was more in keeping with the brewing storm and it grew heavier and darker, as she walked and cogitated. She now forced herself to face the harsh truths she had been so reluctant to admit. The storm clouds had gathered, the threatened deluge seemed imminent.

And then, it hit her. Like a thunderbolt. The photographs! *Oh my God, in the wrong hands they were positively pornographic, utterly demeaning.* Not only was she a bad and neglectful daughter but she was guilty of being party to an unhealthy and repugnant and distasteful relationship. The dawning realisation of the gravity halted her in her tracks; her right hand involuntarily clasped her mouth whilst her left reached out to grip the gatepost, as her knees buckled. She felt physically sick. Her world was spinning out of control…

It took a while to recover some sense of equilibrium, some perspective. As she trudged back to the Vicarage, she did not notice the building intensity of the rain. The deluge had begun, and she was exposed. But she had resolved one thing at least. She needed to discover the absolute truth about H – she had to confront him. The semblance of a plan occurred to her, providing something to focus upon.

As to her father, well, there was no plan that could work; nothing that she could do; nothing that he wanted of her or of anyone else. She did not want to go back to London. In fact, the thought of what lay ahead and what she might finally learn mortified her. She did not want to go – but neither did she want to stay.

37. A New Mandate

Christopher's black cab splashed to a halt on this gloomy, rain-sodden summer's morning. The latest in a series of cloudbursts had hit the capital, flooding many tube stations to cause mayhem during the morning commute. But Christopher had allowed himself plenty of time to arrive early. One could not risk keeping the prime minister of The United Kingdom of Great Britain and Northern Ireland waiting: Uncle Xavier.

He was shown to a private room at The Goring Hotel and was soon joined by Xavier Townsend, who bounded into the room to greet his nephew warmly. Hectic political and business agendas had meant the two mainly settling for snatched telephone calls over the last year.

'How good to see you, Chris. Too long, too long. How the hell are you? Did you get that promotion? What's that old rascal Bill doing these days? And what about Liz? Lovely girl, lovely girl. You need to marry her. Bloody young fool to let her get away. Repaired any fences yet? And…what are you doing?'

'I surrender,' laughed Christopher, waving his white handkerchief in mock capitulation.

'Sorry. Was I peppering you—'

'Yes! And before we speak about anything else, can I just say two things please, Xavier?'

'Of course, of course. Must curb my enthusiasm. Just so pleased to see you, Christopher.'

'Firstly, can we grab a juice? And secondly, I have a small gift as way of congratulating you on your election victory back in April.'

'How thoughtful. My, my – what have you got there?'

Christopher presented Xavier with three parcels. The PM was arguably the most powerful man in the country but was acting just like an excitable young boy with treats at Christmas. Christopher was pleased that the bond between he and Xavier seemed as strong as ever, despite their infrequent meetings; he had looked forward to their breakfast meeting and Xavier gave every appearance of having done so himself. The paper was quickly torn from the first present to reveal a bottle of Winston Churchill's favourite champagne, Pol Roger. The second revealed three famous Churchillian quotes which had been framed:

'A single glass of champagne imparts a feeling of exhilaration. The nerves are braced, the imagination is agreeably stirred, the wits become more nimble. A bottle produces a contrary effect. Excess causes a comatose insensibility. So it

is with war, and the quality of both is best discovered by sipping. Winston Churchill, 1898, Malakand Field Force.

'First things first. Get the champagne.' Winston Churchill, 1931, New York.

'I could not live without Champagne. In victory, I deserve it. In defeat I need it.' Winston Churchill, 1946.

'How wonderful. And so thoughtful of you, young man. Thank you, thank you.' His trademark habit of repeating utterances when in full flow was very much on display this morning, which Christopher delighted in.

'And don't forget the final present, Uncle. Sorry, Xavier.' Xavier looked at Christopher with liquid eyes, his emotions not far from the surface. He was soon holding aloft a montage of mainly historical political figures, under the headline title of *'Moral Crusaders.'* He leant back in his chair and roared with laughter before saying, 'Nelson Mandela, Ghandi and Martin Luther King I get – but Mary Whitehouse? Whatever message are you trying to deliver, my boy?'

'How's the crusade going, Xavier?'

'Well, it certainly doesn't address the subject of pornography and censorship the dear lady here was fixated with,' he said. 'Anyway, I wouldn't call it a crusade and I'm not going there this morning except to say that my colleagues just need to raise their game to recapture the confidence of the British public. But we've talked about this before and the newspapers are full of it. Tell me about your business exploits, but let's charge our coffee cups and plates first.'

Christopher was soon updating him on the progress of the business since his own promotion to the position of MD; on the Skills World sale to Supreme; of the partnership with Ulysses and of the minority equity deal. His uncle was delighted to hear the news and was keenly interested in the details.

'But it's not all plain sailing, I'm afraid.'

'Well, I guess that's business, isn't it? A bit like politics in that respect,' suggested Xavier.

'True enough, but I'm seriously worried. It seems we're being entrapped in a scam that's proving difficult to extricate ourselves from. And to prove. We're worried there may be fraudulent practice which will implicate us. Oh sorry, I don't wish to bother you with such things and you probably don't need to hear about this. I mustn't burden you with anything that might embarrass or compromise you. The less you know…'

'Nonsense. This is a private family meeting. What's bothering you? Let me see if I can help.'

Christopher provided him with an outline of the details and of his fears that both his company's and the government's systems had also been penetrated by sophisticated hacking: of the apparent use of a contemporary digital version of the ancient practice of steganography. Xavier listened wide-eyed, his cheeriness morphing into something darker.

'Do you know Horatio Pilkins?' Christopher asked.

'I don't believe so.'

'He seems to know in advance of government announcements about contract awards. Does he know your minister?'

'I've no idea. This is getting a bit uncomfortable, Chris. What are you suggesting?'

'I can't be certain of this, but Elizabeth's best guess is that Horatio has some sort of influence over one of your ministers and is somehow distorting government tendering processes. We're trying to get a meeting with the senior official responsible.'

'That's a serious allegation. You need to tread carefully and garner proof before expressing such sentiments to anyone other than me, I suggest. Anyway, the DWP will be simply applying European rules on tendering processes and I assure you they give no opportunity for ministers to interfere with results. Are you not being a little impetuous? But I must say a meeting with the officials seems a sensible approach. I will discreetly make a couple of informal inquiries myself, but I really am most fortunate in having such good ministers now. I have complete confidence in the minister heading up this area, Sebastian Frith.'

'Fair enough, Xavier. We'll tread warily but there's definitely something awry. Look, I'm sorry to have mentioned this. Just forget about it.'

'No problem, my boy. You mentioned Elizabeth. Tell me. Is she back on the scene? I do hope so,' said Xavier more brightly, with raised eyebrows.

'You'll be pleased to hear that we're back together. Strictly between you and me, I'm hoping to make an honest woman of her if she'll let me.'

'Oh, my boy, I couldn't be happier. Let's open the Pol Roger and celebrate,' he said reaching for the bottle. Christopher laughed and said, 'A tad early for that and anyway, firstly she's refused to listen to my proposal until we clear up this business crisis; secondly, the champagne will be warm and it's not yet ten o'clock in the morning!'

'All perfectly fair points, Chris. But keep me posted, won't you? Now I really must dash. Let's hope the heavens have relented and the promised Armageddon has stalled.'

Xavier embraced Christopher in a bear hug before striding to the door to be whisked away by aides for his day's commitments in the seat of power.

38. Adrian

As Caroline prepared for the week ahead and tried to come to terms with her situation, she ducked several calls from H, despite promises she had made to herself: to escape her worries about him, about her own conduct, and about her father she turned the television on. Tuning in to an undemanding police drama, she poured another large glass of Macon Villages and curled up on the sofa. At least the antics of DC Tosh Lines on a Golden Oldies channel made her laugh, as he went about his shambolic but often successful escapades in Sun Hill. The Bill served a way of ducking her woes for a while, as the local criminals were relentlessly tracked down by the scruffy DC; an enjoyable, diverting accompaniment to her wine.

The arranged meeting took place in the lounge of the Covent Garden Hotel. At the table that she was taken to by a pleasant young waiter, she joined a handsome man in his late thirties, of black African descent: tall, slim, smartly suited and booted. He was a solicitor whose work took him to London fairly regularly. The meeting was timed conveniently for him between scheduled client meetings, which was fine for Caroline. He was doing her a favour.

'Pleased to meet you, Caroline,' he said in a rich, deep voice, flashing a welcoming smile. He shook her hand warmly. 'I've taken the liberty of ordering coffee. Is that okay for you?'

She was not particularly good with accents but thought she detected the remnants of the nasally Black Country inflection, largely groomed out of him by expensive private education, she guessed. He was reputedly a successful legal practitioner and oozed confident charm, albeit of a quite different style to that which she was more accustomed to with H. Her partner's was more old-school aristocratic, whilst Adrian's carried the hallmarks of the modern-day professional classes: well-educated and equally polite but less paternalistic, less patronising than H, it occurred to her.

'I'm delighted to meet you, and a coffee is perfect, thank you. It was good of you to see me. I appreciate you sparing the time.'

'Absolutely my pleasure. Olivia spoke warmly about you and expressed concern about your well-being.'

'She's been a good friend to me,' she said.

'I gather we have a mutual acquaintance in Horatio?'

'It would seem so. How do you know him, may I ask?'

'Our professional lives crossed, and I came to know one or two people who happen to do occasional business with him and…yes thank you very much. How kind. If you'd just leave it there, we'll pour ourselves, thank you,' he said to the waitress, before continuing, 'An interesting character but I wouldn't claim to know him well.'

'Are you able to say where you met? Was it in a business context?'

'In a professional capacity. As I think you know, I practice family law which may give you a clue. Sorry to be evasive but I need to be circumspect to protect client confidentiality. I'm sure you understand. But I'd like to be able to help as I know you and Olivia are good friends. Olivia's a pal. She tells me you and H see each other?'

'Mm…yes,' she said, pausing to take a drink before continuing, 'You must think this very odd. We've been seeing each other for over a year, but there are times when I wonder if I know him at all. You see, Olivia said something which took me by surprise. Sold his business apparently. He's led me to believe something completely different. In fact, he has sought to reassure me on the point; more than that, he denied it vehemently. It seems disloyal but—'

'You still have your doubts?'

'Which I feel bad about, but the truth is it could be important. At worst, I may have compromised myself professionally and…I need to get to the bottom of it. I'm sorry – this is embarrassing.'

'Not at all. You'd be amazed at some of the things one hears in my line of work,' he said, punctuating the comment with a friendly smile.

The two of them chatted for nearly an hour and he insisted on picking up the tab, apologising that he had to dash to another meeting. She watched his tall, elegant form stride through the lobby, heading off in search of a cab to whisk him to his next appointment.

Caroline sat back with a heavy heart, as she tried to assimilate what she had learnt. Her doubts and worst fears had been confirmed. H was indeed the Managing Director of Ulysses. He had sold HostIT some time ago, as Olivia had suggested. Adrian had been crystal clear and offered sufficiently detailed information to support the assertions. He had also provided one or two contacts with whom she could corroborate his understanding. She did not think she would bother to follow these up. Adrian's information simply had the ring of truth about it; she had enough with which to confront H now.

But when? How? She detested confrontations – but was in no doubt it was now necessary. Where was all this heading? She knew where their personal relationship was going; that was over! But had she compromised herself professionally? How had H used the snippets she had shared with him on so many occasions? *There I go again. I must face up to this, more than snippets, much more.*

Caroline had some homework of her own now. She needed to check the details of the recipients of contracts over the last year or so to get a clue as to the extent to which he had taken advantage. Just how many contracts had Ulysses been awarded? To what value? How she wished the meeting might have concluded with a different outcome. As she picked up her coat and handbag, her mind was assaulted with images: of the two of them, of Caroline lying prostrate on the bed, of…the photographs. She had to get them back. The safe.

She flew up the stairs and let herself into the flat. In the middle of the day, he would be elsewhere, at least she hoped so. Slamming the front door behind her, she stormed into the bedroom. The crime scene. Rushing to the far wall, she pulled aside a poster, fiddled in her handbag before finding the key and inserting it into the wall safe. It would not turn. What was wrong? She examined the key and rummaged in her handbag but there were no others. She was sure it was the right key. At least it was the last time she had retrieved anything from it. He must have…Surely not? He would not do that. But what other explanation might there be? H had obviously changed the safe.

39. Ministerial Appointment

The mundane predictability of office life on this drab Monday morning was reassuringly welcome after the week's revelations. It allowed her to lose herself, put to one side her predicament and the unhappiness crowding in on her.

As the afternoon slowly meandered, she took a late break, intent upon some window-shopping in nearby Victoria. Emerging into the hubbub of Tothill Street, she was approached by a young man. He wore the air of confident authority, brimming with officialdom. Caroline brusquely rebutted his approach and turned to walk away. But there was something compelling about his demeanour that made her pause as he gently reassured her, he meant no harm and simply brought a message of considerable importance.

'What can be so urgent that it requires someone I don't know to accost me in the street? Please leave me alone.'

'Please, Miss Hope, I bring you a request for a meeting with a minister of Her Majesty's government.'

'That's preposterous. Why here? Why clandestinely? I'll call the police if you continue to pester me,' with which she turned her back on the stranger. But his threatening response stopped her in her tracks.

'If you value your liberty and freedom then listen, I urge you. The minister needs to speak with you – off the record and privately. If you insist, I'll report your refusal to co-operate, but I wouldn't wish to be in your shoes – the minister isn't someone to ignore, I suggest.'

Caroline stared open-mouthed, as he released his warnings in a low voice, almost a stage whisper. The words carried a potent threat made all the more sinister by an accompanying smirk. The portent of his words contrasted starkly with the mild delivery. But what on earth could he mean? What was behind all this? Why would a minister invite her surreptitiously to a private meeting? Which minister – presumably hers? Her troubles seemed to be multiplying. He handed her a slip of paper and advised that she attend at the appointed time. With his mission accomplished, he gently inclined his head with the old-world charm of a bygone Edwardian era, briskly wished her a good day, turned and strolled nonchalantly towards Westminster. She stared blankly after him, then down at the slip of paper.

'This evening, St Ermine's Hotel, Churchill Suite 19:30...'

Bemoaning a headache, she finished work early, allowing time to order her thoughts and prepare. Caroline needed to calm down; she was becoming panicked, stressed. She opted for a long shower to refresh and recover some poise – but to little avail. As she dressed and attended her hair and make-up, she selected sombre and formal attire in keeping with the apparent gravity of her situation, recalling the stranger's chilling words. There was nothing for it but to attend at the appointed time and find out what it was all about.

As Caroline approached the suite, she paused briefly to examine herself in the long, gilded mirror. She gently shook her head as if in disapproval, smoothed her skirt, took a deep breath and rapped loudly on the door – louder than intended. It sprung open and she was faced with The Rt Honourable Sebastian Frith.

'Come in, come in. You're late! Sit there.'

He pointed to a single plastic-moulded chair in the middle of the room. It was positioned opposite an imposing high-backed, buttoned red leather Chesterfield. Against the window was a heavy oak sideboard upon which sat decanters of whisky, cut glasses and an ice bucket containing bottles of wine. The minister sipped from his glass of whisky. She would have welcomed some water to lubricate her drying throat but did not ask. She was offered nothing.

As she sat, he slowly circled her before plopping down with a heavy sigh. Taking a further sip, he looked at her quizzically but said nothing for a moment or two. The silence was intimidating, deafening. Her heart was beating rapidly and she could feel the dampness from a rush of perspiration already soaking into her blouse. She kept her arms quite still and was thankful she had decided upon the jacket. It would conceal the stains that even now must be spreading. Caroline stayed quiet, waiting for him to announce the reason for her presence; waited to hear of her crimes and of her fate.

'Well, well who's been a naughty girl then?'

She said nothing, just glared at him. She was resolved to hide her fear and discomfiture as best she could.

'Nothing to say, Miss Hope?'

Nothing. Glare. Silence.

'I don't have all night so let's get to it, shall we?'

Silence.

'We know you've been spilling the beans, Miss Hope; giving away trade secrets, abusing your position of power.'

Silence. Scowl.

She focused on keeping her arms still, anxious that he might smell her fear. He jumped to his feet, strode to the beckoning decanter of amber liquid and refreshed his glass. An ice cube exploded against the crystal like a fired gun. Caroline flinched.

'We have but ten minutes, Miss Hope. Your continued liberty is hanging in the balance and your sullen silence won't aid your cause. Do I throw you to the dogs or are you to be of use to me?'

'You've not asked me anything and I've no idea why a minister should act so obnoxiously and assault me with false accusations. And why here? Why privately? Why not in the department?'

'Good. The lady's found her voice. But you don't conduct yourself like a lady, Caroline Hope – and you the daughter of a vicar as well. Tut tut. I wonder what your father would say about your sleazy life, your dubious morals.'

'Get to the point. Tell me what you want, or I'll walk out of here and you can go to hell – with all due respect, minister.' Caroline was almost shocked by her own utterances which revealed much more spirit and bravery than she felt.

'Feisty too! I like that in a woman, although I prefer mine more attractive, I must say. Sit down!' he shouted, in response to her scraping her chair back, intent on taking her leave.

'You, Miss Hope, will do and act as I say. I know, you see. I know. I have all the evidence I could possibly want. You've been disloyal to your profession, to your department, to your government. You've given away vital information that has skewed open competitive tendering processes in the awarding of tens of millions of pounds. Haven't you? Don't you dare deny it either.'

'I don't know what you're talking about.'

'Yes, you do – here read this.'

He thrust an excerpt from a letter at her, a statement that alleged treachery.

'This could be from anyone. A forgery, a deceit. Why are you doing this to me? What do you want of me? My resignation?' Caroline fought back the tears that welled.

'You will recognise this signature, I believe?'

Caroline stared at the proffered letter and felt sick as she took in the unmistakeable spidery signature of her lover. Her brimming, red eyes could stem the flow no longer. The enormity of her situation overwhelmed her.

'You'll have my resignation on your desk in the morning, Minister,' she whispered between sobs.

'I don't want that. If you resign, the police will be informed of your criminal activity and I need hardly tell you of the inevitable consequences. A vacation at Her Majesty's pleasure would surely beckon. No. You will return to work and continue as if nothing has happened. You will be mine. You will do whatever I will of you and follow my every instruction. Do you understand?'

'No. No, I don't understand. Why all of this if you simply wish me to do nothing?'

'I wanted you to know.'

'Know what?' she snivelled.

He rose to his feet and again walked around her chair, circling like an animal stalking its dying prey. Suddenly, his face thrust down into hers; she could taste his foul whisky breath.

'You now know that I know. That is all – for now! Now get out, you miserable creature.'

40. Torture and Revelation

A restless night's sleep inevitably followed, as Caroline's mind jumped from one torment to another, the appalling meeting with her minister uppermost. There was no relief, no escape from her misery and torture. The daylight hours brought no comfort and precious little insight either. She could not see a way out. Together, the various strands seemed to weave a noose, its stranglehold tightening the more she struggled to conjure an escape, squeezing her life's breath out of her.

Think. Concentrate. Stop panicking.

She tried to put aside her emotions and instead marshal her powers of logic; to analyse her options. But few of her woes seemed to offer the prospect of solution. Her father was dying of his lung cancer – *fact*! She had proven to be a woefully inadequate and unloving daughter who had deserted her sole living parent – *fact*! She had engaged in a disgraceful relationship with an older man who had completely deceived her – *fact*! Furthermore, their expansive sexual activities now shamed her deeply. She had shared commercially sensitive information with H which she was now certain had been used for commercial gain – *fact*! She realised her actions were of a serious nature. She had betrayed trust and failed to maintain minimum required professional standards. This not only threatened her career but, as that dreadful man had insisted, her liberty – *fact*! What could she do? She could not even resign. How could she escape her tormenters? She had no answers. But she must do *something* to find the path to rehabilitation – whatever that price might be.

She lifted the phone to ring her father; perhaps he would be more tolerant of her from a distance. Maybe he had changed his mind to accept treatment. She hoped so.

'Hello, Daddy. How are you? Ooh that cough sounds nasty.'

'What do you want, Caroline?' His throat seemed dry; his voice hoarse.

'Just wanted to talk to you, say hello. Try again to persuade you to have the treatment, Daddy. We all love you—'

'We've been through this. I have a sermon to prepare, so if you don't mind.'

'Just a minute—' Too late. He had put the receiver down. No change on that front then.

What now? Caroline decided to latch upon the one area that did seem open to action; the only aspect that she could seemingly do something about: *H*! She would confront him and end their relationship. That much she could do, and the thought at least mitigated her pain. She resolved to head for Notting Hill that evening. It was quite possible that he would be there, by no means certain, but possible. Should she ring in advance? No – better to visit later that evening and if there, give him a piece of her mind and be done with him.

As she headed towards their shared bolthole, their love nest, she recalled how their coupling had once engendered fulfilment and liberation. But now, as the memories of Kama Sutra gymnastics sprang to mind, she felt degraded.

Pausing briefly at the foot of the steps to the block of flats she looked up and sighed. Fumbling for her keys under the dim porch light, she quietly opened the door. Caroline headed up to their first floor flat, let herself in and switched on a table lamp in the hallway. He did not appear to be at home. Home? It certainly was not that in any conventional sense. She dumped her handbag and coat on the sofa and headed towards the kitchen, intent upon relieving the fridge of the ubiquitous bottle of chardonnay. She poured her favourite straw-coloured nectar generously and was just about to turn the television on to while away the time when she thought she heard something. Caroline stood stock-still and listened but decided there was nothing to listen to. Her ears must have been deceiving her. But just then, she picked up the sound of muffled laughter and simultaneously spotted something in the corner. On closer inspection, she did not recognise the shoes. Ladies high fashion shoes at that. And a handbag and coat, which were most definitely not hers. Unless H was cross-dressing, there could be little doubt another woman was in residence; perhaps a niece or a sister or…

But there was no mistaking the stifled noises of a couple. She crept towards the room from which the sound emanated; her bedroom – *their* bedroom. She moved as if in slow motion, her heart thumping, nerves jangling. Time seemed to stand still, every movement slowly advanced and paused frame by frame by an intrigued voyeur. In the few seconds, it had taken to walk to and open the door, the realisation had hit her even before her eyes provided confirmation.

She took in the scene in freeze-frame snatches…red hair…naked…woman straddling man…her man…H! She stared wide-eyed for a split-second that seemed like ages.

'Bastard,' she exploded. 'Have him and good riddance. *Bastard.*'

She stormed out of the flat, ignoring shouted entreaties.

41. A Friend in Need

Caroline collapsed into Olivia's warm embrace as soon as she was through the door. She sobbed heartily, shoulders heaving, her body shaking; tears streamed from sore, red eyes. The dam had burst. There was no stemming the flow. Her friend held her close, soothing a distraught Caroline as a mother might a teenager tormented by demons, shushing her as if a distressed baby. She held on tightly until eventually the tsunami was spent, leaving a tangled mess of destruction and detritus in its wake. It had taken Caroline days after the last encounter with H to pluck up the courage to contact Olivia, but she felt so lonely and so desperate. She did not know who else to turn to.

'Come on, babe, tell Aunty Liv. Always feels better out than festering away.'

'Oh, Olivia…'

And then, the words began to tumble out in an avalanche of disordered confusion. Something about being duped, conned, cheated. Claims about betrayal, corruption, bullying, naivety, blindness, criminality…Caroline spat out sentiments of hatred and loathing, of resignation and pornography, sin and scandal. The heady mix was directed at multiple targets; herself, the department, the minister and H. Something about being owned, controlled, manipulated. She did not know which way to turn or what to do.

'What do you mean "owned", Caroline? What's happened?'

Gradually, the tears abated, the eyes were dabbed dry and some semblance of rational thought slowly surfaced. She claimed she was ensnared in separate webs spun by H and the minister; paralysed into inaction. Damned if she did, damned if she did not.

'But you still haven't said what's happened, babe. I can only help if you confide in me. You need to share the burden. Let me help…'

Caroline eventually told Olivia everything – almost everything. The extraordinary nature of the private meeting with the minister was explained, H's infidelity also. Of the tawdry nature of her relationship with H and their shared bolthole, she was opaque. And silent over the photographs.

'Oh, Caroline. We'll find a way forward, there's always a way. Come on,' Olivia said gently, her face betraying her depth of concern, empathy to the fore. 'Let's chat this through, shall we? Dry those eyes, have a wash and throw that wine away. We need clear heads on this, babe. I'll make coffee…'

Gradually, the emotion was replaced with a more analytical approach to her woes. The semblance of a plan slowly evolved – one that scared Caroline to death. She realised she had to break out of her torpor and could not passively do the bidding of the minister or H. Whatever they had in store for her could not be good. Olivia encouraged her to take her destiny in her own hands and be proactive. Caroline agreed whilst looking doubtful. Gulp.

She had ducked call after call. But Caroline knew the relationship with H could not rest with her furious outburst on finding him in flagrante. The nightmare scene kept returning to her mind. She could not banish it, no matter how hard she tried. It was as if the image of her man straddled by a rapacious suitor was burned on her retina.

As she undertook her household chores and ventured out to the shops, Caroline constantly broke down in tears as the awful moment replayed. The folly of her actions over the course of too many years engulfed her. Caroline's emotions were fragile, tears flowing at unpredictable moments to overcome her, as if in mourning. Perhaps she was. Perhaps she was mourning for the life she had lost; for the loss of the man she had loved. How she hated him now. She was appalled by his behaviour, distressed by his deception. And yet...

She had rung into the department to report sick, not being able to focus on work just now. Olivia was frequently in touch, the one oasis in the desert of her life. Her friend expressed her concern, fussing one moment, cajoling the next. No matter what she tried, the desired impact was elusive. And prolonged analysis and discussion failed to conjure a plan that would stick; one in which she could escape her entrapment...

Just then, the doorbell rang, and Caroline reluctantly dragged herself down the hallway to open up. And there he was. As bold as brass. She slammed the door in his face, but he was persistent. Realising she had to have it out with him sooner or later, she grudgingly allowed him to cross the threshold. He was as dapper and sharp-suited as ever. The same old H.

'We, err, need to talk, do we not, special lady?' he ventured.

'Ha – special lady? Just...just how special? Who was the other sp...special lady then?' she stammered.

'Are we really going to end our relationship on this sour note? I do so hope not. May I sit down?' he asked. She shook her head, but he did so anyway.

'It's over, H. You disgust me. You've used me. I feel dirty. I hate you.'

'Oh, my dear—'

'Don't you oh-my-dear me! You've cheated on me. You've used and manipulated me. You lied about what you do.'

'I'm sorry you feel like that, Caroline, after all we've experienced together.'

'But you weren't straight with me and what was that statement you produced for the minister. And how do you know him? And why? *Why*?'

'I can see that you aren't yourself, dearest. Distraught even, cuts me to the quick—'

'Oh, quit the smart-arsed, gentleman Jim pretence. You've set me up and I need to know why. You owe me that at least.'

'Okay, I can see there's little to be gained in continuing this conversation...but do take care, Caroline.'

'And what's *that* supposed to mean?'

'Just what I say, it would be sad to see your past indiscretions come back to haunt you.' He rose from the chair, edging to the door, before pausing to offer an afterthought in hushed tones, 'Just continue doing your job and keep your head down. *And* your pretty little mouth shut!'

Caroline stared at him aghast. Never had he been even remotely threatening. Suddenly, the mists cleared, she now knew what she had to do. Gone was all her uncertainty and indecisiveness.

'I *will* tell the truth, H, and be damned with you *and* the minister. You can both go to hell, as can everyone else. If that lands me in trouble, then so be it. Someone needs to do what's right. Someone needs to hear what you've been up to. Seeking personal gain by corrupting public servants will get you ostracised if not thrown into prison. I hope they throw away the keys. Now get out, *get out!* Don't let me ever see you again,' she exploded, her cheeks ablaze. H frowned deeply, his brow furrowing. The pained expression seemed to convey a mix of sorrow, pain and dismay. Good – at last she seemed to be getting through. Recovering his poise, the mask restored, he offered a final threat in his gratingly clipped and now barbed gentility.

'Well goodbye then, my dear, but you should just look at this before doing anything rash. Be assured this is the tip of the iceberg too. Plenty of copies of ever-more explicit material from where that came from. I wonder what your family might think? Or your employers or the newspapers for that matter…' H handed her an envelope, flashed her an oily smile, bade her farewell and swiftly departed.

Caroline looked questioningly at him, as he exited her flat, her eyes burning into his disappearing back. Slamming the door after him, she stared blankly at the envelope. Whatever now. Eventually, she found the courage to delve into it. Her long, slender fingers slowly extricated a single sheet of glossy paper – a photograph. She hardly dared look but slowly turned it over until the incriminating, explicit image was fully revealed. A quick glance was all it took for her to lose every last ounce of composure, as she collapsed into her chair. Utterly distraught. And this time the fog descended more thickly than ever – a real peasouper displacing the clarity of just moments ago.

42. Departmental Business

In the absence of any real plan, and with Olivia's encouragement, Caroline returned to work and resolved to put her head down and simply get on with things. The sharper edges of her pain and humiliation receded bit by bit, as she immersed herself into the operational routine of daily life. There were policy matters to pursue with the various sub-committees, consultations to be had with the industry bodies and frequent meetings with the riled representatives of the Job Centre top brass.

There were also briefing meetings for ministers, but Caroline managed to avoid those personally, choosing instead to delegate the task to other colleagues on one pretext or another. Thank goodness her minister chose not to seek her out. But the storm clouds were gathering with yet another round of competitive tendering in the offing. At least this time, no one would be duplicitously wheedling details out of her.

Personal and professional decisions were shelved for the time being. Deep-down, though, she knew that the situation with H and the minister could not be left to rest; she needed to confront these demons sooner or later.

Caroline had slowly revealed most of the sorry tale to Olivia, who had moved back to her London office. The Hackney situation apparently no longer needed Olivia to be in such close proximity to Marku. As the two settled down for an evening of discovery, as Olivia labelled it, they tried to unravel the various strands. Caroline had become confused and perplexed by the apparent link between H and the minister.

'How had he obtained a statement from H and why?' asked Olivia. 'What had either to gain?'

'I've no idea. It doesn't make sense. We're missing too many pieces of the jigsaw.'

'But didn't you challenge H about his business interests after your meeting with Adrian?'

'I confronted H months ago. But he flatly denied anything to do with Ulysses other than being a supplier. He was so bloody convincing. The man's obviously an inveterate liar.'

'But after your meeting with Adrian, did you challenge him again?'

'I was convinced by what Adrian said and just had to face the reality. I'd been in denial for too long, so I set out to confront him – which is when I found him with…you know…I previously told you.' Caroline began to tear up, but Olivia intervened and encouraged her to carry on. 'Come on, Caroline, what happened next.'

She fell silent in thought and then her face lit up. 'The minister,' she said hurriedly.

'Your private meeting?'

'Yes. Oh, hang on, no. First H denied what you'd told me last year, then...yes, then the Adrian meeting, then the private meeting with that bastard minister, then H screwing the red-headed bimbo and...I think.'

'This is good. The sequence of events is important. And going back to the meeting with your minister was it then that he produced the letter with H's signature?'

'That's right, yes. I couldn't believe it. I didn't want to believe it. Oh, do I have to relive that again? The ghastliest confrontation of my life.'

'Defo. Be brave. Now we've got a handle on the sequencing we need to consider the likely motivation. Why did the minister need to produce such a letter?'

'To persuade me, he knew I was revealing stuff?' ventured Caroline. 'But I never meant to. You do believe me, don't you? Please say you...'

'Course I believe you! Come on, get the emotions in check and let's just work this out,' her friend pleaded, stroking her hand lightly.

'Okay.'

'Right. Well, going back to that signed letter, sight of that certainly made you confront the awful reality of being used; that you'd been deceived.'

'Okay, okay...' she sighed, putting her head in her hands.

'Sorry, babe, I know it's painful but we're on the right lines I'm sure...Let's assume the minister simply needed you to know. He needed you in his pocket. Yes?' pressed Olivia.

'Sort of makes sense.'

'Then we know why the minister used the damning evidence from H. Doesn't that imply he's more dastardly deeds planned for you? But it still doesn't tell us why H played along with this.'

'I wonder if the minister has something over H? Oh, it could be anything, couldn't it?' Caroline groaned, thoroughly exasperated.

'How do the two know each other, I wonder? We could try and find out. A bit of research.'

'Okay we could do that, but is it really so surprising? After all, H has had a long running association with the market in one guise or another.'

The two of them tried to piece the details together, but all it seemed to confirm was that the minister had used H in order to bolster his control over Caroline in preparation for something or other that must be planned. But what? More dodgy contract awards where tender regulations are bent?

'Who's benefited from these awards?' said a suddenly animated Olivia.

'Mainly Ulysses – and we *now* know who the main beneficiary of that is, don't we? Bloody H.'

'But we don't know why the minister wanted that to happen. Rather than he having something over H, it would make more sense if it were the other way around, wouldn't it? And who else has profited?'

'Skills World is the other main recipient; they are well regarded and have a good reputation,' said Caroline. 'Mind you,' she added brightly, 'they were taken over by Supreme, who also won a new contract.'

'So what?' asked Olivia.

'Skills World have just signed a strategic relationship with Ulysses.'

'Oh yes, I think you told me that before. So, Skills World and Ulysses are contractually linked. And Skills World are owned by Supreme. Is there a link between Supreme and Ulysses? Some sort of unholy trinity?'

'Don't know,' admitted Caroline.

'Let's find out...'

Back in the department, the preparations for the next round of tendering were under way. How could she ensure that ministerial interference was minimised? How could the competitive tendering rules be bolstered to ensure fair play? Caroline consulted with her senior colleagues who were astonished any doubts could be harboured. After all, the rules were in line with European procurement arrangements and had stood audit scrutiny. Of course, they had.

'I'd like to raise another concern though,' voiced Adam Harkness, a zealous and hardworking young man in charge of the audit team.

'Yes?'

'You were asking about Ulysses and Skills World. We did an audit of Ulysses and SWL contracts a few months ago. They're all managed by SWL, following a strategic alliance between the two.'

'And?'

'The audit was clean, otherwise you'd have heard about it. But we're perplexed by the statistics of Ulysses. They're way ahead of all other providers,' said the audit team manager.

'Any theories? Any reason to suspect foul play?'

'Not specifically. But the key performance indicators seem unreal.'

'In which areas?' she asked.

'Work-placement and sustainability. Fees being paid out are substantially higher than budgeted due to the exceptionally high levels of claimed performance. Millions higher. It's the result of placing high numbers of long-term unemployed clients into work and somehow sustaining their employment despite the experience of others.'

'But you say they passed the audit.'

'Yes, but this payment-on-results approach is innovative in the market and proving to be very challenging for most providers – for all other than Ulysses actually.'

'I *am* familiar with all this. What's your point?'

'Of course. Sorry. But as you know, the rules for administering the contracts are complex and the overhead in managing the system of checks and balances difficult to navigate. Benefit fraud is an ever-present danger – hence the worry over any warning signals.'

'Thank you for the lecture but—' began Caroline before he hurriedly spoke over her.

'I was wondering if there might be anything wrong with the systems, the actual software systems – either at their end or, dare I suggest, ours.'

'What are you proposing we do? Come on Adam, spit it out. This is painful.'

'We should instigate a technical audit of systems, rather than processes. Get IT experts in forensic analysis to pour over the software and the underlying code in Ulysses' system, DragonFly, and also in STRAP.'

Caroline sat back and looked at him intently. The implications were interesting, potentially illuminating, possibly toxic. For her as well as H. Now she knew that H was in charge of Ulysses; that H had extracted from her commercially sensitive information; that there was probably a tie-up between H and the minister it was very tempting to press on as proposed by Adam. But on the other hand, both men had leverage over her. Freedom to exercise her better judgement seemed to be denied to her. She was damned if she did what was right and yet condemned if she failed to.

'Caroline? Should we go ahead?' pressed Adam.

'Yes, of course. That will be all, colleagues.' She drew the meeting to an abrupt close, grabbed her coat and headed out.

Occupying a corner of the nearest Costa Coffee on Victoria Street, she brooded on her dilemma. What could she have said to Adam? She had authorised the right course of action. But the minister would hardly see it like that. Mind you, it would be a while before he found out, probably not until Ulysses squealed their inevitable protests. The die was cast. She just had to brave it out. Meanwhile, she resolved to work with Olivia on their research; to try and work out the motivations and links between H and the Honourable Sebastian Frith. *Honourable! Ha! As dishonourable and corrupt as they come.*

43. Early News

Someone banging on the front door woke Christopher with a start. He nudged Elizabeth who was still dead to the world. She groaned and turned over, pulling the duvet over her head. He glanced at the clock; it was not yet seven o'clock. Christopher rubbed his eyes, tumbled out of bed and searched for his dressing gown. He settled for pulling on some trousers and a shirt from the piles of clothes strewn across the bedroom. The banging had resumed, and he called out, 'Okay, I'm coming,' as he picked his way bare foot along the hallway, still buttoning his shirt. Opening the front door, he was surprised to find a middle-aged man who turned out to be a policeman.

'DCI Bernard Hales, sir,' he declared, flashing his warrant card, 'and this is DS Rachael Doyle.'

He apologised for the early visit but had some questions he was hoping Elizabeth might be able to help with.

'She's still in bed, but come in. I'll put some coffee on. She won't be coherent until that first kick of caffeine. Like one?'

'No thanks, sir.'

They were soon joined in the lounge by Elizabeth who gratefully took the proffered mug and sat down, wrapping her dressing gown tightly around her.

'May I ask if you know of a Mohamed Khatri?' asked the detective, addressing Elizabeth. She confirmed that she did, although not well. DCI Bernard Hales went on to establish that Mo was working for Elizabeth and Christopher, albeit through an intermediary company.

'Doing what exactly?'

'Technical investigative work. He's a brilliant programmer. Why are you asking? What's wrong?' asked Elizabeth.

'Can I ask of your whereabouts last night between the hours of twenty-one hundred and three o'clock this morning?'

'We were both here, inspector,' interjected Christopher.

'We had dinner after a long, stressful day before retiring for an early night,' confirmed Elizabeth.

'I'm afraid he's been the subject of an assault. May I show you some pictures to verify we're talking about the same man?' asked the detective, reaching into his pocket.

'Of course. Anything we can do to help...'

The photograph was indeed the man she knew as Mo Khatri.

'And when did you last see him?' asked DS Doyle.

'About a week ago, I think.'

'He's suffered a brutal attack. You should prepare yourself for a shock,' said DCI Hayles. He signalled to DS Doyle, who moved in closer to Elizabeth, before he lay three photographs face-down on her coffee table. One by one, he turned them over. Elizabeth recoiled, her hand instinctively moving to cover her open mouth before exclaiming her revulsion. Both of Mo's hands had been mutilated. Most of his fingers had been hacked off, leaving just his little finger and thumb on his right hand. All the digits had been chopped off his left hand, leaving just his thumb.

'Oh my God! Who on earth would do such a thing? Is he all right? Did he survive?'

'He's in Guys Hospital as we speak. He's lost a lot of blood, and the poor man's traumatised.'

'I should imagine so,' said Christopher, nodding thoughtfully, holding Elizabeth's hand. 'Not likely to do any more programming in the future either, I wouldn't have thought. How do you think we can help? Surely, you don't suspect us?' Christopher said, leaning forward.

The detective looked at Christopher and Elizabeth with detached interest. He watched the two of them, presumably to gauge their reactions.

'We aren't yet able to rule anyone in or out I'm afraid, but we'd like to talk with you again please.'

'Of course. Let us dress and cover a few things at the office.'

'Oh, and we have that meeting with Caroline,' Elizabeth reminded Christopher.

'That's fine, madam, make it sometime over the next couple of days please…'

Christopher and Elizabeth's off-the-record meeting with Caroline Hope was held in one of the rooms in the business suite of St Ermin's Hotel. They were shown into the room and helped themselves to a glass of water. A few minutes later, Caroline entered. Christopher noticed that on crossing the threshold she stopped short and looked around uneasily, seeming to shudder before recovering her poise to greet the two of them. The official seemed on tenterhooks but introduced them to a colleague, *Olivia from our fraud department*. He looked sharply at Olivia and forced a half-smile, exchanging glances with Elizabeth.

'Thanks for agreeing to meet us,' said Christopher.

'We needed to meet you anyway,' she said. Her manner was peremptory, the tone icy. She was clearly not in any mood for small talk and indicated that time was tight.

'Fair enough.'

'The thing is, the department has noticed that Ulysses statistics and returns are almost too good to be true,' Olivia began.

'Agreed.'

'Oh, okay. We thought you might protest and point to the clean audit and…' Olivia's voice trailed off.

'Can we speak bluntly?' asked Elizabeth, having exchanged glances with Christopher and received an affirmatory nod. They proceeded to share their concerns about the returns, the nature of the commercial deal with Ulysses that had been foisted upon Skills World and their belief that the returns were somehow invalid. Elizabeth further clarified their strategy of the dual running of systems and then she outlined the early findings of the investigation. Holding centre stage, Elizabeth summarised their steganography findings. She had to explain in simple terms and then went on to outline her fears that the STRAP system may also have been penetrated.

'Oh, my goodness. I'll have to seek advice on this. It's outside my area of expertise. I need to inform the relevant parties of suspected fraudulent practice...' Caroline indicated, then continued in a wobbly voice. 'We've initiated a forensic audit of IT systems at both ends anyway, and your comments seem to confirm the importance...despite being under instruction from the minister to do no such thing,' she murmured as an aside to her colleague.

'What? Why? That can't be right, can it?' said a shocked Christopher. 'What will you do?'

She smiled weakly at him, not offering a response but demanding he write formally to set out relevant details.

'You'll be investigated of course,' muttered Caroline.

Christopher nodded. He knew they were exposed, that events were escalating beyond any realistic hope of containment. He needed to break cover, whatever Horatio or Georgina Harris might have to say.

'There's a couple of other things you probably ought to know,' said Elizabeth. She proceeded to tell Caroline and Olivia about the assault on Mo. They were visibly disturbed.

'What has this to do with us? Or with anything?' asked Caroline.

'We don't know,' said Elizabeth. 'But he was working for us in trying to uncover what we suspect is foul play. We're wondering—'

'If the attack is to stop him,' interrupted Caroline.

'Well, whether that was the motivation or not it will certainly be the effect, that's for sure,' said Christopher, 'poor chap hasn't any—'

'I get the picture,' said Caroline.

'You said two things?' Olivia nudged.

'Oh, yes. A strange thing, but when I worked for Horatio...'

Caroline flinched and said, 'That's enough for one meeting. We are agreed on the way forward. I'll get back to you. I have another appointment. She rose from her chair, snatched her papers up and left. Olivia sat quietly before eventually asking Elizabeth to finish what she was saying.

'Okay. Look, I don't really understand how, but Horatio Pilkins always seemed to know the outcomes of the various tendering rounds before they were announced. He was always so certain Ulysses would win handsomely and Skills World also. And they always did. He occasionally referred to meeting some minister or other. It just seemed untoward and fishy to me, but I've never managed to work out exactly what was going on.'

44. CID

DCI Bernard Hayles and DS Rachael Doyle joined two other colleagues back at the office, Arnold Forest and Simon Sterling.

'Any news on our victim, Arnie?'

'He's not doing too well. Lost a lot of blood. Still under sedation, guv – but he'll live,' said Arnold, proceeding to stuff a sausage roll into his mouth which provoked a glance to the heavens by Rachael.

'Find out when we can speak with him. Did he have sight of his assailant? Does he know him?'

'Or *her,* guv – equal opportunities and all that,' smirked Arnold, smiling at Rachael who raised her hands palm-side up, shrugged her shoulders and sighed. Simon stifled a smile. Bernard ignored the diversionary gestures.

'Just get on with it,' he said. 'You too SS and keep our resident Neanderthal in check, will you?'

Arnie reacted by taking another huge bite from his sausage roll and feigning to pick his nose simultaneously.

'You disgusting animal,' said Rachael, pulling a face.

'Okay. Settle down. What did you think of Elizabeth and Christopher then, Rache?'

'Seemed pretty genuine to me, visibly shocked at the news about Mohammed. Not convinced they were telling us everything they knew though.'

'Agreed on both counts. What was the precise nature of the assignment Mo was engaged on? What progress? How might this link to the assault? Was the nature of the work the motive for our attacker? Let's interview them again this afternoon. Get onto that, Rache.'

'Will do, guv.'

'I'd also like to understand the work that Skills World do. Why engage Mohammed via Elizabeth's own company? Did you get its name, Rache?'

'Hell Hath no Fury,' she confirmed.

'Weird. Why not employ him directly anyway? That seems strange. Let's find out why. And what about the parent company of Skills World? Where are they in all this? Let's do a bit of digging. Anything else guys?'

'It's all a bit thin, isn't it?' ventured Arnold.

'Early days…'

'It seems we've been beaten to the draw, guv,' said Simon, having just taken an internal call.

'What?'

'Elizabeth and Christopher are here asking to meet you.'

'Right oh. Come on, Rache. And, SS, get onto Skills World and find out what you can, will you? Right that's all for now…'

Bernard and Rachael met with Christopher and Elizabeth in one of the interview rooms, taping proceedings for the record. Christopher explained the link with Ulysses, the takeover of Skills World and their subsequent equity participation scheme. He also went on to reveal their concerns about the system the Ulysses contract had foisted upon them to manage all the contracts as a bundle, including those of the parent company, Supreme. Elizabeth developed the theme, telling them about their dual running of systems and the hypothesis she was testing.

'What has this to do with Mohammed Khatri?' asked DS Rachael Doyle. Elizabeth referred to his expertise and prior employment in Ulysses. She also provided an overview of his initial findings and of the steganography techniques employed. Bernard scribbled in his notebook and exchanged urgent glances with Rachael, before verifying his understanding with Elizabeth.

'Let me get this straight. You're saying the system's been hacked, effectively, using this fancy stegan…technique…'

'It's a bit more than hacking into a system. Think of it as being an implant of code that's hidden and acts in a way that the perpetrator programmes,' said Elizabeth.

'Got it. But this code is used to defraud government on a large scale?'

'We suspect so but haven't been able to nail this down yet,' said Christopher.

'And what have you done about your suspicions? Is your company not also gaining fraudulently?' asked Bernard. Elizabeth shuffled in her chair and was about to explain when Christopher took up the challenge.

'We've been conducting our own internal investigation, as Elizabeth has explained, and the DWP has also undertaken an audit, with which we have of course complied and provided every assistance. We passed the audit with a clean bill of health.'

'And who else knows about your stegan…steganography theory?' pressed Bernard, referring to his scrawled notes.

'We've just met with Miss Hope to share our suspicions, our concerns with her.'

'Who?'

'Caroline Hope at the Department of Work and Pensions. We told you earlier we had a meeting with her,' Christopher explained.

'Mm. Okay. And you employed Mohammed Khatri, who's found this hidden code?' he enquired of Elizabeth, who confirmed that was correct.

'Could it be a motive for the assault on Mo?' asked Christopher. His question was answered only by a penetrating look from the inspector.

'Why did you engage him through your own company and not Skills World,' asked Bernard, rifling through his notes before adding, 'Hell Hath No Fury. Strange name.'

'To protect Mo. He has restrictive covenants which he may be breaching by doing this work,' explained Elizabeth.

'So, you had him undertake this covertly?' Rachael pressed.

'I guess so.'

'And you own this company, Elizabeth?' asked Bernard.

'I did some consulting a while back so formed my own company. But SWL pick up the costs so it's employment once removed really. The point is that Mo has rare skills plus the experience of having worked at Ulysses, so was uniquely placed to do a forensic examination of the code base.'

'And we suspect Supreme and Ulysses are somehow linked,' added Christopher.

'How? Why would you suspect that? How does that have any relevance?' asked Bernard.

'We've suspected foul play for some time. And the only logical explanation is a link between Horatio at Ulysses and Georgina Harris,' said Christopher.

'You suspect them of being in cahoots? Tied into this hidden code thing?' asked Rachael.

'They play dirty, so we wouldn't be surprised. I just don't trust them *and* I'm getting to the stage where I don't want anything to do with their approach to business,' he added.

'What proof have you?'

'Of some sort of illicit partnership or criminality? None at all. Just a gut feeling. Too many instances when the messages emanating from both have been too similar. Choreographed. If I were you, I'd dig deeper into this.'

'Mm. Thanks for the advice,' sighed Bernard, casting his eyes to the heavens. The interview concluded with Christopher and Elizabeth providing more details about their meeting with Caroline Hope at the Department of Work and Pensions…

It was early afternoon, as Bernard gathered his team to review progress. Simon and Arnold delivered the good news that Mohammed seemed to be improving and was no longer under sedation. It was possible that a short interview might be possible tomorrow.

'Okay, Rache and I will cover that. SS and Arnie – get onto the Ulysses, Skills World and Supreme arrangements. Something fishy's going on there. What's it got to do with Mohammed Khatri's attack? We need something concrete. And fast.' He then updated the team on the salient points from the interview with Christopher and Elizabeth, identifying a possible motive for the attack on Mohammed.

'But even if Horatio and Georgina are conspiring to defraud the authorities and on the make, how does this link back to Mo's attack? Do we really think either of these characters would bloody their own hands or even instruct someone else? It's all circumstantial, isn't it? We've nothing to lay a glove on either of them, guv…' said Rachael.

'I know, I know,' Bernard confirmed, before changing tack and addressing Arnie. 'I've a job that's right up your street. You and SS go and speak with Horatio. An upper-class twit by all accounts, so unleash your Neanderthal-man on him. Let's shake the tree, see what falls out.'

'Will do.' Arnold smiled, and rubbed his hands together.

'Good. Let's not waste time. We need to join the dots. Finally, Rache, arrange a meeting with Caroline Hope. Soon as you can – we'll go to her office. That's it.'

45. On the Edge

Following the meeting with Skills World, Caroline and Olivia caught up that evening.

'Where'd you get to after the meet, hon?' asked Olivia.

'Decided on the spur of the moment to speak with the head of the Skills section in fraud, Fred Ingle. Do you know him?'

'Know of him but he's above my pay grade. Your boss was okay with you doing that?'

Caroline pulled a face.

'You did clear it with him?'

'Since when did you get so picky about protocol? I didn't want to be dissuaded. I simply had to do something. Every time I decide to do one thing or another, I'm bullied by either the minister or by H – or I change my mind when I work out the potential repercussions.' She needed to unload some of this and had opted for the confessional, the sentiments coming out in a rush.

'How'd it go?'

'Not well,' she grimaced. 'It'll be reported up the line and the likelihood is that I'll be suspended from duty. But at least it's out there,' Caroline said, shrugging her shoulders. She felt drained, and let out a big sigh before saying, 'Let fate and justice take their course.'

'Why will you be suspended?'

'Potential fraud in my area. Standard approach to suspend the person closest, the manager in charge. No presumed guilt, no stain on your record. So, they say.'

'What exactly did you discuss?' Olivia pressed.

'The whole steganography thing, over-payment on contracts...'

'And the question about contract awards?'

'No.'

'Why? If you're going to get all this out in the open, surely it has to be the whole thing?'

Caroline lapsed into a sullen silence and tuned out.

How can I?
Why can't I raise this?
The minister!
H!
Those wretched photographs.
It would crucify me personally and professionally.
And God knows what it'd do to my dad.

'Caroline? Talk to me,' Olivia pleaded. 'Is there something you haven't told me?'

Yes! But how can I? Not even you, dear friend.

'I've had enough. Don't want to talk about it anymore. I'm going to jack it all in.'

Caroline was in a dark place, as she wandered into the office, the weekend's reflections still reverberating. She was frustrated that for all her powers of logic…so she consciously tried to stop thinking altogether but failed to do even that. She felt depressed, ever more withdrawn. *Whatever next? The minister? H? Suspension?* With the blows seemingly raining down on her from all quarters, she felt punch-drunk.

Having muttered her good mornings to the team, she slumped in her chair. Her office staff had imparted the news that major benefits fraud had been uncovered; the police were close to cracking a scam that had defrauded millions by the use of false identities, foreign workers and bogus benefits claims. She was so fixated with her own problems it did not occur to her that this was Marku's scoop. She was just relieved it was not in her area. Thank goodness for that at least. Perhaps it would divert the fraud investigation service from her. *Ha! That's false hope girl and you know it. Nothing will make this go away. The only solution is to disappear.*

Just then, her reverie was broken by news that she had unscheduled visitors: DCI Bernard Hayles and DS Rachael Doyle. They met in one of the utilitarian rooms dotted around the Spartan offices of the department. Having shown their warrant cards, Bernard Hayles said, 'You met recently with Christopher Townsend and Elizabeth Standing, I understand?'

Caroline confirmed that was the case and enquired as to what interest this was to the police. DCI Hayles outlined the nature of his enquiries with reference to the attack on Mohammed Khatri and the potential link with Skills World and Ulysses but was sketchy on details. Caroline told them the meeting with Christopher and Elizabeth had revealed concerns about potential fraud. She also indicated that this resonated with some disquiet in the department that payments, mainly to Ulysses, had been excessive but that no evidence of any malpractice had been uncovered. Elizabeth had shared with Caroline her hypothesis and early findings about the hiding of illicit code in the various Dragonfly installations under Skills World's management control, a troubling revelation.

'And how do you know Horatio Pilkins?' asked Bernard, changing track. Caroline twitched before explaining the professional association.

'We hear Ulysses has been successful in winning business over the last year or so,' said Rachael.

'Yes.'

'Why do you think that is?'

'They won via competitive tendering processes, so I guess they had one of the best offers,' ventured Caroline, eyes cast down into her lap, intently studying her interlocking fingers.

'You manage those processes, don't you?'

'Yes.'

'You would know then?'

'Yes.'

'No need to guess then?'

'Just a figure of speech.'

'Do you not think it improper you and Horatio have a personal relationship as well?'

Silence.

'You do, don't you, Miss Hope?' demanded Bernard.

'Not any longer,' Caroline answered quietly.

'But you did?'

'Yes.'

'Do I have to spell this out for you? Can't you see how it looks?'

'What's this got to do with the matter you're investigating? The Mohammed assault.'

'We don't know yet – but there seems to be a link. We're trying to understand what it might be and whether there's a motive associated with these contracts which might take us to our *killer*.'

'*What*?' responded Caroline, raising her head sharply to establish eye contact with Bernard.

'Yes, Miss Hope. Mohammed unfortunately died a few hours ago from complications. This is a *murder* investigation now and we'd appreciate your assistance. You need to be a little more fulsome in your answers. So, what can you tell us – or do I have to insist on you joining us down at the station?'

'Oh *God*!' she exclaimed before breaking down…

Rachael stepped forward and offered some comfort, whilst Bernard retreated into the recesses of the room for a few moments, reviewing messages on his mobile. Once some degree of composure had been restored, Caroline was more forthcoming about the nature of her relationship with Horatio and of her shock at finding his circumstances had changed; that he was no longer the owner of HostIT and had become the CEO of Ulysses. She explained the consternation this had caused her, pleading with them to believe her.

'You didn't know he was heading up Ulysses?' he asked. The tone was one of incredulity. The question felt like a verbal assault. *How could I have been so naïve? So stupid?*

'Whether you believe it or not…' Her voice trailed off.

'Did you report this relationship formally, Miss Hope? To your superiors.'

'No.'

'Are you still in a relationship?'

'No.'

'Why, Caroline? What happened?' pressed Rachael.

'I found out. That and a red-headed bitch…'

'You mean you found out he was lying to you?'

'Yes,' she said.

'Who was the red-head?'

'No idea. Don't want to know. She's welcome to the manipulative, lying, scheming bastard.'

'Did anyone in the department know of your relationship with Horatio Pilkins?' asked the detective sergeant.

'No one. Except the minister,' Caroline added.

'Minister?'

'The secretary of state for work and pensions. The so-called Rt Honourable Sebastian Frith.'

'Not a fan then?'

'*No*!' she replied. 'He's a repugnant, bullying reptile.'

'Would you like to elucidate?'

'No.'

'Tell me, Miss Hope,' intervened Bernard, 'how did the minister respond? Was he surprised?'

'No. Seemed to know all about us.' She spat the words, as if clearing her throat of bile.

'Did he demand your resignation?'

'Quite the reverse. I offered it but he refused. He forbade me from reporting any indiscretions I may be guilty of and threatened me. *Bullied* me.'

'How?'

'Just threatened to destroy my career unless I did what I was told. He's not content to see my career in shreds, he's destroying me,' she said, tears rolling down her cheeks to form black mascara tracks. Caroline's distress made further discussion difficult, although Bernard managed to establish that she had met with the fraud investigation unit. She expected a team fraud investigator, or TIO, to be appointed to explore the matter further. Caroline felt fragile and exhausted – hardly able to answer their questions, unable to think straight at all. Thankfully, the meeting was suspended.

46. Time to Act

Christopher called an early morning impromptu meeting of his top team: Paul and Elizabeth. Whilst their strategy had yielded some evidence of malpractice they still did not have cast-iron evidence of over-payment and skulduggery. But they were surely only a step away from that; so close.

Elizabeth insisted the only way of proving the hypothesis was to either run dual returns from the two systems or to penetrate STRAP, effectively hacking into the government's system. Christopher and Paul recoiled in shock as either option had potentially damaging repercussions, but acknowledged her logic was flawless. But now, following the attack on poor Mo, the police were involved, and the government had been alerted to potential fraud.

'Mo's attack just has to have something to do with all this, doesn't it?' said Christopher.

'I think so,' answered Elizabeth, 'suggests he was close. *Too close.*'

Furthermore, it seemed certain that Caroline Hope would involve the fraud team inside the Department of Work and Pensions as well, and they had extensive powers; and she had already instigated a forensic audit of IT systems, Elizabeth reminded Paul and Christopher. The next decisive step doubtless had to be taken by either the police or the fraud team, probably by both acting in tandem. They could no longer pursue their own investigation in isolation. They had been sucked into this unholy mess and it was time to extricate Skills World. The situation was spiralling out of control; time to act decisively.

'What do you think, guys?' asked Christopher, wanting to see what solutions occurred to his team, testing his own thought processes and conclusions. The mood was sombre.

'First up, we need to write that formal letter to the department and take care in doing so,' suggested Paul.

'And we need to make clear that it's only Ulysses and Supreme returns that have been made via Dragonfly,' asserted Elizabeth, a smile lightening her features.

'What?' said Christopher and Paul in unison. 'That's not true, is it? We've been reviewing this whole situation for months now and—'

'I was *always* certain Ulysses were on the make,' interrupted Elizabeth, with venom in her voice. 'I didn't trust the unholy trinity of Horatio, Gregory and Eleanor. To hell with implicating Skills World!'

'Well, I'm staggered. Did it never occur to you to tell me, to share with both of us what was happening? We're supposed to be a team,' said Christopher, wide eyed.

'Are you complaining, or do you want to thank me?'

'Oh, for God's sake, Elizabeth. Sometimes…Look, Paul, draft that letter and check it out with both of us. Let's get that off today. We need to make it crystal clear we were coerced into adopting the Dragonfly system by Ulysses and strong-armed by Supreme. It was Skills World who decided to explore this matter at our cost. And we then took our preliminary results to both the police and the DWP. We're the good guys. Agreed?'

They nodded grimly.

'What about the legal letter threatening reprisal if we fail to comply with the Ulysses contract?' asked Paul.

'I've called in Jane Smith of Entwistle Partners to handle that.'

'Oh, have you indeed?' said Elizabeth.

'She's a bloody good corporate lawyer and knows the details of our deal. She'll also deal with the threatening letters.'

'And Supreme?' asked Paul.

'I have a plan,' declared Christopher with a look of fierce determination, 'but first I need to check it out with Jane and Ernest…'

Supreme Group HQ: 15:30

Christopher was joined by Paul and Jane Smith at the hastily arranged meeting with Georgina. The two Skills World executives had spent the morning with Jane working out their approach and checking through the legalities. As they waited for the summons into the CEO's office, the three conferred. Paul and Jane engaged in the technicalities and finer points, working out their likely legal and financial impact. Christopher sat back and looked around him, gathering his thoughts. He had found an inner tranquillity with the realisation he was pursuing an endgame to draw a line under this traumatic period. Christopher was at peace with that notion and his mind-set was philosophical, having set aside his driving ambitions for now. *I'll be back*, he promised himself. How, and in what field, he did not know.

As they waited, his mind meandered, before alighting on his legal adviser sitting just opposite him, calmly discussing key points with Paul, shapely legs crossed, skirt riding high. He could not help but admire the coiffured and striking image Jane presented; her curly blonde hair set off by a stylish black suit and scarlet blouse. A highly respected corporate lawyer with a razor-sharp brain who was content to display her femininity; she oozed confidence and sensuality. He wondered how the chemistry might work with Georgina. The assured CEO had more than a touch of arrogance, imbued by success in heading up a large and wealthy corporation. He imagined some sort of explosive chain-reaction and smiled at the prospect. Just then, his thoughts were interrupted by news they were to be granted admittance.

The Skills World team encountered a frosty reception, the greeting curt. Alexander Russia was present, as was a Supreme in-house legal advisor.

'Please meet Peter Henry,' said Alexander.

189

Handshakes ensued. Christopher swallowed his surprise at the unprepossessing man in their midst: a short, stocky character wearing a shabby brown suit and thick-rimmed spectacles. He sported long, grey hair that looked as if it had not been washed in weeks, scraped back into a short ponytail. The bedraggled image contrasted sharply with the power dressing of the two female executives and the business suits.

'What is it you want, Christopher? I'm not used to being instructed to attend emergency meetings,' said Georgina, fixing him with a hypnotic stare. Her striking red hair, now worn longer, flowed over the dark green and lace wrap dress. Her freckled face was set in a frown and her eyes seemed to be flashing warning signals.

'Thank you for seeing us at such short notice. I realise you have a limited amount of time so, let's get down to business. We aren't happy, we want *out*.'

'Oh, do you now? And why might that be?'

'I'd rather not get into the details but suffice to say Supreme's style of doing business isn't ours. Our values are different – *wholly* different.'

'What are you implying? You must be careful, Christopher. It won't have escaped your attention that our legal adviser is present. We won't hesitate to sue the arse off you,' she said. It was as if an anger was bubbling away in the magma centre just below the surface; a volcanic eruption seemed imminent.

'And nor will it have escaped your attention that I've mine present too. Look, I don't want a spat. We simply want out. I'm triggering the parachute clause,' said Christopher. His face was set, and his jaw thrust forwards.

'Well, you have to say something about your reasons,' indicated Alexander. Christopher sighed and carefully provided an overview of the findings of illicit code embedded in the Dragonfly systems, of their contingency plan, of the Mohammed Khatri assault, the involvement of the police and of the meeting with the DWP.

'I note that our hand was forced to sign the deal with Ulysses; of the pressure you placed me under to sign both that deal and the one with Supreme.'

'No pressure was exerted, and we observe that you signed. *Willingly*. No doubt driven by commercial opportunity and personal financial gain – so you can't grab some sort of moral high ground. You have contractual commitments, Mr Townsend,' said Alexander Russia.

'Supreme and Ulysses have a sinister, almost certainly criminal relationship; Ulysses has definitely engaged in criminal action and—' But the surprisingly aggressive intervention from Paul was cut short by a rapid-fire exchange between the lawyers. Paul also received a sharply rebuking aside from Christopher. He had allowed his frustration and emotions get the better of him, the last person Christopher would have expected this from.

'Please, let's all calm down. All I have to say is that we're intent upon executing the parachute clause within our contract. You will recall that we fought for the inclusion of that at the last moment before signing up to the equity share scheme. Let me be clear. I'm not making any allegations or offering any explanation as one isn't required by this clause. What I have said is simply contextual in the cause of openness and transparency. I'm disappointed to have reached this point but all I'm doing is executing the clause we signed up to.'

Georgina nodded silently, looked pointedly at Peter Henry and then slowly shook her head before addressing Christopher directly.

'So be it. You disappoint me. You realise you will only get a small return on your investment, don't you? You could have made millions had you the balls to see this through. I misjudged you.'

Turning to Peter and Alexander, she said, 'Sort it out, gents, and get these lily-livered people out of my hair.'

Georgina Harris then stood, leant forward over her outsized desk, hands planted, fingers splayed and fixed her stare on Christopher Townsend with fire blazing in her eyes. 'You now sacrifice one hundred percent of Skills World to *my* company, Christopher Townsend. You spineless coward. Get out of my office.'

She continued to stare at Christopher whilst instructing Alexander, 'Suspend him immediately, Alexander. Then sack Paul and Elizabeth and put in interim management. Get this all finalised within the week…'

The execution of Georgina's instructions brought to a close an era that had promised so much. Christopher's relief was tinged with a sense of unrequited promise. As they trooped out, Christopher caught hold of Jane's arm, telling Paul he would catch up with him shortly.

'Thanks for your support, Jane. A shame it has to end like this.'

'And that we weren't able to share another celebratory bottle of Bolly,' said Jane, reaching up to kiss him lightly on the cheek. 'Another time, Christopher,' she said, leaving him with his thoughts.

Christopher caught up with a solemn Paul. 'What are your plans this evening?' he asked.

'I intend to take Isobel to her favourite restaurant for a date-night as a surprise – all starched white tablecloths, candlelight, good food and a decent bottle of wine. I plan to celebrate. After all, we've made a small amount of money, we've got our severance deal to look forward to and we've been relieved of a whole lot of stress.'

'After that?'

'Dunno. Think about that tomorrow, but whatever I do will be after a short holiday, if I can persuade my nearest and dearest to take time out too. The promise of the Caribbean should do the trick. And you?'

'I'll check with Elizabeth and take it from there. To be honest, I don't feel like celebrating. It seems to me there's unfinished business here. And we should expect to hear more from DCI Hayles and Caroline Hope I guess…'

He and Elizabeth opted for a drink at one of their favourite pubs on the river at Teddington. Elizabeth settled for a Start Point gin served with tonic, lime and a sprig of rosemary. It was one of the small-batch gins that were on-trend, this one a London Dry Gin with spicy tones of juniper, coriander and cubeb punctuated with fresh citrus. Christopher opted for a pint of Fullers ale. As they sipped their drinks, they reflected upon the day's events. Elizabeth was seething with anger at Georgina's reaction, but relieved to get out from under the malign influences of both Ulysses and Supreme; to get away from Horatio and Gregory, from Georgina and Alexander.

'What does the future hold for you, Chris?'

'I've no idea professionally. But now, a line's been drawn under this there's a certain young lady who I need to ask a certain question of.'

'Oh yes? Anyone I know?'

'*Will* you, Elizabeth?'

'Will I *what*?'

'You know damned well. Please marry me, Elizabeth.'

She looked at him with a sparkle in her eyes and a smile playing around her lips.

'No special location or down-on-one-knee antics then? No romantic gestures? Right here in this packed pub? You want this to be the venue we will always remember when we look back at this seminal moment in our dotage?'

'You will then?'

'Mm. Okay then.'

'You *will*? You'll be my *wife*?'

'Yes, Georgie Boy.'

He sat motionless with a silly grin on his face, as Elizabeth studied him intently. Then the emotions released, tears flowed, and they embraced.

'Come on, Chris, let's go home. I need a shower and then you can take me somewhere special. Nice and expensive please.'

'Anything for the future Mrs Townsend,' he declared, swigging back the remnants of his beer and taking her by the hand.

Christopher and Elizabeth went back to his flat. Elizabeth was on cloud nine, they both were. They chatted animatedly about engagement rings, when and where to hold the wedding. They both favoured a small ceremony and a short engagement.

'But a nice big diamond ring, Georgie Boy. You don't get out of that. And let's have an engagement party. Just our best friends. Nothing fancy. They have a room at the Anglers in Teddington.'

'Or we could do it at The Wharf Restaurant,' suggested Christopher.

'Great idea. And an autumn wedding and...'

The evening proceeded in that vein until they eventually returned to business matters. Reflecting on the events of the day, Elizabeth turned to him.

'Are you really going to just walk away?'

'In the short term, I don't seem to have a choice.'

'And then? Start up another company?' she wondered, reaching for the champagne.

'No, I don't think so. I might try my hand at politics. I've always hankered after a political career and events seem to point to a change in direction. But first...'

'Yes?'

'There's unfinished business. I want to find out what's been going on. Who's behind this scam?'

'Surely the police will handle that. And the DWP's own fraud team?' suggested Elizabeth. She put her glass down and studied him. 'What can you do now?'

'I need to think about that but let's see. I'm not sure I share your faith that this whole business will be unearthed. I can't help wondering if there aren't malevolent political forces at work deep in the weeds. But come on, let's finish our champagne and before the future Mrs Townsend falls into a drunken stupor…' They chinked glasses and finished the contents swiftly. Christopher put his glass aside, took her hand and the two of them stumbled upstairs.

47. Clash of Cultures

11 July

As they waited in reception, Arnie and SS looked around their lavish surroundings. They sat opposite each other on deep, soft, black leather sofas with a glass-topped chrome table between them. The charcoal-grey carpet was topped by a rust-coloured Persian rug which lent a splash of colour, as did the red carnations on the table, reception desk and in the window recess. Various prints adorned the walls and a bronze statue held centre-stage in the Ulysses reception area.

Arnie prowled around the room, picking up and thumbing through various magazines – of high-fashion, design and travel. His shiny, weather-beaten suit, over-flowing belly and egg-stained tie jarred with his surroundings. He filled a glass with chilled water from the dispenser, took a deep draught and belched. Simon cringed, and the receptionist looked up with ill-concealed disgust. Arnie grinned at her, but she looked away scornfully.

'Who's this supposed to be then?' Arnie said, gesticulating towards the statue.

'Eros?' replied Simon, shaking his head.

'Who?'

'Greek mythology not your strong point then?'

'Missed that bit at my sink-school. Cover it at Eton, did we, Mr la-de-da?'

Their banter was soon interrupted with the news that the CEO was ready to see them, and they were waved through the doors and escorted to the inner sanctum to be met by a cheery Horatio Pilkins.

'Good morning, gentlemen. Please do take a seat. Can we get you anything? Tea? Coffee? Yes, do help yourself to the biscuits, inspector.'

'Detective Sergeant,' grunted Arnie. 'DS Arnold Forest and this is DS Simon Sterling.' They showed their warrant cards, but Horatio did not look.

'Quite, quite. Well, gentlemen, how might I assist you good fellows in your esteemed enquiries?'

'Well, first cut the bullshit and posh Tory-boy crap,' said Arnie. 'Doesn't wash with me.'

Horatio allowed an ingratiating smile to adorn his features, cocking his head to one side.

'And for starters, you can tell us about your crooked dealings, the bedding and corrupting of public servants and your dodgy corporate shenanigans,' Arnie added.

'My, my – do I see a throwback from the good old nineteen-seventies in my midst? A DI Regan or is it a lowlier DS Carter, I wonder?'

'Smart-arse cracks don't work either.'

'May I suggest a more civilised conversation,' suggested Simon, dimming the smile that had grown during the exchange.

'Ah ha. Is that the cultured voice of reason I hear? Very welcome too. Quite a team, aren't we, gentlemen? But really, I must gently press you to get to the point. As remarkably insightful as it is to be in your delightful company, I have duties I must attend to soon, I fear,' said Horatio, throwing a radiant smile at Arnie.

'What's your interest in Dragonfly and HostIT?' asked Simon.

'I used to run HostIT – and now I don't. They are merely suppliers to Ulysses as I'm sure your enquiries must have revealed. They also supply Skills World, if that's of any particular interest?'

'Not true!' barked Arnie, rubbing his belly whilst stifling a burp.

'I assure you, my good man, they do. They provide the system to Skills World which—'

'HostIT. You have a financial interest in that company,' interrupted Simon, his tone lighter.

'I have a small shareholding. Insignificant really.'

'But you *are* a shareholder, aren't you?'

'Well, yes, I suppose I am but, really, I carry no influence. I'm a passive pawn on that particular chess board,' offered Horatio, waving a hand in lofty dismissal.

'Would you call twenty-two percent insignificant, Arnie?' asked Simon, referring to his notebook.

'Wouldn't have thought so.'

'No. So that's a lie then. Let's move on, shall we?' Simon proposed.

'By all means. Yes, let's do that. Are you sure you gentlemen are comfortable? Any more coffees?'

'Got any instant?' asked Arnie.

'I don't believe so. Nothing but the real McCoy. But don't worry, I'll ask them to water it down for you. More biscuits as well, what? Yes, I think so.'

'Where's your system developed, sir?' Simon asked.

'System?'

'*Dragonfly!*' Arnie said, throwing his hands up and sighing.

'Let me remind you that I don't manage HostIT these days, but one likes to be helpful, so let me see. Mm, I believe it's developed in Blighty. Home-grown talent you know. Rather expensive, but there we are.'

'Lie number *two*. Racking them up, aren't we?' Arnie effected a false sickly-sweet smile. Horatio returned it. Simon revealed that they knew the software had been developed overseas, in Bangalore mainly. 'By "IT Mania" we understand,' he further clarified.

'You do seem to know rather more than me, gentlemen. I really can't imagine how this is helping you. But of course, I'm delighted to do my civic duty in assisting our admirable public servants,' he beamed.

'Tell us who the other shareholders of HostIT are,' demanded Arnie.

'All a matter of public record, I imagine, but let me see…I can't say that I know any of them particularly well, but I do believe the main shareholder is a lady called, err, June. No wait a minute, maybe Gloria? Yes, I'm pretty sure that's the dear lady's moniker – but what's her surname now?'

'Rogers?' suggested Simon.

'No, I don't think so. Doesn't ring a bell. Watson! Yes, that's it.'

'And so, we arrive at lie number – what is it Arnie?'

'Three. Three strikes and you're out,' ventured Arnie, leaning forwards, slowly shaking his head in mock disappointment.

'I do believe that is what the Guv said. We really aren't making much headway here are we, Mr Pilkins? So, we'd be grateful if you'd accompany us to the station to continue our chat,' said Simon.

'That means we get your smart-arse downtown and interview you on tape,' clarified DS Arnold Forest.

'Let's make an appointment for tomorrow, shall we? I really am most frightfully busy today and—'

'Nope. *Now.* You can help us voluntarily with our enquiries or we'll arrest you for obstructing the course of justice which, by the way, is now a *murder* investigation. So, *Mr Pilkins*, what's it to be?'

'Well, of course, if you put it like that, I'd be only too pleased to accompany you, err, gentlemen. I'll just make a call to my solicitor if I may?'

48. Breakthrough

DCI Bernard Hayles pulled his team around him to review proceedings, take stock and determine their next steps. They had a breakthrough which had persuaded his bosses to expand the team; even so they could only muster twelve detectives. Bernard welcomed the new team members, one of whom asked, 'Is this it? Is this the sum total of manpower on a murder investigation, Guv?'

''fraid so. I expect to see the numbers swell very soon, but in the meantime let's press on,' answered Bernard. He turned to Arnie and Simon. 'Where's Horatio?'

'Cooling his heels awaiting the arrival of his expensive lawyer.'

'Good. Let him stew a while.'

The murder weapon had been found, although forensic confirmation was yet to be received: an old rusty hunting knife. They had picked up the owner as well, a well-known drug addict and general low-life, Peter Green. He also confirmed that a used syringe had been located nearby.

'Pimply Pete?' cried Arnie and SS in unison.

'He's no murderer, is he? A petty thief and druggie yes – but a murderer?'

'It just looks as if it all went wrong. Rusty knife, a used syringe and the poor sod gets sepsis and God knows what else. Need to wait for the post-mortem results.'

'But surely, Guv, that can't be the whole story? What possible motive could he have?' asked SS.

'He was flush with cash, loaded with drugs and high as a kite when picked up.'

'So, what are you thinking? Paid to lop off his digits and it all went tits up?'

'Succinctly put in your inimitable style, Arnie, but that's about the size of it as far as I can see. He's with the medics and it's going to be some time before we get much sense out of him. But he keeps muttering something about a Hindu Boy. Mean anything to any of you?'

They all shook their heads.

'Nor me. We may well have the culprit who plunged the syringe and hacked off his fingers – but let's treat this as the next lead to follow up. I want the bastard behind this. What's the bigger picture? What's the motive? If it has anything to do with the steganography scam, then that's likely to rule out Pimply Pete as anything but the poor sod chosen to do the foul deed. He's certainly not bright enough to mastermind the fraud Christopher Townsend and Elizabeth Standing think is taking place. Where's the link back to Skills World? Ulysses? The delightful Horatio? And what about our minister? Arnie and SS, how's the tracking of corporate structures going?'

'Pleased you asked that, Guv,' said Simon. 'The easy bit is that Supreme acquired Skills World…'

'We know that, Mastermind,' interrupted Arnie.

'Yeah, yeah. The links are interesting, though. Look, I'll draw it on the board so even you can get your head around it.'

Simon proceeded to draw the various links between the different companies and then drew dotted lines to HostIT, the supplier of Dragonfly. He further explained that Gloria Rogers, nee Watson, was the majority shareholder married to none other than the minister of health. That drew a murmur of interest from his colleagues. Two ministers now seemed to feature in the wider panorama. He had also discovered that most of their software development was sourced from overseas companies. These were proving difficult to track down. Some were registered in the Cayman Islands, but with their operating teams based in Bangalore and Delhi in India.

'Company names and shareholders?' asked Bernard.

'A work-in-progress, I'm afraid, but I'd put money on them being none other than our slippery Horatio and the minister or his wife, Gloria. Working on it,' Simon responded.

'Hindu Boy?'

'No idea, guv.'

'And what's the link between Horatio and the other minister, Sebastian Frith?'

'We dunno yet,' said Arnie.

'Let's find out.'

'Need more resource on this,' grumbled Tracy, a middle-aged detective: one of the new team members. Bernard threw her a withering look.

'Been thinking, guv…' said Arnie, wearing a quizzical look.

'First time for everything,' offered Rachael.

'We don't even know there's a link between the Mohammed thing and Skills World, do we?'

'We don't have proof, but it appears that this was the only work he was doing,' said Rachael.

'But this could just be some sort of revenge attack for something personal. Drugs related or an argument with pimps or whatever. Just saying.'

'We're currently looking at Mohammed's various computers. He had a couple of pcs', a desktop pc and other external drives too. We should have an audit trail any time soon, so let's check that out, shall we?' said Bernard. 'Anything else?'

'Why don't we shake the minister's trees? Both of them,' suggested Simon.

'No. I don't want to go there until we understand these links better. But let's get on with the Horatio interview, the corporate structure and ownership strands. And I need to see the fraud guys in the Department of Work and Pensions. I'm meeting the head honcho later. We also need to get back to Caroline Hope. Right let's get to it guys and gals.'

49. Ministerial Intervention

Caroline was still expecting to be suspended, but in the meantime she was beavering away at everyday departmental business. The minutiae were mind-numbingly dull, anaesthetising her from the sinister, grubby realities. Hearing a commotion, she looked up sharply as the door burst open, slamming shut behind her unwanted, uninvited guest.

'A word in your shell-like, *Miss Hope*,' the minister sneered. The emphasis he placed on her name was laced with unspoken insult, his facial expression suggesting his sensitivities had been affronted as if by rancid, rotting detritus.

'Minister,' she answered flatly, her hand instinctively reaching for her mobile. She had suspected a visit was likely, sooner or later.

'Listen carefully,' he hissed, appearing to control his temper with difficulty. 'I warned you, Miss Hope. You wouldn't listen. You can only blame yourself.'

'What?'

'After this, the next step will be to the press and thereafter—'

'*What* are you talking about?'

'You know very well. If you are to limit the damage, then you will call off your internal audit people and their ridiculous investigation. Then you will speak with the fraud team that you so unwisely contacted yesterday. You will tell them your fears and allegations are without foundation – brought on by stress and over-work. You got your wires crossed.'

Caroline was shocked at his demeanour. His contorted face was scarlet red with blue veins standing prominent on his beak, spittle forming at the corners of his mouth. His venomous words were delivered in a loud, muffled whisper, as he evidently struggled to keep a lid on his inner fury.

'As if they're likely to believe that, and in any event the police are investigating. Somehow it's linked to a murder.'

'Oh, I think you'll find they have more pressing matters to pursue than this nonsense,' he said, a sardonic smile forming, slowly mutating into a forbidding sneer.

'Using your corrupt influence to pervert the course of justice?' Caroline said, with false bravado. The observation was met with a knowing grin.

'You have rather more to worry about when your misdemeanours become public,' he said.

'Just exactly what do you mean – what have you done?' asked Caroline. She was shaking, working hard to keep her emotions in check, determined not to break down in front of the minister.

The Rt. Honourable Sebastian Frith threw an envelope onto her desk, from which spilled two photographs. Of her.

X-rated.

Pornographic.

Filthy, shameful images.

Caroline gasped.

'Wh…What have you done?'

'It's what *disgusting* things you've done young lady. Copies of those were sent in the post to Reverend Hope. Special delivery. He should get them any time soon…' He delivered the news with a cruel leer as he bent over to take a closer look. 'My, they're revealing, aren't they?'

'You haven't? You *bastard*. Please, no. Please tell me you haven't. I'll do anything, *anything*. Please.'

'Already done. Next one goes to—'

'You bullying, first-class bastard. I quit…'

Caroline flew at the minister and struck him before he could react – and with such force, he fell backwards, knocking a chair and various files flying to land in a crumpled heap on the floor. Pinpricks of blood appeared above his eyebrow where he had caught the chair on the way down.

'You vicious little *whore*. Prepare to see yourself in the red-tops, *slut*.'

Caroline pulled the door open and stopped in her tracks, the gathering office staff gawping at the prostrate minister who sported red wheals across his face, a cut above his eye, blood dribbling down his cheek. She tore her eyes away from her nemesis and faced her team, before angrily declaring to them, whilst pointing at the Rt Honourable Sebastian Frith.

'That corrupt bastard has been threatening me, blackmailing me. He's ruined me—'

She stormed through the office, her entire staff staring open-mouthed.

50. Cul-De-Sac

It was mid-afternoon and the breakthrough with the arrest of Pimply Pete had given the team fresh momentum. Adrenalin was coursing through their veins as they pursued the various strands of the investigation.

'How far have you got with the corporate structure, Simon? Ulysses and Supreme first.'

'Supreme is a successful global company operating in this market space. A highly credible corporation with a reputation for delivering great results for shareholders. It's driven by a ruthless, flame-haired beauty called Georgina Harris. She transformed the company and is hugely admired. Doesn't suffer fools gladly.'

'Got the hots for her then?' said Arnie.

'Let's quit the smart-arsed cracks.'

'Sorry, guv.'

'As far as we can see, Supreme has no formal relationship with Ulysses other than via the Skills World alliance,' Simon elaborated.

'Any common shareholders?'

'Nope.'

'Turning to HostIT – who developed their system?'

'We know that 'IT Mania' wrote at least part of it. They operate mainly out of Bangalore, but also have bases in Delhi and Singapore. Again, there is a complicated corporate structure which seems to track back to a Cayman Islands registered company.' Simon paused, and banged his fist on the table, shaking his head in apparent frustration.

'Shareholders?' demanded Bernard.

'Dunno, guv. Need a bit more time and some co-operation from the authorities…' Simon shrugged his shoulders and sighed.

'What about Hindu Boy then? What have you got, Arnie? Rache?'

'Some news here, guv. Hot off the press. The geeks have unravelled the security on Mohammed's pcs. Found several threatening messages. Most of them are pseudonyms but there is one from someone called Anirudhh. May be Hindu Boy? But we can't find any link back to "IT Mania" or to "HostIT",' explained Rache.

'Can our Indian friends help?'

'Where do we even begin to look, guv? There are thousands of Anirudhh's in Bangalore, let alone elsewhere. I made some tentative enquiries, but they have so much crime. In Bangalore alone over five-hundred kidnappings every year, three-hundred murders, the second highest number of rape cases in India, the highest…'

'Okay, I get the picture. Any news from forensics yet?'

'The provisional indications are that he got sepsis from the knife wounds, plus HIV, which may have been from the used syringe. And hepatitis B. They can't prove that HIV was from that particular syringe though. He was a regular drug user and could have contracted it years ago. But, apparently the attack on the immune system left him with no chance once he contracted sepsis. The report will be a few more days whilst they run other tests,' said Rachael.

'Arnie, what did you get from your upper-class twit?'

'Lots of hot air, lashings of smugness and an expensive lawyer to rub salt into the wounds. He's guilty of something but Christ knows what. He's a lying bastard but we've not got much to go on, Guv. Mind you—'

'Yes? Spit it out.'

'It's not much but, checking my notes, he does seem to have had a fling with the gorgeous Georgina in the dim and distant—'

'For Christ's sake, Arnie, why didn't you say so earlier? Follow it up. Do they still have a dalliance? Are they in cahoots somehow? And keep him here in the meantime.'

'Will do, guv. Sorry,' said a downcast Arnie.

The team went on to discuss their findings about the ministers under question, the minister of health and the secretary of state for work and pensions. Apart from the obvious link of being from the same political party and working in government together, they had also been at University together. There had been rumours of sordid activity by Roland Rogers who allegedly had an unhealthy interest in children. But there was no evidence to substantiate this. All they had managed to prove was that Roland Rogers was effectively the major shareholder of HostIT through his wife, Gloria. But it was not even clear that he had breached any parliamentary rules let alone been responsible for corrupt or criminal activity.

As for Sebastian Frith, he had clearly upset Caroline Hope, but her claims seemed to be of bullying rather than anything more sinister. They needed to pick up the interview with Caroline, but she seemed to be an unstable, emotional wreck. Then there were the claims of fraud which were now being investigated by the team within the DWP, working co-operatively with the police.

They were not making the progress DCI Hayles demanded. He rubbed a furrowed brow. His superiors were breathing down his neck and the pressure to close the investigation down and simply focus on Pimply Pete was becoming hard to resist. The team had spent much of the day in this small office, which was littered with mugs, take-away cartons, half-eaten pizzas; the air was fetid from the proximity of adrenalin charged, tired, sweaty bodies. It was a warm, airless day so the open window did not greatly help. The atmosphere was heavy.

Bernard looked up as the door opened and his superior's boss, Chief Superintendent Harriet String, poked her head in, wrinkled her nose and signalled she would like a word. He glanced at his team – who had all stopped their discussions mid-flow – and then followed her out of the room. This would provide the opportunity to press for more manpower. There were still many strands to investigate and too little time and resource to do so.

DCI Hayles returned twenty minutes later in a dark mood, and declared to the assembled detectives, 'Last chance saloon guys. Unless we have a breakthrough by close of play today, we are to deal with Peter Green first thing tomorrow. Then we're being re-assigned to a new case.'

'What? That's bollocks,' blurted Arnie, throwing his bulk back into his chair which creaked its protestations.

'Why, guv?' asked Rachael.

'Dunno.'

'I smell political pressure from above. I bet we're getting too close for comfort and one minister or another is wielding his influence. It stinks,' said Arnie.

'Mm. That's as maybe, but let's not waste time with speculation. We have work to do...I hope none of you were planning an early night. Let's give it one last push,' said Bernard.

'Where'd you like to start, guv?' asked Rache.

'Pick up Caroline. Rattle her cage. She knows more than she's said so far. Get over there before she signs off for the day. Bring her in Rache. You join her Arnie. And SS, you and I'll go and speak to Sebastian Frith. Let's see what he's got to say.'

'I thought you wanted to save that until—'

'We no longer have the luxury of time on our side. Okay, it's nearly five o'clock, let's move.'

51. Interception

Caroline stormed past her team and grabbed her jacket, sending the coat stand crashing as she burst through the door. Heading for the lifts, she fumbled in her pocket to extricate her mobile. *I must ring Daddy. Must get there before the post. He mustn't open that envelope.* She was perspiring freely now, her breathing shallow and panicked. She was all fingers and thumbs. Desperately, she scrolled for the contact. The realisation that he was not even in her 'favourites' struck like a splinter of guilt.

Found it.

She hit the green phone.

Nothing. Just a dull monotone sound. She hit it again. Same result.

Oh, Christ you've not paid the bloody bill, have you? Cut yourself off. Please, no, please, Daddy. She tried yet again but the result was no different. *I have to get up there. What time are the trains? I'll just dash to the station, but no. I need to go home, pick up a few things and…*

'Miss Hope, we'd like a word please.' Caroline looked up to see DS Doyle and DS Forest.

'Not now,' Caroline half-shouted.

'It won't wait, Miss Hope,' said Rachael. 'Are you all right?'

'No, I'm not and, please, I have no time. You'll just have to wait.' With that, she tried to push past, but Arnie's considerable bulk blocked her path.

'We can't take no for an answer, Miss Hope. If you won't come voluntarily…' said Arnie. But he stopped abruptly, as a dishevelled Sebastian Frith, holding a bloodied handkerchief to his face and muttering profanities, rushed past them and down the stairs. Rachael had also taken in the scene and stepped to one side to ring Bernard Hayles.

Caroline implored the detectives to allow her to make a call. But it was another failed attempt to reach first her father and then Edith. The detectives encouraged her into the car and took her to the station. In the rush-hour traffic, progress was slow. By the time they arrived, it was past six-thirty.

Caroline lapsed into silence. She could not rid her mind of that disgusting image of herself. Whatever had she been thinking of? Her father would be mortified. In his weakened, cancer-ravaged state, he might not withstand the shock. She was so full of shame and remorse. She disgusted herself. *I can't bear this. If he sees those photographs…*

'Had you been meeting with the minister, Caroline?' pressed Rachael.

'Yes. Please, I need to go.'

'What was it about? Did you argue?'

'He's a reptile…bullying…ruining me.'

'You had an argument?'

Caroline nodded.

'Did you hit him? We saw his bloodied face—'

'Got out of hand. I might have pushed him, and he fell.'

'Nothing else?'

'No.'

Eventually, the police decided to let her go. It was gone eight o'clock and the evening seemed to be leaching away. It would take another half an hour before Caroline emerged from the police station.

52. Forest Towers

Bernard took himself into his private office, Rachael following.

'We're running out of time, Rache. Too many unanswered questions; too many tenuous links. If only they could…but they were interrupted by Arnie, who seemed unusually animated.

'I think we have something, guv.'

'About bloody time—'

'I've been looking into the links between Horatio and Georgina and the ministers. Guess what? Horatio went to the same boarding school as both Roland Rogers and Sebastian Frith, a place called Forest Towers. It's an exclusive school in Surrey with both preparatory and upper schools spanning the ages of eight to eighteen.'

'And?'

'Our two ministers and Horatio were there at the same time. Sebastian and Roland are a bit older, so the overlap was only a couple of years.'

'Okay…where are you going with this?'

'I tracked down the headmaster, now retired. It seems he also recalled the three of them; he positively paled when I challenged him about the rumours—'

'Arnie, time's running out. What have you got?'

'I'd like you to meet Agnes, a retired cleaner from Forest Towers. The headmaster helpfully suggested I might like to speak with her…I had to lean on him a little, but he came good,' Arnie explained, smiling broadly.

'Okay, where is she?'

'In a meeting room down the corridor—'

'Let's go then.'

'Just before we do that…'

Arnie proceeded to tell Bernard that he had tied Horatio to Sebastian Frith. He had a report from his questioning of the reception team at the DWP offices in Westminster of the two meeting there recently. He also had CCTV film confirming that account.

'I've managed to track down footage of the two piling into a black cab outside the DWP offices and heading off together, and of them entering a building some twenty minutes later. Sebastian's flat.'

'Good work, Arnie. Now let's see what Agnes has to say for herself.'

On entering, Bernard was met with a frail, wizened old lady sitting primly at the table, hands together as if in prayer. Arnie was gentle with her, coaxing her in conversation, empathetic. Arnie asked Agnes to tell her story. She smiled at him and sensitively recalled an incident of more than three decades ago as if it were yesterday…

'I'll never forget it. The poor mite. I was a cleaner you see and always did earlies. First stop was the boys shower rooms in the upper school. Boys are such messy, untidy creatures you know. Anyway, there he was. Naked as the day he was born, sat shivering in a corner, all bloodied. A pathetic sight. We'd always hear of these awful tales of bullying and buggering and all of that sort of stuff…' Agnes paused and reached for a tissue to wipe away a silent tear forming in the corner of her eye. She was clearly reliving the moment. Arnie refilled Agnes's glass with water and encouraged her to continue in her own time.

'He wouldn't say a word. He was shaking, almost comatose; his hands drawn around his skinny knees. A pathetic, heart-rending sight to behold, I'll tell you. Of course, he shouldn't even have been there. He'd be about eight or nine and should have been in the prep school dorm. How he got there and what he experienced…well, I'll leave you to imagine.'

'What did you do then, Agnes? Can you remember?'

'Of course I can,' she said. 'I could hardly forget, could I? I got a blanket, wrapped it around him and carried him to the sick bay. He was all skin and bone, no weight at all and anyway I was a bit bigger in those days,' she chuckled, before continuing. 'He never said a word and didn't for the next two weeks. His physical injuries soon cleared up although I'd skin the little bastard alive if I knew who'd done it.'

'What was his name, Agnes?'

'Horatio. Horatio Pilkins…'

Arnie glanced at his boss. Bernard returned the look and then asked Agnes if the culprit had been found but she thought it had all been hidden away to protect the school's reputation. She had little more to add and after signing a statement was taken home by one of the detectives.

Arnie further revealed that he had spoken with the headmaster at length, a Hugh Jenkins-Smyth. He had initially stalled but in the end admitted that the school had a difficult problem with sexual malpractices, as he put it, but never an incident as serious as the one involving Horatio; not that he could recall. The culprits were never identified; they had covered their tracks well and Horatio could never be persuaded to identify them. Arnie recalled the next dialogue for Bernard's benefit, reading from his notebook:

'Plural?' asked Arnie.

'Sorry?'

'You said culprits – not culprit.'

'We know there were two of them. It's all very unsavoury, I'm afraid. It seems that one held the poor child whilst the other acted…if you see what I mean.'

'Who did you suspect?'

'Mm. Rumours abounded but nothing concrete and to be honest we didn't look very hard. Boys will be boys you know. I know how that sounds but—'

'It's bloody disgusting, that's how it sounds…you should be ashamed of yourself…'

Bernard and Arnie joined the rest of the team and gave them the heads-up on the latest turn of events. Simon had also made some progress on uncovering the corporate structures, having secured some assistance from the financial regulatory authorities. It seemed that not only had HostIT's Dragonfly system been partially developed by IT Mania, but they had also been sub-contracted in the development of STRAP, the DWP's system. Through an elaborate structure of ghost companies, he had managed to identify three key shareholders: Gloria Rogers, an Anirudhh Sharma and a certain Georgina Harris.

'Bingo! Both Georgina and Gloria. Effectively establishing a link with not only Horatio but also with Roland Rogers,' said an excited Rachael.

'There's more, guv,' Simon declared, smiling at Rachael's interjection. 'IT Mania's parent company is a "Zzz Limited". Interesting name, don't you think? Anyway, about forty percent is owned by Gloria, fifty percent by Anirudhh and the remainder by Georgina.'

'I've got a theory, guv,' interrupted Arnie.

'I'm all ears.'

'It seems to me we're close but about to be timed out. Yes?' He received a curt nod from Bernard. 'Let's take a risk. Let's go for Horatio aggressively and tell him we have a search warrant for his home and business premises,' suggested Arnie.

'But we don't. He's not daft, why would he swallow that?'

'You suspect Roland and Sebastian were the Forest Towers culprits, don't you?' speculated Rachael.

'Yup,' said Arnie, 'a bit of a leap in the dark I know, but what else do we have? Just lots of circumstantial evidence; nothing of real substance. Can't we seek that warrant anyway? I can't see what we have to lose...'

53. Horatio

Arnie and Bernard pulled Horatio into an interview room. They had decided to marshal their arguments as persuasively as possible, citing what little evidence they could muster. This time, Bernard led the session.

'Sorry to keep you waiting all this time, Horatio. Are you happy for us to continue?'

'My dear chap, do we really have to go over all this yet again – and at this time of night? You've nothing on me, so either charge me with some trumped-up allegation or let me go.'

'I can't do that. There've been developments which seem to cast you in the role of victim, actually.'

'Intriguing.'

'Would you like to relate your experiences of Forest Towers, Horatio? Can you recall the bloodied and buggered eight-year-old, I wonder?'

Horatio blanched.

The detectives pressed Horatio, but he soon recovered his poise. In the end, he admitted there had been some sort of incident, claiming it was just horseplay that had got out of hand.

'Who were the abusers, Horatio?'

'Goodness me, it was so long ago…'

'Roland Rogers and Sebastian Frith, by any chance?'

'I've no idea who you're talking about.'

'Ministers of the crown; acquaintances of yours?'

'Certainly not.'

Arnie leant forward and hissed, 'Stop pissing us about.' He showed him the CCTV evidence; of Horatio with the Rt Honourable Sebastian Frith at two different venues including the one outside the minister's house.

'You see, Mr Pilkins, we know that you have dealings with the two ministers; we know you were the victim of a serious assault that left you traumatised. You didn't speak for weeks. We've spoken with Agnes and your ex-headmaster.'

'Who?'

'You know who your assailants were…' said Bernard.

'And you determined to get your revenge, didn't you? We also know that you and Georgina Harris go back some way. Lovers still, aren't you?' prompted Arnie.

'I can't think what that—'

'I've had enough. Last chance, Horatio. If you want any sort of leniency, then come clean. I have a search warrant for your flat,' Bernard said, waving it in the air.

'Let me see that,' demanded his solicitor. A valid search warrant had indeed been issued.

'What will we find?' demanded Bernard.

But for once, Horatio had nothing to say and lapsed into thoughtful silence.

'I need a few minutes with my client...' said the solicitor.

'By all means. Take as long as you like. Meanwhile, we have a search to undertake, gentlemen. Oh, just one thing before we go. Keys? Or would you prefer that we...'

Horatio sighed, reached into his jacket pocket and tossed them over.

54. Northumberland Bound

Rushing out of the police station into the squally summer's evening, rain swept in to drench her as she hailed a cab. Just then, her mobile beeped to indicate several missed calls. Olivia. She ignored them.

'Kings Cross Station, and quick, please.'

'Right you are, love. Hold tight.'

There was no time to go home and grab a much-needed shower or pack a case. She had already missed the last flight to Durham, so had to rely on a train. She would certainly miss the 21:00 to Newcastle so she was aiming for the last train at 22:00. She was going to be hard-pressed to catch even that. It was not due to get to Newcastle until gone two o'clock in the morning, and it would be about another hour to get to the rectory.

In the event, Caroline caught it with minutes to spare. *Oh, please God the special delivery has failed to arrive. Maybe the minister was bluffing?*

As the train pulled out of the station, she went to the toilets. She removed her top and washed under her arms as best she could, splashed water on her face and dabbed herself dry with paper towels. Delving into her handbag, she extricated her cosmetics bag, made up her face, applied lipstick and sprayed perfume. Hopefully, the scent would counter some of the odours, the ravages of her day. Smoothing down her skirt and top, she returned to the carriage.

As the train headed north, she grabbed her mobile. Time to catch up with those missed calls. Most were from Olivia, who had left three messages.

18:05: What the hell's going on, babe? Did you really hit SF? Well done, you! Call me.

19:30: Where are you? Getting worried about you. Call me. Please!

20:43: You're freaking me out! Call! Please Caroline.

One was from a number she did not recognise. She did recognise the voice though:

20:53: Delivery made, bitch. You'll pay for this. Next envelope goes tomorrow morning. Then for the general release – bound to go viral.

55. Notting Hill

21:25

They entered the Notting Hill flat, snapped on the obligatory disposable blue nitrile gloves and began a painstakingly thorough search.

'What exactly are we looking for, guv?' asked Rachael.

'Anything to do with Ulysses, Supreme or Skills World; any communications, data, information that might suggest illicit…You know the loose ends and suspicions as well as me. We need some concrete evidence.'

They started in the hall. Nothing in the table drawers, nothing in coats other than old bills, receipts, sweet wrappers. Nothing in the cupboards except books and mundane business papers; nothing suspicious or interesting. Then in the lounge: books, ornaments, newspapers, magazines, bottles of gin and whisky, glasses, TV controls, keys. Still nothing out of the ordinary.

They were more hopeful in the bedroom.

'Blimey,' declared Arnie, at the sight of the over-the-top, mirror-ceilinged room. The initial search found little in the wardrobes and drawers, other than male and female clothes. Presumably, Horatio's and Caroline's? Or Georgina's? They would check that out. Turning to one of the bedside tables, Arnie opened it and stepped back momentarily, focused his eyes and then delved inside.

'The dirty get.'

He had found adult sex toys, pornographic DVDs and filthy magazines. The other bedside table revealed a similar horde.

'Consenting adults and all that,' said Rachael.

And beyond this, there was nothing remotely interesting or sinister concerning the ministers, Horatio, Georgina Harris, or of any evidence indicative of fraudulent or criminal activities. Suddenly, a cry went up from Rachael and Simon.

'Guv. Over here.'

Behind a poster of the Kamasutra, was a large wall safe. Sure enough, one of the keys Horatio had handed over worked, and Simon carefully extracted the contents, handing them to Rachael to place on the bed. A cursory glance was enough to convince them they had found a horde of incriminating material. The printed photographs were the most immediately shocking, showing extraordinarily explicit images of a young woman.

'Who's that?' asked Arnie peering over Simon's shoulder.

'No telling…wait a minute, there's one here of her face. Oh my God – look who it is.' They looked at each other, eyebrows raised before carefully placing the material in an evidence bag along with numerous documents, flash drives, a PC and an external hard drive.

'Let's get it back to base, guys. We can grab coffees and something to eat on the way; an all-night shift is in store for you lucky people,' said Bernard.

56. Slow Progress

The journey seemed to be taking for ever. As Caroline settled back into her seat, her mind turned over the twists and turns of her life, particularly the last few years during which so much had gone so tragically wrong. Just then, her musing was shrilly interrupted…

22:45: Her mobile chirruped and this time she answered it, speaking quietly. Her energy had completely drained away, her voice flat. It was Olivia, of course.

'At *last*! Where are you, Caroline? I've been around to your flat twice but…What on earth's going on. I heard from the girls in the office about your fracas with the charming Sebastian. Caroline? Where are you? Speak to me…'

'It doesn't matter anymore,' Caroline whispered, slumping in her seat, as she watched the countryside go by all too slowly. 'I just hope I'm not too late.'

'For what?'

'Oh, forget it…nothing to do now…'

'Just tell me where you are. You're not making any sense, babe.'

'Thanks for being my friend. I'm sorry, I'm truly sorry. Goodbye, Olivia…'

Caroline hit the red button and turned her mobile off.

She glanced around her immediate surroundings, taking in her fellow passengers for the first time. Something to focus on, a distraction. There were very few in her carriage – a couple of businessmen had consumed a few beers, the tinnies littered around them, and were now slumbering and snoring; a group of noisy students who, she gleaned from their drunken conversation, had been partying; an old lady who had fallen fast asleep, her book resting in her lap, glasses sitting atop her silver curls.

The East Midlands cities of Leicester and Derby slid by, and as the crooked spire of Chesterfield appeared, she reached for her PC. Her time could be used to pen emails: to that right honourable scoundrel, The Rt Honourable Sebastian Frith, to H and to Olivia.

As she busied herself, Sheffield and Leeds slipped past, before it was time to change at York. Composing the emails, firstly in her head, helped while away the time. It was diverting, almost cathartic. For now, at least, Caroline had spent all her tears and her feelings were numb, as if some narcotic had snatched away her senses. She was becoming philosophical about what lay ahead. *I've brought this all on myself. But I'll let the minister and H both know what I think of them: bastards!* She was determined to do what she could to ensure that justice prevailed; she would face the inevitable consequences of her own sins and considerable shortcomings. But she would also ensure that others would similarly meet the full force of the law for their crimes, for their sins. *But how Christian is that?* she asked herself with a jolt. Retribution or forgiveness? Caroline sat back and tussled with conflicting notions that she weighed on virtual scales of justice. How to act in this most precarious of predicaments? There could be no doubt that she had fallen foul of several of the Christian capital sins: lust for sure; pride in pursuing her own career advancement; gluttony and greed in the literal consumption of fine food and alcohol, but also in pursuit of higher rewards. And now, she was set on committing another sin: wrath in the pursuit of revenge. But there was only so much anyone could take. Eventually, she set aside these conflicting thoughts to focus on her task, pounding the keyboard at first tentatively, but soon getting into her flow as the pent-up feelings transposed into prose. In what little time was left, she would set the record straight, ensuring that those who had been so utterly corrupt – cruel even – were held accountable for their acts. And then, she could meet her own destiny. She finished her work and re-read them for the umpteenth time:

Caroline
To H,
Cc Christopher Townsend; Elizabeth Standing; Olivia; Margaret Shanklin
Re Bastard!
*Good morning, **BASTARD**. You have a few shocks in store today. I thought I once loved you, H...that you loved me. How wrong could I have been? You <u>cheated</u> on me with some red-haired bimbo. I can still see the two of you. You <u>used me</u>, <u>manipulated</u> me. Joined forces with the **<u>despicable Sebastian Frith</u>**. I am ashamed of our relationship, disgusted with what we did and <u>appalled at your criminally corrupt behaviour</u>. Contracts were outrageously and unlawfully awarded to Ulysses. I know you're ripping off the government. I know you've embedded code in your systems and penetrated STRAP. You've been **<u>grossly overpaid at Ulysses</u>**. I know you're in cahoots with the minister. Don't you dare try and blame Christopher Townsend or Elizabeth Standing either! They are decent people who reported their findings and suspicions. You've destroyed my career. Destroyed my life. I loathe you. You are a **<u>CORRUPT,</u>** manipulative **BASTARD** of the first order under all that posh, upper class twaddle you use to deceive. <u>Rot in hell,</u> H.*
Caroline

Caroline Hope
To Sebastian Frith,
Cc Christopher Townsend; Elizabeth Standing; Olivia; Margaret Shanklin
Re Bastard!
I will get to the point swiftly. You've <u>destroyed</u> my career and <u>my life</u>. You've constantly subjected me to bullying and harassment. At a private suite in St Ermins hotel, you <u>bullied</u> and <u>threatened</u> me – assaulted me. Under your instruction, I was forced to breach competitive tendering rules and award contracts to those you wanted to win...mainly to <u>Ulysses</u>. You've instructed and

bullied me to block attempts by our internal audit teams to uncover the <u>*corrupt over-payments to Ulysses*</u>*. I can only assume you have a direct kickback arrangement. The photos you bribed me with are disgusting and taken under duress. Sebastian Frith – you are a **CORRUPT BULLY** abusing your power for your own ends. I can't cope anymore. You sought to destroy my father. You've destroyed me. May you go to **<u>hell</u>** for eternity…You disgust me! People need to know about you. Goodbye and good riddance.*

Caroline

She saved them to her drafts folder. Finally, she was happy with the result. *Happy? Ha!*

Half an hour out of Newcastle, she packed the pc away. The emails would save until later. A final check in due course and then maybe she would hit send. *Maybe?* Of course, she would, and she took a moment to imagine how they might be received. How smugness might be replaced by shock and a dawning realisation that their sins had found them out, their crimes had been exposed. But it was now time to focus on the here and now, on the immediate future. How would she find her father? Caroline wondered to what extent his health would have further deteriorated. It suddenly occurred to her that he should be fast asleep at this time. Hopefully, he still kept a spare key in the usual place.

Stepping onto a nearly deserted platform, she shivered and pulled up the collar of her coat to afford some degree of protection from the bitter easterly wind. Whipping in from the North Sea, it was bitingly cold even at this time of year. She made her way through the station and emerged to find the taxi rank. Fortunately, a sole taxi was there for her to climb into. Glancing at her watch, it was now nearly two-thirty in the early morning. Her turban-attired driver told her it would be about forty minutes to reach her destination. Caroline sighed and fell back into the seat, exhausted. It was as if she was sleepwalking through the horror story that had been her life.

57. Piecing Together the Jigsaw

On reaching the office, they divided into two teams, Simon and Rachael taking the flash drives and computers, Bernard and Arnie the documents and photographs. They had called in reinforcements to assist with the process but they knew they had more work to undertake than time available. Nonetheless, they soon pieced together enough to be able to confront Horatio…

02:40: Bernard reconvened a meeting with Horatio and his long-suffering solicitor. This time, he took Simon with him as the team's resident technology expert.

'Okay, Horatio, the game's up. We've got enough to put you away for a long stretch.'

Horatio looked at him askance, seemingly gauging the extent to which they were bluffing. He would have known they would find the safe, but he played dumb, presumably holding on to the last vestige of hope. Bernard sighed, and then proceeded to lay out several of the explicit photographs. His solicitor's eyes grew wide, as he took in what lay before him.

'Now do you believe us? Tell us who this is, Horatio,' he demanded, banging his fist on the table.

'Caroline,' he said quietly.

'Speak up for the tape. Surname as well, if you please.'

'Caroline Hope. But she was a consenting adult. No crime there…' he suggested, but his response was shorn of its customary confidence.

'And can you explain these messages please, sir,' asked Simon, putting various emails and documents in front of him. Horatio gave them a cursory glance before slumping in his chair. After a pause, he quietly answered the detective.

'Yes, I can…look, I only wanted retribution. They had to pay for what they did.'

'Which was?'

'You know full well. The bastards raped me.'

'Names?'

'Sebastian Frith did the wicked deed, whilst Roland Rogers pinned me over a table.'

'But it's not just these two paying the price is it? It's the British taxpayer. What possible justification can you have for that?'

217

'Can we do a deal?' Horatio asked, eyes now pleading. All his upper-class complacency, swagger and chutzpah having dissipated.

'*No!*' thundered Bernard. 'The best you get is to co-operate and maybe, just maybe, the courts will take that into account as a mitigating factor in sentencing you.'

Over the next two hours, the story slowly came together. He revealed how he had gained competitive advantage by a combination of his wooing and corrupting of Caroline, and by the hold he had over Sebastian Frith and Roland Rogers. How contracts had been illegally awarded by ministerial intervention and the corrupting of a departmental official – Caroline; how the various returns via Dragonfly had skewed payments from STRAP. Money had been misappropriated from government by illicit contract awards in contravention of European tendering rules; from over-payment by manipulating returns of vocational training and welfare to work activity; from insider knowledge.

'Not to forget the blackmailing of Miss Hope as well.'

'I only ever intended to persuade her to stay quiet. I genuinely meant her no harm. She was a naïve innocent in this drama, I'm afraid. I do feel sorry for her.'

'A bit bloody late for contrition, isn't it?'

'Mm.'

'Tell us about Georgina Harris.'

'Oh hell. I promised I'd never…look, I employed people to investigate Roland and Sebastian. You will have found the evidence, no doubt. It's all there. Sebastian's a disgusting, depraved, evil paedophile with a penchant for small boys; Roland's a misogynist cad and paedo with a sexual predilection for teenage girls.'

'Tell us about Georgina?' said Bernard. Horatio looked up at the two of them and raised his eyebrows in a look of ill-concealed disgust.

'She was one of the girls abused by Roland?' Simon said, slapping his hand on the table.

'Yes,' he said forlornly, shaking his head. 'Roland raped her repeatedly. She was only thirteen at the time. I found her, and together we vowed to wreak our revenge. In our way, not through the authorities…'

'And you've known about all this criminal abuse for how many years? You let them inflict their havoc on how many young people? You're just as bloody evil as them. Aren't you? *Aren't you?*'

Horatio glanced up at him before turning away. They took a short break to allow the points to sink in, and for the detectives to check and assimilate their information…

Resuming, Bernard changed tack.

'Now tell us about the numerous bank accounts…one-hundred and five and still counting. False identities, I'm sure we'll find. You can help us short-circuit our enquiries, Horatio.'

'That might count for something…' suggested Simon.

'Oh hell.' H paused and placed his head in his hands before slowly nodding his assent.

'It was run by Roland mainly – and Rupert, with input from Sebastian…'

'Rupert?' prompted Simon.

'Rupert Watson, Gloria's son. They ran a scam to rake in benefits using Romanians, Bulgarians and Poles who they armed with false IDs...they couldn't speak much English but were promised work...took out bank accounts that benefits were paid into. They were quite creative about the numbers of children and the nature of housing benefits claimed as well as out of work allowances, I believe.'

'The bank accounts were controlled by Roland and his merry band I assume?' said Simon.

'I doubt Roland would get his hands dirty...but yes, essentially.'

'And the immigrants?' asked Bernard.

'Just turned out on the streets or dumped back in Dover with a ferry ticket. Never got work and paid a small fraction of the benefits claimed—'

'Imprisoned and enslaved?'

'I guess you could say so.'

'And you received a cut?' probed Simon.

'I had nothing to do with it. They simply paid me a fee; the price of their reprehensible actions all those years ago.'

'But why were you given copies of these accounts. I assume they are copies?' pressed Bernard.

H confirmed that was the case and explained that it was part of the price he had extracted for having collected a cache of incriminating photographic evidence of their sordid, criminal proclivities over many years. 'I'm sure there would have been many more accounts they chose not to share with me...' Horatio muttered, disconsolately.

'But again, you kept all this information to yourself. Allowed innocent immigrants to be enslaved, used, corrupted and then cast aside...to say nothing of defrauding the nation. All to exact revenge and line your own pocket. You really are a piece of work, aren't you?' said Bernard.

'Anirudhh Sharma?' interjected Simon. 'Tell us about him.'

'I can't...I've heard the name and know of his reputation.' He shuddered before continuing. 'He's a big time evil one by all accounts. I doubt you'll find him...Roland and Sebastian won't dare lead you to his door...'

'Mm. We'll see about that,' said DCI Bernard Hayles.

As dawn approached, the outline of the story had been pieced together. It was enough to earn the team the extra time needed. Horatio was eventually released with the warning that he would be required to continue to help the police with their inquiries. Charges would subsequently be brought to bear; he was required to remain in the country pending the completion of their investigations and voluntarily released his passport to their safekeeping.

Subsequent investigations over the following days were to uncover a breadcrumb trail to Roland Rogers and Sebastian Frith. The flash drives and computers were full of incriminating details of bank accounts, messages, emails and criminally disturbing images of young and teenage children. The detectives painstakingly assembled the evidence, specialist agencies assisting their urgent efforts.

58. The Rectory

12 July 2001, 03.15

As the car pulled up, she awoke with a start. Caroline had not intended to fall asleep and now rubbed her eyes, yawned and stretched. With her fare paid, she turned and watched the taxi disappear around the bend towards the heart of the hamlet. Sighing, she pulled her coat tighter around her as shivers took hold. She turned to face her childhood home. Caroline stared at the house, taking in the weather-beaten, forbidding stone rectory; the rotting windows and green stained walls; the fractured guttering and broken downpipes; the holes in the roof.

The persistent fret had developed into something heavier as the wind swept it sideways. Caroline hardly noticed. What she saw was a little girl playing on her swing, dressing her dollies, making cakes in a shower of flour and icing sugar. The tomboy in her playing with the Meccano set and her favourite red truck. Now singing nursery rhymes in front of a coal fire and laughing with her mother; now being comforted from a fall onto bare knees, leaning into her mother's ample bosom for comfort. So many memories flitted through her mind. How she missed the warm embraces, the hugs and kind words. But love had departed with her mam, her life so cruelly taken by the cancer, recollection of which sent shudders through her. Love had deserted Caroline, true love that is. Her father did not know how, and as for H…

The happy memories contrasted with her current plight, bringing it into sharp focus. It was overwhelming. How could things have come to this? Where had it all gone so wrong? Tears coursed down her face, merging with the rain that drenched her. Gazing at her memories, she was transfixed. It was as if time itself stood still. How she wished it could be turned back. Slowly, reluctantly she walked up the driveway. The house was in darkness, except for a dim glow emerging from the lounge window. Perhaps he had forgotten to turn off the lights on going to bed.

On reaching the front door, she rummaged in the third plant pot on the right, the flowers long since having been replaced by weeds, woodlice and slugs. She pulled the key out and turned back to the front door. All the urgency and panic of a few hours ago had disappeared, replaced by a quiet dread. She had exhausted herself, was emotionally spent, fearing what was before her.

Caroline turned the key and the door slowly, noisily creaked open. She stood motionless for a few moments, allowing her eyes to become accustomed to the dark. Her senses were assaulted. The house smelt damp and dank and dirty: the odour was noxious. She recoiled. Caroline reached out to the hall table to steady herself. Willing her feet to move, she shuffled forwards to push open the lounge door.

A lamp on the side-table shone dimly, a bible and prayer book sitting alongside a half-drunk mug of coffee. The coal fire had withered and died; the embers barely glowing. Her nose twitched. That smell again, but unpleasantly sweeter. The odour of old age and sickness assailed her. Caroline gagged, but just about retained control. Inching forwards, she saw a prone figure in the worn, leather chair.

Her father.

He appeared to be asleep.

She tentatively reached out to him.

Crouching down, she touched his hand. It was cold.

On the coffee table was a pile of unopened post, in his lap was a few papers, some of which had tumbled to the floor. She feared the worst. Not daring to inspect the papers, she swept them to one side and knelt to her father.

'Daddy, oh Daddy.'

His skin was pallid, almost parchment thin, his clothes dishevelled and stained. She gently reached for his wrist to feel for a pulse. Nothing. Or was there? It was faint, but yes, there was a flicker of life. But he felt so cold. Grabbing a blanket from the sofa, she wrapped it around him.

'Daddy.'

Caroline gently shook him and received a faint mumble, but he seemed barely conscious. There was no stirring him.

She scrambled in her bag and found her mobile. *'Emergency service, which service do you require please?'* She was told an ambulance would be with them within the hour, sooner if possible.

Caroline set about resurrecting the fire and it was soon blazing. What to do now? She had to check those papers and with a dread set about her task but there were no photographs, thank goodness. Turning her attention to the unopened post, she found a suspicious package and ripped it open: incriminating material spilled out. Her hands shook, as she poured over the various images. She stared unbelievingly at them: naked as the day she had been born, spread-eagled. What had she done? What sort of life had she lived? Had the quest to forge a career, to gain advancement and recognition made her feel any better about herself? Of course not. And she had deserted her terminally ill father; turned her back on him. The shame was hard to bear, impossible. There only seemed one course of action open to her. But first, she knelt down and fed the flames, watching her former life go up in smoke. And now for those emails and then the work would be done, and she could finally draw a line under all this. Once and for all.

04:00

Caroline sank into a chair opposite. She needed to cry, but the tears simply would not come now. She was awake but barely sentient, a zombie-like demeanour enveloping her. It was still early – sunrise an hour or so away.

Mechanically, she reached for her pc. It was time to expose those who had hurt her; those whose misdemeanours had played a role in her demise. Oh, she had been more than culpable herself and bore the guilt with a heavy heart; a cloak of despair that she could not cast aside; nor did she want to. There was no delusion or denial. That would be pointless now. But she was equally determined that those who had behaved so despicably would pay a price as well, worrying in the next instance about such un-Christian sentiments.

The machine came to life and she selected her Outlook email file. A series of emails immediately pinged into the inbox – time to renew contents insurance, an electricity bill, dating web sites advertising their services, unsolicited advertisements inducing her to buy. It all seemed so prosaic. She did not care about all that junk, the electronic detritus of modern-day life. But a series of emails from Olivia caught her eye. She scanned the last two:

Olivia
To Caroline,
Re Speak to me...
You must be heading to your father's house, Caroline. Going home. I'm really, **REALLY** *worried about you – ring me! Text me! Get in touch. Please, please get in touch, babe.*
Love
Olivia Xxxx

That was followed by another:

Olivia
To Caroline,
Re Please ring...
On my way, Caroline. Driving – with you by 06.00 latest...please don't do anything daft. **PLEASE** *ring me.*
Love,
Olivia Xxxx

As she read, a plop of water splashed onto the keyboard, taking her by surprise. She glanced up to the ceiling, imagining a leak. There was – it was her. The tears were flowing involuntarily and freely. Her body shook violently. She sobbed her heart out. She put her head in her hands, leant forward and rocked backwards and forwards. The grief, shame and guilt were crushing...

Oh, Daddy! I'm so ashamed, I'm so sorry...

Just hang in there for a little longer, she told herself. She had work to do. It would not take long. Caroline grabbed her pc and located the draft emails. She quickly scanned them. No, they would not do. Did she want retribution to be her legacy, the summit of her achievements on this mortal coil? She set about composing brief emails that struck a different chord and hit send just as the flashing blue lights cast an eerie light into the room.

59. Birmingham

12 July: 09.00

Christopher's slumbers were brought to a premature, ear-splitting end. 'Chris. *Chris*, wake-up, get down here. *Fast*,' shrieked Elizabeth. 'You won't believe this…'

Moments later, an unshaven Christopher appeared at the doorway in his striped pyjamas, rubbing his eyes and ruffling his hair, which comically stood on end.

'What's up? It's only eight-thirty or something, isn't it? Thought we were going to sleep in today?'

'Shit, Chris. Just look at this.' Elizabeth swung her pc around so he could read it himself, looking at him askance.

Caroline Hope
To H,
Cc Christopher Townsend; Elizabeth Standing; Olivia; Margaret Shanklin
Re Forgiven
I thought I once loved you, H…that you loved me. How wrong could I have been? I am ashamed of how we conducted our relationship, disgusted at what we did. Furthermore, you cheated on me.
I can never forgive myself – but I forgive you.
You used and manipulated me in exploiting my knowledge.
I forgive you – but can't forgive my own naivety and appalling judgement.
You clearly joined forces with the despicable Sebastian Frith with criminally corrupt intent. Contracts were outrageously and unlawfully awarded to Ulysses. I now know you're defrauding the government. I know you've embedded code in your systems and penetrated STRAP. You've been grossly overpaid at Ulysses.
For all this, I forgive you – but can't forgive my own behaviour.
I would instead recommend you consider the conduct of Christopher Townsend and Elizabeth Standing who can show both of us standards of behaviour we can admire and aspire to. That's too late for me – but not for you. They are decent people who reported their findings and suspicions. You've destroyed my career. Destroyed my life. But I've played my own part in that.
I reach out to you in forgiveness.
I shall pray for your redemption, H.
Caroline

'And look at this – to the minister.'

Caroline Hope
To Sebastian Frith,
Cc Christopher Townsend; Elizabeth Standing; Olivia; Margaret Shanklin
Re Path to Righteousness
I will get to the point swiftly. You've destroyed my career and my life. You've constantly subjected me to bullying and harassment. At a private suite in St Ermin's hotel, you bullied and threatened me – verbally assaulted me. Under your instruction, I was forced to breach competitive tendering rules and award contracts to those you wanted to win...mainly to Ulysses. You've instructed and bullied me to block attempts by our internal audit teams to uncover the corrupt over-payments to Ulysses. I can only wonder about your motivations. The photos you bribed me with are disgusting and taken under duress. They reflect badly upon me. I can never forgive myself and don't ask anyone to condone or even understand my behaviour. But, Sebastian Frith – you are a corrupt bully. You've been abusing your power for your own ends. I can't cope anymore. You sought to destroy my father. You've destroyed me. It's too late for me. The end.
But I forgive you.
I will pray for you.
Caroline

'See what you mean. Christ, the proverbial is really going to hit the fan.'
'What do you make of it?' Elizabeth asked.
'It seems to be consistent with your theories, and look, she's saying the minister is in cahoots with H in corrupt contract awards and overpayments. This is dynamite. And it's gone to a Margaret Shanklin. Who the hell's that, Elizabeth?'
'Clever girl,' she declared moments later, having googled the name. 'She's only an investigative reporter at The Sunday Times. As you said, the shit will certainly hit the fan. At least it's all out in the open now. But there's something here to be more immediately worried about. Look at the construction of the note. The accusations are explosive, but the language is almost cool, dispassionate.'
'And what's with all this forgiveness? And praying. Is she religious?'
'I believe she's a vicar's daughter, but who knows? Look at what she says about herself. No forgiveness, too late, the end. Christ, Chris.'
'She's obviously at the end of her tether.'
'Oh, how very perceptive of you, Mr Empathy. Its threat is of someone on the precipice, about to jump,' mused Elizabeth, concern etched on her face. Poor Caroline. What can we do?'
'Not sure there's anything we *can* do is there? We don't really know her that well, and it all sounds pretty messy to me.'
'Which is exactly why we should try! I'm going to contact that Olivia we met at the meeting.'
'Oh, good idea.'

Just then, they were alerted to an incoming email: Olivia. The message suggested they speak urgently, provided a mobile number to contact her on and was accompanied by a forwarded email:

Caroline
To Olivia,
Re Sorry...
*I love you, Olivia. I can't ask for your understanding. I don't understand me. Nobody can forgive me. I don't deserve it. I'm <u>so</u> sorry. Thank you, Olivia. You were **my only true friend** in this despicably evil world. Thank you for your love and friendship. Sorry, I let you and everyone down so wretchedly. I'm truly, **truly sorry**. Goodbye, my friend. Goodbye. God bless.*
Caroline

Elizabeth read out the number, Christopher punched it in. He was soon speaking to Olivia, who was speeding north, having stopped for a coffee for a much-needed caffeine fix. Olivia seemed on edge, fraught. He put it on loudspeaker. Olivia told him she had been trying desperately to speak with Caroline since yesterday, but without success, and was now edging into the village where Caroline's father lived.

'I'm almost there, so don't have long, but did you see the last message from her? The past tense? The tone seemed so final. She's never said goodbye to me like that. Never,' said Olivia.

'Have you read the messages to H and the minister?' asked Christopher.

'Yeah. At the moment, I'm more bothered about getting to Caroline whilst she's in one piece. God knows what she's going to do.'

'What can we do to help?'

'Don't know...but...I just needed to speak to someone who knew what was going on and—'

'Hi, Olivia. It's Elizabeth here.' She had grabbed the phone and shoved Christopher to one side. 'Men are no bloody use at this stuff. Here's what we'll do.'

Within minutes, Elizabeth had indicated that Christopher would somehow get through to both the CID's Bernard Hayles and to Caroline's bosses at the department. They would also contact Margaret Shanklin at the Sunday Times.

'We'll get up to Newcastle, but it may be tomorrow or the day after. If you'd let us know what is happening at your end?'

'Oh my God!' said Olivia.

'What is it?'

'Just arrived, ambulance, blue lights...what's she done? Gotta go, Liz.'

The line went dead before the Liz thing could provoke comment from Elizabeth and the exchange galvanised them into action.

60. Bedside

A Few Days Later

Christopher and Elizabeth were warmly welcomed by Caroline at the front door of the rectory. She ushered them into a large room where Olivia was stoking the fire. The late summer's day was warm with the sunshine filtering through the fluffy clouds but was yet to permeate the old stone rectory. And the main resident needed warmth. The room had been turned into a large, downstairs bedroom with a lounge area to one side. In bed was Caroline's father, Reverend Hope. He appeared to be asleep, propped up on pillows to aid his breathing.

Caroline explained that the ambulance had rushed him to hospital. It had been touch and go. His illness had entered a final stage.

'I'm now his carer and his nurse. When he's lucid, we've found a connection that was beyond us, following mam's death. I never truly understood the full impact on him. Or me for that matter,' she said. Her tone was quiet; there was a serenity which surprised Christopher.

'And, how are you?' asked Elizabeth, reaching out to squeeze Caroline's hand.

'It's not about me, it's about Daddy, but I'm okay, thanks. I just had to get away from London; I've resigned, which will have been a relief to them – saves embarrassment all round. I need to be here, with Daddy…Home at last.'

'She's become a nun, haven't you, babe,' interjected Olivia.

Caroline smiled, and moved the conversation on to the aftermath of her emails and the police investigation. 'Did you speak with Bernard Hayles?' she asked Christopher.

'Of course. He'll be in touch, but whilst I understand that charges are to be made against Horatio, they're being coy about their plans on the ministerial front. We've been warned not to say anything as that would be regarded as interfering with a police investigation; perverting the course of justice.'

'So, you've not spoken with Margaret Shanklin?' asked Olivia, frowning.

'Oh yes, I have. In confidence of course.'

'Cool, I like it, the bastards all deserve to be screwed,' said Olivia.

'Now then. Retribution is beneath us—' began Caroline.

'See, I told you she'd become a nun. It might be beneath you, but certainly not me!'

'You'll have to forgive my irreverent, sin-laden friend. I pray for her daily,' she smiled.

'Take more than a few prayers, hon.'

'But seriously, what does the future hold for you?' asked Elizabeth. But before Caroline could answer, she needed to attend her father who had woken up spluttering. She gently eased him up, plumped the pillows and lifted a feeding cup with a lip spout to his mouth for him to sip water, then moistened his dry lips. They had all pulled their chairs around his bed now that he was awake.

'The Lord spoke. Found her calling…' said Reverend Hope in a croaky, faint voice. He could not continue and needed another sip of water, but he reached out to hold his daughter's hand and suddenly his face lit up with a beaming smile. The warmth between father and daughter was touching in his final hour of need. Turning to Christopher and Elizabeth, she spoke quietly, 'It's true. I'm lucky. The Lord saved me when all seemed…well, impossible. I have a calling to follow my father into the ministry and the Bishop has kindly agreed to spend time preparing me for ordination. I'll attend a selection residential, known as a Bishop's Advisory Panel and, once selected, a theological college for four years.'

'That's a big move. Have you thought it all through?' asked Christopher.

'Ignore him, he always asks the wrong questions at the wrong time,' said Elizabeth, gently punching Christopher's arm.

'And sometimes the right question – *eventually* at the right time!' responded Christopher. Elizabeth smiled at him, and raised her hand to show Olivia, Caroline and her father the diamond ring now sported on the third finger of her left hand.

'Congratul—' said Reverend Hope, not quite managing to complete the sentiment.

'That's amazing news, congratulations to both of you,' said Caroline.

'Must call for champagne and a cup of tea for Mother Theresa here,' added Olivia.

'But first, I have a little something for you, Olivia,' Caroline added, passing her an envelope. Olivia looked quizzically, noticing that Reverend Hope was alert and paying close attention.

'What are you up to? What's this, babe?'

'Take a look.'

She shook the contents into her hand and stared open-mouthed at the sapphire and diamond ring that she had so often admired.

'I could not possibly—'

'Yes,' spluttered Reverend Hope, reaching out to enclose Olivia's hand around the ring that had been his wife's and her mam's before her.

Epilogue

Well House – Drawing Room 2045

Christopher and Elizabeth were joined by Margaret Shanklin in the latest of their fireside gatherings, all part of Margaret's painstaking assembly of the various strands of The Hope Affair. Micky, their faithful golden retriever, lay prostrate in pole position in front of the roaring fire as the three of them picked their way through the convoluted juxtaposition of events.

'As I recall,' began Christopher Townsend, pausing to cough. He was suffering from a heavy winter cold and Elizabeth fussed around him.

'As I was saying…all hell broke loose when news broke of the police swoop on the homes of both Sebastian Frith and Roland Rogers.'

'A co-ordinated raid that was captured on the television cameras and by leading newspapers. Somebody must have tipped them off,' smiled Margaret.

Both ministers had been led away for questioning as their various residences, including holiday homes in France and Spain, were searched, the result of a co-ordinated operation across Europe. The searches yielded a rich vein of digital and paper-based materials which were to trigger their admissions of guilt to odious crimes of paedophilia. Their subsequent resignations accompanied by lurid newspaper articles brought down the government of Xavier Townsend amid a cacophony of public outrage.

'A good man trying to restore faith in our public servants,' reflected Christopher, shaking his head sadly at the memory.

'Do you realise that in this period nearly twenty thousand sexual crimes were committed every year against children under the age of sixteen: hundreds with children under the age of thirteen? But only about ten percent of reported crimes led to a conviction. Shocking!' said Margaret.

'But our two ministers were convicted, weren't they?' prompted Elizabeth.

'Oh, yes. And they received relatively long sentences given their abuse of trust from positions of high office: five years.'

Christopher had been stunned that crimes of this heinous nature were punished so leniently. In due course, both Sebastian and Roland secured early release, having served less than four years each. Of course, they had been forced to sign the sex-offenders register and their political careers were in shreds. Sebastian's wife left him as soon as the news of his misdemeanours surfaced, later divorcing him. Gloria proved more loyal and her marriage to Roland somehow survived. The question of corrupt practices and blackmail by Sebastian were never proven as all focus was on the headline paedophilia crimes.

'And Caroline Hope's allegations of having been bullied and manipulated by both Sebastian Frith and Horatio Pilkins were surely true, if overtaken by more serious crimes. That she was naïve was incontrovertible, and that she resigned from her position let the department off the hook in a sense. My book will expose this dimension of the whole affair as well, it being part of the subtext of abuse of power by political figures. The inadequacy of government during this period will be revealed for all to see. I've assembled corroborating evidence from dear Olivia and from a number of her colleagues of that time.'

Olivia had gone on to channel her energy and zest for life into a political zeal to promote compassionate capitalism. She worked tirelessly to expose any corrupt, overbearing, manipulative practices in the corporate world over the two decades that followed. As minister for business under Christopher Townsend's One Nation government, she had worked assiduously and been a driving force in exposing tax avoidance schemes of large multi-national corporations; she had worked hard to promote the cause of corporate social responsibility, equality of opportunity and social justice.

'She was a quite brilliant minister,' confirmed Christopher. 'Not only that, but she founded the charitable Hope Foundation to support the disadvantaged into the workplace, the emphasis on physical and learning disabilities, mental illness and homelessness. All originally funded from the proceeds of her family businesses, which she sold on inheriting them. It was a privilege to work with her and to have the honour of regarding her as a friend.'

'And Caroline opted for ordination. Four years of studying followed, and then another four years curacy before, eventually, becoming the vicar in her father's parish, recalled Elizabeth.

'Where she remains today,' said Margaret.

'And thank God for divine intervention when she was on the point of...' said Elizabeth.

'Amen to that,' agreed Christopher.

Horatio Pilkins was never taken to court. The Criminal Prosecution Service regarded the evidence as being too flimsy and refused to pursue the prosecution.

The existence of widespread fraud of welfare benefits, stolen identities and the abuse of immigrants from Eastern Europe was discovered but the evidence was considered too flaky. Details of fraudulent bank accounts were found, but the police could never link the whole scam back to Roland's stepson, Rupert, to Gloria or to Roland.

'So, Horatio got away with it all,' Elizabeth commented, a statement not a question.

'I'm afraid so, although his reputation was sullied by the newspaper reports and he soon resigned from his various directorships. Ulysses began to fail and never won any more contracts from the DWP, unsurprisingly. It withered on the vine and eventually went bust,' said Margaret.

'What about the whole business of steganography?'

'You've got a good memory. Again, none of this was ever proven, I'm afraid. By the time experts accessed the STRAP system, all traces of any hidden code had vanished. The best theory is that there was a self-destruct element to the code which was triggered. By whom – we can never know. Of course, the system was quickly de-commissioned and replaced. Without the hidden code in the government's system, it was impossible to prove any fraud and eventually even the DWP gave up trying. As for Anirudhh Sharma, he was never found, as predicted by Horatio Pilkins…*Until now*!' declared Margaret, sitting forward in her chair, a triumphant, radiant smile lighting up her features.

'I give you advance notice of a scoop which will appear in the Sunday Times this weekend. We've got him! He divides his time between London and Bangalore and has blood all over his hands. We've meticulously pieced together the story which reveals his role behind the whole steganography and benefits fraud scams, implicates him in arranging Mohammed Khatri's murder and draws in Roland, Gloria, Rupert and Sebastian. Who knows, we may even ensnare Horatio in the end. I've been fighting to secure legal clearance with the paper for weeks now but at last we're ready to go.' She sat back and watched their elated reactions with undisguised glee.

That there were hundreds, if not thousands, of enslaved, poor immigrants from Romania, Bulgaria and Poland was almost certainly true. Flaviu had been just one of the many sad human stories resulting from this corrupt practice. He had made it back to mainland Europe but was never reunited with his wife and daughter. He was trapped in the slums of Paris and failed to return to Bucharest, eventually being drawn into crime in order to survive. Flaviu served several short prison sentences for petty offences and was eventually murdered in the back streets of Paris: the victim of a gangland feud, it was thought. Of Taara and Dannie, there was no news.

Horatio and Georgina Harris eventually married and set up in business, Georgina having been forced to resign by her board at Supreme. Their business was designed to service the welfare to work agenda, but they failed to secure any government contracts. Horatio may have escaped the full force of the law but clearly, government had drawn their own conclusions and were not about to award public monies to an organisation run by these two disreputable characters.

Christopher Townsend and Elizabeth had unwitting minor roles in this drama, and they recalled how close they had come to being embroiled in the whole affair. Margaret was encouraged to state the events as she found them, revealing their roles in Skills World and their early departure from the venture. They had nothing to hide and had acted entirely properly, although the small financial gain weighed heavily upon Christopher Townsend's conscience. He had subsequently donated an equivalent sum to Olivia's charity, The Hope Foundation.

'This experience, as uncomfortable as it was, became a major influence on my future life. It was the catalyst for embarking upon a political career and shaped the values and policies I advocated as best I could thereafter,' said Christopher.

'And there's no denying the impact you were to have on breaking the mould of British politics. Your One Nation government was transformational, and its influence remains strong today. You will go down in history as one of the all-time great British prime ministers,' claimed Margaret, with Elizabeth nodding vigorously.

'That remains to be seen. History will be my judge and jury – but the job is far from done. There is much left to do…'